Kelly

Enjoy the adventure.

J. M. Shaw

THE ASCENSION

First Novel in the Callum Walker Series

J M SHAW

ISBN: 978-1-7778839-4-2 (print)

ISBN: 978-1-7778839-0-4 (e-book)

For my husband, Henry and my kids: Morgan and Avery
I love you dearly, forever
Thank you to Paul, Kaliegh, Chad, and the rest of my family and friends
for staying loyal, teaching me to be patient, and listening to me ramble.

CHAPTER ONE

A miserable evening wind signals the onset of winter, and weary pedestrians hurry their steps to escape the biting cold. Snug inside a small coffee shop, Callum Walker intently studies the herd of rosy-cheeked people from a seat next to the window. Observing the frosty chaos on the crowded sidewalk from his padded stool, he luxuriates in the warmth of a glowing fireplace.

The commuters clutch their coats tightly around their bodies to ward off the icy wind. Callum thaws his chilled fingers around a steaming cup of deluxe, dark-roast coffee—an unusual extravagance. The flow of travelers spills onto the street when their fervent prayers for a green light are answered.

Callum can only see small slivers of faces peeking from beneath hoods and scarves. A few of the bundled bodies push through the mob so roughly that tempers might have flared if not for the urgent mutual need to escape the merciless cold. From the comfortable atmosphere of the coffee shop, he scans the movements of the huddled pedestrians.

Callum frequents the window stool at the end of each workday, sitting at his claimed spot to examine the throngs of people. His calm demeanor gives no hint that he is constantly alert to

1

the possibility of unexpected danger only he can identify. This venue provides an ideal vantage point for Callum's watchful eye. He delights in the mingled aromas of coffee, pumpkin spice, wood smoke and mentally prepares for his own hour-long journey home.

Callum lives far south of the city center and does not look forward to battling the numbing gusts of late autumn during the rush hour swarm. Instead, he prefers to take refuge in the cozy cafe until the drove thins out. Watching and waiting, he hopes each day that nothing threatening will happen to drag him away from the tranquility of his chosen oasis.

Even though his gaze never leaves the street scene, Callum is very much aware of the low hum of voices at his back. At this time of day, small tables are crowded with other commuters reluctant to face winter's blast. A cluster of worn leather chairs forms a semicircle in front of the fireplace, where a group of well-dressed business folk eagerly discuss their plans to vacation in sunny Cuba. The fire's heat permeates so effectively that the vacation planners shed their tailored jackets and drape them over the chair backs. Callum is quite envious that they can afford such extravagant attire while he shivers in a thin, zip-up hoodie. Even now, he hunches his shoulders against the current of icy air that blows through the door as another over-chilled patron enters. Callum wears several layers under his light jacket to help him survive the frigid temperatures but still suffers during cold snaps like today.

His expression turns sour as he cups his hands around the half-filled cup. The coffee's heat transfers to his belly with each welcome sip of the unadorned dark brew.

In a brutal world that offers little security, this modest coffee shop is Callum's haven, especially after a challenging day at work. It is his chance to regenerate before facing an equally trying evening.

Unlike most of the other customers, Callum does not enjoy a prestigious, well-paid career. Callum can barely afford the luxury of premium coffee. Still, it gives him an excuse to linger until the early evening.

Callum works at a full-time job in a high-rise business tower that offers twenty floors of legal and financial services to many affluent, big-name companies. He is accustomed to seeing people wearing an air of privilege and looking down on the world with arrogance and contempt. The city of Duncaster is not the largest in the country, nor is it a capital city, but it is prosperous and offers great potential for business growth. A population boom over the past decade has pushed Duncaster's size to over half a million jostling inhabitants. There are thousands more who commute downtown from surrounding communities, so the city works hard to attract companies looking for desirable head-office locations.

Regretfully, Callum is not fortunate enough to earn a fat paycheck. He is only a lowly maintenance worker who keeps a high-rise tower operating faultlessly for its corporate tenants. Callum usually labors behind the scenes, staying invisible to the building's tenants unless a problem arises and requires his presence. It is a demanding and thankless job that sends him to every nook and cranny. So, occasionally, he suffers the wrath of a patronizing tenant if their air conditioning fails or the toilets clog. It is both depressing and demeaning to be railed at by business owners and then admonished by a supervisor who orders him to appease a jerk in pinstripe. If both sides remain happy, Callum gets to keep his miserable job.

He only earns enough to afford a one-bedroom apartment with paper-thin walls, so overtime hours are necessary to pay for groceries and other necessities of life. His home is in an older area of the city, about three miles south of the downtown core, in a community he less–than–affectionately refers to as "Gangsters' Paradise." His neighborhood has been left to decay, creating a place where crime rates soar, but rent is cheap. Callum feels lucky that at least he has a roof over his head.

Despite this, Callum is such a regular patron that the barista, a perky young blonde with cheerful blue eyes, knows his simple order by heart. She always offers him a smile and a friendly comment. Yet, despite her kind gesture, he never feels comfortable returning the favor. His daily presence here is just an interlude before facing the merciless world again. If the pretty barista knew about his dreadful situation, she would turn a blind eye to him as so many others have done. It is the reason why he ignores her attention and savors his coffee while maintaining his post at the window, mindfully scrutinizing the people passing by.

This evening, weary and emotionally spent from his workday, Callum wants nothing more than to escape to the relative comfort of his bed, but he knows that his day is far from over. Observing the convoy of pedestrians has lessened significantly, Callum pulls a cellphone from his jacket pocket. He checks the time and can hardly believe that he has already spent an hour lost in thought. His half-finished coffee is now cold, but he gulps down the last few mouthfuls because he knows he will welcome the caffeine boost before his night is done. Callum drops his empty disposable cup into the trash as he rises and pulls the hood of his jacket over his short, mocha-brown hair. Shoving his hands deep into his pockets, Callum drags himself out the door and into the bitter night air. It is another good night for hunting.

CHAPTER TWO

A few pedestrians remain outside, and they hardly notice when Callum's solitary, lithe figure joins them in the cold twilight. He hunches his muscular shoulders and lowers his head against the biting wind that has lessened during his evening vigil.

The mist caused by Callum's breath swirls before being whipped away. Halos of light from streetlamps cast deep shadows across the pathways of trampled snow. Callum walks for several blocks, occasionally glancing over his shoulder to ensure he is not being followed. Then, at an intersection, he turns south and continues for another half-hour.

All traces of the warmth Callum had gained from the coffee are long gone, and he starts to shiver beneath his meager layers of clothing. At least the cold keeps him alert and diminishes the dreadful effects of fatigue—or worse, hypothermia.

When he passes the edge of the downtown office district, no more security cameras monitor the streets or businesses. The police are noticeably absent unless called to an actual crime in progress. The farther he travels from the center of Duncaster, the more obvious the changes in infrastructure become.

Office buildings and department stores give way to family

restaurants and strip malls, and beyond those, into tall condominiums that occupy entire city blocks. They, in turn, yield to liquor marts and all-night convenience stores with heavy bars protecting their windows. These changes remind Callum that he is approaching his own neighborhood. Like most cities, Duncaster has an unmarked divide that segregates its lower-class residents and criminal element from the respectable neighborhoods. The south district is a domain where people are looking for opportunities to either make a dollar or rob someone else of theirs.

Callum has been beaten and mugged more than once on his way home from work. Being left with bruises and a wounded ego is nothing compared to some of the other, more hazardous threats he routinely faces. But tonight, Callum is not heading home. Instead, he diverts his path and anticipates something far more sinister and dangerous than a roving gang of south-end thugs.

The last few pedestrians have disappeared, and Callum finds himself walking alone past the entrance of a narrow alley between two decrepit buildings. An eerie yellow glow from a bare bulb casts a patch of light at the opening of the twenty-foot-wide lane.

Callum halts as a shiver runs down the back of his neck, making the hairs stand on end. It has nothing to do with the frosty weather, but instead, it is an ingrained instinct warning him to be on guard. An undeniable primal fear confirms Callum's sense that he is being watched by something evil hiding in the shadows. This intuitive reaction, which protects against potential threats, is an innate part of his humanity. For Callum, however, the perception is much stronger. It generates a powerful physical reaction that confirms danger rather than suggesting it. It makes him far warier of this hidden passageway then he otherwise would be. His awareness is a unique attribute that now sounds deafening alarm bells within his mind. Callum's heart rate and breathing quicken, and every fiber of his being warn him to run like hell. Yet, he ignores the burning desire and turns toward the uncertainty hidden in the shadows.

The alley extends the entire length of the buildings on either side, its far end reaching another puddle of light marking the neighboring street. The glowing light fixtures are too far away to penetrate the dark midpoint, but Callum spies a battered green dumpster resting at the closest fringe of the shadowy interspace. Aside from a brief weekly visit from the sanitation trucks, the lane is virtually abandoned.

Pressured by intense feelings of dread, Callum must consciously work to steady his resolve and face a threat his eyes cannot see but his sixth sense is still keenly aware of.

The first steps toward danger are always the hardest. Anything that feels so frightening cannot possibly be good, but the initial momentum is necessary to confront it. Callum cautiously moves forward and pulls his bare hands from his pockets, ready to defend himself against anything concealed in the darkness. He passes the usual alley debris dropped from the rusted fire escape, clinging to the upper walls. Callum notices sheets of plywood and other construction materials leaning beside the nearest doorway but can barely make out nebulous shapes in the lightless zone. They create a void large enough for concealment. An enemy could be tucked inside a recessed door frame farther down the alley or crouching behind the fetid mounds of overstuffed trash bags.

Intuition draws him toward the ugly, olive-colored bin, but gut feelings are rarely specific. But this is not his first hunt.

Callum faced many hazards in the past, and each time he dreads the silent anticipation before an attack. He hates the anxious seconds that tick by while he watches and waits for his unseen quarry to pounce. His heart beats a heavy rhythm against his ribs, and his eyes dart from one dark corner to another. Nevertheless, Callum faces these unnatural perils with courage, not because he has a death wish but because he has an advantage —one born from the supernatural power of magic.

Although he conceals his abilities from the world, Callum believes that his unique gifts should be used for good. After fleeing foster care during his early teenage years, Callum used his arcane talents to provide for himself in less than legal or ethical ways. Creating simple distractions, he would steal food or money, eventually escalating into more serious activities. But when Callum neared adulthood, he began to experience a strange awareness—a powerful psychic intuition that manifested over time. At first, it was a vague feeling that made him take notice, but as his ability developed, he was compelled to seek out the sources of those malign impressions.

Callum is not immune to fear. His magical skills do not always provide a confidence boost when he approaches unknown malevolence. Something terrible is waiting, and he presses on despite his apprehension.

Right now, vile magical energy permeates the atmosphere of this place, like smoke revealing the presence of fire. It activates Callum's ethereal insight. He aspires to use his magical talents to rid the world of the worst kinds of evil and help those defenseless against such unnatural foes.

Closing his eyes, Callum pauses for a few seconds to take in the energy of the space rather than just seeing it with his eyes. Then, in a flash of perception, he feels hostile wickedness emanating like pulses of frozen air from the direction of the dumpster.

The squat, rusting bin faces him. Two heavy plastic lids cover the top as if guarding its precious contents. At almost six feet wide and chest-high, it seems an adequate hiding place. Callum silently moves to the front of the grubby steel container. Despite his hands shaking from both cold and anxiety, Callum tries to steady his nerves and focus on whatever might be lurking. He clenches his jaw and grasps the edge of one lid, inching it slightly upward. With the other hand, Callum retrieves his cellphone and activates the flashlight. Holding the lamp against his chest, he readies himself for the moment he needs to use it. Callum tenses, and in a single quick motion, flips the lid up and beams his flashlight into the pitch-black inside the container.

The light reveals a few bulging garbage bags, remnants of rotting food that assault his nose, and a few patches of greasy, steel floor. Callum allows himself the slightest sensation of relief and lowers the lid.

Pull yourself together, Callum. He cannot shake the feeling that evil is nearby while tingling fingers of dread continue to tickle his neck. *If it is not in the bin...then where?*

Callum had not set out on this hunt without reason. He heard news reports and read victim testimonies on social media, describing terrifying encounters with something large and deadly inhabiting isolated corners of the city. Frequent portrayals of strange occurrences drew media attention. Thrill-seekers ventured into the night to prove they are daring, or possibly because of some morbid curiosity. Soon after, reports about gruesome deaths began to appear in the news. While the hearsay was dismissed as fear-driven fantasy, Callum knows better.

The attacks, claiming five victims over the previous four days, were all reported to have happened within a three-block radius of where Callum now stands. The unfortunate souls died after suffering injuries thought to have been inflicted during a vicious animal attack. Few other details were provided.

When Callum heard about an eyewitness account of a massive, wolf-like creature with red eyes, he gave credence to the story and started planning his quest to track it down. Now, facing the foul-smelling garbage bin, he suddenly feels a rising sense of imminent mortal danger.

Hearing a deep, guttural growl, Callum backs several paces away from the dumpster. He realizes his mistake in assuming this creature would be inside the bin and curses his stupidity.

Peering past the dumpster into the region of shadows, Callum sees blood-red eyes glaring at him. If not for his practiced ability to push aside immobilizing fear, Callum would be paralyzed by panic. But instead, he remains focused on the looming confrontation.

He takes another step backward as the snarling beast leaps atop the garbage bin in an effortless bound. The plastic lids buckle and pop under the creature's weight. Callum studies ancient stories and folklore regarding monsters, and they have proven to be both informative and surprisingly accurate. The beast presently threatening Callum with an intense, ravenous stare resembles Fenrir—a giant dire wolf from a Norse legend. The wolf with glowing eyes is taller than a bear and infinitely more ferocious. Callum recalls dire wolves were actual animals that lived a thousand years ago. Still, it is not until the creature speaks that Callum truly understands what he faces.

"You think yourself worthy of hunting *me?*" the wolf growls. It pulls its lips into a snarl and reveals rows of glistening, murderous teeth.

This creature, though a formidable opponent, is not a dire wolf. There is only one wolf in folklore that possesses the ability to speak like a human—Amarok.

"I can't let you keep killing people, Amarok." Callum musters his courage and swallows the lump of fear rising in his throat.

"How clever you are to know my name, and how foolish of you to come hunting me without a weapon." Amarok's voice rumbles as it drops down from the bin, landing without a sound. Vicious eyes lock on Callum as it pads toward him, sizing up its prey. Amarok stops, sniffs the frigid air, and squints its scarlet eyes.

"I can smell your fear, *human,*" the wolf says, looking down its long snout and taking obvious pleasure in toying with its intended victim.

"We all feel fear," Callum says. He lifts his chin and stares back while trying to control his quavering voice. "It's what we do in spite of it that defines us."

"And what do you plan on doing, human?"

"I plan to kill you so you can't take another life." Callum tenses, pulling his shoulders back.

"Ha!" Amarok snorts, spraying Callum with a thin mist of snot that immediately freezes. "And how are you going to kill me? Humans have no fangs or claws to fight with. Your kind are all so timid and weak."

Callum wipes his face with his sleeve and stifles a gag after the unwelcome shower.

"Perhaps you plan on killing me with laughter?" The wolf taunts, keeping his gaze on Callum while beginning to circle him.

Callum holds his ground but steadily turns his head to watch the great wolf as it loops around him. Amarok slaps the back of Callum's thighs with its heavy tail and emits a deep-throated chuckle.

"You assume that I'm unarmed," says Callum. "That's not very smart." He clenches his jaw to keep from wincing at the sting across his hamstrings.

"You *are* unarmed. I see no weapon in your hand, and there is nothing of danger to me within your garments." Amarok sneers as it completes the circle, stopping with its great wet nose and bared fangs less than an arm's reach from Callum's face.

"I'm not as weak as you think, and I *am* armed, but you can't see my weapons," Callum says. He lifts his right hand and quickly cups his palm over the top of Amarok's muzzle. As he has instinctively done before, Callum visualizes the power he wants to employ, and a magical word enters his consciousness. "*Pyrovium!*" he shouts, vowing to remember the spell for future use—if he survives this confrontation.

Instantly, the image of flames manifests from his mind, and the skin of his arm and hand brighten with crimson light. The beast's snout beneath his palm ignites. Callum yanks his arm back as Amarok yelps and thrashes in panic, wheeling, lurching, and pawing frantically at its burning face. Callum is not fast enough to avoid being knocked in the chest by the wolf's spinning hindquarters. He lands unceremoniously on his butt in a slushy pool of filthy water, partially frozen in the alley's central gutter. He attempts to shake off the unexpected blow. A hissing sound turns his attention to Amarok, awkwardly straddling the trough of icy water with its scorched head pressing into the shallow trench. Once the fire is quenched, Amarok lifts its head and scowls at Callum with savage, animal fury.

"How is it possible that you have magic? Only my master, Kincaid, possesses that kind of power," Amarok spits. His rage is now past the point of control.

"Kincaid?" Callum questions in a whisper. He never gets an answer.

Amarok charges with its head low and maw gaping wide, each ugly yellow fang ready to slash and rend human flesh. With no time to think, Callum lifts both arms and extends his fingers toward the wolf.

"*Pyrovium! Pyrovium!*" He exclaims, repeating the incantation that is still fresh in his mind's eye. Orange flame bursts from Callum's fingertips, covering Amarok in a blazing shower as the wolf barrels forward. His arms feel heavy, and he is briefly light-headed after casting his spell. Still sitting in the icy channel, Callum sees Amarok careening closer, its entire body engulfed in fire.

"Shit," Callum mutters. He rolls over the wet pavement, desperate to escape the four-legged fireball bearing down on him. He comes to a stop on his belly just as a wave of heat rushes past.

Blinded and senseless, Amarok slams headfirst into a wall with a sickening crunch. Staggering, the tormented wolf flails against the brick, struggling to end its searing torture. Its screams are abruptly silenced as arcane fire consumes its face. After several excruciating seconds, its efforts become feeble, and it slumps to the ground in stillness.

Callum covers his mouth and nose with his wet sleeve to avoid the nauseating smell of burning fur and flesh. He clumsily pushes himself to his feet and approaches the blackened and smoking form. Even as the flames burn out, the dying wolf tenaciously clings to life. Amarok, oozing blood from its charred hide, still glowers at its would-be prey.

"I'm sorry it came to this, but I can't allow you to kill anyone else," Callum says, feeling a flicker of sympathy for the wretched predator.

"You will face my master's fury," Amarok warns. His voice is hoarse and weak. "He is coming."

The wolf tries to rise, but its strength fails, and it collapses again. Amarok's ruby eyes close, and a final breath rattles in its lungs as its massive chest deflates.

Callum feels guilty for inflicting such misery on the beast, even though it killed humans and would happily kill again. Protecting defenseless people against evil makes Callum an instrument of punishment, leaving him to grapple with the moral implications of his actions. So far, his desire to defend is stronger than his remorse.

Moments after Amarok's death, its body begins to shimmer with white light. A consuming radiance emanates from the seared corpse and illuminates the alley with intense brilliance. Callum shields his eyes and squints until the glare subsides. It takes a few moments until the wolf's body is reduced to bits of gray ash floating in the frosty winter air. The only residual evidence of Amarok's existence is an oddly shaped patch on the gray concrete—a random shadow detached from a life source. The alley again plunges into dark obscurity, bound by the sentinels of yellow light at both ends.

Callum tucks his frozen hands into his sodden pockets and limps back toward the street. He is aching, cold to the bone and soaking wet, but continues his frigid walk home and contemplates a new mystery.

Who is Kincaid?

CHAPTER THREE

When the alarm on his cellphone goes off the next morning, Callum pulls the blankets over his head to stifle the unwelcome sound. After safely making his way back to his apartment last night, he shed his frozen clothes and stood in a steaming shower until all traces of grime were expunged, and a pleasant warmth returned to his weary body. Callum then lumbered off to lie on his bed—a sagging, second-hand mattress on the floor that reeks of mildew. Crawling beneath the folds of his covers, he quickly fell into an exhausted, dreamless sleep. Now fully awake, Callum notices soreness in his back, chest, and butt, all of which feel severely bruised.

His night's rest, however short, is enough to restore the expended energy used in his nocturnal magical assault. Callum rolls over with a grunt to shut off the alarm, then gingerly sits up and wipes away the last traces of sleep from his face. It will take quite a while to feel like his usual self, but the morning is already in full swing, and Callum must be at work in under two hours. He stands and gently stretches before heading to his closet to rummage through a meager pile of unfolded clothes acquired from neighborhood thrift stores. Callum gathers a wrinkled pair of blue jeans, a loose-fitting sweatshirt, and a cotton T-shirt. Carrying the clothing to the bathroom, he hurriedly shaves and showers before dressing.

Wiping a towel across the steamy mirror, Callum examines his injuries beneath his lifted shirt. He is shocked to see a broad patch of red and blue skin over the center of his chest. The spreading bruise reaches both collarbones, a reminder of where the Amarok's hindquarters struck him. No doubt he has other contusions just as colorful on the rest of his body.

Despite his battle damage, Callum knows he received far less punishment than he inflicted. His muscles protected him from more acute trauma. A daily regimen of endless walking, plus the rigors of a physically demanding job, raises Callum's overall fitness, strength, and endurance to the level of an athlete.

Callum finishes his bathroom routine and takes a pain pill. Traces of sunlight filter through the broken slats of Venetian blinds. The grungy, single-pane windows provide a hazy brightness that barely enlivens the faded and peeling wallpaper.

He sighs with dismay and plops down on a time-worn loveseat beside the grimy window. Scraps of plywood, plastic milk crates and a stack of old phone books create a makeshift coffee table. Its surface is buried under neat piles of newspapers and dog-eared collections of fairy tales—the product of endless scrounging in second-hand stores and yard sales. An assortment of chipped dishes and unwashed coffee mugs attest to the table's use as the main dining area as well as a study desk. Callum grabs an open box from the floor beside his sofa table and scoops handfuls of the stale, sugary cereal into his mouth.

Furthest from the window, the tiny kitchenette is barely used beyond boiling a kettle or heating canned soup. Its cranky mini fridge no longer works well enough to keep food cold. Only two steps away, a child's folding table sags beneath the weight of magazines and worn reference books on ancient mythology, culled from city library discards. A pair of blue plastic lawn chairs flank the table with strips of red duct tape holding their cracked legs together.

Although Callum's shabby apartment is furnished with junk and stocked with food bank donations, it feels like home to him. He does not care that his clothing and spartan comforts were purchased second-hand or rescued from someone's trash. This is how he survives on his meager earnings. The great city of Duncaster prides itself on recruiting large, successful companies. Still, that policy makes the city unaffordable for many residents living on the edge of poverty.

Before leaving on his long trek to work, Callum grabs two slices of white bread and slathers them with a thick layer of peanut butter. He stuffs the paltry lunch into a plastic grocery bag and into a threadbare backpack. Pulling on another hoodie, Callum then skims the morning news headlines on his cellphone as he heads for work on foot, as always. This part of Callum's morning routine allows him to find out whether there are any new reports of strange, unexplained occurrences. Thankfully, nothing was mentioned about his harrowing adventure last night.

The possibility of witnesses to his supernatural battles worries Callum far more than any remaining physical evidence since it never lingers long after a creature's death. He is grateful for the unexplained process that governs the mythological monsters and helps him to deal with the aftermath. All the slain creatures simply dissolve in the brilliant white light, and Callum regards this as the ultimate proof of a successful hunt.

A few months ago, Callum was unfortunate enough to have been caught on camera casting magic against an undead spawn. Since the video was shot at a great distance, its quality was poor and is easily brushed off as a hoax. Callum cannot always control the location of a magical confrontation but hunting at night dramatically reduces the chance of being seen. Last night's battle with Amarok seems to have escaped any unwanted attention, so he pockets the phone and continues trudging with a sense of relief.

It would be nice to be appreciated, and hopefully rewarded, for his efforts, but Callum knows it would cost him his day job and make people suspicious and fearful of him. It is much easier to stay invisible than it would be to hide from a world that knows who he is and what he can do. There would never be another peaceful moment, only the downside of fame. This is why Callum keeps his magical power hidden and why he chooses to remain aloof and alone. Secrecy is the safest alternative to a lifetime of running. He prefers to be the hunter rather than the hunted.

Callum's head is pounding, and his muscles are complaining, but he hurries his pace. He cannot afford to miss any time at work, and it is not the first time he shows up exhausted and sore from a night of hunting. Unfortunately, today will be another miserable day.

Inhaling the wonderful aroma, Callum passes the cheery coffee shop and wishes he could stop in for a quick cup. He looks through the window and is surprised to admit disappointment when he does not see the amiable barista. Although he chooses to be alone, there are occasionally longings for a human connection. The young woman is the only person in his complex life who offers even the slightest hint of a social bond.

Continuing a block farther, Callum arrives at the high-rise Marcs Building where he works. He steps through the large glass doors into the open area of the lobby, thankful for the warmth after his long trek on such a frosty morning. The sun streams through the three-story glass wall of the atrium, bringing the daylight into the immense space. Footsteps and voices echo from the towering walls and vaulted ceiling. Workers clad in trench coats and blazers hurry toward their offices, oblivious to his presence.

Callum weaves a path across the busy lobby. He slips down a quiet hallway to reach a bank of service elevators reserved for staff. Using an employee key card to summon the elevator, he impatiently waits and visualizes the lengthy to-do list needing immediate attention. Deep in thought, Callum fails to notice the determined footsteps of his approaching supervisor.

"It's going to be another busy day, Cal," Robert says abruptly, startling Callum.

"Good morning to you too," Callum replies sarcastically. He tries not to show his annoyance at being caught off guard.

Robert is not a small man, so Callum knows he must have been deep in thought to not see or hear him coming. It is a mistake that could get him killed on a hunt, and he chastises himself for the lapse in attentiveness.

"You're going to be training the new guy today."

The elevator arrives with an electronic ding. Callum follows Robert inside the car, wondering when and why they hired a new employee. The last staff meeting was less than a month ago, and it centered on the necessity of reducing their budget. A year before that, there was a wage cut rather than layoffs, and Callum hoped his overtime would not be cut as well. Under these circumstances, how can the company afford to add a new member to the maintenance team?

"What floors am I covering today?" Callum asks, slouching beneath the oppressive weight of his duties.

"You're working in the basement. The heating unit needs work, and emergency generator three is scheduled for replacement," Robert replies over his shoulder as he punches the elevator button for the lowest level.

Callum closes his eyes and sighs at the thought of the heavy workload ahead. Much of it is well beyond the scope of his job description, but voicing his concern is not an option if he values employment. Callum will have to muddle through as usual.

"With Liam's help, I'm sure that you can get it all done by the end of today," Robert adds cheerfully.

"Liam?"

"Yeah, the new guy."

The doors slide open to reveal a drab world of gray pipes lining unpainted, cinder-block hallways and the monotonous hum of unseen machinery. Compared to the grandeur of the lobby atrium they left, this claustrophobic environment feels like a gloomy prison.

Flickering fluorescent lights lead Callum as he follows Robert through a maze of dreary tunnels until they reach the staff room.

A few travel posters fight a losing battle to transform the space into something cheerful. Several employees sit around cream-colored folding tables, chatting while they finish breakfast. Others pause and look up at the new arrivals, offering a friendly nod or small wave to greet them. Robert responds while Callum merely hangs his head and averts his eyes.

Robert continues toward the back of the staff room. Callum inhales the intoxicating scent of fresh coffee brewing on the counter as he follows the boss. The rich aroma mixes with oatmeal and bacon. He subconsciously presses a hand over his grumbling belly, embarrassed at the recollection of his own pathetic breakfast.

Banks of battered army-green lockers line the back wall with scarred wooden benches in between. Sitting by an open locker, a well-muscled, dark-haired man in his early twenties, around Callum's age, bent over tying bootlaces. Noticing the two men approaching, he stands and meets Callum's gaze with the slightest flicker of recognition. The man's expression is so fleeting that Callum almost misses it and becomes instantly suspicious.

"Liam, this is Callum," Robert says, waving his arm toward each man as he makes the introductions. "He'll be doing your training today."

"Good to meet you," says Liam. He extends his hand in a friendly gesture.

Callum eyes his outstretched hand, rough and calloused, suggesting Liam is not a stranger to physical labor. Reluctantly,

Callum takes the hand and feels the strength of Liam's grip snuggly clasping but not crushing.

"Nice to meet you, too." Callum returns stoically.

He holds Liam's brown-eyed gaze, wondering what lies beneath the man's neatly trimmed and shaven exterior. The trainee's strong posture projects an air of authority that seems out of place, like pretending to be something he is not. Callum retracts his hand and battles the urge to step back.

"Well, you have your list of duties for the day," says Robert. He hands Callum a clipboard as he pats his shoulder and departs.

Callum bites his lip to conceal a wince when Robert's hand unwittingly touches bruised muscles. Once his supervisor is out of sight, he turns without a word toward his own locker, leaving the trainee to follow like a lost child.

"What experience do you have in working building maintenance?" Callum asks flatly. He deposits his pack into the locker. After removing a couple of clothing layers, he retrieves a thick, tan coverall from a hook and pulls it over his faded T-shirt and jeans.

"Mostly electrical, but I'm a fast learner," Liam says, perking up and looking relieved to finally be brought into a conversation.

"It'll be a crash course for you today because we have a lot to get done." Callum trades his sneakers for a pair of steel-toed work boots.

"I'm looking forward to it," Liam says, a little too gleefully.

Callum ignores the unusual degree of exuberance.

Once fully garbed, the two men leave the staff room for a quick tour of the concrete labyrinth of identical gray halls. Liam intently listens to Callum's instructions, sticking close to his trainer's side until the tour brings them to their destination. The furnace room is their first assignment of the day.

The moment Callum and Liam enter the room containing the massive, roaring heating unit, Liam stops in his tracks and gawks at the behemoth. The industrial heating unit is a beast of a machine the size of a small house, squeezed into a room barely large enough to contain it. It is connected to the intricate ventilation system that links every floor in the building. With serious winter weather on its way, it is essential to keep it fully operational. Unfortunately, it has failed intermittently over the past few weeks. Tasked with diagnosing the problem, Callum is expected to troubleshoot the electrical system for a frayed wire or loose connection.

The complex device intimidated Callum when he first locked eyes on it. After a few years of getting well acquainted with the mechanical beast, it no longer poses such an insurmountable challenge. A little magic also helps when faced with a problem too difficult to fix the regular way.

Today, Callum starts by removing various access panels covering the machine's components. The activity proves difficult and strenuous, yet he manages to hide his discomfort from his trainee. Pointing out and describing each section' function and maintenance history, Callum tries to focus Liam's attention on the areas that require regular monitoring. Liam follows so close that Callum nearly trips over him a few times and treads on his toes more than once. Glaring at his new co-worker rather than yelling at him, Callum gets the message across, and Liam takes a few steps back.

"How long have you worked here?" Liam shouts to be heard over the din of the colossal furnace.

"A while," Callum yells back without looking up or pausing in his examination of the machine's vital parts.

Callum does not make a habit of extended conversation at the best of times. Something about the trainee provokes a sensation of warning or perhaps even danger, so he has developed an instinctive mistrust of Liam. Callum finds it wise to heed any such impressions, no matter how unfounded they might seem.

"I worked at Power Plus for five years before applying here. I wanted to learn more than just electrical," Liam says, trying to keep the one-sided conversation going after Callum refuses to contribute any small talk.

Callum half-listens as Liam yammers on to recite his work history. They have an arduous day of labor ahead, and Callum is already fatigued and aching. He fervently wants to be left in peace to finish the job, end his shift, and go home to bed.

"Is that so," Callum says. He tries to give the impression that he is still listening despite focusing on the task at hand.

For the next couple of hours, Liam follows Callum like a puppy, chattering all the while about his job skills, education, and hobbies. Periodically, Liam asks a question that forces Callum to stop working and answer or risk betraying his complete lack of interest. After all, Robert expects Callum to mentor this trainee. Silence is not a smart option.

Callum does not want to offend Liam. Instead, he does his best to ignore the monologue.

When Callum finally diagnoses the problem with the furnace —a hole in a conduit located in an isolated crawl space behind the machine—he is silently overjoyed at the prospect of finishing this task.

Bombarded by noise from the roaring heating unit, Callum tries to get comfortable in the cramped tunnel. Tucked in behind the main motor, with only his booted feet sticking out of the access port, he is finally free of Liam's constant narrative.

Unscrewing a metal panel just a hand-width above his face, Callum checks out the fist-sized hole in the heavy plastic pipe that houses a rainbow bundle of wiring. He considers leaving the repairs to Liam—he is an electrician after all—but the man has not stopped talking long enough to take instructions.

Besides, the small space allows Callum to lie down and rest his sore muscles.

Holding a pocket flashlight in his mouth, he can see the rough edges of the hole in the conduit and peers inside. He can hear the hum of high-voltage electricity flowing through the lines as he sits up and leans on one elbow to inspect what he can see of the wire bundle.

Callum wonders if a rat might have chewed its way into the

conduit and is hiding somewhere in its dark recesses, so he expects to find a charred, dead rodent.

Looking closely, he spots a couple of slices in the wire insulation. Carefully reaching through the hole to grab the damaged line, Callum hopes to pull out some of the slack, so he can make an easy fix with electrical tape.

He calls to mind protective magic, whispering the incantation as his fingers tingle in proximity to the live wires. With the protection of magic, he can safely feel his way around inside the conduit and shield himself from electrocution. He grasps the damaged wiring between two fingers but is startled to feel a swift, sharp sting in the side of his hand. Thinking he was shocked despite his protective spell, Callum jerks back and out of the hole. He inspects his hand and realizes he is bleeding from a small puncture wound.

What the hell?

Callum props up on both elbows to peer deeper into the conduit. The last thing he expects to see is a miniature human-like face, the size of a dime, appearing at the edge of the hole. Startled, Callum's elbows collapse under him, and the flashlight falls out of his mouth. It lands at an angle, illuminating a finger-length, cyan-blue, hominid figure cautiously peering from inside the tube. In its hand, the pocket-sized intruder holds a pin-like sword, aiming the point toward him as though intending to convey a serious threat.

"Do not touch me, or I will cut you again!" a squeaking voice screams over the noise of the machinery.

Callum retrieves his flashlight from the floor and aims the beam back at the hole. Aside from its pale blue skin, the creature possesses a delicate pair of transparent wings rising from its upper back. Overly round blue eyes unblinkingly stare back at him. With a heart-shaped face and dainty features, it closely resembles a miniature girl. Callum recognizes the personage as a fabled fairy. Her panic-stricken expression seems to be pleading for mercy.

"I'm sorry. I didn't mean to scare you," Callum raises his voice as the fairy retreats back into the safety of the pipe. "I know you're there, and I'm not leaving until you come out."

After several seconds, the face peeks over the edge of the hole again, still brandishing the needle-sized blade in her trembling hand.

"You are not going to hurt me?" she asks cautiously.

Callum knows very little about fairies, other than stories of their childlike shenanigans. However, he understands they are magical creatures who can be extremely dangerous. Like humans, some fairies are self-serving and cruel, while others are benevolent and gentle. Callum is unsure of this fairy's disposition. He reasons that she could have already attacked him with a spell if she wanted to. But since there is no maliciousness in her behavior, he is inclined to dismiss the possibility of a threat.

"You have nothing to fear from me, but you can't stay here," Callum explains, offering her a friendly smile.

With that statement, the fairy seems to relax, and she flickers her wings. Floating out of the safety of her hiding place, she then sheaths her glinting blade in an ornate scabbard at her hip. Following her smooth descent with his flashlight, Callum rolls onto his side as the fairy flutters down and hovers a hand's width from his face.

Now outside of the shadows, he can see her navy-blue hair is pulled tight into a braid at the back of her head, exposing her elongated and pointed ears. She wears tan-colored leggings around her spindly legs, and her body is covered by a jacket of soft, cream-colored fur that matches the trim of her ankle boots. Her svelte limbs and wiry body give her the appearance of being malnourished. While he studies her, the fairy scrutinizes him in return with an apprehensive expressive on her youthful face.

"I have nowhere else to go," she says somberly. Her voice is laced with a tone of desperation.

Callum feels pity for this wee person who appears to need his help. He is used to hunting evil magical creatures, but this is his first encounter with one lacking the malevolent energy his psyche is attuned to. Callum drags his tool bag closer, opening its mouth to allow the fairy to climb inside.

"I know it's not very inviting, but you can hide inside until it's time for me to leave work. When I'm done, I'll take you to my home. You'll be safe with me."

"Th...thank you," the fairy responds, taken aback by his unexpected kindness.

She starts toward the tool bag but suddenly halts and looks back at her would-be savior. The fairy darts up to Callum's face and quickly plants a soft, nearly imperceptible kiss on his nose before pivoting and diving into the bag.

Callum is stunned by the unusual display of gratitude as he closes his tool bag. Now that he knows the problem with the heating system, he quickly finishes his repairs and slides out of the crawl space, carefully sliding the precious case with him.

Too bad his other encounters with magical creatures cannot be solved so easily.

CHAPTER FOUR

I t is one o'clock when Callum and Liam break for lunch. Liam makes his way to the upper lobby, now almost vacant, and finds a secluded corner. Liam leans against the granite tile decor and eyes the lone receptionist across the expansive foyer, who shows little interest in him. The bespeckled brunette is too engrossed in her work to even notice him while typing away on her computer. Liam is confident he chose a position far enough away from any prying eyes or eavesdropping ears.

He tried all morning to befriend his new co-worker, but Callum seems determined not to engage in any conversation beyond what is necessary for his training.

Liam is fed up with standing around and talking to someone who remains so firmly aloof. He wonders what else he can try and decides it is time to report the lack of progress in hopes his handler might have some suggestions. Liam dials the number and waits for the call to connect.

"Hello, Liam," says the other end of the line. "Have you found out anything about your target?"

"It's not looking very good right now, Eric. Walker won't say more than a few words—no more than he has to, anyway—and he seems suspicious of me for some reason." Liam keeps his voice low so his words do not echo across the atrium. "Do you think he knows we're watching him?"

The success of his mission banks on Callum's ignorance about Liam's clandestine organization.

Liam has spent the past couple of months preparing to infiltrate Callum's workplace, and he hopes his efforts have not been in vain. Liam anxiously waits for an answer to his query while eyeing the busy receptionist. At worst, he sees this operation as a chance to observe his target. If Callum really is involved in sorcery and refuses to talk, studiously watching the young man may be the only way to confirm his suspected magic.

"Lucy has not had any luck either. Walker comes into the coffee shop every day but never talks to her. No matter how friendly she is, he barely even acknowledges she is alive. We all know how charming Lucy can be, so his lack of interaction is strange. Have you learned anything at all about him?" Eric asks. His voice betrays the defeat he feels over their collective shortfall.

The Order's intelligence department is certain this is the same man who, four months earlier, had been caught on camera defeating an undead creature using magic. The video evidence was very fuzzy, but an amulet of sight provided guidance to their leader, Desmond Quinn, and confirmed Callum as their correct target. With this information, a covert team of hunters Liam currently leads are focusing their attention on this workplace location. He sent in unmarked stalkers to determine whether Callum really does have magic. Throughout the past couple of months, only Lucy has managed to make superficial contact. Liam's entire team is frustrated by Callum's secrecy.

It seems their target is determined to remain isolated. Without any surviving family members, there is no other identifiable source they could use to glean further information.

"I think he might have suffered a recent injury," says Liam, mentally reviewing his morning's interactions. "Walker's trying to hide it, but I've seen him flinch a few times when he moves too energetically. I wonder if he had a run-in with Amarok, who we detected in the area a few days ago."

"Hmm. That could be important. Do you think you could somehow turn the conversation in a way that lets you find out? Try to be smart about it so he does not become even more suspicious."

"I'll try, but it could be a while before he starts to trust me. He has been working here for a few years, and even his co-workers say Walker never talks about himself." Liam can hear the obvious frustration in his own voice as he warns Eric about the difficult task of discovering Callum's concealed arcane exploits.

"Just watch him closely. That is all we can do right now. Maybe he will slip up on his own, and we will catch him. Master Quinn is still consulting the sight stone for advice," Eric says with a sigh, sounding as hopeless as Liam does about their chances for success.

Liam ends the call and makes his way down to the basement staff room to eat his lunch. He needs to devise a plan to bring Callum's injury into the conversation without sounding too inquisitive.

Liam's orientation continues after lunch, and he watches Callum closely as they work through their list of maintenance and repair tasks. Callum displays immense knowledge, demonstrating that he is intelligent and task-oriented. Beyond that, there is simply nothing of a personal nature Liam can detect.

Covering a lot of ground early in the day, Callum and Liam finally reach the generator room by mid-afternoon.

"We're going to need some serious muscle on this project," Callum explains as he leads them both into a massive concrete room, roaring with the deafening drumbeat of machinery.

The chamber is nearly as large as the main floor lobby. Although the ceiling is not nearly as high reaching, it is just under two stories tall to accommodate the three large, boxy machines, each the size of a minivan. Bright white walls and glaring lights give the room an atmosphere of sterility. The combination of pounding noise and stark lighting disorients Liam.

Callum's raised voice snaps Liam back to the present reality of his mission.

"The third generator needs a hefty part replaced. That thing weighs over a hundred pounds," Callum shouts. He points toward a metal ladder attached to the side of the farthest unit.

Callum lessens the cacophony via a control panel and activates a shutdown of the third generator. He heads straight toward the waiting ladder, and Liam dutifully trails along. When Callum reaches upward to the rungs, he stalls, and a grimace of pain briefly transforms his face. The occurrence does not escape Liam's notice.

"Are you okay?" Liam asks, hoping the concern in his voice sounds genuine enough to persuade Callum to open up and talk.

"Yeah. I slipped on some ice yesterday, but I'll be all right," Callum says, holding a hand to his chest and softly grunting.

Liam does not buy it, but at least it is more conversation than Callum has offered up to this point.

"You're looking a bit worse for wear," Liam remarks. Callum peers over his shoulder and gives Liam a questioning look at his sudden interest in his well-being.

"I'm just a bit sore, is all. I guess my pain meds are wearing off." Callum skeptically frowns and studies Liam's reaction.

"It's a good thing this is the last job for today, then," Liam says. He realizes that his attempt to alleviate Callum's suspicion may have backfired entirely.

After a brief pause, Callum curtly responds. "Let's just finish our work and go home."

He carefully climbs the ladder, leaving Liam with a sense of relief that his inquiry is not challenged further.

As Callum warned, the grueling job does require significant effort. Removing a top panel, both men employ the power of brawn to reach into the space and unbolt the malfunctioning part. They pause only when Callum leaves to hunt down a wayward hoist. It takes nearly two hours to replace the faulty component and finish all the day's objectives.

Leaving the generator room, Callum is visibly exhausted. Dark circles rim the young man's eyes, and his ashen complexion confirms his weariness.

Liam quickly changes out of his coveralls, intending to follow Callum out of the building, but his target is elusive. Callum leaves without anyone noticing, and Liam loses track of his quarry.

Because it is Friday, Liam knows he will have to wait until Monday to continue spying on Callum at work.

He decides to put the weekend to good use by continuing his team's surveillance in their target's neighborhood. If Callum so much as steps outside of his apartment building over the next two days, Liam plans on being there to tail him.

CHAPTER FIVE

Entering his apartment and locking the door, Callum carefully pulls his fist out of his jacket pocket and opens his fingers to reveal the tiny blue fairy curled up in the palm of his hand. She stretches her translucent wings and floats upward to inspect the place Callum offers as a sanctuary. He sheds his hoodie and throws it over a hook on the back of the door. At the same time, the fairy freely explores the apartment, darting from one corner to another and hovering over each new discovery.

Callum wearily indulges his guest's inquisitiveness as he heads for the bedroom. He wants nothing more than to sink onto his makeshift bed and forget this long day.

The fairy seems interested in every detail of Callum's human world home, and he cannot suppress an amused grin at her childlike curiosity. Her tiny wings buzz without pausing as she zips around the entire apartment before taking notice of Callum's retreat.

"You are hurting," the fairy says anxiously. Her glassy wings suspend her in a blur of motion in front of Callum's nose and obstruct his path toward sleep.

"I'll be fine. I just need to rest," Callum says softly, resisting the urge to brush her aside.

Instead, he maneuvers around the fairy and enters the bedroom, not bothering to switch on any lights. Lowering his aching body onto the pitiful mattress, Callum kicks off his boots and slowly leans back until his head rests on a lumpy pillow. Too tired to undress or even climb beneath the inviting blanket, he is content to close his eyes and lie still.

Callum hears the fairy fluttering above his face and forces his eyelids open.

Observing his obvious discomfort, she peers down at him with a worrying expression and questions. "How can you say you are well?"

"Don't worry about me. I'm a survivor. Give me few good hours of rest, and I'll be right as rain." Callum hopes he is correct and closes his eyes again.

The fairy lands on his chin, but he is too fatigued to care. Callum does not react even when he feels the gentle tickling of her lightweight feet moving from his chin to his sternum.

"I do not understand how sleep will make you better." The fairy puzzles as she sits down in the middle of his sore chest.

"Sleep is how I recover my strength and energy at the end of my day," Callum says listlessly. "I need about eight hours each night just to stay healthy—although I rarely get that much. Don't fairies sleep?"

"We do...just not every night. So, what do *you* do when you...sleep?"

"My body stays still, and my mind dreams," Callum explains, then considers, "Hey, maybe I can ask you a question. What's your name?"

Callum lifts his head and tucks his chin to look down at the three-inch-tall fairy sitting cross-legged in the middle of his chest. She gazes at Callum with owlish eyes and tilts her head. It is such an unusual sight that he nearly laughs.

"You can call me Frey," she says. "What should I call you?"

"My name is Callum." He rests his head back and drowsily squints at the patched and stained ceiling.

"Thank you for welcoming me into your home, Callum. I have never spoken to a human before. You are kinder than I expected," Frey says politely. She curls up as though preparing to spend the night atop his chest.

"Humans aren't all kind."

"Nor are all fairies. But you are kind, Callum." Frey yawns. "I will not forget that you helped me, and I will let you sleep now. In the morning, your generosity will be repaid."

CHAPTER SIX

Liam enters the cafe and pauses, soaking in the comforting aromas of freshly baked cinnamon buns and fragrant coffee.

Taking his place in line, he watches the sprightly, blonde barista as she prepares a latte for her customer. When Liam steps up next in line, her eyes brighten with surprise and delight at seeing his familiar face.

Liam knows it is not easy stepping into a role for the sole purpose of covert surveillance. He may be a man of many talents but still finds it hard to maintain the illusion of his assumed persona. It is always a struggle to perform a pretend job amid the fear of losing the advantage provided by an insider's position. At the end of a long day, Liam calculates it would be in character to venture into this delightful cafe.

The attendant behind the counter is not really a skilled server, nor does she aspire to work in a coffee shop. But for the past couple of months, she played the part well.

Of course, Liam is not an electrician by trade either, but he was recruited to play a role in this investigation. He spent months studying electrical manuals and working with mentors who prepared him with adequate abilities to convince a prospective employer that he can do the job. In truth, Liam and the blonde have a shared history.

They knew each other long before the start of this mission. Both are highly accomplished at hunting and killing monsters and other magical creatures the Order deemed dangerous to mankind. In addition, each possesses unique training, making them formidable soldiers against arcane terrorists.

As he stands at the counter, Liam's heart pounds with joy at the prospect of spending a few scarce moments with Lucy, his girlfriend. Grinning broadly, he waits for this opportunity.

"Are you allowed to be here?" Lucy asks in a whisper. She flashes a glance at her co-workers to ensure no one is eavesdropping on their conversation.

Lucy bites her lower lip to keep from breaking into a beaming smile. Her twinkling blue eyes hesitantly leer at Liam. Lucy desires to hug him but battles to preserve her composure and maintain an illusion of unfamiliarity.

"He's not here, and my shift is over. As far as anyone else is concerned, I'm just another customer chatting up a pretty girl. What time are you finished?" Liam asks, elated that they are lucky enough to be stationed close together.

Their work tends to keep them far apart—often on opposite sides of the country—so they frequently go for months without contact. Liam will not squander this chance to spend even a few precious minutes together.

"I have another hour left. If you order coffee, you can stay until then." Lucy's voice is soft and melodious as she absently tucks a loose lock of flaxen hair behind her ear. Her eyes flit up from the countertop to meet his, then shift away just as quickly. Lucy's bitten lip fails to control her coy grin.

Liam chuckles to himself and smirks. "Well then, I guess I'll have a coffee."

Taking his cup, he sits alone at a corner table, sipping until Lucy finishes and says goodbye to her co-workers. When the exit door closes behind her, Liam pauses for a full minute before leaving the cafe's relaxing warmth and following Lucy into the frosty night.

Anyone watching would never suspect they knew one another—until they traveled well beyond the spying eyes of Lucy's workmates. Liam increases his pace to position himself at Lucy's side, escorting her beneath the halos of streetlights and along the empty downtown sidewalks.

"I'm not sure we're ever going to get anywhere with Walker," Lucy tells Liam.

"Yeah, he's definitely not the sharing type. If Quinn says Walker uses magic, then it must be true. We just have to keep trying until they tell us otherwise," Liam says with a shrug. He reaches down to take Lucy's gloved hand in his own and gives it a gentle squeeze. She turns to him, rising onto her toes to plant a warm kiss on his cheek. Liam peers down into her affectionate eyes, and his heart skips a beat.

Liam knows Lucy has the physical prowess and agility to easily shove him away if she wants to. Her fitted winter coat accentuates her deceptively delicate figure and hides a muscular, toned body. It breaks his heart to know that her assignment is centered around enticing Callum with flirtatious advances. She is not a woman who seeks emotional attachment blindly. Her demonstrated devotion to Liam soothes his weary soul and chases away distant longing after a prolonged separation.

"Quinn knows he has magic. We'll succeed, Liam. Have a little faith."

Lucy hugs Liam's arm and leans her head against his shoulder as they meander through the late evening. They treasure this stolen moment of closeness.

Liam's cellphone buzzes, and he regretfully sighs as Lucy releases his arm. Then, looking down at the caller's number, Liam frowns.

"Duty beckons," he huffs before putting the phone to his ear.

"Liam, we have received word of an undead spawn near your location," Eric announces. "Is it safe for you to act?"

"Yes," Liam says, casting a telling glance and secretive wink at Lucy. "I'm alone at the moment, and Walker is clear of my location."

Liam notices Lucy's concern and reassuringly smiles at her after realizing she only hears one side of the conversation. He knows Lucy can detect the intensity in Eric's voice even if she cannot hear his words.

"I need you to contain the threat, and if possible, capture a live specimen for us. I will text you the address."

A moment later, Liam's phone chimes to let him know he has his instructions.

"I'll report back after the task is completed and the undead is ready for extraction." Liam ends the call. He looks at Lucy with obvious disappointment and poses a question, "Are you in the mood for some hunting?"

"Only if it doesn't involve coffee," Lucy says with a snicker.

After a half-hour walk through the maze of skyscrapers and deserted streets, Liam and Lucy arrive at a small, downtown park. It is a three-block island of greenery surrounded by asphalt parking lots and high-rise condominiums. The area is dotted with mature trees and shrubbery, punctuated by winding foot-paths. Picnic tables and benches invite daytime visitors to linger amid the natural beauty.

Much of the park is covered by a sprawling canopy of barren branches, although a few brown and yellow leaves still cling to their anchors. Because of this, the park lacks the advantage of any lighting—only stray hints of moonlight penetrate the dark-ness of the wooded domain.

Lucy and Liam arrive at a graveled pathway disappearing into the treelined depths. Liam holds out his cellphone flashlight to brighten their route. The hunters move cautiously, straining to catch any sound indicating trouble. Rustling leaves and wind-blown debris create plenty of noise, so nothing can be differentiated between normal fauna or unnatural foe.

Lucy walks close behind Liam, matching her steps with his to better determine if something approaches. This is the right place, according to Eric's texted directions. Still, the hunters do not see any sign of the expected undead threat.

His anxiety rising, Liam reaches into a jacket pocket to withdraws a stone the size of a quarter—a yellow gem infused with magical energy.

Humans lack the vital life force to meet the energy requirements of magic. So instead, they must harness arcane forces, stolen from other magical creatures, into vessel stones. Verbal incantations direct the manifested mystical power from the stored stones into a variety of unique forms.

He holds the stone in the palm of his open hand and whispers a familiar incantation, memorized after years of training. "*Transformare ferrum.*"

As Liam utters the incantation, the stone glows and immediately transforms into a glowing bastard sword with the yellow trinket embedded in its hilt. Holding his conjured weapon at the ready, he hears Lucy whisper the same command and knows that she is also on standby for whatever comes their way.

But the night does not freely give up its secrets.

The hunters continue along the path through the woods, scanning the darkness with a flashlight and the soft golden glow of two arcane swords, but fail to find the loathsome creatures that should be there. Liam starts to think this is a wild goose chase when he hears footsteps on the gravel path ahead.

Liam extinguishes the light from his cellphone and pockets the device, freeing both his hands and relying on just the amber glow of his sword to guide him. In the scattered moonlight that filters through the foliage, Liam can distinguish two approaching forms.

"Behind us," Lucy whispers. Liam is suddenly aware of footsteps also approaching from the rear.

It is a cunning trick for an undead being, and they should never be underestimated. The undead spawn, or lich as they are commonly known by the Order, are supernatural creatures conjured by something even eviler than the monsters themselves.

Liam has seen an increasing number of living dead manifested in this region of the country over the past five years. No matter how many are destroyed, their numbers grow relentlessly. Creatures of malevolent natures are attracted to other magical forces. This makes Liam wonder if the local prevalence of lich—and other magical monsters—is due to the presence of a powerful source of supernatural energy: Callum Walker, the suspected warlock.

"*Lux*," Liam says. His sword blade glows brighter and illuminates the path ahead, exposing two liches shambling straight toward them.

Glassy, white eyes stare out of their pallid faces, and patches of putrid, rotten flesh hang from their bodies.

Glancing over his shoulder, Liam's heart sinks when he spies two more liches approaching from behind. There are never this many undead in one place. They normally lack the brainpower to plan a coordinated attack, but there is no denying that this appears to be an ambush.

"Eric's crazy if he thinks we're going to try to capture one of these things," Liam mutters. Lucy nods in grim agreement.

He regrets inviting her on this hunt, but Liam knows he would have no hope of surviving if he had been alone. Liam turns to face the horrific abominations in front of them, fervently hoping more liches are not lurking in the shadows.

Without warning, the rotting creatures charge into battle, their shrieking wails rending the frigid night air. Liam rushes to engage the two undead monsters before him, his magical weapon blazing with light. He swings the blade in an arc that easily carves through the decaying flesh of the nearest lich and severs the animated cadaver's arm with brutal force. The lich's mouth opens, not in a cry of pain, but in a screech of rage as the limb drops from its body. Liam pivots to the side, his arms and shoulders flexing, and swipes his blade across the lich's throat, freeing his head from his neck.

The head topples from its perch and lands on the gritty pathway with a dull thud, yet momentum keeps the creature's body lurching forward for a final step. The headless corpse begins to glow with white light even before it topples to the ground. Within seconds, it disintegrates into ashes and is scattered by the winter wind.

Turning, Liam sees his second foe dart toward him. The hunter swings his deadly sword to counter the attack, missing by a hair's breadth as the lich crashes against him. Liam falls backward under its weight, and the weapon flies from his hand, landing just beyond reach.

Scrambling to shove the lich up and off his chest, Liam dodges its snapping, snarling jaws. The rank smell of the monster's festering body makes him gag, but Liam does not dare release the stalwart force holding the beast at bay. Even as black chunks of congealed blood drip from its sickening mouth and land on Liam's face, he remains focused on the battle.

"*Strenuitis!*" Liam grunts.

He feels an expanding warmth against his chest, where a magical talisman hangs from a neck chain and releases its stored energy.

Liam's incantation hurls the undead lich ten feet through the air. Panting from exertion and fueled by adrenaline, Liam vaults to his feet. He raises one hand to clutch the talisman through his coat while thrusting his other palm toward the spawn, staggering upright.

"*Crepitus!*" Liam shouts, channeling every iota of his willpower into the spell.

The lich lifts its head. Its fixed eyes are wide with shock. Then, a half-second later, it explodes into thousands of rotting fragments, splattering globs of sour tissue against trees and rocks in a shower of fetid chunks.

"Yuck!" Liam gasps in disgust. Looking down at his clothes and skin, he is adorned in black slime and scraps of lich flesh. Luckily, he knows the white light will consume every molecule of the slain creature.

"That is *so* gross," Lucy says while wrinkling her face.

She is visibly appalled at the sight of her beloved Liam peppered with bits of meat and rancid fluids and relieved that they are already dissolving into light and ashes.

"Let's not tell anyone about this mess," Liam suggests as he examines his now-unsullied clothing with a scowl. Looking past Lucy, he notices the torso of a lich lying on the gravel path.

She had hacked away the creature's arms and legs, so it could neither fight nor escape. In this condition, it remains free of the equalizing light that dissolves any dead creatures conjured by dark magic and restores the natural balance of life.

"You chopped off its arms and legs. Smart. Sick, but smart." Liam chuckles as he sits up and grabs his phone to give the report.

"Now, you can call Eric and take credit for my brilliant work." Lucy huffs, crossing her arms over her slender chest and bestowing him a sly half-grin.

CHAPTER SEVEN

Callum wakes to the savory scent of food, and his stomach growls at the prospect of a decent meal. Opening his eyes, he stretches life into aching arms and legs, expelling the stiffness that has built up overnight. He is feeling better after a good night's rest. But in his sleep-addled state, Callum wonders about the source of the delicious aroma.

Hearing unexpected noises in the tiny kitchenette, Callum jolts upright in alarm and bounds from his bedroom.

Frey is proudly standing on the table next to a breakfast plate heaped with scrambled eggs and buttered bread—Callum's reference books pushed aside to make room. She waits patiently for him to join her.

"How? Where?" Callum mumbles the questions as he takes in the scene and tries to figure out how the mouse-sized fairy could have prepared such a meal and where she acquired the ingredients.

"I found eggs in a neighbor's cold box and brought them back for you." Frey slyly smiles. "We fairies have magic of our own."

"Oh...well...thanks, Frey," Callum says after pausing to appreciate this welcome surprise while ignoring the unlawful procurement.

Giving in to his hunger, he pulls up a fragile plastic chair and attacks the mouth-watering meal with gusto.

"You have shown me kindness, and I promised to repay the favor," Frey says as she takes a seat on the edge of his plate.

"Have you eaten?" Callum asks after swallowing his third mouthful of buttery-soft eggs.

"I have, thank you." Frey nods her appreciation for his consideration. "I do have a question for you."

"What would you like to know?"

"Why do you possess magic?" Frey asks bluntly.

Callum almost chokes on a mouthful of bread. He had not revealed his gift to her, yet Frey seems aware of it.

"What makes you think I have magic?"

Frey cocks her head curiously at his response. "Fairies are magical, and we can sense magic in others. It is very natural for us, although I am surprised to find a human with such powers."

He always wondered how and why he had been blessed with such powerful abilities and would welcome any information that might explain this mystery. Callum endured a life of isolation because he fears what others might think or do if they knew what he is. But in doing so, he deprived himself of any possibility of friendship. Callum had not even told his foster parents before he ran away the week after his fourteenth birthday. Fear has kept Callum from talking about his unexplainable powers, but it has also made life painfully lonely.

Since Frey shares the experience of being magical and can detect magic within him, Callum wonders why he keeps denying his secret.

He considers that it might be a relief to talk to someone who he can relate. The years of self-imposed solitude have become an ingrained habit, but Callum is starting to enjoy Frey's company.

"I was born with it," Callum explains, attempting to sound like it is the most natural thing in the world. To admit even that is difficult, and Callum forces himself to push beyond his comfort zone. He doubts that Frey will be satisfied with his simple answer, so he decides to occupy her with his own questions. "Where did you come from, Frey? Why were you hiding in a pipe?"

Frey's cheeks flush bright pink, and she averts her eyes when she answers. "I have been fascinated by humans all my life, studying your species from a distance. So...I left my home to learn more. I saw you many days ago and sensed your magic. I was curious about you. Humans are not supposed to have magic, but you do. So, I...followed you to your place of work, but I became lost. I grew frightened when I could not find my way out, and I tried to hide. Fairies are good at hiding."

Callum is uneasy about the thought of being observed without his knowledge. He clears his throat and hastily rises from the table, picking up his dirty dishes and carrying them to the cluttered sink.

Frey flutters up from the table after him but keeps her distance. "Have I upset you?"

"There aren't many people who like the idea of being watched," Callum says. He busies himself at the sink so he does not have to face her.

He is shamefully aware of the irony, knowing how guilty he is of the same behavior he is now objecting to. It is one thing to be the watcher and quite another to be watched.

"I am sorry. I did not mean to make you angry. I do not understand much about humans, but I am trying to learn."

Callum turns and looks at her. "I'm not mad at you, Frey. I'm just a bit...embarrassed, especially since I've been so careful about not being noticed or followed."

"I do not understand all of these different feelings humans have. Can you please teach me?"

"Tell you what, you can stay here, safe in my home, for as long as you want. I will answer all of the questions you have about humans, and you can teach me about the magical world."

Callum proposes. He carefully watches her small, hovering figure over his second-hand dining table.

Looking closely, Callum can see the hilt of the fairy's sheathed dagger hooked to a leather belt around her narrow waist. The weapon's protruding handle digs a groove into the velvety fur of her furry vest. Her braided hair loosened during the night, allowing wisps of dark blue to form a halo around her cherub face. Frey thoughtfully stares at Callum and purses her mouth as she considers his offer. The fairy clasps her hands beneath her chin, and her expression transforms into delight.

While Callum endured a life of strict seclusion, ignoring an instinctive desire for belonging, he secretly aches for friendship. Frey is the first person, although not exactly human, he has ever confided in. Not wanting to risk losing this one social connection, Callum yearns for Frey to accept his invitation. Besides, he has known for years that he sorely lacks insight into his connection to magic. It would be wonderful to have someone who could teach him.

"I agree." Frey enthusiastically bobs her head, and her lovely face brightens into a cheerful smile. She circles swiftly around Callum's head before fluttering over to the couch and landing on the armrest.

Callum releases a slow breath that he did not realize he was holding.

Quinn sits, cross-legged and eyes closed, on the stone floor before a crackling fireplace and savors its radiating warmth. He has been motionless for over an hour, and his muscles are starting to cramp. The black stone talisman around his neck pulses a purple light as Quinn focuses on the images in his mind.

Quinn is confident that this human, Callum Walker, is the one he seeks. The written prophecy foretells, *"A man of born magic will carve a path for change. He will bring about a judgment and end the reign of darkness, casting open the doors of the realm and uniting the powers that be.*" Sometimes prophecy is unclear. Even so, the face in his vision is undeniable.

Despite diligently studying Callum, the Order had no success in obtaining proof that the human possesses or uses magic. Still, Quinn is certain his vision is correct. He can still see the image in his mind of the hearty young man standing over the dying beast, Amarok—a scene so vivid it is hard to push from his thoughts. He knows that the sight stone, resting against his chest, has never failed.

Quinn always followed the stone's visions and predictions faithfully. Many times, it has shown Callum Walker with increasing clarity. After months of frustrating searching, Quinn finally found his target. Now, it seems he may be denied the evidence he urgently requires.

He wants to cast away all of humanity's rules and send his hunters in to capture the warlock. To do so prematurely would defy the edicts that the Order operates under. A hasty decision would nurture hostility within the echelons of the Order and threaten his position. Quinn may be the governor of this organization, but he is still expected to uphold the ancient laws to safeguard humans. While he delicately walks this fine line in his pursuit of Callum, it is now a race against time. The war waging against him is starting to gain ground.

Sighing in defeat, Quinn opens his eyes. He knows there is no choice but to follow the Order's mandated code of conduct. Quinn must maintain humanity's blessed ignorance of the parallel magical world—for their own protection. His team of hunters are among the few citizens aware of magic's existence, and they can call upon it with the aid of artifacts. But they are powerless without these items and would have to rely on their physical combat prowess in such cases. Each hunter is a costly investment. Adopted at a malleable age, they are indoctrinated over time with false beliefs to ensure tight control. It takes many years to mold these young men and women into a loyal army ready to do Quinn's bidding without hesitation.

The foes his hunters face, however, are not so limited in their use of supernatural powers. If Callum Walker can cast magic unaided, as Quinn's visions indicate, his power could become a great asset to the Order's cause. The sight stone already confirmed Callum fights evil rather than siding with it, so there is some hope that he may come along willingly.

Still, proof of Callum's ability is necessary. Without this physical evidence, Quinn's plan cannot proceed. He is bound by the laws of men. Quinn must carefully manipulate these directives to avoid being thrown from his apex of hard-earned authority.

Quinn rises to his feet, fighting the numbness that invades his legs and buttocks. Squinting his beady eyes against the brightness of the firelight, he limps his overweight frame toward the couch and flops down. Straightening both aching legs along the cushions brings some feeling back into his muscles. Quinn hisses through crooked, yellow teeth and snarls a bristling mustached lip at the unwelcome tingling and cramping. At least his suffering proves worthwhile. The stone answered his burning question: How can he expose Callum Walker?

The stubborn, secretive human has eluded their investigation for months, and it is taking far too long to extract the information Quinn needs. These are desperate times, and equally desperate measures are now required.

Quinn waits until the pain in his legs subsides, then crosses the room to a massive, ornate, wooden desk.

Having worked his way up to this powerful position through years of dedication and perseverance, Quinn is determined not to fail this personal mission to capture and extract the warlock's power. He takes a seat in a high-backed leather chair and picks up the phone to call his assistant for updates.

"Eric speaking," a voice responds.

"This is Quinn. I have a sensitive matter to discuss." He

fingers the magical charm dangling from the chain around his pudgy neck as he speaks.

"Umm...yes, of course." Eric tries to conceal his surprise at receiving an unscheduled call from his superior.

"We have a shapeshifter in our custody, correct?" Quinn asks. He is about to suggest an action that borders on infringement of the Order's rules, ones that have been followed for over two hundred years.

"Yes, we do," Eric says tentatively.

"Good. I need you to make a deal with our shapeshifter. See if he will help us expose Walker in exchange for freedom," Quinn orders in his usual commanding way. "Do you think you can arrange that?"

Eric is loyal to the Order, and Quinn is his general. But their objective is to capture or kill conjured evils and other magical beings, not to release them back into the world. An anxious silence occurs at both ends of the call, and Quinn wonders whether Eric might dare to refuse.

Ending the protracted pause, Eric responds, "I think I can arrange it. I'll prepare my team on the ground to follow him closely and set up the encounter."

"Excellent. Update me immediately once the interaction occurs with our warlock."

"Of course," Eric says in earnest.

Quinn loudly exhales after ending the call. He rubs a hand over the crown of his greasy scalp and slumps against his chair back.

Quinn is pleased Eric has proven himself a loyal subordinate or appears to see the logic in the plan. Either way, this is the best option for success. It will not be long before his hunters gain the coveted evidence and take the necessary steps to capture the warlock. Sooner or later, he will add the young man's power to his arsenal.

CHAPTER EIGHT

Time quickly passes while Callum enjoys the company of his new friend. Frey respects Callum's reluctance to talk about his past. She still asks plenty of questions, but she does not press further if he is not forthcoming with an answer.

They eat meals together and talk for hours. Frey is unaware of the many social intricacies of human etiquette, and Callum knows next to nothing about the world of magic, so their companionship benefits both. Until Frey starts explaining things, Callum does not realize how much there is to learn.

Frey educates Callum about the great dividing veil of magic that separates the humans and a co-existing magical realm. It is a planet-wide segregation of massive territories and isolated pockets. She tells him about creatures that most humans have never heard of, even in tales and legends.

Frey explains the consuming light and how it vaporizes any supernatural corpses conjured through dark magic. Like an ethereal equalizer, this mystic force restores the balance of life, magic, and nature. It is an automatic process rather than a conscious entity, comparable to the force of gravity or magnetism. Conjured creatures should not exist, so their bodies cannot linger in the natural world after their life force is removed.

If humans were aware of the number of magical beings roaming in secrecy, mass panic could ensue. As a species, humans have shown they refuse to tolerate things they do not understand. Those with magic can be curious about humans and occasionally show up in the natural world—as shown by stories of such encounters appearing in legends and fables.

Frey tells Callum a great deal about her homeland and her life there, reminiscing about family and friends to the point she seems homesick. She shows such eagerness to relate her personal history that Callum starts to feel comfortable about sharing some details of his own.

Watching as she sleeps curled up on his pillow, a realization dawns on Callum. He feels a growing fondness for the tiny fairy. They enjoy a degree of mutual acceptance that Callum has never experienced. He is pleased that Frey accepted the offer to share his home.

By the second morning, Callum's head is heavy with the information he needs to process.

Frey's fairy-specific knowledge is generously shared as she paces along the makeshift coffee table. Holding her hands clasped behind her back like a professor, she routinely pauses to ensure Callum pays attention. He perches on the edge of the couch, leaning over a stack of papers and scratching down notes as the fairy talks. He occasionally stops Frey to request clarification when she introduces unfamiliar terms. It is like being back in grade school, but with Frey teaching him, Callum is more diligent in his efforts to learn. He understands that her knowledge will be helpful for staying alive.

Frey explains the origins of magic and how it is closely tied to creation. Like energy, magic is an existential force—it ignites the spark of life. It is completely invisible, yet felt by those sensitive to its nature, like Callum and herself. She also teaches him that all forms of magic must invariably consume energy. Hearing this,

Callum realizes why he feels so drained after invoking his own arcane force.

"I could sense your magic when I first saw you, and I could also see the goodness of your soul. That was why I trusted you when you offered to take care of me," says Frey, grinning sheepishly.

"I think it's time for a break," says Callum. Setting down his paperwork, he leans back on the couch and rubs his eyes. They have talked for hours, and the young warlock is feeling overwhelmed under the deluge of newfound knowledge.

"I need some fresh air." Callum stands and stretches before starting for the door.

As he pulls a hooded sweatshirt over his ragged T-shirt, he hears Frey's soft voice. "I want to come too."

Callum looks at his friend. He considers the risks of exposing her to the dangers of the outside world and wonders whether he can keep her safely concealed.

"Will you promise me that you can stay hidden?" he asks firmly, deciding it would not be fair to expect her to stay while he is free to leave. Besides, Frey is too free-willed to accept any such arrangement.

"No one but you will see me," Frey assures him.

Floating upward from the coffee table, Frey flashes him an eager smile, then zips down into the folds of Callum's hood before he can object.

He sighs and yields to her determination, feeling strangely protective of her.

Callum strolls down the bustling sidewalk. A light dusting of snow fell throughout the morning, but it is already melting in the warmth of the late afternoon sun. Vehicles slosh along the sloppy roads, splashing pedestrians who dare to walk too close to the curb. The air is crisp but well above the freezing point, allowing Callum to leave his hood down so Frey can see more from her hiding place. It is pleasant to feel the sun on his face and even more so to share it with someone else. At this time of year, much of his commute occurs at dawn or dusk, and this interlude on a lazy Sunday makes Callum feel almost normal.

He smiles at the constant gentle tug at his collar as Frey squirms around to steal glimpses of Callum's world.

Frey enlightens him on reclusive nature of fairies. They prefer to dwell in deep forests, small caves, or flowering meadows to remain concealed from other potentially threatening creatures. Fairies seldom venture across the veil into the human world because it is difficult to avoid discovery. Unlike most other fairies, Frey is far too curious for her own good. She refused to stay away from Duncaster since it proximally corresponds to her home beyond the veil.

When Frey became lost in the Marcs Building, she resorted to basic survival instincts and found a dark place to shelter in. But the fairy's unquenchable interest in humans kept her venturing out at night to observe the janitors and watchmen. She might have been able to survive there for quite some time, if not for the accidental damage to the wires that drew attention to her hiding place.

Now, Frey rests in Callum's cozy sweatshirt, completely in awe of her surroundings. Callum chuckles at her sense of wonder.

Callum has no destination in mind, just a desire for fresh air. He decides to give his inquisitive companion a tour of something that will genuinely pique her interest. He heads toward the North Gateway Mall to warm up from their urban trek.

Frey tickles the back of his neck as she climbs higher up his collar to see all the sights.

"There are so many humans," Frey remarks. She inches her way to the top of his shoulder while huddling in the folds of his hoodie.

"This is where people like to gather to eat or shop. Sometimes they just walk around and look at things through store windows."

"Is that what we are here for, to eat or shop?"

"I wish I had the money for that," Callum says, ruefully shaking his head. "No, I came here to get warm and show you this place."

"What is...money?" Frey asks with profound interest.

Callum grins at her innocent curiosity. "It's something of value humans use to trade for items or services. Don't fairies have anything like that?"

"No, we share everything and work to help everyone in our community," Frey says in a matter-of-fact tone.

"That sounds like a fair system if everyone pulls their weight."

"Those who do not are punished. If it continues, then they are banished."

"Oh." He considers how unforgiving this system must be.

Callum is pleased that Frey is relishing their excursion. Her astonishment never fades, even after they make an entire circle through the complex and start around again.

On their second circuit, he is alerted to magical energy much stronger than Frey's. Callum can detect something following him through the mall's main artery, but there are too many people to determine a precise location.

Concentrating on the supernatural energy, he senses a presence approaching from multiple sources in front and behind. His skin crawls when he realizes they are surrounded.

Callum cautiously scans the crowd for someone who might be acting unusual or giving him unwarranted attention. However, all he can perceive is an endless flow of unfamiliar faces.

"I can feel the magic too," Frey murmurs with concern.

Callum continues to walk at a normal pace to avoid drawing any attention. "I can't see it."

He cuts across the main promenade to a broad branching hallway, a shortcut to the opposite side of the shopping complex. Picking up his pace while trying to remain inconspicuous, Callum notices the magical energy is matching his speed and direction. As he reaches the end of the hallway and turns into the flow of the main promenade, he feels a secondary force closing in on him.

"Don't use your eyes. Use your power." Frey utters an incantation, "*Visus spectuculm.*"

He never heard this spell before, but he can feel the arcane power of the words washing over his face.

Callum's vision immediately changes. The throng of people is enveloped by a hazy cloud of colored mist. He blinks and rubs his eyes, thinking he suddenly went blind, but the manifestation does not fade. Callum quickly understands that his eyesight is not failing him. The effect is due to a clever spell, courtesy of his miniature friend.

Some figures are surrounded by pastel-pink or sky-blue clouds, while others radiate deep greens and rich purples. As individuals pass, their auras mingle to form swirling, multi-colored mists before reattaching to their owners. The entire scene resembles an abstract painting, so it is difficult for Callum to discern the human details at the core of each cloud.

"What the hell!" shouts a stranger when Callum bumps into him at the center of the swirling, green vapor.

"Watch where you're walking, idiot!" snarls the angry man, hurrying away.

In response to their minor collision, Callum watches the man's green aura turn crimson. Then, backing himself against a shop window to avoid running into anyone else, Callum stops to observe the psychedelic illusion.

"I cast a spell on your eyes, but it will only last a few minutes. I gave you the ability to see the life energy of those around you, but the intruding magic will mask the effect," Frey explains with urgency. "This will show you where the threats are coming from."

"Thanks for the warning," Callum grumbles. He is relieved that he will not see the world as vivid hues of color forever.

"I am sorry, but time was too short to warn you."

"Let's make a rule that you ask before using magic on me."

He scans the river of colorful blobs moving past and wonders where and how fairies learn to use their spells. Is their power inspired by creative thoughts, as his abilities seem to be, or do they commit the words to memory?

Unfortunately, Callum has no time to ponder this mystery.

While most of the crowd is highlighted in rainbow shades, each color indicates their emotional state. A small handful possesses no aura at all, making them highly conspicuous. The magic in their possession must have a dampening effect on the visual spectrum.

Knowing this makes it easy for Callum to locate the unmistakable men and women tracking him. A few shops away, he sees two on his right, plus three more an equal distance to his left. Five young adults lurking, all wearing nondescript clothing to blend into the mass of weekend shoppers. But Callum's intuition combined with Frey's magic exposes them all.

He makes mental notes of faces and locations just as the spell wears off and the auras dissipate. Keenly aware that this danger is occurring within range of a hundred cellphone cameras, Callum is indecisive about how best to deal with it. He cannot confront the magic-users openly unless he wants to wind up on the evening news.

"There is a small passage across from us," Frey says in a shaky voice.

Callum scans and spies an access corridor that leads to public washrooms and beyond. There is probably an exit somewhere in that direction and far fewer people.

If Callum cannot quickly get away, at least he might be able to wield defensive magic without drawing attention. He is not concerned about maintaining secrecy when it comes to the trackers pursuing him. They already possess their own magical powers and are obviously quite aware of his.

Taking a couple of deep breaths, Callum crosses the mall's main artery, weaving through the throng and plunging down the side passage. As he passes the entrance to the washrooms, he senses his pursuers closing in from the rear. A few confused shoppers leaving the washroom, curiously eying Callum as he rushes past, but no one interferes. Scanning ahead to the sharp turn at the end of the corridor, the warlock breaks into a run.

Just as he rounds the corner, Callum risks a backward glance and discovers his pursuers have stopped. Instead of continuing their chase, they stand guard at the hallway's entrance as though waiting for further orders.

Concerned with the danger behind him, Callum overlooks the threat awaiting as he takes the turn. After a few long strides, he slides to a halt at the head of a utility corridor with white cinder-block walls. An emergency exit at the end of the hall offers an escape. Yet, to reach that salvation, Frey and Callum are forced to confront a menacing mountain lion in all its terrifying glory.

The blood drains from his face, and Callum considers backtracking but remembers the stalkers blocking their retreat. He realizes now why they opted to keep guard. Callum has been herded into an ambush.

"I have been looking for you," growls the cougar. Callum tenses.

"It is a shapeshifter," says Frey, her shaking voice heavy with surprise.

Callum is thankful the fairy can provide information about the creature pacing before them. As the cougar rises on powerful haunches and starts to alter its shape, Callum whispers, "You need to get to safety. Go hide in the ceiling panels."

Before the shapeshifter finishes transforming, Frey slips from his hoodie, shooting upward and away from Callum.

The cougar's limbs elongate, fingers and hands form, and feet extend from the ends of long legs, producing an odd-looking humanoid. It lacks the facial details needed to complete an exact replica of a person, but the shifter makes a valiant attempt at mimicry. Its smooth skin stretches over a bland face, and the result resembles a cheap, featureless mannequin. A pair of blood-red eyes unwaveringly glare at Callum, no less intimidating than the cougar had been moments before.

"What do you want?" Callum demands. He watches the shapeshifter for any sign that it might transform into something even more petrifying.

Callum curses his lack of knowledge about this creature. Yet, he is grateful Frey had the presence of mind to identify it for him. Everything Callum read about shifters was about werewolves, but this creature does not seem to be a moonstruck beast. He realizes his current lack of knowledge is a serious disadvantage.

"I want to know how you have stayed hidden for so long, *warlock*," the shifter demands, throwing the last word at Callum as an insult. Then, it takes a step closer.

"I don't know what you're talking about," Callum lies. He counters his foe's advance with a matching step backward.

"You know exactly what I am talking about," the shapeshifter says with a sneer.

It occurs to Callum that the shifter is trying to goad him into betraying his secret. He starts to suspect there is a larger game in play. Callum is an unwitting pawn, and it may explain why he was funneled down this passage toward this confrontation. For whatever reason, someone wants to expose him and is willing to go to extreme measures to do so.

Stalling for time, he turns the question on his foe. "Why do you call me Warlock?"

The shifter is taken aback, confused by Callum's unexpected tactic. It furrows its fabricated brow, revealing deep thinking is not the creature's forte. Unable to muster a satisfactory reply, the shifter abandons its verbal approach. Narrowing its eyes in anger, the creature lunges, transforming as it leaps. Callum dives out of the way and presses himself against the wall. The shapeshifter, now a colossal grizzly bear, lands on four massive paws.

Callum is quick to recover after dodging the bear and charges toward the exit. The grizzly looks around, puzzled by a missing victim beneath its feet. Hearing its would-be prey's footsteps racing toward freedom, the grizzly reverses course to pursue.

The colossal bear barrels after Callum, who only manages to cover half the distance to the door before feeling a giant paw strike his right shoulder. The brute force slams Callum against an unforgiving wall. He bounces off and slides across the smooth tile floor.

The bear charges again but stops short, rearing onto its hind legs and thrusting its forepaws into the air with a wild bellow. Callum manages to roll away just before the weight of the grizzly hammers down to crush him. He scrambles to his feet and turns to face the rampaging beast. Knowing he cannot hope to outrun or outfight it, Callum is stuck with a panicky dilemma and reconsiders his hesitancy to use magic.

The bear now rises before him on two legs, opens its maw wide, and emits a deep-throated laugh.

"How can you be the man that Quinn is trying so hard to find? You are nothing but a frightened child," the shifter's voice rumbles.

"Who's Quinn?" Callum asks. He wonders if he is somehow connected to Amarok's master, Kincaid. He does not really expect the shifter to answer, but he tries anyway, hoping to distract it.

The shifter responds with another transformation. Seeing a chance, Callum makes a break for it and sprints for the emergency exit.

He now knows it takes several seconds for the shifter to complete each conversion, so he takes full advantage of that brief interval. It does not matter what the creature changes to next. Callum is only focused on escape. He thinks of Frey, hoping she is safe. Will she wait for his return if he leaves her behind to save his own life? Surely she will understand how desperate his situation is.

Callum is a stride away from the door when a set of teeth

clamps deep into the calf muscles of his left leg. He screams in shock at the searing pain and topples face-first onto the floor.

The embedded teeth pull at him, rolling Callum swiftly onto his back. He writhes in agony and scrambles to clutch at his wounded leg. A frighteningly large, flat head of a Burmese python fills his vision. The giant serpent clinches its broad mouth around Callum's calf. The snake's body is already coiling around him, moving steadily up his leg.

The python slides its corded body past Callum's hips and encircles his waist. Callum desperately thrashes to free himself from a horrifying fate, but the shapeshifter's new facade is too powerful. Helpless, he is trapped in its strangling embrace.

Callum battles a rising dread as the snake's coils reach his chest. It releases Callum's lower leg as it slithers its powerful, spade-like head along the floor and wedges its muzzle underneath his back.

The shapeshifter finally captures the warlock's flailing arms, pinning them against his torso. Shoveling its head beneath his neck, the python starts to wrap another muscular coil around his throat.

The thought of being crushed to death petrifies Callum. His eyes are already bulging and his vision darkens. There is no longer any point in concealing his magic. He must use it and deal with the consequences of discovery later.

Callum scours his memory for any useful spell. His creativity has never failed him in the past, and he prays it will save him now. With no time to hesitate, Callum decides on the lethal power of electricity. The warlock can barely extend the fingers of his trapped hands, and when he tries to speak, his tightly constricted throat cannot get the incantation out. Denied his voice, Callum's thoughts create the word—an ability he did not even know he possessed.

Fulgur! His thoughts scream, and the warlock feels a surge of high-voltage energy crackling outward from his chest. A wave of vibrant blue magic radiates from his entire body, tingling like a static charge across his skin. Much like the flame spell he cast at Amarok, this power does not harm him in the slightest.

Deprived of oxygen, Callum begins to fade into unconsciousness when he hears a sizzling noise and smells the stench of roasted flesh. The python's coils go limp, allowing him to wriggle free from the pile of convulsing, scaly skin. Slowly, the reptile reverts to its original form of the mannequin with red eyes. The skin on the creature's face and arms blisters and chars, and its crimson eyes are wide and lifeless.

Callum gasps and coughs, gulping mouthfuls of air. Staggering to his feet, he leans against the wall for support and looks down at the shapeshifter's electrocuted corpse with disgust.

He only wanted to escape, but this creature intended to force Callum to defend himself with his only weapon—magic.

Although the dead shifter now looks humanoid, Callum knows it is only an illusion. It is a conjured magical creature, confirmed by the familiar white light consuming its body.

Callum hears footsteps approaching along the corridor. He realizes that the magic-users guarding the entrance will investigate the unexpected silence, so he limps as fast as possible to the exit.

He pauses at the door, waiting for the flicker of delicate wings to brush past his ear before shoving it open and vanishing into the evening gloom.

CHAPTER NINE

Liam sits in a nondescript white van parked near the mall and listens to reports over a two-way headset. He chooses to remain uninvolved in the operation because he would be easily recognized. Knowing there is a possibility Callum could escape the shapeshifter, Liam does not want any connection to the incident. He needs to preserve his ability to interact with the target undercover. He already made direct contact with Callum at his workplace. Although there was little conversation between them at the time, Liam still has an opportunity to form a bond. Liam nervously drums his fingers on the steering wheel while monitoring communications between team members.

The capture squad kept their distance while Liam followed Callum from his apartment during his aimless Sunday stroll. After a time, though, Callum made a straight path toward Northland Mall. Liam waited until they were within two blocks of the shopping complex before calling his team to mobilize. Once Callum entered the mall, his fate was sealed.

Liam ordered his crew to keep their distance. While the shapeshifter moved into position, a technical team gained access to the security office. Using a sleeping spell to incapacitate the personnel, they observed and recorded Callum's movements via the mall's surveillance cameras. The next step was to surround Callum and gradually drive him toward the trap.

Acting on a hunch, Liam moved his van to this new location across the street from the emergency exit door. Now, he patiently waits for his team to fulfill their mission yet hedges his bet by watching the door in case the warlock manages to escape.

When Callum easily detected the team's presence amid the crowd of shoppers, Liam was troubled. It occurred well before Liam's squad had been ready to close in, and they nearly lost track of Callum because of it.

The trained hunters can blend into a crowd and conceal themselves well. They are experienced in covert surveillance, and it should have been impossible for Callum to discover them. Even so, he pinpointed their positions as if they had all been waving flags.

Liam almost called off the mission at that point but decided to let it play out. They still needed definitive proof that Callum uses magic, and Liam hoped their quarry might offer unquestionable evidence if he felt threatened.

And now, his choice to carry on appears correct. Liam is ecstatic when Callum inevitably takes the bait and heads for the only escape route available. Liam's team closes off any chance to retreat while their target steps directly into their trap.

The keen hunter watches the encounter on his cellphone, receiving a live feed from the cameras in the corridor, courtesy of his gearheads inside the security office. The shifter is neither trustworthy nor loyal to their organization, so its participation in the operation is considered an unreliable element. Eric, however, has assured him that it is necessary to use the creature, and Liam does not question his orders. As he watches the live video, Liam fears that the shifter might lose self-control and kill Callum. But when the warlock finally takes action to defend himself, Liam realizes that Quinn was right. The shifter was badly overmatched against Callum's unleashed power.

Regrettably, the creature is now dead, but the asset has served its purpose. At last, the Order possesses the verification needed to move forward. Moments later, Liam watches Callum emerge from the emergency door, limping across the parking lot on an injured left leg. Liam leaves the van and follows him.

Although this is not part of the original plan, the hunter anticipated this scenario and prepared for a necessary adaptation. This is now a scouting mission. Liam suspects Callum uses some arcane charm to sense the magical trinkets his team carries. That would explain why the warlock had initially been alerted to their ambush. Quinn predicted this from his vision, but it remains conjecture.

Liam is about to test Quinn's theory by leaving his magical talisman and amulets behind, but the lack of protection leaves him uncomfortably vulnerable against a powerful adversary. Given that he plans to follow Callum alone, Liam hopes he will not find himself in a situation where he needs protection.

"Do not pursue the target. I'm currently tailing our warlock. I need you to regroup and prepare for the target's new location and capture on my command," Liam radios to his team as he trails Callum at a respectable distance. Callum is not moving quickly because of his injury, and his limp is evidently quite painful.

"Confirmed," Anthony replies. As second in command, he was the first to enter the hallway when the battle was over.

Liam does not consider Callum's escape to be a failure. Their dynamic plan included plenty of room for error, and Liam had fully anticipated this outcome.

At least now he has a chance to learn what Callum might do in a desperate situation. The truest self is usually revealed when a person is most challenged. So, Liam is exceedingly curious to see what kind of man their warlock really is.

"Are you all right, Frey?" Callum asks, feeling her trembling body pressing tightly against the back of his neck.

Frey zipped into Callum's hood during his pause at the mall door before fleeing into the gathering dusk. As Callum hobbles along the edge of the parking lot, she crawls up and onto his shoulder, ignoring the cold.

"I am fine, but you are in pain, and you are bleeding," the fairy says, stating the obvious.

Callum is immensely relieved to hear Frey's tiny voice again.

In the heat of the moment, he could allow only a brief hesitation as the hunters converged on his position. The tickle of her wings brushing his neck was the reassurance he needed before abandoning the scene of battle.

Even though he is relieved to know Frey is safe, Callum is concerned by the evening's events. A skilled band of men and women are clearly stalking his movements, but Callum temporarily pushes this worry aside. The immediate priority is to reach a secure place where he can deal with his injuries.

"I know, but there's nothing I can do about it right now," Callum says, huffing a discouraging sigh.

He grits his teeth in a futile effort to ignore his throbbing leg and awkwardly climbs a set of stone steps to a sidewalk near a bus stop. Taking a bus is an option. Callum would have to wait for the next one, but he does not feel safe enough to stop moving. He cannot detect any magical energies pursuing him. Still, it is far too soon to feel confident about his escape.

"How did you kill that shapeshifter? I did not hear you voice a spell?" a puzzled Frey asks.

"I just thought about what I wanted to do, and the incantation happened in my mind," Callum says quietly to Frey once beyond earshot of a couple of giggling teenage girls.

Frey ducks back under the edge of Callum's raised hood when they approach other pedestrians, diligently keeping her promise to stay hidden.

"That is not a usual ability." She observes. "Have you ever done that before?"

"No. It's the first time that's happened."

Frey continues. "Magic requires words of power to direct its focus and form. Some elite mages practice for centuries, but only a few ever master soundless spell casting. You seem to do this in an instant," the fairy says in amazement. Her flickering wings create a breeze against his ear while she hovers to consider this information. "You seem to be instinctively drawing upon arcane and psionic magic at the same time. They are two different branches of sorcery and rarely cross over."

Callum hangs his head and despondently sighs. "I wish I had someone to teach me all this instead of having to learn as I go. I've had to rely on my imagination and memory to compile a list of new and old spells."

"I must say, as a human and a creature of magic, you are... curious. You must be very special, Callum Walker," Frey says. Her minute hand gently pats the side of his neck.

"Apparently, you're not the only one to notice my peculiar skill," Callum adds, glancing around them. He has a nagging sensation of being watched but cannot see anyone following. Callum shrugs it off as anxiety and exhaustion playing with his mind.

Frey falls silent for a moment. When the fairy speaks again, she presses her tiny arms around the side of his throat in a hug. "I am so sorry that I did not help you, Callum. I was frightened."

Callum tries to reassure his friend. "It's over now, so don't worry about it."

It suddenly occurs to him that she had the opportunity to abandon him during his fight but did not. The fact that she chose to stay nearby, despite her fears, and rejoin him is comforting.

"I wish I had done something to help you. I am ashamed of my lack of courage," Frey says with a sniffle, holding back remorseful tears as she sinks into the depths of his hood.

Her sorrow is heartbreaking to Callum, who wants to say something to make Frey feel better. But after years of avoiding any meaningful relationships, he is woefully ignorant about counseling others in emotional pain. Instead of comforting Frey, Callum just totters on in silence, searching for a place to hide.

His leg throbs with each agonizing step, and his upper arm burns where his shirt is torn and wet with blood from the bear's powerful swipe. For now, Callum can only guess at the seriousness of his injuries.

The sky shifts from pink and orange hues to murky ebony as the hours pass. Callum is apprehensive about returning to his apartment. He is aware that the unknown enemies are probably still dogging his footsteps and decides to look elsewhere for warmth and first aid.

With night approaching and the temperature steadily dropping, Callum is unsure about where to go. He does not have money for a hotel room, and though he thinks about going to a hospital, he knows that his wounds will raise questions that he cannot answer. He continues to lurch onward, block after block, passing through a suburban neighborhood and arriving at a small shopping plaza that might offer a faint promise of help.

Looking down the row of storefronts, Callum notices small restaurants, a hair salon, and, at the very end of the strip, a dentist's office. A closed sign hangs on the office door, so Callum cautiously peers through the large front windows into a vacant waiting room.

The left side of the lobby contains neat rows of empty chairs. The seats cast elongated shadows from the streetlights, filtering through the gloom. Callum spies a reception desk decorated with brochures and posters promoting various dental procedures available to clinic patients. In direct line of sight to the front entrance, a long hallway stretches into the gloomy recesses of the treatment rooms. The very end of the corridor is painted in a faint red glow created by an exit sign mounted above a rear emergency door.

"What is this place?" Frey asks. "Why do they need so many chairs?"

"This is where people come to have their teeth fixed," Callum explains. He pulls his face away from the window and carefully scans the nearly empty parking lot.

"Is it safe to go inside?" Her wings twitch against his ears as she lies prone on the top of his shoulder.

"There aren't any lights on, so it's a good sign this place doesn't have a weekend cleaning crew. But I don't like the idea of entering through this door. It's too easy for someone to see us," Callum says with a discerning frown. He is apprehensive about trusting their luck after the harrowing day they already suffered. "There's another door around the back. I'm going to try it."

"Are we permitted inside?" Concern strains Frey's quiet voice as Callum makes his painful way around to the rear of the building. "Are the humans of this tooth business afraid of the dark? Is that why they are gone?"

"Frankly, no, we're not permitted," Callum explains, trudging toward the edge of the building and slipping around the corner. "They're only here to work during the day. Right now, the business is closed. We're not supposed to go inside, but I really don't know what else to do, Frey. This place should have a first aid kit or some other medical supplies to treat my injuries."

"Do you have no healers in this expansive city?"

"Of course, we do. We call them doctors, and they work in hospitals. But that's where those people from the mall would expect me to go. I don't believe it was an accident that I ran into the shapeshifter today. Especially since he knew about my power."

Callum lumbers as cautiously as his leg allows, reaching the back lane and locating the emergency door.

He is thankful there is no trace of the magical energy they encountered at the mall. Finally, it appears he and Frey have evaded any pursuers. After hours of limping, Callum is exhausted, sweating heavily from his slog through the city and shivering in the cold.

The angry clouds dust the ground with snowflakes and muffle the city noises. Callum expects the office to be protected by a security system, but he has silenced alarms in the past with his magic. He and Frey plan on being inside only long enough to find some bandages, maybe a warmer jacket, and some gloves if they are lucky. Even a blanket would be welcome. However, before Callum is prepared to invade the secured interior, Frey speaks from the safety of his shoulder.

"*Patentibus,*" the fairy whispers. The locks click, and the door is thrust open with the unseen pull of magic. An instant later, the shrill alarm bursts into life.

"Dammit, Frey," Callum mutters as he scuffles inside the dark dental office and closes the door behind him.

"I do not understand why you are upset. You wanted inside, so I helped," Frey says above the blaring siren as Callum hurries down the dim hallway leading to the front waiting room.

He frantically searches until he finds the control panel located behind the reception desk. Between the shrieking alarm and its flashing lights, it makes Callum's head hurt.

"*Tempore constringitur,*" Callum commands, waving his hand over the device and repeating a spell he learned years prior. Then, the alarm is abruptly silenced.

Callum exhales in relief. "I wasn't ready to deal with the alarm yet," he explains irritably while starting a frantic search for first aid supplies.

Frey departs the warmth and safety of Callum's hood yet flutters close to him. "You mean that screaming box?" she asks, sounding a little less offended by his outburst.

"Exactly." Callum hunches down behind the reception desk and searches every drawer he can find. "The box alerts others that someone has entered this office, and they'll want to make sure this building is safe. We won't have a lot of time before they arrive."

"Oh," Frey says. "I did not know. I am sorry."

Just then, a telephone on the desk begins ringing, but Callum ignores it. He knows it is sure to be the monitoring company calling to check if a staff member accidentally triggered the sensors. The security officers will soon investigate the possible break-in, and Callum estimates that he has twenty minutes at most before they arrive.

Thankfully, he locates an emergency kit and hurries to one of the washrooms halfway down the hall. Frey follows and watches him from a perch on the edge of the sink.

Callum pulls off his shirt and uses the mirror to check on a pair of gashes across his upper arm. The wounds started to crust over before he removed his shirt, and his action opens them up again. Fortunately, the cuts do not appear deep enough to require stitches. Callum struggles to reach the shallow slashes, twisting his upper body to clean and bandage them himself.

"Perhaps I can place some bandages?" Frey asks.

"I can manage this part alone. You've done enough already." Callum's reply is a bit sharper than he intends. He regrets his angry tone, especially when he sees Frey shrink at his harsh words. He drops his arms and peers at her apologetically. "I'm sorry, Frey. I know you didn't mean to make trouble, and I appreciate that you were just trying to be helpful. I shouldn't be raising my voice at you."

Looking up, her feathery lashes rapidly flutter, and Frey seems lost for words.

Callum continues his expression of regret. "I'm used to doing things alone, which is my problem, not yours. This day has been very...difficult. Still, you've shown me great kindness, and I shouldn't have talked to you like that. I guess I'm just discovering what it means to have a friend. It seems I have a lot to learn. Please forgive me, Frey."

It occurs to Callum that his "people skills" are as lacking as Frey's understanding of human social intricacies.

"I will forgive you. I am not perfect, any more than you." A warm smile lifts the corners of Frey's mouth. She flits her wings as she levitates from the sink to hover in front of his face. "Now, please let me help you."

"All right." Callum weakly grins, still choking on guilt but heartened by her acceptance.

While Callum washes his shirt one-handed in the sink and dries it with paper towels, Frey places a gauze bandage over the cuts on his arm and tapes the edges down. When she finishes, Callum pulls his garment over his head. It is damp and ripped but no longer blood-soaked.

His leg wound appears less gruesome but is far more painful. Multiple fang piercings ooze small dots of blood on the surface and are rimmed by heavy purplish bruising. Callum knows there must be deeper damage. He inhales sharply and grimaces while pouring half a bottle of hydrogen peroxide over the wound.

Frey attaches more dressing pads over the puncture wounds. Callum wraps a compression bandage tightly around his lower leg to minimize the swelling. The stricture makes walking easier and the pain marginally more tolerable.

Frey zips away to explore, returning almost instantly with good news.

"I found a room with a table...there are some clothes. Perhaps you can find something warmer to wear." Frey says excitedly.

"All right then, lead on."

He follows Frey's zigzag flight into a staff lunchroom near the rear door. Seeing a small kitchen, Callum succumbs to his hunger and makes a fruitless, hasty search for any food left in the refrigerator or cupboards. Now keenly aware of time constraints, he turns his attention to the closet. There are a couple of long lab coats, but Frey points out a puffy nylon jacket much too much large for him. It is a nasty olive-green color, but burglars cannot be fussy. Callum pulls on the jacket over his thin hoodie, already grateful for the warmth it provides.

"Come on, Frey. The guards will be here any minute. It's time to leave." Callum urges, and Frey zooms into the warm safety of his hood.

Turning to leave, Callum freezes when he hears an insistent pounding at the front door. Glancing at the wall clock, he realizes he and Frey have lost track of time and lingered far too long. Security officers are knocking at the windows and shining flashlights down the dark hallway, so Callum cannot leave without being seen.

"Who are they?" Frey asks.

"They're the men who protect this building," Callum hastily explains. "They're here because of the alarm. We have to find a way out before they come inside."

He carefully peeks around the doorframe and can make out the silhouettes of three men at the front door. One is sorting through a large ring of keys.

"Shit," says Callum under his breath when he realizes they are trapped for the second time today.

They need to reach the emergency exit, but there is no way to avoid being spotted if they do. Being in no condition to run, escape seems impossible. Callum does not desire being arrested or going to prison.

"What is shit?" Frey asks, not realizing the proper use of the term. Callum would have laughed if not for their predicament.

"We're trapped, Frey. Those men are coming inside, and they'll find us. We can't get away now." Callum ducks back into the staff room and closes the door.

He leans against it, sinking slowly until sitting. He wraps his arms around bent knees and despondently stares at the floor, trying to think of some magical enchantment that might help. His knowledge and ability is limited, and under pressure, he is unable to devise any means of escape.

Frey flutters down and floats close to his face, just above his nose. She looks into Callum's eyes with great concern.

"I am sorry—" she begins to say.

"It's not your fault," Callum interrupts, sighing in resignation to his fate.

"—that I do not have time to explain or ask for permission."

Now alerted to the fact that Frey intends to cast another spell on him, Callum straightens.

"Wai—!"

"*Parvus,*" she incants, ignoring his protest and smiling happily at him.

Callum is blinded by a burst of blue light that instinctively makes him shut his eyes and shield his face. The intense light fades fast. Callum lowers his arms and attempts to blink away the bright white spots dancing across his vision.

The room around him has changed, frighteningly so. Its dimensions appear to have expanded, and the furniture now towers high above his head. Frey, who hovered at Callum's eye level mere seconds ago, now slowly descends and lands before him, wringing her hands and studying his shocked expression. She is nearly as tall he is now, and Callum realizes that the room has not grown. Instead, he has been reduced to the size of a fairy.

"What the hell!" Callum mutters, awestruck by the gigantic proportions of the staff room.

Everything is huge and intimidating when seen from this floor-level perspective. Even if Callum and Frey can somehow get to the exit now, they cannot open the door. There are no gaps along the door sill, so crawling underneath is not an option. Alarm addles his thoughts, and Callum's chest tightens. Frey has effectively caged them in the building like mice.

Callum's fear spirals into near panic as he hears heavy footsteps approaching. The warlock has a horrible vision of being squashed under a security guard's colossal boot. They would not even realize what they had done.

Frey can fly to secret nooks behind ceiling tiles, but Callum is at the mercy of vast open floor space to get to the nearest hiding spot. He bolts to his feet, dizzy with fright and panting, now aware of how a mouse must feel.

"I am sorry, warlock. I needed to shrink you to this size to take you to my people," says Frey.

The fairy's fine, impish features are easier to distinguish now that Callum perceives her at a comparable size. Her bright blue eyes and gentle face are lovely.

From his present point of view, he can see hints of red streaks and elegant wisps of hair hugging her pale blue cheeks. Her pointed ear's part her hair, and she has a sparkling gem piercing her right earlobe. Once semi-transparent wings, seemingly as fragile as an insect's, are now visible as a sturdier structural frame of flexible cartilage—half as thick as his own finger—decorated with a delicate network of veins. Her studious round eyes beseechingly stare.

"I don't understand," Callum stammers. "You're taking me to your home?"

He backpedals until stopped by the door. She approaches with her arms outward.

"Yes. I believe you are the one that is spoken of in prophecy, and I need to take you to my clan queen," Frey explains, closing the space between them. "I need you to trust me now. Please."

She calmly gazes into his eyes, yet Callum is apprehensive about this plan. He knows, however, that Frey is a proven friend, so he relents and nods.

Frey hugs her arms around Callum's taut shoulders and whispers an almost imperceptible, "*Domun.*"

The staff room vanishes as Callum and Frey are surrounded by a swirling white fog. Fairy and warlock are no longer imprisoned in the dental office.

CHAPTER TEN

L iam watches Callum enter the dentist's office through the rear entrance and suspects he used magic to gain entry. Approaching the door himself, Liam hears the security alarm blaring and then abruptly fall silent. He considers calling his team to descend upon the building but holds back because he does not want them connected to a break-and-enter situation.

A tripped alarm means security guards will soon be on the scene, most likely before his team can assemble. However, Liam calls for Anthony to mobilize the other hunters to hurry to the strip mall's location and monitor the front door. Liam takes up a position around the back.

All he can do for now is wait for Callum to emerge and continue tracking him. Eventually, the warlock will find a place to rest for the night or risk dropping from exhaustion, and Liam will have his opportunity to strike.

"Security has entered the front of the building," Anthony reports by headset radio.

Liam comes to attention, watching vigilantly for Callum to flee through the rear exit.

After several minutes, the back door opens. Two perplexed

security officers emerge into the snowy night. They shake their heads in bewilderment and mumble something to each other before stepping back inside and closing the door.

Liam is baffled.

He did not see Callum leave the building and is certain Anthony would have alerted him to any escape attempt out front. If the guards are checking the rear entrance area, a thorough interior search must have been fruitless. Callum seems to have simply vanished.

As a veteran hunter skilled in using magical artifacts, Liam knows some incantations can transport a person between locations. Nothing about his quarry indicates that level of expertise. Liam has used such artifacts for five years yet still struggles to achieve total mastery of translocation spells. It seems unlikely that the warlock left the building under his own power. Perhaps someone is helping him, but who? Liam suddenly realizes he needs to re-analyze the video from the mall in case something has been missed.

"The guards are locking up. What's your order, sir?" Anthony asks.

That is a good question, Liam thinks, wishing he had a satisfactory response.

Finally, he touches the headset and issues a command. "Let's call off the hunt for tonight, but I need a team to watch his apartment building in case he returns home."

"Understood," Anthony replies.

Feeling defeated and depressed, Liam reluctantly departs. He had been so close to his target, yet Callum managed to slip from his grasp. There is no doubt that the man uses magic, so now his team just needs to track Callum down again. The rules of engagement have changed, and Liam can proceed with the next step. Permission was granted to take measures to capture but not kill the target. Quinn seems to have a determined interest in obtaining this man.

As Liam leaves the surveillance location, he dials his handler's phone.

"Report," Eric says sharply.

"The shapeshifter is dead, but Walker remains at large," Liam announces, getting straight to the point.

"How the hell did that happen?" Eric is predictably furious.

"We've confirmed he practices magic. The shifter forced Walker to expose his usage when it tried to kill him." Liam is frustrated by the shifter's lack of self-control.

There was a moment during the fight when Liam almost ordered his team to intervene—his mission to catch the warlock alive is paramount. When Callum killed the shifter, Liam was relieved that not only had their theory been proven, but the warlock had shown he is capable of effective self-defense.

"I don't care about the shifter!" Eric roars. "I want to know how Walker escaped?"

"He has to have used a relocation spell or had help from someone that could transport him," Liam postulates. Without evidence, whatever he says at this point amounts to pure speculation.

"What measures are you taking to find him again?" Eric asks. Clearly, he struggles to regain his professional demeanor.

"We have his home under surveillance, as well as the coffee shop and his place of work. The minute he returns, we'll know about it."

"If he is spooked, he might not return to any of them," Eric says, almost as if talking to himself.

"Is there any way your technicians can track the magical energy Walker is using? It's how the Order tracks us. Why not Walker?"

"You do not understand. Walker..." says Eric, his words tapering off in a long, exasperated sigh. "I think it is time to debrief you on this mission objective. You have attained greater proximity to the target than anyone, and there is something important you need to know before you proceed. You left your amulets behind, so I need you to text me your location, and I will send someone to pick you up. Keep this between the two of us...for now."

Liam is intrigued but does as he is ordered and waits. Forty minutes later, a black SUV pulls up to the curb. Liam hops inside. The estate is less than an hour's drive north of Duncaster, reachable through a maze of rural roads cut between fields on one side and deep forests on the other. The wait and ride to the estate will provide ample time to think.

The hunter had already been thoroughly briefed on this mission when it was assigned. His objective is simple enough—make contact to prove that Callum uses magic, then oversee his capture. Now, Liam is wondering what his handler hid from him.

The long ride is nerve-racking, and Liam runs multiple possibilities involving any withheld information through his mind. By the time the SUV turns onto the long, very private driveway, Liam is completely lost in thought and fails to notice darkness has fallen since leaving the glow of city lights behind.

Led by the intense beams of its headlights, the SUV crunches along a graveled driveway that penetrates the woodland barrier. Once breaching the far edge of the trees, they pass through a shimmering and undulating hidden wall.

This invisible magical border surrounds the entire compound, and only those who are invited can see beyond it. Trespassers are enchanted by a charm that reveals nothing but an empty field. Those permitted to enter must confront the intimidating presence of a massive mansion, its grounds patrolled by vigilant hunters.

Constructed a century ago, the five-story fortress has a facade of pitted, once-red bricks now faded by weather and age to a filthy russet color. Both wings of the building feature imposing towers, complete with sentries maintaining a constant watch. The mansion's windows are ablaze with light, and curious silhouettes cast moving shadows on the manicured lawn.

The SUV proceeds slowly along a sweeping curve driveway to

the base of a wide stone staircase. A giant fountain burbles at the center of the grassy expanse. Sconces on the mansion's walls cast light upward along the rough, antique brickwork and downward to a dense, thorny hedge surrounding the structure's base.

This occasion is Liam's first nighttime visit, so he feels the eerie effect the dramatic lighting adds to the magnificent old structure. It is as if the builder used light and shadow as architectural elements to maximize the intimidation factor.

Eric is waiting to receive Liam at the top of the stone steps. The middle-aged handler is a clean-shaven and balding man with an ample midriff. His thick neck rises like dough from the snug collar of a slate-gray, custom-tailored suit, with an elegant silk tie coming dangerously close to strangling him. Eric, however, is unfazed by his painfully uncomfortable attire or at least pretends not to notice.

"I am sorry for the abruptness of this meeting, but I could not discuss this over the phone," Eric apologizes as he leads Liam through the open foyer.

Liam follows behind, quietly marveling at the elaborately carved pillars, detailed moldings, and decades-old period decor. He is led across a spacious foyer, its ceiling soaring above two levels of balustrades and linked by a colossal staircase of polished redwood. Liam marches in silence through a maze of grand hallways lined with dozens of closed doors. Everywhere he looks, the balance between colorful wall adornments and rich accents of furniture and woodwork is exquisite.

Liam is dutifully compliant yet tenses his shoulders against the oppressive authority this building represents. Liam nervously glances around, knowing each passageway has hidden cameras observing his every movement. His pulse races and his eyes flit back and forth, aware of the severe fealty required of him. By the time Liam reaches Eric's office, he is on edge and disoriented by his hasty tour.

Eric settles into a white leather armchair and waves Liam toward a matching couch with his pudgy arm.

"You are a smart man, Liam. I am sure that by now, you realize there is more to this mission than meets the eye." Eric begins. "You were only given details that were pertinent to your task, but you have proven yourself very capable. Quinn feels that it is time for you to become fully informed."

Eric rests his elbows on the arms of the chair, netting his fingers over his lap. He guardedly gazes at Liam as if wondering where to start.

"Okay, what is it that I haven't been told?" Liam asks bluntly. He is curious to know what has been concealed and hopes it will answer his growing list of questions.

"I think you should know that our target does not use magical artifacts. He does not need them to cast spells. He was born with this remarkably rare ability." Eric narrows his eyes slightly to underscore the seriousness of this information.

Liam listens, sitting upright with eyebrows arched and mouth agape. This news goes against his innate understanding of the relationship between magic and humanity.

The hunter hangs on Eric's every word as his handler explains. "While we have strongly suspected Callum Walker to be a warlock, we could not prove it without your valuable efforts. You know first-hand how secretive he is. During tonight's tracking, you have confirmed Walker's uncanny ability to detect any magical threat encroaching upon him. We now have the validation we need to move to the next stage in our planning— capturing the warlock."

Liam immediately realizes why such effort has gone into finding Callum. He knows only one other human who shares such capabilities, and his existence was thought to be a fluke. If Callum shares this capability, then it is a lucky occurrence, one that seems beyond impossible.

Liam serves the Order faithfully, hunting supernatural creatures that cross the mysterious veil separating the humans from the magical realm. He and his fellow hunters always return their defeated quarry to Quinn. Liam believes the blind promise that doing so advances the Order's decades-long research into the delicate and deadly art of magic.

Like all his comrades, Liam was adopted by the Order as a toddler after his parent's death. Welcomed into the arms of this surrogate family, his childhood apprenticeship included learning about the nefarious lord of dark magic, David Kincaid, who stubbornly obstructs the organization.

Kincaid is the instigator of this hellish war for supremacy over the magical kingdom. This war has spilled over to humanity's side of the great divide. Many thought this dark lord to be the only human to possess inborn magic. Now, Liam is learning that Callum has the same limitless abilities as the Order's adversary.

Liam always considered his hunt for magical beings to be a noble calling. His organization is learning about the magical nature of the captured creatures and ridding the human world of their dangerous, unchecked power.

The Order emphasized that any being with such ability represents a potential threat to humankind. Magical creatures wield weapons that cannot be taken away. Whether intended for good or evil, they are an inherent menace that needs to be either controlled or terminated. Or so Liam has been told ever since his initiation into the Order.

"So, Quinn considers Walker to be an indispensable asset," Liam says thoughtfully, trying to grasp the importance of his assignment.

He knows now that his role is just a single element of a complex mission that can help the Order turn the tide in this magical war. Callum's exceptional talent makes him the most important prize Liam could ever present to his master. So, the hunter is more determined than ever not to fail him.

"An asset, yes. But Walker is a dangerous man. He wields the same power as our sworn enemy. There is every reason to believe he is just as evil-minded as Kincaid."

"I see." Liam frowns, reflecting on this possibility and feeling uneasy about this unvalidated claim.

"You have proven yourself successful in identifying this target's capabilities. You predicted his movements and tracked him effectively." Eric looks far more pleased than he sounded on the phone. "You have confirmed our theory about his perception of magical energy, which will greatly aid us in his capture. Quinn approved of this briefing because you have displayed a profound adeptness in your work and loyalty to the Order. With your continued dedication to our cause, we will acquire our target and discover how he can use magic without a talisman."

"If we're comparing Walker to his counterpart Kincaid, then he'll resist us, as aggressively as the necromancer does now. How does Quinn expect to gain Walker's cooperation?" Liam asks. He is careful with this inquiry, fearing insubordination. Yet, his burning curiosity is ravenous.

Besides, this new intel does not seem to match what Liam has personally experienced in his interaction with the warlock. Callum was an ass during Liam's first day of training, but there was nothing to suggest he is a malicious monster.

Eric's expression hardens. "Your job is not to question, only to obey! Or is Quinn mistaken in trusting your advancement from team leader to commander?"

Liam flinches. "No, sir. Sorry, sir." He drops his gaze to his lap and inwardly curses his troublesome inquisitiveness.

"While Quinn does not appreciate such curiosity, I am not so closed-minded." Eric proudly raises his chin and peers at Liam. "Since you are so keen to know, I will tell you this, Walker will never become our ally. He will be captured, and the magic will be drained from his body like all the dangerous creatures you and your fellow hunters deliver to us. We will use his magic to imbue our gems and keep our arsenal stocked in the battle against our nemesis."

"Walker is human, and he won't survive the extraction." A spark of dread causes Liam's heart to race—Callum is a man, not a monster. Nevertheless, the young hunter masks his reservations behind a purposefully blank expression.

"Is that a problem?" Eric scrutinizes Liam with piercing eyes.

"Of course not." Liam steels his expression, although his conscience is suddenly conflicted by Callum's condemnation to death. "I'm a devoted servant to the Order. I will not fail in my mission."

Eric seems convinced by Liam's firm declaration and calls an end to their meeting. Liam's mind is so absorbed with this unexpected moral dilemma that he barely notices his return trip to the cave-like solitude of the SUV as he leaves the mansion behind. The best conclusion his jumbled thoughts can produce is that there is nothing virtuous about warfare.

Liam rationalizes that Callum Walker is just one life among many who have fallen victim to this destructive war. The warlock's death will serve a valiant purpose. It will help the Order save many others from Kincaid's evil bloodshed—even if the warlock dies painfully and in ignorance of his great sacrifice.

Or so Liam tells himself.

CHAPTER ELEVEN

Callum spent years studying fables and mythology, hoping to glean an understanding of the tantalizing magical world just beyond comprehension. Without expert guidance, much of what he discovered through painstaking research is unreliable at best.

The world of the fae has been particularly elusive until the moment Callum opens his eyes to behold a world he only ever imagined. This mystical domain is given little credence in written tales and far-fetched encounters. Nothing learned through his meager resources prepared the young warlock for the magnificent spectacle before him.

Callum stands on the peak of a hill—likely an ankle-high hump on the forest floor, but now immeasurably larger given his mouse-sized stature. With Frey at his side, Callum gawks downward into a depression large enough to be considered a valley. A quaint fairy village nestles between the protective roots of a massive tree. Thick, fibrous roots encircle the tiny community and safeguard it from unseen hazards lurking in the surrounding forest.

An invigorating aroma of pine and musky, damp soil wafts to Callum and Frey on a chilly night breeze.

Above the village, overhanging spiny branches are illuminated by the glow of many floating orbs. The wispy spheres cast a ghostly light across the rooftops of nearly fifty fae dwellings. Some homes are carved right into the sturdy roots. Others are built from sticks, clay bricks, or stones and roofed by layers of bark and moss. A web of pathways, trodden hard and flat over centuries, surrounds the cozy huts. Between the trails, Callum can spot patches of yellow lichen, resembling well-tended gardens.

Although he can only see a short distance beyond the radiant orbs, Callum notices a host of teardrop-shaped structures hanging amid the branches. Resembling Christmas ornaments made from twigs, each one shimmers with light through small circular windows. Callum can occasionally see the shadows of moving figures within. Dozens of more lights float at multiple levels, and the warlock realizes this marvelous fairy community extends much higher up the monolithic tree.

"This is your home, Frey?" Callum breathes incredulously.

"Yes, it is," Frey says proudly. Then, she remained silent, allowing Callum to absorb the breathtaking scenery on his own.

He is surrounded by serene calmness and soothing magical energy that makes him momentarily forget his physical pain.

"If you had the power to come back here whenever you wanted, why didn't you return when you got lost?" Callum asks, confounded over why anyone would want to leave a place like this.

"When I saw you and sensed your power, I followed you. I was sad when got lost in your work building, but I stayed because I wanted to find you again."

Frey looks at Callum with tears welling in her eyes. Her pale blue cheeks are flushed pink, yet she does not look sad. Instead, Callum sees an overwhelming worry expressed in her delicate features.

"I could see the loneliness in your face," Frey says. "I felt bad for you." She pauses, and a roguish expression appears. "For my part, it has been very nice having someone to talk to."

Callum smiles back at Frey. He appreciates her unhesitating acceptance of him and his odd human ways. Callum found the freedom to confide things to her that he never told another soul. In exchange, Frey taught him things about himself he might never have learned otherwise. And she rescued him from inevitable incarceration in a human jail.

Frey is his first trusted friend.

"I have grown to like you in our few days together, Callum. I...care about you very much." Frey confesses, looking down at her feet and clasping her hands over her midsection.

Callum knows that he feels the same about Frey, but he is unsure how to tell her. A lifetime of introversion is a lot to overcome.

"I do not have much time to explain." Frey takes a steadying deep breath and returns her indigo eyes back to Callum's. "I will be punished for bringing you here, but our magical realm is at war. I have saved you from the security men by bringing you across the veil, but it is not safe here either."

"Is that why there's been an increase in magical monsters attacking people in my city?"

"Yes. They are conjured by a human with powers like your own. A prophecy tells of a human with natural magic who will appear when things are at their darkest. This person will bring an end to the war and save us all." Frey moves closer and takes Callum's hands, fixing him with a discerning gaze. "I believe you are the one foretold in the prophecy. I am certain of this, which is why I took the risk of bringing you here."

Callum is speechless. His heart pounds, and his thoughts race.

How can Frey possibly believe such a thing? There is nothing special about him other than an ability to cast spells. He is not even particularly good at that. He is not as powerful as she thinks. Callum is just a man, working at a menial job and living in near poverty with no family or friends. Hell, he cannot even muster the courage to ask a girl on a date. How can he possibly be the person Frey is thinking of? Callum did not even know there was a war going on, much less how to fight in it.

Callum pulls his hands away and steps back, leaving Frey distraught by the sudden rejection. He starts to reply but stops when a horn blares from the valley below.

"Intruder!" A stern shout echoes through the night air, joined by other voices that relay the cry.

Callum spins to face a dozen fairies zooming down from the canopy of branches. Several fae—armed with formidable spears and bows with nocked arrows—spot the unwelcome new arrivals and converge.

"Listen to me!" Frey glances at the advancing aerial squadron, then quickly back at Callum. Her face is full of fear. "Humans are never supposed to see this place, and I have broken a great law by bringing you here. You must promise me that you will not resist them, or they *will* kill you! I need time to talk to my queen and explain why I have brought you here."

"I don't—" Callum starts to speak, but Frey lunges into his arms and kisses him.

His first instinct is to pull away, but instead, he falls into her kiss and closes his eyes. Callum's head is swimming with questions as she steps back and tenderly smiles at him.

The fae troops descend, each clad in leather pants and jackets of ivory fur that make them look bulkier than their lanky frames. They gracefully land and surround Callum in a swift, coordinated maneuver.

One of the soldiers grabs Frey by the arm and yanks her away from their circle of leveled spears, leaving Callum to confront the stone-faced sentries.

"Do not resist them!" Frey shouts insistently and struggles to free herself from the soldier's grip.

"That is enough, Frey!" a fairy demands as he lands on the hilltop and takes charge.

This fae is older and carries himself with an air of authority that suggests a powerful command. He glares at Callum with dark brown eyes, huffing disdainfully before turning to Frey.

Callum sees alarm in Frey's eyes as this domineering fairy steps toward her. The soldier releases her arm while still guarding from behind.

"What is the meaning of this, Frey? First, you defied your queen by leaving, and now you bring a human into our midst!" the older fairy thunders at her.

Frey meekly bows her head. Her slim shoulders slump under the weight of the furious reprimand. "I am sorry, Captain Marcus. I know I have broken our laws. But this man needed help and...and I believe he is the one from the prophecy." She steals a quick glance at Marcus before continuing to wring her hands and twists her fingers.

Callum seethes, wanting to protect Frey from Marcus's verbal onslaught. It takes all his willpower to resist launching the devastating spell forming unbidden in his mind. Because of his hasty promise, he finds himself helpless to defend or even comfort her.

"You will be severely disciplined for this violation," Marcus proclaims with stoic authority. "The queen will decide the fate of this human. If he is sentenced to death, then his blood will be on *your* hands."

Frey covers her face and starts to sob.

"You will face your judgment at morning light. Until then, you will be held in isolation. Is that understood?"

Frey nods. She wipes her eyes with the back of her hand and sniffs, lifting her head to meet Callum's apprehensive gaze.

"Forgive me, Callum," she says as the tears resume flowing down her cheeks. "My heart tells me you are the one destined to save my people. I know you will succeed."

Callum attempts to step toward his friend, heedless of the ten razor-edged spears threatening to pierce him. He only stops when a fae soldier blocks his path by thrusting a spear within a hand's width of his throat. The fairy soldier scowls with assertive intensity. Callum's hands twitch at his sides, desperate to explode with raging magical energy.

Discretion wins. Raising his hands in surrender, Callum retreats to his original position in the circle of lances. With his jaw clenched in suppressed fury, he watches Frey take flight accompanied by an armed escort. They fly over the sleeping village before ascending into the canopy and darkness beyond.

Marcus turns his attention to Callum. "Frey has made a great claim in your defense," he says, waving aside the circle of warriors.

Callum feels like he is under a microscope, his every action scrutinized. Prudently, he keeps his hands raised as he faces the fairy captain. A needle-sharp spear point stings the small of his back as an unspoken warning that any sign of aggression will not be tolerated.

Marcus halts before Callum. "I can sense your magical energy, and that intrigues me," Marcus says. His eyes never leave Callum's face.

Callum decides his best choice is to be open and honest. Defiance will only lead to more holes in his flesh. "It's been with me since birth," he says bluntly.

"It has to be a trick. You must be hiding a magical talisman," Marcus mutters. The captain motions for the fae soldiers to search him.

Callum feels a sudden kick across the back of his thighs, knocking him to his knees and causing his injured leg to spark and throb anew. A second shove leaves him pinned facedown on the mossy ground with a spear against the nape of his neck.

Callum remains motionless as every stitch of his clothing is examined. The searchers find no rings, neck chains, or other suspicious adornments. Still, they do rob Callum of his apartment keys, wallet, cellphone, and coat before hauling him back to his feet.

Satisfied that their captive carries no obvious weapon or magical artifact, they give an all-clear nod to their captain.

Marcus says, holding the cover open. "You will not be harmed if you cooperate."

"I'm not going in there."

Callum sharply pulls and manages to free his left arm. He is rewarded with a clout across the back of his head, applied by the thick, blunt shaft of a spear. A blinding pain explodes inside Callum's skull, forcing his knee to buckle. He wraps his free arm around his head to ward off a second blow but is instead seized and lifted, then dropped unceremoniously down the dark shaft.

Callum falls for several seconds, then lands with a thud on a hard-packed dirt floor. Crumpling into a groaning heap, he remains inert, absorbed by the pain radiating from several wounds. Eventually, the exhausted warlock rolls onto his back and peers up at the circular opening far above. The last trace of light is extinguished when the woven cover is lowered, and darkness engulfs him like a suffocating blanket.

Alone, aching, and blind to his surroundings, Callum cradles his throbbing head and succumbs to a wave of hopelessness. His thoughts turn to Frey, and he worries whether his friend will receive more gentle treatment than he is now enduring. He wonders what tomorrow will bring and if he will freeze to death before dawn. Finally, Callum surrenders to the blessed mercy of sleep, the only remedy for his pain-racked body and weary thoughts.

CHAPTER TWELVE

E arly morning brings precious little daylight into Callum's earthen cell as he wakes from a fitful sleep. Shivering on the clammy floor, he looks up and sees sparkles in the dirt walls of the pit, caused by ice crystals reflecting traces of light. Curling onto his side with his knees drawn up and his arms wrapped tightly around his torso, Callum curses the fairies for taking his coat.

He awakened several times during the night, shivering, and his hands and feet stinging from the biting cold. But as the sun fully rises, his thoughts turn to the human world and the Monday work shift he is now missing. Callum doubts his manager will be understanding of the current plight that keeps him from his job. Many others are qualified to perform his work, so his unexplained absence is unlikely to be forgiven. Callum will be unemployed by the end of the day. Without a paycheck, his apartment will be lost within a couple of weeks, leaving him destitute and homeless.

When he finally gives up on huddling for warmth, Callum stretches his sore muscles and sits up. He scoots over to one of the frigid walls and leans his back against the hard, cold earth, crossing his legs and buries his painfully cold hands in his armpits. In the scant light, Callum notices occasional wisps of threadlike roots dangling from the curved sides of the hole. There are no handholds, ropes, or a ladder to use for escape. Scaling the walls is not a viable option, and any attempt to escape would undermine Frey's adamant defense of him.

Callum lets out a dismayed sigh as he resigns to his miserable situation. With his fate in the hands of his unsympathetic captors, he can only wait and endure. Callum rests his head back against the wall and watches each breath gently spiral upward. He tries to focus on anything other than the numbing cold permeating his weary body. Even gnawing hunger and thirst are preferable to the hypothermia that keeps him continually shivering.

He watches the finger of sunlight trace a faint path across the floor. The sun is nearly dead center above the pit when Callum hears voices. The language is foreign to him, but after hours of silence, he listens intently to the comforting signs of life above.

When at last he hears someone unlatching the gate that covers his cell, Callum grows hopeful. As it lifts, the full brilliance of the sun explodes down the shaft, and Callum shields his eyes until they can adjust to the light's assault.

"Callum Walker!" Marcus' voice calls down to him.

The fae captain's head and shoulders appear in a dark profile as he leans over the entrance. Callum is surprised to be called by name but takes it as confirmation that Frey's account of their adventure has at least been heard. He wonders if she revealed his entire life story—a tale he shared in confidence.

"Please tell me you brought a warm blanket or maybe some food." Callum croaks. His parched throat causes his voice to crack.

The shadow of hope vanishes when Marcus draws away from the entrance and sunbeams return. Seconds later, the sun is blocked again, and Marcus descends with fluttering wings into the icy pit. He gently lands, wearing thick boots and a fur coat, and he carries the puffy green jacket confiscated at the time of Callum's capture. Marcus tosses the coat to the warlock.

"The queen has called for an audience with you. She wants to know for herself if Frey's claims are correct."

"Where is Frey?" Callum asks, pulling the jacket on over his trembling shoulders.

"Frey is in good health. She is being held in the education center, awaiting her sentence while she spends her time in service."

"I want to see her," Callum says firmly. He felt a deep emptiness since the fae troopers seized Frey, and he longs to see for himself that she is being treated well.

"You can ask the queen's permission when you speak with her," Marcus says, deflecting Callum's request. "Are you ready to proceed?"

Callum looks up at the distant portal above and wonders how he is expected to leave the pit. Marcus offers no explanation and once again hugs him tightly before beating his glassy wings and flying them both up into the warm sunshine.

Callum gasps a request to walk rather than fly. Marcus grudgingly agrees and lands in the heart of the fairy community, guiding him toward an intricate network of paths.

"Do all fairies fly?" Callum asks.

"No. The magical realm is home to a multitude of different beings, but very few can fly. Among the many types of fairies, only sprites, pixies, and common fae are blessed with wings," Marcus explains. He marches close as Callum limps on his wounded leg. "Frey is not the first of our kind to cross the veil and study your kin, but you are the first human to step foot in Whitshell."

Crossing the village on foot subjects him to many shocked and awkward stares from fairy folk unprepared to witness a miniature human. The sprites whisper curious questions and comments to each other. Callum keeps his head down and tries to ignore the intrigued gawking.

"Is that why you can speak English? You've been watching us?" Callum asks. He ponders how long human society has been oblivious to the existence of these secretive creatures. Except, of course, the select few who go on to write fairy tales about their encounters.

"Actually, it is the other way around," Marcus replies with a new tone of civility. Though the captain carries a rapier strapped to his belt, he is far less intimidating in both posture and presentation. Perhaps his monarch accepted Frey's explanation that Callum arrived here against his will. That would hopefully make him a guest rather than an invader.

"The races of this realm have lived millennia longer than humans. There was a time when we did not conceal ourselves from your kind," the captain narrates as they walk. "In fact, we taught your human ancestors our parent language. Your predecessors shared our dialect with successive generations, eventually renaming it as 'English.' At least in this part of the globe."

"Oh." Callum feels insignificant in the grand picture of human existence. He cannot help wondering whether fairies have influenced other aspects of human societies and cultures.

A whirlpool of questions occupies Callum's mind, but he does not get another chance to inquire. Prisoner and escort halt at the foot of an enormous conifer. The rugged and scarred coarse tree bark is cracked wide enough for Callum to step into—if he does not mind the stretched silk of spiderwebs or skittering beetles as long as his forearm. Last night, he saw this gargantuan evergreen as a looming wall rising from the earth. Now, standing at its base, Callum swallows a sense of dread. One way or another, his route is now upward.

He sizes up a stairway of sculpted steps chiseled into the outer husk of the tree, noting without enthusiasm that it endlessly spirals up the trunk. There is no sign of handholds or a protective railing. Callum looks skyward through the gaps in the foliage and sees dozens of pendulous buildings dangling from ascending levels of branches. The aroma of pine sap is pungent, and the ebb-and-flow of a rustling breeze causes the tree to sway and creak gently. Rather than admiring this arboreal beauty from his miniaturized perspective, Callum feels lightheaded at the prospect of a grueling climb up the narrow stairway to unknown heights.

"It will take much less time if I can carry you," says Marcus.

Callum hesitates. "Can I trust you not to drop me?" he responds, confronting his petrifying fear of heights.

"You have my word." Marcus confidently nods. Callum has no alternative but to accept his captor's assurance.

It feels like an eternity before the pair soars up to the community's highest level, nearly halfway up the tree. Callum's heart is jackhammering, and his legs are shaking by the time Marcus finally alights on a broad branch.

"I did not drop you," says Marcus, confused by Callum's intense anxiety.

"I appreciate that," Callum replies breathlessly. "But it doesn't change the fact that I'm terrified of heights."

Marcus tilts his head and studies Callum with curiosity, baffled at this odd declaration of fear. He says no more despite his apparent fascination with Callum's strange and foreign phobia.

The captain leads the way toward a grand entryway carved into the tree trunk. When Marcus knocks and requests entry, the doors swing open. Callum is dazzled by the chamber's interior, a spacious room that resembles the inside of a log building. Blond woodgrain patterns dominate the walls, and the tree's circular growth rings give the floor the look of a giant braided rug.

"This way," Marcus beckons to Callum, who unexpectedly pauses to admire the magnificence of the place.

The warlock rejoins his warden, and together they climb a staircase that curves along the wall. Callum limps after Marcus as they ascend three levels and arrive at a tall door covered in elaborate carvings. Marcus swings the door open, holding it for Callum to enter first.

The enormous chamber feels alive. Masses of colorful blossoms in wooden planter boxes form a fragrant perimeter. Windows cut into the side of the tree allow sunlight to flow into the room and create a bright aura. A shallow pool of water in a stone-sided cistern is framed by tall, slender windows, so the day's natural brightness dances across its surface in patterns. The only furniture in the circular room is a plain, round table placed between two simple chairs.

Seeing no one else, Callum pauses in the room's center to absorb the tranquil light and beauty. As the door gently clicks shut behind him, he realizes he is now alone in the room.

Uncertain of what is expected when meeting a fairy queen, he wishes Marcus had stayed to offer helpful advice. Nervously, Callum begins a slow circuit around the circular room, examining each planter box in turn. Most of the flowers are undersized, while others are exceedingly large, reaching the ceiling and bowing back toward the floor. It seems that even the towering plants were carefully selected to adorn the room without overwhelming the space.

Callum leans over some plants, parting a few leaves and petals to peer out a window and savor the heat of the sun. After warming, he removes his jacket and hangs it over the back of one of the empty chairs.

His slow circle around the room continues as he frets about meeting the fairy queen. When he finally reaches the reflecting pool, Callum stops.

Peering into the pristine water, he can see the intricate mosaic of tiles covering the bottom of the knee-deep cistern. Callum has an odd feeling about the pool, but it is so vague that he cannot identify anything specific. Puzzled, he leans toward the water to examine it in greater detail.

"I made the pattern myself," a quiet voice says over his shoulder.

Callum jumps and spins around to see a young fairy girl standing behind him. The sudden movement throws him off balance, and Callum stumbles, nearly falling into the water. The fae reaches out in a flash and grabs his sleeve to save him from the plunge.

"Thank you...um, your majesty," Callum says, trying to regain both his footing and composure.

He looks down at the smiling child, who seems unmoved. She looks no older than thirteen, but her eyes are dark and deep, hinting at profound wisdom.

"You are welcome, Callum Walker," she says as she moves purposefully toward the polished woodgrain table.

She gracefully tucks the fabric of her flowing white skirt beneath her, then takes a seat at the table. Wavy sorrel hair falls over her slim shoulders as she leans forward to sit. Once settled, the fae girl cocks her head at Callum, studying him with sagacious, violet eyes.

"I...Uhm...You *are* the queen, right?" Callum asks. He is confounded by this fairy, who appears adolescent at most. Outwardly, she seems far too young to possess the qualities necessary to rule a community.

"Where are my manners?" she says, nodding. "I am the appointed Queen of Whitshell, but you may call me Daphne."

Callum cannot imagine her as a sovereign leader, but he really does not know much about fairies. She could, in fact, be hundreds of years older than she appears. Ignoring her youthful features, Callum notes that Daphne carries herself with the high intellect and confidence of someone who has experienced many challenges and rises above them.

"I see that I am somewhat of a surprise to you," Daphne observes. "Perhaps you were expecting someone who looks older?"

"I don't know what I was expecting," Callum mumbles.

"Let me ask you something, Callum," the girl-queen says as

she lifts her chin and addresses him in a tone of inquiry. "What do you see when you look around this room?"

"I see lots of beautiful flowers and sunlight," Callum says. There is something about the queen's innocent question that signals a need for him to be wary.

"Are you able to sense an energy here that does not belong?"

Callum now feels very uneasy over Daphne's strange queries. She has a purpose, but what? "I don't understand what you're asking."

He first assumes the queen is referring to his empathic sense that alerts him to the presence of good and evil, a fact he only shared with Frey. Or perhaps she is alluding to his perception of magical energy.

"This room abounds with life, but there is something here that intrudes. I have planted a foreign invader as a test to see whether you are indeed the warlock that Frey believes you are."

Daphne stares at him, calmly awaiting evidence on which to pass judgment. She may doubt his possession of magical gifts, despite her own ability to sense his powers. But like Marcus, Daphne requires confirmation.

"Frey probably also told you that I'm not very experienced," he says. Callum knows his knowledge and capabilities are limited, and he might not be able to do what is being asked of him.

After experiencing her soldiers' rough brand of diplomacy, a thought occurs to Callum. Failing the queen's test might mean immediate banishment to a dark, freezing pit for the rest of his days. Despite his involuntary arrival, Callum doubts they will simply let him leave. Most importantly, Frey is counting on him to pass this test and prove her claims about him. If he satisfies Daphne's examination, it might reduce the severity of Frey's punishment.

"She did, but that should not matter," says Daphne evenly. "Even a novice can do what I am asking. Please, take your time."

"All right then." Callum sighs.

Feeling very unsure of himself, he begins to make another slow, deliberate circle around the chamber. He concentrates carefully on each planter, looking intently at each bloom, leaf, and stem before moving on to the next box. His intuition does not reveal anything nefarious among the flowers. Nevertheless, he is disappointed as he leaves the final planter box and heads directly for the reflecting pool.

Callum stops at the edge of the water and feels drawn by something he cannot explain. He stares down at the pattern of tiles lining the bottom and ponders what makes this shallow bath so special.

The blue and white tiles are laid out in a pretty montage of mountains and sky. But, upon closer inspection, the image beneath the rippling water is slightly unclear. Callum remembers the vague sensation that drew him to the water before Queen Daphne startled him. Now, leaning over the pool once more, his eyes continue probing. A disturbing sensation of energy grows in intensity. Something is hidden beneath the water, potentially dark energy, but not enough to be glaringly obvious to his senses. That would have made Daphne's test far too easy.

"There's something here in the pool," Callum whispers. He rests a hand on the edge of the cistern while reaching toward the water's surface.

Daphne remains silent and watchful as his hand hesitates above the liquid. Callum feels a compulsion to find what lurks below its surface, yet he is frightened by what he might discover. As usual, the pull to investigate overpowers his fear of the unknown. Callum takes another deep breath and warily touches the pool.

The instant his fingers contact the water, an opalescent shimmer surges as a spell breaks. Callum can now make out a small, dark form in the pool, gazing up at him with ebony eyes. Whatever it is, the creature was concealed in the basin by an enchantment until his touch released it.

Seeing a chance for freedom, the unknown creature springs

to life. It leaps from the water and rams its head with a hard thump against Callum's chin. The blow knocks him backward onto the hard wooden floor.

The small, vile beast pounces onto Callum's chest, clawing with feral violence at the warlock's face and neck using talon-like fingernails and a snapping mouthful of brown, curved teeth.

Callum grabs the creature's middle with both hands, and it squirms and thrashes in his grasp. Snarling in high-pitched squeals, it flails its short arms and twists, trying to wriggle free. Callum gapes at the up-close view of the grotesque creature's tiny head and large pointed ears. While holding the enraged beast at arm's length to avoid its sharp claws and snapping jaw, Callum manages to identify the monster.

This wild thing is unquestionably a goblin and a furious one at that.

It whips its head around to bite Callum's arms and stomps on his ribs with deceptively powerful legs. The goblin's ear-piercing screams reverberate throughout the room. Callum must subdue the goblin or risk being kicked, chewed, or clawed to death. He forms a solution and now forces himself to concentrate regardless of the pain and rising panic.

"*Glacies!*" Callum shouts the moment his thoughts coalesce into a single word in his mind.

The goblin's eyes bulge in terror as a vapor of frost burst from Callum's fingers and penetrate its green body, freezing it into a solid chunk of ice. Within seconds, the squirming beast is lifeless as a stone. Callum heaves it away, and the frozen goblin cracks into pieces when it strikes the floor. Its beaky nose and both arms skitter across the room while the rest of its body lands facedown with a heavy thud.

Laying on the floor, Callum gasps to catch his breath. It takes nearly a minute until he can regain his feet. He winces at the dozens of stinging scratches that decorate his face and neck and holds his chest, now bruised and tender after the rough hammering of sturdy goblin feet.

"Well, Daphne, did I pass your little test?" Callum asks angrily. He meets the queen's wide-eyed, shocked expression, now displaying the most emotion he saw on her childlike face so far.

She looks down at the shattered, frozen goblin. "Yes, Callum, you have certainly passed," says Daphne.

The chunks have already started to glow a brilliant white as it fades from existence. Based on Frey's prior explanation, this goblin must be a creation of dark magic meant to wreak havoc on Whitshell's fae folk.

Daphne seems uncertain. Clearly, she expected him to fail.

"Since antiquity, there have been humans born with powerful magical abilities like yours," Daphne finally explains. "They have always appeared in singularity, and many of them used their gifts for self-serving purposes. But some were truly noble, and their journeys were written in your history books. Now, very few even know where to look."

"So, there have been others before me?" Callum asks, now reassured that his gift is not so strange after all.

"There have been others, born centuries apart and always alone." Daphne carefully watches Callum for a reaction. "Frey said she told you about our version of a prophecy, written five centuries ago. It alludes to '*a sign in our most desperate hour. Two humans will arise, both born with the power of magic. One will serve himself with the darkest of desires, and the other will bring an end to the reign of evil. Both will be judged, but only one will succeed, and in this way, the protector will set the entire world free.*' Although this is only a portion of our interpretation, and each race of beings has their own rendition, I believe, as Frey does, that you are our protector."

Callum remains silent. He does not want to accept that the prophecy is about him. It is too vague to offer a concrete identification, and Daphne herself says there were others born like him throughout history. Maybe the prophecy was already fulfilled hundreds of years ago by someone else.

"You doubt this?" Daphne asks, carefully observing him.

"Of course, I doubt it." Callum snaps. "I can't bring an end to evil."

He paces the floor while Daphne's eyes track his movements. Callum is overwhelmed by the queen's expectations, which are beyond anything he can imagine for himself. He wants to close his eyes and forget everything he has seen and heard and wonders if he can just walk away from this new knowledge or even find some way to disprove it.

After all, Callum knows he did use his powers for personal gain and survival before he started hunting. Could he be the one who has served his darkest desires? He shudders the idea of being judged for his many past mistakes.

"There is no denying that our world is at war. It was contained within the magical realm until recently when Kincaid began to send his creations into the cities of men," says Daphne. A note of pleading in her voice compels Callum to listen.

"Kincaid. I've heard that name before." Callum halts his pacing at the recollection. He turns to meet her gaze.

"The evils that you have been fighting were conjured by this man. He seeks domination of our world. His name is David Kincaid, and he is a human born with natural access to magic, just like you. Whether or not you choose to accept your role in this prophecy is up to you. Still, I must tell you that Kincaid knows of your existence, so you and your human world are already in great danger."

Of all that Frey has taught Callum about fairies, he most remembers her strict assertion that fae do not lie—they are truthful to a fault. But even knowing this, he does not want to trust the information that Daphne is revealing. Stubbornly, Callum tries to ignore it and cling to the possibility of this whole thing being a cruel joke at his expense. But, as hard as he tries to deny it, Callum's intuition drives him toward belief.

Reluctance to accept his part in this prophecy is not totally fueled alone by disbelief. Callum cannot imagine he is meant to play such an important role simply because he judges himself unworthy. He spent the past few years trying to make up for the crimes he committed as a young teenager. Callum believes his sole redeeming quality is the decision to use his gifts to protect those who cannot fight the magical monsters he finds.

"Callum, I would like you to sit with me," Daphne says to him.

He hesitates before trudging to the table and slumping into his seat. Callum is dazed by his jumbled thoughts, lost in a reality that weighs him down with unbelievable facts.

"I understand how you must feel," Daphne sympathizes. "When I became queen, I felt ill-prepared for the task. We can never be fully prepared for our challenges until we choose to accept them. The trials teach us about ourselves, and when we embrace the path before us, we discover the strength within to overcome obstacles."

Callum meets Daphne's kind eyes and finds some comfort from her compassion. His entire life has been filled with secrecy and solitude. He lives alone to avoid discovery while also trying to survive within the constraints of acceptable human behavior.

"You must find conviction, and your journey will guide you," Daphne adds.

Callum sits quietly for several minutes, reflecting on her advice.

There was no hesitation in hunting monsters. How is this different? Callum does not desire adventure and is not looking for the thrills from facing mortal danger like some people relish. He ventures out alone at night to fight monsters because he believes his magic comes with a responsibility to fight for the defenseless—Callum simply feels compelled to help others. Frey has shown him that he is not alone. Others in this realm share his gift of magic.

Realization suddenly dawns. Callum was so wrapped up in his own effort to survive that he almost missed an entire world just beyond his doorstep. Now that world looks to him for help, and he is faltering.

"I understand if you require some time to think," Daphne says as she presses her palms on the table and rises to her feet.

As the queen starts to move away, Callum speaks up. "I'm willing to hear you out, but on one condition."

"Which is?" Daphne asks, pausing and turning toward him again. There is a glimmer of anticipation on her face.

"Frey was protecting me because she believes in this prophecy of yours. So much so that she was willing to break your laws. I want assurances that she won't be punished, and I want to see her again." Callum fixes firm eyes on Daphne, determined to accept nothing but agreement.

He is now aware Kincaid will continue to inflict monsters on the human world, and he is already a hunted man because of his own power. Callum is far past the point of deniability, and he knows it. He hopes he has earned enough favor from this fairy queen to make this request.

"We do not endorse physical punishment, Callum. Rather, we prefer a term of re-education for those who violate our time-honored directive. Frey will still be disciplined, but she will not be hurt or imprisoned. She will go to our mother city, Ursona, where she will be re-taught the values of cooperation and obedience. I cannot change our traditional methods at your request. But if it means so much to you, I will allow a meeting with Frey before she is sent away."

"Then, tell me what I need to do next," Callum says. His voice is hesitant yet determined.

Daphne smiles broadly at him and sighs with relief as she sinks gently back onto her chair. "I can tell you what I know about the prophecy. It is my hope that you will use this knowledge to save our world and yours."

CHAPTER THIRTEEN

Callum spends a head-spinning afternoon engaged in deep conversation with Daphne. Thankfully, their discussion is accompanied by an abundant meal of soup, fruit, and unusual fae versions of bread and cheese. After enthusiastically devouring his meal, the food restores much of his spent strength and improves his mood.

The queen is keen to educate Callum on theories surrounding the imprecise prophecy written five hundred years ago. The timeline disproves Callum's argument that others could have previously fulfilled the forewarning. For over six centuries, no other empowered humans like him have existed—other than Kincaid. These realizations add stress to his burdened mind and banish further doubts of its validity. Callum wishes he could deny his importance and free himself from the unknown anguish awaiting him.

"I wish there was more I could offer you about how to set forth along this path," Daphne says sympathetically. "The history of the prophecy is filled with mystery, and its vagueness leaves open-ended questions that have not found answers. The best counsel I can give is to have faith that the high gods will direct your path."

The sun long since vanished below the horizon, leaving the garden room bathed in reflected moonlight from the cistern. Callum gathers his coat while Marcus is summoned. Daphne clasps Callum's hands in farewell and reaffirms her promise that he will be reunited with Frey. As the captain escorts him out of the queen's inner sanctum, Callum notices how Marcus' level of respect has subtly increased. Anyone granted an extended private audience with Queen Daphne must be important indeed.

The fairy and warlock retrace their path down the winding staircase and through the ornate natural palace carved into the heart of the evergreen. When they emerge through the double doors onto the tree limb, Callum is once more caught off guard by Marcus.

Without warning or time for objections, the fae commander embraces him from behind and swiftly rises into the air. Seizing Marcus' spindly arms, a terrified Callum holds on for dear life as they swoop and plunge through gaps between pine branches. An icy wind whistles past his ears and bites his face and fingers. Rather than heading for the base of the gigantic palace tree, Marcus's beating wings sweep them toward a teardrop-shaped building hanging far above the ground by the point of its tented roof. A thick cable of twisted vines rises from the peak and secures the dangling structure to a sturdy evergreen limb.

The flight ends when Marcus deposits Callum gently on the rustic front porch that protrudes from the tiny, oddly shaped cottage. Before them is an inviting door made of twigs—the size of planks to fae folk—fastened together by interlaced ropes of root tendrils. Chinks between the boards betray the yellow warmth of an inviting fireplace within. A round window cuts into the upper face of the door, offering a glimpse of the homey interior through a lattice of willowy sticks.

Marcus approaches the unlocked door and opens it. "You will wait inside until Frey arrives," he declares with a hint of deference.

His movements cause the entire structure to sway slightly.

Callum inhales sharply, throwing himself against the birchbark siding that covers the curved outer walls.

Marcus motions with an outstretched arm, pausing and tilting his head at the sight of Callum stricken with near panic. "This building is sound. You will be safe here."

Callum involuntarily glances beyond the edge of the railless porch. With a hand pressed against his hyperventilating chest, the warlock can feel his thundering heart. His head is spinning at the petrifying view of the distance between himself and the ground far below. He snaps his eyes closed and desperately hugs the wall.

"Come on, inside with you," Marcus says with a vexing scoff. Callum's phobia about heights is becoming an annoyance.

Marcus takes hold of Callum's puffy coat sleeve and guides him away from the wall and across the threshold. The warlock shuffles obediently through the doorway. Once inside the dangling cottage and the illusion of security, Callum relaxes and opens his eyes upon hearing the door close behind him. He is alone.

The cabin's curving timbers and rustic surfaces combine to create an organic beauty. The ceiling of the circular room rises into a cone of sculpted boards and beams, sanded smooth to reveal the wood's intricate grain patterns.

The room's focal point is a stacked-pebble fireplace opposite the doorway with a cheery blaze crackling inside. Callum gravitates toward the warmth. A pair of handcrafted armchairs and a wide sofa are positioned around the hearth, each topped with feather-filled cushions wrapped in wool. The intimate sitting room is smaller than his apartment but far more welcoming.

Surrounded by the tranquil atmosphere, Callum soothes his prior panic. He settles on one end of the couch, lifting his throbbing leg, now swollen significantly.

Pulling his pant leg up to his knee, Callum removes the rough bandage. He sighs in dismay at the crimson heat of his inflamed skin around the black scabs of the shapeshifter's bite marks.

Moments later, the door to the quaint cottage flies opens. Frey rushes into the cozy interior bearing a small satchel slung over her shoulder. A slender fae soldier follows close behind, entering the room and closing the door behind them. He stiffly stands and stares at Callum with a suspicious gaze.

"Callum!" Frey squeals excitedly when she sees him. She streaks across the room to him, wrapping her arms around his neck and pressing against him in an emotional hug. She buries her face into his chest and murmurs, "I have been so worried that you were hurt or sent away, and I would never be allowed to say goodbye."

"Yeah, me too," Callum says. He awkwardly embraces Frey in return and feels her slight frame quivering. "I spoke to Daphne about you. I wanted her to promise that you wouldn't be punished for trying to help me. I guess I'm a bit confused about how your law-and-order works around here."

Frey pulls away from him and wipes away tears with her slender hands. Callum lowers his leg from the couch, and Frey gladly takes a seat beside him.

"We do not hurt or imprison our own kind, but I am to be taught a lesson about servitude. I have been assigned to work as a servant to a sage scholar in the great city of the Seelie court," Frey explains, giving Callum a half-hearted grin as reassurance. "I am to leave this night, and I will not return for thirty years."

"What? Thirty years is outrageous! This isn't right, Frey. You were only trying to help me," Callum thunders.

"Fairy folk live for centuries, Callum," Frey says patiently. "Thirty years is a short time by our standards. Daphne *has* asked the Seelie court for leniency, and they have given me this shorter course," Frey explains with reverence, despite Callum's protests. "I knowingly broke our laws by leaving Whitshell in the first place, and I did it again when I returned with you. I accept my actions and do not claim innocence. I will not argue for mercy I do not deserve. It is against the nature of fairies to lie."

"Honesty to a fault," Callum huffs sarcastically, glaring at the stoic sentinel by the door. The guard's persistent stare never leaves the two figures on the couch.

Such unmovable scrutiny makes the warlock uneasy. Callum doubts the fae will grant them a private moment together. So, instead, he does his best to ignore the observer and focus on his troubled friend.

"I have brought you something from our druid," Frey says quietly, sniffling away lingering tears.

She opens the satchel at her hip, retrieves a corked jar containing a thick gray paste, and removes the stopper. Callum questioningly eyes it, wrinkling his nose in disgust and apprehension.

"Sprites do not have magic strong enough to heal your wound," Frey says. "We can protect small animals and help plants to grow, but we are not healers. The druid in our village is trained to use herbs and plants to treat ailments. This ointment will take away your pain and lessen the swelling. However, it will not be enough to mend your injury but will numb it until you can get proper help from your human shamans."

"Oh," is all Callum can reply. But he also trusts Frey and allows her to examine his leg.

Frey kneels at his feet, sliding her fingers into the open jar and scooping out a big glob of the ugly, gray cream. Callum gags at the odious aroma of mold and other horrible smells, wincing as the cool salve stings his feverish skin. He does not recoil. Instead, he permits Frey to gingerly slather his angry-looking punctures with the rank concoction. When she finishes, Frey corks the jar and retrieves a roll of white linen from her bag. She wraps the fabric in layers around his leg to cover the gray plaster and ties it firmly in place. Her medical task complete, she returns to Callum's side on the couch, bashfully smiling.

"How does that feel now?" she asks, casting him a fleeting glance.

"It feels better," Callum says honestly when he notices the

pleasant lack of pain. He lets his pant leg fall back into place. "Thank you, Frey."

"You are very welcome." Her pastel-blue cheeks cannot conceal a warm pink blush, and she lifts her eyes hesitantly toward him. Fresh tears glisten.

"Frey Pearvale, it is time to leave," the fae guard finally intones. Frey flinches at his commanding insistence.

"What? No!" Callum exclaims, but the stalwart soldier returns a narrow-eyed stare that is as inflexible as his determination. "She's only been here for twenty minutes."

"He is right," Frey sighs. Her body slouches in submission, and her eyes express heavy regret. "The queen granted me a long enough stay to treat your wound and wish you goodbye."

"No!" Callum shouts. He bolts to his feet to position himself between Frey and the sentry. "You can't do this. Not yet!"

The warlock shifts his weight, making a move toward the soldier—in protest rather than confrontation—hoping to argue his position. The fairy guard responds by withdrawing a slender but lethal sword from a scabbard at his hip. Its fine blade narrows into a deadly, glittering point.

With a couple of whirlwind flaps of his wings, the warden lifts from the ground and advances toward Callum. He lands with skillful agility, leveling his blade to the warlock's throat and stopping just short of impaling his Adam's apple. Callum freezes in place, every muscle flexed. His eyes widen like saucers at the sentry's rapid hostility, but the warlock's surprise quickly shifts to anger. Callum glares down the length of the gleaming rapier and into the stern eyes of the fairy sentry.

"Nova, wait!" Frey shouts, jumping up and hurrying to aid Callum.

She pushes the warlock aside with surprising strength and places herself at the point of the sword. Her self-sacrifice baffles the soldier, and confusion engulfs his willowy face.

Frey addresses the sentry with a placid yet firm entreaty. "He is a human, Nova. They are prone to outbursts of emotion. You know this from our teachings. Right now, this human is *very* distressed, but he means you no harm. The warlock is unfamiliar with fairy law, but the queen decrees that he is the Prophesied One. He cannot rescue our people from this war if you kill him now."

"He challenged me. I am within my right to run him through." Nova mutters.

He scowls at Callum while continuing to hold his blade pointed at Frey's heart. There is a hint of conflict in the watchman's golden eyes as they flit between Frey and Callum.

Callum feels lost in an archaic world of unjust rules. He is aware that attempting to implore the guard for more time was immediately taken as an aggressive act. His arcane power is useless in this tense situation, likely to cause more animosity than harmony. He chooses not to lash out and make the situation worse for Frey. Instead, Callum tries to rein in his emotional upheaval rather than letting his anger control his volatile magical energy.

Even knowing little about fairy magic, Callum would willingly fight to protect them both. But a small army of formidable fae soldiers, plus an entire community of fairies outside the pendulous cabin, gives him a reason to re-evaluate. Finding themselves in a vulnerable standoff, Callum swallows his aggravation and tries his hand at diplomacy.

"I didn't mean to threaten you. I only meant to ask for a few more minutes, that's all," Callum beseeches the guard, tempering his tone and relaxing his expression. "If I will never have a chance to see her again, I need a little longer. Please."

The sentinel gives Callum a dubious look, and his right eye twitches with the strain of indecision. This silent consideration lasts for several tense moments before the soldier reluctantly pulls back and lowers his sword.

"I am only allowing this reprieve because our queen believes you to be the Prophesied One," Nova explains to Callum. He then turns his attention to Frey. "You have five minutes. I will be outside. Do not give me a reason to remove you by force."

With that statement, the dutiful guard departs, slamming the door closed behind him and allowing Callum and Frey a moment of privacy.

"Callum, I do not want you to worry about me," Frey says the instant Nova leaves the room before Callum has a chance to speak. She turns to him and grabs both his hands with her sylph-like flingers. "I am capable of taking care of myself. Just know that I will always cherish our time together, and I consider you my dearest friend. Thirty years is a short time for fairies, but I understand it to be many years of your human lifetime. It is painful to say, but we cannot be together. Even so, I care deeply for you."

"Frey, I..." Callum wants to explain the conflicting emotions coursing through his mind, but the words are a jumbled mess. "I mean...Uhm...I've never really had a friend before you. I appreciate your kindness, and I... Dammit. I really suck at saying goodbye." Callum huffs at his lack of poise and for stumbling over his words. "What I'm trying to say, Frey, is that I'm very glad we met. I care about you, too."

She smiles serenely, leans in closer, and bows her head to rest her forehead against his chin. "I will be in Ursona. You will not be able to enter the city without invitation or merit. If you should earn either one, please come find me."

"Frey," Callum says as inspiration blooms. "Why can't we just leave Whitshell? Sneak out the window and fly away together right now."

His desperate thoughts are conceiving wild plans of them living on the run—a stressful life but one at least they would share.

Frey tearfully shakes her head. "My kin would hunt me down, and I would be forced to return to more severe punishment.

They would kill you for defying the court's order." Squeezing her friend's hands tightly, the fairy locks her anguished eyes on his. "You have to let me go, Callum. The high queen of the Seelie Court has given her commands. I must follow them or risk being stripped of my wings."

There is so much more Callum wants to say, but with precious seconds vanishing, he decides to simply hold Frey in his arms. He embraces her and inhales her flowery scent until Nova raps on the door and demands her departure. Callum grudgingly releases her, his eyes glazed as he fakes a smile.

"Goodbye, Frey," Callum whispers.

She nods, biting her lower lip to keep from sobbing. Sorrowful pain draws lines on her lovely, blue face.

Watching Frey turn from him and disappear through the doorway is gut-wrenching and crushes Callum's heart. His first true friend has been taken from him in an unfair turn of events he can barely comprehend. Callum stands staring at the door for several insufferable minutes before he returns to the couch to sit with his face buried into his hands.

An hour later, the shadows have lengthened, and the untended fire is dying. The once-cozy cabin is now diffused in a gloom that matches Callum's despair.

Marcus returns, letting himself inside without a knock or invitation. "It is time to return you to your home across the veil," Marcus announces. A sympathetic expression replaces his normally apathetic one when he sees Callum's somber face appear from his hands.

"What?" Callum asks.

He did not expect to stay in Whitshell forever, but he hoped for more guidance before being evicted. Thus far, all he received is a history lesson from Daphne, a few imaginative theories about the origin or meaning of the augury, and a painfully brief reconnection with Frey. So, now, he is being shoved out of the magical realm with more questions than answers.

"I have no idea what I'm supposed to do with everything I've learned. And that isn't much."

"It is not our place to tell you what to do. The queen has given you all the knowledge you need, and it is up to you to find your path and trust the powers that be to design your future. No one in this realm knows how the Prophesied One will end the war any more than you do." Marcus points out while standing in the doorway.

This captain of the fairy guard is evidently unaccustomed to dealing with the range of emotions that Callum exudes—or his questions and objections.

"So that's it, then. You throw me in a hole when I arrive and leave me to nearly freeze to death. Then your queen lets a goblin attack me just to prove my worth. I jumped through your damn hoops only to be told I'm the greatest hope this realm has. Then I get sent away with nothing but a 'good luck, fated one,'" Callum fumes, abandoning all emotional restraint and projecting his rage.

"This is the way it must be. We cannot interfere, or we risk altering the outcome," Marcus says, standing his ground and studying Callum cautiously. "This is your journey, not ours. We fairies cannot involve ourselves. We must stay concealed to protect our people from the conflict that threatens us."

"Whatever."

Callum gives up on this endless debate. Furious to the point of losing rational thought, his heartstrings are stretched and raw. But Marcus is only following orders, and, to his understanding, Daphne is also subservient to her own deciding authority among the enigmatic spearheads of the mysterious Seelie court.

Sighing in submission, Callum stands and approaches Marcus. "Let's get this over with."

Marcus stiffly nods in silent response and steps out to the porch. Callum follows, burying his mounting depression and replacing his emotional void with a fierce determination to survive.

He vows to somehow find his way to Ursona and revisit his captive friend. But for now, he needs to focus his thoughts and energies on avoiding the organized forces hunting him or risk falling victim to an insidious enemy that wants him dead.

CHAPTER FOURTEEN

L iam lost access to a supporting team of hunters when Eric ordered them to other missions. Even though it has been over twenty-four hours without any sign of the warlock, Liam is told to stick with his assigned role for another two weeks.

He has been told to discard all his artifacts since Callum can detect their presence. It would be logical to assume other magical beings can sense the presence of magical energy, but whether it is true or not remains to be proven. Liam feels naked and defenseless without his talismans, but this measure is necessary given the current situation.

While at the estate, Liam received critical information about Callum's true value to the Order. The warlock is one with powers equal to those of their hated enemy, and this knowledge gave Liam the resolve needed to work even harder to find him.

When he returns home after his Monday work shift, Liam uses a laptop to re-watch the footage from the mall's hidden camera at least a dozen times. The hunter searches each second of action in slow motion, scrutinizing the video for any clue of how Callum eluded him—it is the only irrefutable evidence available.

Liam eventually spots something. A tiny flicker of light rises out of Callum's jacket hood just before the confrontation with the shifter. The twinkling object appears to float upward and disappears into a ceiling tile. The flash of light could be discounted as an anomaly, but since it reappeared after the shifter's defeat, only moments before Callum fled the building, it gives credence to Liam's hypothesis. The warlock may not be operating alone.

Working online with the Order's computer technologists to confirm it is not a digital glitch, Liam narrows down a list of magical culprits. He surmises that Callum must be in the company of a fairy.

The simplicity of Callum's spells during the shapeshifter battle suggests the warlock is not advanced enough to cast a spell as sophisticated as a portal. But a fairy, on the other hand, is more than capable of transporting him out of harm's way.

Proud of his revelation, Liam leaves his thin-walled apartment to have a private conversation outside on the sidewalk. He crosses the street and stops at a desolate bus stop. Brushing away a layer of snow from the bench, Liam takes a seat and calls Eric. He listens impatiently to the ringing hum, always keeping his eyes glued to the front door of the downtrodden apartment building. When Eric finally answers, Liam reports his findings.

"Hmm," Eric says, pondering this new information. "If this is the case, it narrows down the list of places that he might be since fae can only travel by way of magic to their homeland. Faehame, I believe it is called."

"Where's that?" Liam asks.

"It is an old Scottish term for a fairyland, but it is impossible to say where it is unless we know more about the fae who cast the spell. Fairies can live in forests, mountains, lakes, and even underground. So, unless we know where this fairy hails from, there is no way of knowing where Walker was taken. But I will deliver this information to Quinn. He will be very pleased."

"So, that's it. The warlock is out of our reach," Liam says

with resignation. He had been so close to his target, yet Callum slipped away. Liam cannot help but feel disheartened and anxious about this failure.

"It's actually very good news."

"How so?"

"Fae folk will not permit strangers to stay in their midst for very long. They will *have* to return him home within a day or two."

"It's already been over twenty-four hours, so if you're right, he should be back within another day," Liam says. The frustrating delay in completing his mission might soon be over after all.

"We know that he was injured in his confrontation with the shifter, and that might work in our favor when he returns. If Walker's moving more slowly, he should be easier to catch. But be assured, there will be no more excuses for failure," Eric warns. His voice carries the hint of a possible threat, indicating his expectation for success at any cost.

Liam has been forgiven once for allowing the warlock to slip away, but the hunter knows any other failures will be met with drastic punishment. Quinn is reasonable to a point, but if angered, his wrath is vicious and deadly.

Liam swallows hard. "Fairy folks are known to care for animals and plants. How likely is it that they'll help Walker by healing his wounds?" he wonders aloud.

"Have faith, Brother," Eric declares in a heartier tone. "There is no one more knowledgeable about the magical realm than Quinn. He has also foreseen the warlock's reappearance in the city of men. If he says the fairies will send Walker home, then you can rest assured. That is what they will do. As for his injuries, well, the sprite fairies are not very adept at healing humans. They may try to help, but they will not be able to offer Walker a full recovery."

"Thank you, sir," Liam replies and ends the call.

Eric's assurance of Quinn's irrefutable knowledge of Callum

Walker sets the hunter's mind at ease. Of course, he has no way of knowing how Quinn obtains his knowledge, but it is his sworn duty to trust and obey without question—whether he agrees or not.

It has been a long day for Liam. He needs to preserve his cover as a maintenance worker and keep up with his other responsibilities as a hunter. It is late in the evening, and Liam is ready to get some sleep before another long day of surveillance and work. He must maintain his cover job just in case Callum graces their employer with his presence long enough to be fired.

At the beginning of his mission, Liam took the initiative and rented an apartment in Callum's building. While he would have preferred a suite next door to the warlock's low-budget rental, he managed to acquire a single-room apartment on the same floor. Now, Liam stands across the street from the decrepit building, cold hands stuffed into his coat pockets. He pauses when movement catches his eye—someone is walking toward the main entrance.

The trim figure shuffles down the opposite sidewalk, shoulders hunched against the cold, despite the protection of a bright green winter jacket. Liam notices the stranger limping as he tramps through the snow. It seems too good to be true that Callum would make this fortuitous appearance. Still, Liam studied his quarry well enough to recognize him at a distance.

Trying not to draw attention to himself, the hunter resumes his seat on the bench, sitting casually as though waiting for the next bus. He casts occasional sideways glances toward the shadowy figure to confirm Callum's identity.

The warlock does not appear to notice he is being watched. His only concern seems to be getting out of the cold.

When Liam's quarry enters the apartment building, the hunter finally crosses the deserted street and hurries toward the entrance. Waiting for a couple minutes before stepping inside, he allows his target enough time to climb the empty stairwell.

Unfortunately, the elevators are not functioning in the dilapidated building.

Liam quietly moves up the stairs, straining to listen for movement. He hears the metallic screech of the heavy access door on the fourth floor as it opens and the corresponding thud of it closing. Liam bolts up the remaining levels and peers through a tiny window in the door, confirming the hobbling figure enters Callum's apartment.

The young hunter hurries down the hall, unlocks his own door, and slips inside. He rushes across his barren bachelor suite, jumping over an inflatable mattress covered in a messy pile of blankets. Then, going straight to an old computer desk, he impatiently waits for his laptop to wake up so he can check the concealed cameras in Callum's apartment. When his surveillance feed pops up on his computer, the hunter watches Callum pack his belongings, apparently preparing to leave the apartment, possibly for good.

Realizing that it is now or never for him to capture the warlock, he fumbles his phone in frantic excitement as he dials Eric's number to call for reinforcements. Liam vows not to waste this precious second chance to complete his mission, doubting he will get another.

CHAPTER FIFTEEN

Callum is chilled to the bone but ignores the coffee pot and kettle in his kitchenette. Instead, he burrows into his closet to find an empty tote bag trapped beneath a mound of clothes. Callum begins to sort his meager belongings, packing only those few items that he will need most. There are still many unanswered questions, but he doubts Daphne would grant him the answers he desires.

The gray paste's numbing effect on his injured leg is already wearing off, and the bite wound is throbbing and burning. But it does not hurt nearly as much as his aching heart knowing he might never see Frey again. Callum is infuriated with Daphne for offering him so little time to wish his friend farewell. The queen could offer Callum kind words but little practical insight, and the young warlock feels wholly unprepared for the mission he reluctantly accepted.

Being unceremoniously dumped back in Duncaster and restored to his proper height, Callum is wretchedly cold and alone once again. The familiar surroundings magnify the deep isolation that has been his sole companion for so many years. After witnessing the close-knit community of fairies and hearing

Daphne's descriptions of the faefolk's family-centered culture, Callum longs for such fellowship.

It feels odd for Callum to admit, but Frey provided him with a feeling of peace. Now with forced separation, it adds more anguish.

Callum's return to Duncaster was so sudden that he had no time to prepare. Without warning, Daphne simply gave the command to deliver him back. The fairy captain cast a return spell and restored Callum to his former stature. The warlock found himself standing in ankle-deep snow, then Marcus left him alone in the darkness of a cold night. The captain did not even offer a single word of encouragement before vanishing in a blink of light.

Lacking any real plan of action, Callum ventured home to pack what little he would need to leave his life behind, and given his poverty, it was not much. He cannot stay in Duncaster if unknown magical adversaries are actively pursuing him. It is time to leave this old existence behind and embark on his new journey.

Callum finishes stuffing clothes into the tote bag and gathers what little food and medicine he has on hand. His thoughts churn as he scurries around his small apartment. His scavenged and makeshift furniture must be abandoned, and whatever does not fit into his bag will be lost to him.

The last thing he grabs is a small box tucked away behind the bathroom cabinet. Callum pulls a strip of rotten wood away and reaches into the dark cavity to retrieve his small parcel—a tin of money that he has been squirreling away. There is not much cash, but it might be enough to buy a bus ticket to take him away from Duncaster and escape the people pursuing him. As he tucks the collection of bills into a tote pocket, he is unexpectedly aware of a sensation that he is being watched.

Callum stands motionless and scans the room, his ears probing the quiet night for any stirrings of life. He cannot hear anything out of the ordinary, but the eerie feeling of eyes upon him is unshakable. Callum does not sense any magical energy, but his intuition alerts him just the same. Despite knowing it was a calculated risk to return to his apartment, he had no choice. He needed clothes and money to support his escape. However, his instincts demand caution and cannot be ignored. So, Callum hastily collects the rest of his required belongings and leaves his home and refuge for the final time.

Liam left his coat on when he entered his apartment and now grabs his go-bag at the sight of Callum frantically packing. Eric promised to send in a team of hunters, but they are driving on icy roads from the mansion and are still at least half an hour away. Their target will be long gone by the time they arrive.

Based on Callum's hurried behavior, it is evident that the warlock knows he is being hunted and plans to quickly flee the city. Liam must be ready to follow him alone rather than waiting for backup. After shedding his magical artifacts, he hides a pistol in his pack and hooks a sheathed knife to his belt. Liam knows he cannot fight Callum with magic and is reassured that the warlock is merely a human who is vulnerable to bullets and blades. Not that Liam has any intention of killing Callum. Quinn wants him alive, but the threat of death is a great motivator for cooperation. The weapons are only there as a last resort, and the hunter hopes he will not be forced to use them.

Liam swallows the last of a mug of cold coffee and watches his target pause for one final look around his apartment.

The hunter has always followed his master's orders without question, and he accepts the claim that his work is ultimately in the service of protecting mankind. Most of the creatures crossing over from the realm are not a threat to humanity, but Kincaid's growing dominance with summoned monsters has created a shift in loyalties. Factions among the inhabitants of the magical realm are taking sides in this war, and the evil that

Kincaid conjures is encroaching on populated centers, threatening the people Liam swore to defend.

His present assignment is in stark contrast to all others because he is ordered to hunt one of his fellow humans rather than protecting. Naturally, this weighs on Liam's conscience. Regardless of any power he possesses, Callum Walker has done nothing wrong or evil as far as Liam can tell. More than that, his actions align with Liam's own profession. He is also a hunter who happens to have a powerful gift Quinn wants to utilize.

Still troubled by these thoughts, Liam shoulders his pack and adjusts the knife on his hip. This is a time of war, and humanity's survival hangs in the balance. Quinn assigned Liam to this mission because he never failed in the past nor questioned his orders. And because Callum has something that can help end the conflict forever.

Embracing this reasoning, Liam prepares himself for whatever he must do to subdue the warlock, even if it means confronting him face-to-face. Liam needs to use swift, disabling force to avoid any retaliation. If he can prevent Callum from casting his magic, he might succeed in capturing him.

Watching through the peephole in his door, Liam hears footsteps approaching. He holds his breath and waits until Callum passes the door and enters the stairwell. Liam keeps his distance inside the building and continues his stealthy tracking in the frigid night.

The vacant streets make it easy to follow the warlock's limping footsteps through freshly fallen snow. Maintaining nearly two blocks of space between them, Liam takes a moment to text the incoming team an update with his new coordinates. A team member responds that their vehicle ran off the road after hitting a patch of black ice.

"Dammit," Liam forcibly sighs.

The veteran hunter confirms that he is now utterly alone in his mission.

After another couple of blocks, Liam notices several additional sets of footprints in the pristine snow, all of them crossing the road to join in the direction of his own pursuit.

Given the lack of visible bystanders, the hunter is suspicious that someone else may be seeking his warlock. Liam quickens his pace to reach Callum before this unknown competitor does, breaking into an ungainly sprint that leaves him slipping on snow-covered, icy patches. The medley of footprints soon overlaps Callum's own route, disappearing around a corner half a block from where Liam started his frantic race. There are no diverging footmarks, so he is confident he can still intercept the warlock.

Liam's mind is running through terrible scenarios where Callum's life is snuffed out, depriving the hunter of his quarry while incurring Quinn's fury. There is no way of knowing the objective of this new challenger. In the context of the ongoing magical war, there is a high likelihood it involves murderous intent. Liam must reach Callum immediately. If the warlock does hold the key to ending this war, he must be found alive.

Liam skids around a blind corner, trying to balance caution with urgency. It turns out to be an unsuccessful combination. A squat, bearded man in leather clothing delivers a hefty swing with a club Liam cannot avoid. It strikes the hunter firmly across his belly. Winded, Liam doubles over. He hugs his aching abdomen and falls to his knees, fighting an overpowering urge to vomit.

"I have never liked hunters," the scruffy assailant growls.

Liam glances up at his assailant. Recognizing the brawny character spoken of in fables, Liam is confused. He never expected to meet a mountain dwarf in the middle of a populated human city because dwarves try to avoid humans at all costs. Mountain dwarves are a solitary race that chiefly dwells in vast, underground settlements carved out of rock and earth. These magical creatures are physically formidable without resorting to arcane forces, which most dwarves shun as a form of cheating.

"I bet you are surprised to see me," the dwarf gloats. He sets one end of the club weapon on the ground and leans on it.

Despite his short stature, the dwarf looks down at Liam. The corners of his wild mustache rise slightly, hinting at a malicious grin beneath the wiry red bead hiding half of his face.

"What the hell are you doing here?" Liam grunts. Still incapacitated by the hollow ache in his gut, he strains to keep his eyes locked on the looming dwarf. Despite their stunted build, dwarves are powerful and able-bodied, so Liam wants to avoid another unprovoked attack at all costs.

The dwarf leans forward and speaks in a quiet, dangerous voice, "You are not the only ones interested in the warlock."

"Why are you after him?" Liam's mind churns out theories that might explain this odd behavior from such a reclusive race.

"We have our reasons. Now, the thing you should be asking yourself is what we will be doing with *you*," the dwarf replies, both cheerfully and menacingly.

"We?" Liam asks. He frightfully recalls the jumbled footprints in the snow indicating multiple members of a hunting party.

The sound of movement behind him makes Liam's blood run cold. He twists his head in time to see another scruffy dwarf closing in with a broad stick raised high above his shoulder.

Far too late, Liam realizes he allowed himself to be distracted by curiosity and failed to notice his stocky assailant was not alone. There is only enough time to squeeze his eyes shut and brace himself before receiving another assault.

The second dwarf's club strikes Liam's head, triggering an explosion of sparks behind his eyes. Sprawling and senseless on the icy sidewalk, Liam is at the mercy of the two burly attackers.

"I guess you hunters are not as good as you think you are," the first dwarf chuckles as he crouches next to his inert victim.

The last thing Liam remembers is the feeling of slush pressing against one side of his face and warm blood trickling down the other.

CHAPTER SIXTEEN

Callum estimates he has several miles to go before reaching the bus station and sighs at the thought of the cold, painful journey ahead. He is determined to leave Duncaster behind, including the merciless trackers bent on capturing him.

The confrontation with the shapeshifter was well-planned, so Callum is far more cautious of people who could easily trap him. He was lucky that Frey's spell at the mall helped him visualize the threat, but Callum can no longer count on her assistance. He lumbers on, tote bag slung over one shoulder, through ankle-deep snow in worn, wet sneakers.

Callum is thankful for the warmth of his stolen jacket and a semi-clean sweatshirt from the final visit to his closet. Unfortunately, he lacks dry, insulated boots, mittens, knit cap, or anything that would protect against the elements. Even though he can tuck his hands into pockets and pull his thin hood over his head, Callum's feet have no defense against melted snow soaking his socks and stinging his toes. The extreme discomfort makes it hard for Callum to focus, blinding him to the sensation of magical energy. Therefore, he is unaware of any invading presence until he takes a shortcut through a vacant parking lot.

Halting near the center of the empty expanse, Callum surveys the area, now beginning to sense that he is in a very uncomfortable spotlight.

He can feel arcane energy emanating from the shadows but cannot isolate its precise location nor see anything beyond the line of trees and shrubs bordering the lot. Closing his eyes, he concentrates on the impressions. Callum's intuitive senses immediately detect that whatever follows him is not inherently evil and definitely not human. He also perceives purpose that is creating emotional conflict.

Someone or something is fighting a natural disposition to perform this present action, and that inner conflict is causing distress. Callum believes this is a different sort of energy than the type he felt radiating from his opponents at the mall, so he is slightly relieved.

Opening his eyes, he scans the shadows. "I know you're out there!" Callum shouts.

He is vulnerable standing in the open, but at least he will not be caught unaware by someone sneaking up on him. With unknown adversaries waiting to confront him, it is the safest place for the moment.

Callum spies movement at the edge of the shadows, and an undersized man steps forward. He wears a patched leather coat that hangs to his knees and a pair of baggy brown trousers tuck into furred boots. A shock of greasy black hair is pulled into a tight bun, and a braided beard hangs halfway down his barrel chest. Callum recognizes this character as a member of the Dwarven race.

The dwarf holds his head high and squints at Callum. His hands grasp a wooden cudgel with a bulbous knot on one end. It is an effective and intimidating weapon.

"Who are you?" Callum asks firmly.

As soon as the question is uttered, Callum catches movement around him as more well-armed dwarves emerge from the winter night's shadows. They all share the first man's hairstyle of braided beards and topknots, and all are dressed in some combination of leather and fur. Each wields a hand-carved club that they either rest on a shoulder or set with one end on the ground like a leaning post.

Twenty brawny dwarves step forward in a solid offensive, and Callum instantly sees his chance of escape vanish. Swallowing a lump of fear and dread, his adrenaline surges. He wants to run, but an injured leg makes this option impossible. Callum's mind sifts through any possible spells that might offer protection, but he is dangerously outnumbered. With his depleted strength—an accumulation of several days of mental turmoil and physical exhaustion—Callum lacks the vitality to power a spell strong enough to conquer this large of a threat. He might manage to subdue a couple of the dwarves, but the rest could easily pound him to death.

"I am Grumneth Steelbeard," the first man says in a deep, booming voice. "I am the commander of this dwarven militia, and our government has struck a bargain for your capture."

"What?" Callum asks in equal measures of anger, confusion, and terror.

What he knows of dwarves paints a picture of secretive mountaineers that live in seclusion.

"Our government has ordered us to return you to Bombiher, in the southern mountains beyond the veil," Grumneth adds. "There, you will be handed over as a prisoner of war."

"How am I a war prisoner? I only learned of the conflict last night, and I've never even taken part in it." Callum is bewildered by the accusation and afraid of what the allegation means. The dwarves all look like they came prepared for a tremendous battle.

"That is not my concern. I am following my orders. A treaty was arranged with our allied master, and you have been promised as an offering by our leaders." Grumneth speaks as though he expects Callum to understand and accept this arrangement.

"What allied master?" Callum asks. He is frustrated that his life has become nothing more than a bargaining chip in some unethical exchange between people he never met. Steelbeard and his comrades see him as a piece of currency to be used in barter for someone else's benefit.

"Master Kincaid is our ally, and he wants you delivered to him. *Alive*," Grumneth explains, raising his tone at the end to emphasize intention. A chorus of grunted affirmations from the other dwarves echoes his sentiment. "We do not wish to damage you, but we will not hesitate if you resist."

"That doesn't sound very reassuring."

Revising the idea of using magic to escape, Callum considers whether he has enough arcane potency to disorient this formidable band and hobble away. He quickly dismisses this idea, knowing he will not get far on his throbbing leg. Any direction he takes will be easily discovered by his tracks in the fallen snow.

He wears a tense frown and sweeps his eyes across the line of determined dwarven militiamen. Nearly two dozen pairs of eyes watch him with restless zeal. A twenty-foot span across a slippery parking lot is all that separates him from this unexpected opposition.

"We are prepared to subdue you, Warlock," Grumneth warns as he brings his club down from his shoulder and threateningly slaps it against the palm of his free hand. Callum has no doubt that he would be pummeled into unconscious compliance.

"Doesn't look like I have many options," Callum reluctantly sighs.

Despite the dwarf's outward resolve, Callum senses his adversary is attempting to hide his profound nervousness and fear. He hates this feeling of helplessness and wishes he could fight. But until he can rest and recharge his strength, Callum is powerless.

"You can choose to come along quietly," says Grumneth. Though conveying a strong facade, his eyes show a pleading hope that Callum will not fight.

Callum discerns that these tough dwarves are as afraid of

their prisoner as he is of them. The dwarven commander is merely a loyal servant playing his part in an action he does not entirely approve of. Steelbeard's intense conflict of emotions is as obvious to the warlock as a red flag.

"What do your people get out of this arrangement?"

Whether he wants to or not, it seems he will be joining these mountain folks on a journey to their homeland. He can already see some of the dwarves closing in, but Grumneth lifts a hand and shouts a command to hold their positions.

"We have a promise from Master Kincaid that our people will be excluded from this bloody war if we turn you over to him," admits Grumneth. "It will save the lives of many of our kind." He frowns as he speaks, underlining his displeasure with this arrangement. "We are without a choice as well."

"Then I guess I'm going with you," Callum says with a heavy heart.

The next hour provides a stressful trip through the sleeping city. The dwarves travel through Duncaster's darkened side streets and across snow-covered yards, parks, and open fields. Steelbeard's soldiers venture along a winding path through the human city, anxious to avoid any nocturnal residents who brave the weather for a nightly stroll.

Callum is roughly hustled along by the band of furtive abductors until they reach a shadowed alleyway where Grumneth's squad halts in the dead center of the lane. They pause long enough to remove a manhole cover before applying a forceful shove, coercing the warlock down through the pitch-black hole into the bowels of the city.

Grumneth's troop travels for over an hour, traversing the city's underbelly network of sewage conduits, all the while splashing through fetid water. Then, led by Grumneth's uncanny sense of direction, the dwarves have no trouble finding their way through the maze of dark, stinking tunnels.

The dwarven commander calls a halt at a peculiar, rustic door that looks out of place amid the modern environment of gray concrete. The entryway is fashioned from blackened planks anchored with iron bolts, welded by dampness and rust. There is no handle or latch visible, but when Grumneth knocks on the wooden panels, the door swings inward from the other side.

"Get moving, Warlock." The stern order comes from an irritable dwarf standing behind Callum, backed up with a bruising prod to his lower back from the end of a club. Exhausted, soaked, and shivering from hours of limping through wet snow above ground and liquid muck below it, Callum obeys without defiance.

He approaches the odd-looking entrance and follows the line of thick-bodied, little men. When it is his turn to pass through, Callum sees nothing but a continuation of the dismal drainage channels beyond the doorway. There are no signs of another person, not even evidence of the other dwarves who preceded him, making Callum wonder who opened the door. His over-wrought mind is too weary to focus on this mystery, so the warlock shrugs it off and keeps limping forward.

The moment he reaches the threshold, Callum is startled by a creeping sensation not felt since childhood when he had accidentally blundered through a wall of cobwebs. He pauses with fright and shivers at the uncomfortable tickle, but the dwarf at his rear offers a nudge to keep him moving.

"What the hell," Callum says, stumbling forward through the wall of unseeable filament.

Past the door, Callum thrusts out a bracing hand against the wall, instantly yanking it back at the feel of cool, clammy clay rather than smooth concrete. The unpleasant tingle vanishes, as does any sign of the sewer tunnel extending beyond the doorway. Callum gapes in puzzlement at a high ceiling cavern he is sure was not there moments ago. Neither was a small army of nearly fifty rugged dwarves staring curiously at him.

"Welcome to the magical realm!" The sarcastic chortle is echoed by most of his comrades, clearly relishing the warlock's startled reaction to crossing the veil.

Callum is hastily directed through the unsympathetic crowd toward a cart, pulled by a pair of mountain goats, waiting at the far edge of the cavern.

The warlock's hands are tightly bound with coarse rope and tethered to the back of the flat top cart. Despite his pronounced limp, the dwarves have no intention of letting their captive ride. Trailing behind it, however, gives Callum plenty of opportunity to observe the lone, unconscious figure who sprawls, silent and unmoving, across the cart's rough-hewn planks. The dwarves sort themselves into a single-file procession, lighting smoky torches as they prepare to trek through one of the many tunnels that branch from the cave.

Callum is tugged along as the group marches into a cramped, dwarven-sized passageway that scrapes his head unless he stoops.

After a couple agonizing hours of their journey, Callum inevitably stumbles to the stone floor of the tunnel and is dragged for several paces before he can regain his footing.

"Pick yourself up," a dwarf grumbles.

"For someone of such great reputation, this human appears a wee bit overrated," another dwarf chuckles behind Callum. The insult is answered by an echo of belly laughter.

Rather than venting his anger with a verbal retort, Callum inhales a steady breath and opens his lashed hands toward the ground. He whispers under his breath, "*Labellum.*"

The ground in front of the warlock's feet sinks into a sudden depression. Callum staggers over the tripping hazard, jolting his throbbing leg in the process. But his sniggering abductors are caught unaware and collapse over each other in a heap of flailing limbs and outraged curses. Now, it is Callum's time to snicker, which he does, imperceptibly.

"Get up, you pair of useless blockheads!" Grumneth bellows, having backtracked from the head of the line to the source of the uproar. The bumbling culprits scramble out of the shallow hole to face the wrath of their irate commander.

"I suppose that was your fault," Grumneth grunts at Callum after the two oafs wander further down the convoy and away from the guffawing witnesses to their clumsiness.

Callum clamps his lips together to stop his own smirking. Staring intently at the back of the cart and his rope leash, he refuses to answer their questions.

"I see. Well, it does not matter. Those dolts likely had it coming."

Grumneth barks some dwarven commands up the line of troops, and the procession starts moving again.

"What time is it?" Callum asks. The moment of levity vanishes, and the grim reality of his situation returns.

He gauges the passage of time by the active drying of his jeans and sneakers and is thankful for the muggy warmth of the hand-dug network of passageways.

"Don't worry, there are still several hours before sunrise," Grumneth says, clearing his irritated throat at the choking torch smoke thickening the stale air. Although Callum has not broken into a fit of coughing, he is suffering a raw burn in his throat and chest from the smoggy tunnel. "At least another seven hours by my count before we hand you over to Kincaid."

Callum cringes at this thought and regrets his decision to surrender, even though defying this sizable squad would have been pointless. The entire ordeal leaves him frustrated and depressed over his terrible luck. While his captors chatter in their native language, Callum can only ponder the remainder of his life, however short it may be. Oddly, he also considers the motionless passenger on the wagon.

"What's their story?" Callum asks in hopes of keeping the commander talking enough to spill a few answers. He nods toward the lifeless body on the cart, noticing a bloodied burlap sack over the victim's head.

"We found this hunter following you," says Grumneth, panting from his effort to keep pace with the procession.

The unconscious figure is dressed in dark jeans, a black canvas jacket, and military-looking laced boots. The similarity to the trackers from the mall is undeniable. This unfortunate stranger appears to have suffered a violent encounter with his subduers.

"Why are you bringing him along?" Callum asks, trying to understand Grumneth's motivations. Would it not have been easier to just leave this person alone while they ambushed their target?

"Master Kincaid likes trophies, and these cursed hunters are a nuisance to him. He will be pleased to accept this gift from us," Grumneth says between puffing breathes.

"Why doesn't he like hunters?" Callum probes. He hopes to glean as much information from the dwarf as possible.

"They serve his bitter enemy opposing him in the war," Grumneth answers.

"Who is his enemy?" Callum casts Grumneth a curious sideways glance.

"The Order," the commander replies, then breaks into a coughing fit that leaves him breathless. "We do not know much except that they hunt our kind and others. They cross the veil uninvited and kidnap magical creatures who are never seen again."

"If Kincaid wants me, why is the Order sending this hunter after me?"

Since Grumneth has limited knowledge of the Order, Callum decides to stick to the dwarf's close ties to Kincaid's side of the conflict. The more he learns, the more questions he has, so Callum will keep posing them for as long as Grumneth is willing to talk.

Callum recalls Queen Daphne's claim that Kincaid knows of his existence and is actively searching for him. He wrongly assumed that the hunters in the mall worked for Kincaid. It now appears he is being hounded by more than one faction in this violent campaign. Even the normally peaceful dwarves are betraying their reclusive nature to serve a more powerful enemy. It makes the warlock wonder how many others are after him—or soon will be.

"You and Master Kincaid share the same organic source of magic. The Order is an assembly of men and women pretending to be sorcerers," Grumneth says, inclining his head toward the cart and its insensible passenger. "Like this human hunter, they need their trinkets to cast spells. But their leader wants to learn how *you* can do this without the help of magical objects."

"So, the Order wants to study me?" Callum asks, realizing how ridiculous this conversation is becoming.

"This hunter, like many who serve the Order, kill and capture innocent beings so they can gain magical knowledge from all of the races and refine their own power." Grumneth speaks with obvious contempt for the Order and all those who are part of it. He glares at the unmoving man jostling on the rolling cart. Callum can easily perceive the dwarf's hatred of the hunter and the organization he serves.

"How do they gain this knowledge?" Callum asks.

He feels the ground descending on a sloping path, taking them deeper beneath the surface world. Callum stumbles on the barely visible and uneven terrain, but Grumneth's powerful arm reaches out to catch him before he falls.

"Thank you," Callum gasps, feeling rather embarrassed about his clumsiness.

His swollen, infected leg relentlessly throbs, and the forced marching adds to his misery. Callum starts to grow envious of the catatonic hunter on the cart.

"All we know is that no one escapes the Order. Once they

target you, it is only a matter of time before you become their prey." Grumneth continues. "I lost my wife to the Order a few years ago, and I have not seen her since."

Grumneth becomes visibly distressed by recounting his personal sorrow, his chubby cheeks growing red-hot with buried rage. Callum sympathizes with this dwarf's loss, but he doubts Kincaid is a better ally than the forces behind the mysterious Order. He begins to understand that this hidden realm of magical beings is caught between two equally aggressive warlords bent on domination.

"You called me a warlock when we first met. Does that mean you're aware of the prophecy that the fairies believe I am part of?"

"We know of the prophecy." Grumneth nods, wiping his bulbous nose on the back of his sleeve and struggling to repress his display of grief over his lost wife.

"Then why are your people handing me over to Kincaid when I might be able to help them?" asks Callum, puzzled by the dwarf's conflicting motive.

"We cannot wait any longer or gamble on a hope," Grumneth says dismissively. "We are caught between enemies, and only Kincaid has offered to give us amnesty. He has promised to protect us from the hunters in exchange for our loyalty to him."

"And you believe *him*?" Callum asks in utter astonishment. He knows little about Kincaid but remembers that human history is full of power-hungry leaders that use fear, threats, and false guarantees as solid motivators for obedience.

"As I said, we are without a choice. This was not my judgment to make." Grumneth's shoulders hunch at his admission of helplessness. "Kincaid's monstrosities have invaded our homeland. They are holding our family's hostage to ensure our obedience."

Callum momentarily forgets his status as a captive, allowing anger to creep into his voice.

"Dwarves do have a choice—we all do. You're making the decision to abandon who you are and do Kincaid's bidding. Your people have great strength, but you'd use that power to take me hostage rather than defend your home and families?" Callum cannot hide his irritation, and Grumneth flinches at the truth in his sharp accusations.

The conversation ends when Grumneth hangs his head and increases his pace, leaving Callum stuck hobbling behind a long line of dwarven troops. He resents the commander for walking away rather than admitting the fault of his people's action. Still, there is nothing he can do except watch him go.

The intricacies of this war may be a mystery to Callum, but he can tell that the dwarves are not happy about fulfilling their mission. The entire squad is apprehensive about his presence in their midst.

The troop trudges onward, navigating a maze of narrow tunnels for another hour. Callum has no idea what time it is. He is exhausted and trips so often that he resorts to holding onto the back of the cart to stay upright. Finally, after what seems like an eternity of stumbling over treacherous footing, Callum feels an unexpected blast of fresh air washing over his face, and the congested passage opens into a massive cavern.

Callum looks up as he follows the line of dwarves into the underground expanse. Torchlight illuminates towering walls formed by decades of toil, clearly visible from the scars of countless tools that moved dirt and broke rocks. The ceiling is too high to be reached by their feeble torchlight, so it hangs over them like a dark, oppressive blanket. The sound of agitated voices resonates all around him, and the cart abruptly jerks to a halt.

There is a significant surge of activity throughout the cavern, and Callum finds himself unguarded but still restrained. He grabs the opportunity to climb aboard the cart to sit and rest. Callum has no idea how long they will be stationary but hopes no one will object to him hitching a ride for the rest of the trip. The deteriorating status of his damaged leg makes Callum doubt he can walk much farther.

The man on the wagon started to stir over the past hour. Callum clambers onto the cart, and the resulting movement seems to prod the hunter out of his unconscious state.

"It's probably better if you lay still," Callum says in a whisper when he sees that the hunter trying to roll onto his side.

Although the man does not reply, he seems to heed the suggestion as he relaxes and lies motionless on his back once more.

After several minutes the hunter asks in a straining, hoarse voice, "Where am I?"

Callum looks around at the pools of torchlight that cut through the shadows and show an ample space filled with bustling motion.

"All I can tell you is that we're underground in a giant cave," Callum mutters. "It's been a very long walk, so I hope you don't mind if I share your cart."

"I'm really not in any position to argue about it." The hunter groans, reaching to the side of his head where the thick burlap sacking is glued to his hair with dried blood. The man winces when he touches his injured scalp through the rough fabric. "You wouldn't happen to have any painkillers on you?"

"Sorry, I'm all out," Callum says, only half-listening while he watches the activity around him.

From what he can see, it looks like the dwarves are occupied with unloading cargo from other carts that have traveled with the convoy. The heavy boxes are passed hand-to-hand in an assembly line, then stacked in neat piles near the center of the cavern. After watching the purposeful movement for close to twenty minutes, Callum jumps with surprise when the sound of a piercing whistle rises above the commotion. It is the unmistakable sound of a train announcing its approach.

Craning his neck, Callum peers over the heads of the

dwarves and makes out a distant tunnel slowly being illuminated by the blazing headlamps of an arriving locomotive. The whistle shrieks once more as it emerges from the depths of the Earth, and with a thunderous chugging, it slows to a stop. The engine lets out a terrible hiss that releases a cloud of steam.

Callum now realizes that this cavern is more than an immense cavity in the Earth. It is a waypoint for an underground rail line. While he marvels at dwarven ingenuity, he is startled when two stout men rapidly approach his cart.

"Back on your feet!" shouts a husky, blond-bearded dwarf as he grabs Callum by his bound wrists and yanks him from his perch.

The warlock slides off the wagon, landing hard on his feet and wincing at the jolt of pain that shoots up his leg. The blond dwarf pulls a knife from his belt and holds the blade up for Callum to see.

"Will you behave, warlock?" the dwarf asks in a growl. His words are more of a warning than a question.

Callum glances at the torchlight glinting off the deadly blade and nods his head in compliance. With that acknowledgment, the blond dwarf motions for Callum to lift his hands. Then, in a single stroke, the warrior slices through the bindings to free his wrists.

Another brawny dwarf steps to the end of the cart and grabs the hunter by his knees to slide him off. The injured man reaches out wildly with his arms, blind to what is happening as he slips off and lands brutally on the stony ground, gasping to regain his breath.

While Callum rubs the raw flesh of his wrists, the hunter is lugged to his feet and shoved toward him.

"Keep him standing, warlock," the blond dwarf barks.

Callum reaches out to steady the unsteady fellow captive, who can barely remain vertical under his own power. He manages to hobble onward while supporting the man's weight but staying upright is a precarious proposition.

"How's your leg?" the hunter asks weakly. Leaning heavily on Callum, he then struggles to find a measure of strength in his own limbs.

"Better than yours, it seems," Callum mutters in reply, wondering how the man knows about his leg wound with his face still covered by the blood-soaked bag.

Callum also wonders if the hunter feels his faltering steps as he supports the weight of two people. There is no opportunity for Callum to further comment on the hunter's odd question. An insistent dwarf jabs him in the back with the end of a club, reminding him to keep moving.

The pair of human prisoners are directed toward the train and its line of open boxcars, most of them being hastily loaded. The fourth car in line is left wide open, and Callum is prodded toward it. They pass crews of tireless dwarves absorbed in their task of transferring hundreds of wooden crates onto the cars.

"Both of you, over here," Grumneth growls at the prisoners from his station beside the gaping doorway of the ominous, unoccupied car.

Drawing nearer, Callum spots unfamiliar red markings crudely painted on the boxcar's battered exterior. They radiate cold energy that makes him shudder.

"Help the hunter inside," Grumneth orders when Callum finally staggers up to the door with his burdensome acquaintance hanging off his shoulder.

With the help of the other two dwarves, Callum hauls the semi-conscious man up through the central door and into the boxcar. He enters next, crawling on hands and knees to the opposite wall. The warlock flops down on the dusty floor of the empty car, props himself against the scarred wooden wall, and looks back toward the door.

Grumneth almost appears apologetic as he meets Callum's furious glare yet remains silent. With a wave of one hand, the door is rolled shut and latched, and the boxcar prison plunges into darkness.

"Great!" says Callum with vehement frustration.

"What's great about this?" the hunter grunts from across the black expanse.

Callum stifles a sarcastic laugh and answers, "I was just thinking that my luck can't get any worse."

"I bet it can."

"Why do you say that?" Callum asks.

"Because I'm the hunter who was sent to catch you. But I was ambushed by these lunkheads."

Callum tenses. "Who are you?"

A wave of dread washes over Callum as he stares into the darkness. He can hear movements from the hunter lying somewhere across the empty train car. But both men are exhausted, wounded, and temporarily as blind as bats.

"Relax," the hunter groans after an agonizing effort to move. "Do you really think I'm in any condition to fight you?"

Callum can hear the cloth being pulled from the man's head and a half-stifled yelp of pain as it rips free of the crusted blood. There is no point in trying to hide what he is any longer. The warlock closes his eyes and focuses his mind on creating an illumination spell.

He lifts his hand, palm upward at the roof. "*Lux lumen,*" Callum says.

In an instant, a steady flow of brilliant white magic flows down his arm and collects in his open hand. Then, swirling into a baseball-sized orb of light, it floats freely from his hand like a glowing helium balloon. The sudden presence of light chases away the boxcar's gloom and dazzles both passengers. Finally, the orb slowly ascends until it bumps against the ceiling.

Callum's squinting eyes are still adjusting when the train lurches forward and tosses him off balance. He catches himself with his elbow before falling flat and painfully pushes himself back to his place against the wall.

Looking across the rolling train car, Callum sees his companion struggling to heave himself off the floor. With great difficulty, the man returns to a sitting position and lets his damaged head rest against the wall with his arms weakly hanging at his sides. The instant Callum sees the man's bloody face, he recognizes him.

"Liam?"

CHAPTER SEVENTEEN

"Bet you're surprised to see me," Liam says. There is no trace of a smirk. He looks deathly pale as fresh blood from torn scabs trickles down the left side of his face.

Callum's bewilderment quickly turns to anger. He clenches his jaw and stares at the man who deceived him, stalked him, and is responsible for his gruesome leg wound. From what Grumneth told him, Liam's allegiance is with an organization that indiscriminately kills and kidnaps magical beings—evil and innocent alike.

"What are *you* doing here?" Callum snaps, hotly glaring at Liam.

"I'm guessing the dwarves told you what I really do for a living," Liam says.

Wincing as the train accelerates and bounces over an uneven stretch of track, Liam's shoulders tense, and he bows his head until the wave of pain passes. When he returns his gaze toward Callum, Liam's eyes are watery and glassy.

"You didn't answer my question," Callum growls and narrows his eyes.

"All right then. Not that it matters now," Liam says, enduring Callum's hard look of contempt. Then, taking a deep breath and expelling it to steady his resolve, the veteran hunter explains his ties to the organization that brought him to this current predicament. "My master had a vision about a human warlock with natural magic. He started searching for you eight years ago, but it's only been in the past few months that his visions began to show details of your identity. Because you refused to interact with any of our other agents, I was sent in to open a line of communication with you in a familiar setting. When you wouldn't respond to my effort, my superiors ordered me to set a trap for you. So, we intercepted you at the mall. We needed to confirm that you do have magic. Our plan was to capture you after we had proof, then take you back to our headquarters for more investigation."

"I guess I threw a wrench into your plans when I disappeared." Callum is pleased that he caused Liam's organization so much difficulty.

"Yeah, that was a bit of a mystery. But I eventually spotted the fairy in the video from the mall security cameras. I figured out that you'd gone to the fairy homeland." Liam shifts his legs, grimaces, and continues. "It was just a matter of waiting for you to return. We knew the fairy laws wouldn't allow an outsider to stay more than a day or two before forcing you to leave and come home. They're very loyal to their ancient rules and predictable to a fault."

Callum does not bother to hide his animosity. "So, the shapeshifter that tried to kill me was a happy accident?"

"If it's any consolation, I didn't approve of the shapeshifter. I was overruled. The shifter wasn't supposed to take it that far. The creature swore it would push you just enough to make you use your powers and give us the confirmation we needed."

"Well, the damn thing lied, and it nearly killed me," Callum blurts out.

"You handled yourself pretty well from what I saw. But it looks like you're still recovering." Liam nods toward Callum's injured leg.

"I'll survive," Callum mutters, feeling uncomfortable about Liam watching his epic battle with the shapeshifter. He notices how unwell the hunter appears to be, so Liam must be suffering his own version of misery. "You're the one looking a little worse for wear now."

"Yeah, well, those dwarves didn't fight fair." Liam winces again and gives up on his effort to sit upright. He carefully lowers himself to the floor so he can rest on his back. Blinking slowly, he stares up at the ceiling.

Callum's expression softens as he turns his eyes toward the orb of light caught in the space between the low roof's wooden braces.

Despite everything he experienced in the past few days, he is still surprised by the irony of the situation. How many people get to have civil conversations with an enemy plotting to capture them? Yet here they are. Both imprisoned by the same captors and severely handicapped by injuries, the two opponents are now thrown together by bad luck.

He doubts Liam will live another day, let alone a few hours, with his untreated head injury. If he survives to the end of this train ride, Liam will be handed over to his mortal enemy, and that will undoubtedly be a death sentence. One way or another, the hunter is fated for a miserable end.

"You know the dwarves are going to give us to Kincaid." Callum watchfully glances at the hunter's reaction.

"Yeah, I expect so," Liam says, creasing his forehead and flinching at the mention of his impending doom. While Liam seems resigned to his emanant death, the prospect still frightens him.

"What's this war actually about, anyway?" asks Callum, keenly disappointed that his life is again in peril over a situation he barely understands.

"It started as a feud between two brothers. Now it is a battle for power and control, over everything and everyone," Liam sighs.

"I assume one of the brothers is David Kincaid."

"You assume correctly. The other is my master and leader of the Order, Desmond Quinn. Quinn is actually his middle name, but he separates himself from his brother by refusing to use their common last name."

As the train rumbles over some debris on the tracks, the boxcar sways roughly before steadying itself. Liam feebly moans, and it takes a moment for him to recover. His breathing is weak, and his ashen face betrays extensive internal injury. Callum cannot help but feel pity for Liam, despite his outrage.

"Kincaid has gifts just like yours, but he uses his powers to conjure monsters," Liam continues. "I've been fighting for years to kill his creations when they threaten the lives of humans."

"Yeah, apparently so have I," Callum says, surprised that he feels a bond rooted in their shared purpose.

This recognition somehow reduces his rage. Callum curses his pang of sympathy for the hunter who caused him so much grief. He can appreciate that they are indirectly fighting a similar cause—although the Order appears to assign final judgment to all magical beings, regardless of wickedness or benevolence.

Despite his conflicting emotions, Callum recognizes that Liam is a desperately needed wealth of information. Nonetheless, he cannot allow himself to forget this man is his enemy. In a reverse situation, Liam would not hesitate to rob him of freedom.

"Quinn wants to learn how you access your powers so he can do the same. Kincaid's just plain scared of you because you represent a threat to him. He wants you dead, so you can't challenge his plan for domination." With that last detail, Liam closes his eyes and is motionless.

If not for brief pain spasms across his face, Callum would think the hunter is dead. Maybe the need to remain conscious is what keeps Liam talking, or perhaps he wants to make amends by imparting his knowledge before death arrives to claim him.

"So, we're both dead men when this train stops." Callum is

aware of deep fear for his own well-being. He knows that Kincaid is searching for him. Hopeful optimism keeps Callum from acknowledging it would probably result in his own demise. "Quinn would turn me into a guinea pig, and Kincaid just wants to make me a corpse. What about these dwarves? They do Kincaid's bidding, and then what?"

"They become collateral damage. Kincaid won't protect the dwarves just because they obey him. He'll demand more and more until they fail. Then he'll annihilate them." Liam's voice is faint and strained, but he continues to respond.

"That sucks."

Callum reflects on why Frey had taken such a significant personal risk to deliver him to her queen. The war is far bigger and more important than his solitary fight for survival. Those touched by it are being manipulated or victimized. Prophecy or not, the odds are stacked heavily against Callum.

"It was simpler when I thought I was just killing monsters," Callum scoffs.

"The magical realm has been in chaos for centuries," Liam says softly. "This war threatens to annihilate it."

His voice trails off, and his head slowly rolls to the side. Liam finally drifts into unconsciousness. Considering his declining condition, the odds are slim that the hunter will awaken on his own.

Callum thinks about just letting Liam sleep. It would be a simple thing to sit and let the man pass into an endless slumber. The hunter has undoubtedly done terrible things to others, himself included. No one would question why he let nature take its course rather than attempting to wake the dying man. The dwarves seem unconcerned about the hunter's state of health. Liam's death would not trouble them.

He wrestles with the dilemma for only a moment, but it seems much longer. Despite resenting Liam for his role in causing present misery, Callum knows he could not live with himself if he let someone die without trying to help. He recalls

Frey telling him how shamans use magic to heal wounds and sickness. Callum wonders if warlocks might also have this ability. In any event, Liam's past crimes hold no weight in the final decision to save his life. He is, after all, just a human being who is suffering.

"Liam!" Callum shouts but receives no response.

The hunter is still breathing, but it is shallow. Cursing under his breath, Callum drags himself across the floor of the small boxcar toward his former would-be abductor, who is otherwise lifeless.

Mindful of his own condition, Callum then shifts to sit on his hip so he can keep his swollen leg extended while supporting himself with his right arm. He raises his left hand and slaps the hunter across the uninjured side of his face.

"What the hell?" Liam asks sharply, his eyes snapping open. Raising a hand to his cheek, the hunter peers up in shock at the unexpected assault and sees Callum at his side.

"You have a head injury. Sleep isn't your friend right now." A serious frown paints Callum's face while he brushes Liam's hand aside.

He grasps the hunter's bristly jaw to turn his head for a better look at the laceration. A black scab has formed across the finger-length gash over his left temple, still seeping blood around its edges. Liam's hair is plastered to the side of his head, and his face and neck are sticky with semi-dried blood. Even his jacket collar and shoulder are soaked.

"Is it still bleeding?" Liam asks, submitting to Callum's examination.

"It's not the cut that I'm worried about. They knocked you out cold for several hours at least, and I'm willing to bet that you have one hell of a headache."

"That slap you gave me didn't help." Liam scrunches his face and squeezes his eyes closed. "Please don't hit me again. I just need to shut my eyes because that light's right in my face."

Callum shakes his head. "I must be crazy," he whispers to

himself, placing his left hand over the bleeding head wound.

Feeling the touch, Liam's eyes fly open again. "What are you doing?"

"Just shut up before I change my mind." Callum clenches his eyes shut to stop the distractions of noise and light around him. He directs his thoughts to focus on healing—convincing himself that if shamans can use magic to heal, so can he.

The warlock concentrates intense mental energy on a magical power that is completely unfamiliar to him. He never had cause to heal anyone before and is not even sure he possesses this skill. Callum can sense some unexplained internal wisdom guiding him. So, he must at least try.

Callum can feel the heat radiating from Liam's head and visualizes the slow buildup of blood beneath his skull, pressing on the hunter's brain. With his eyes still tightly closed, Callum focuses every bit of energy he can muster on isolating and repairing the internal damage.

After a couple of minutes of forceful mental strain, Callum finally grasps the essence of strong magic he never used before— like a vast, hidden wellspring within him. He holds on to the fleeting power and hears himself utter a strange incantation. Words pour through him like water from a vessel, and warm energy flows down his arm and into Liam's battered skull. Though the language he speaks is unknown, Callum understands its general significance. It is not just a single phrase but an ongoing idiom that breaks the droning rumble of the freight car.

Rather than delivering a verbal spell, it is as though the warlock is reciting an ancient story that tells of gifting powerful healing. The instant Callum begins speaking, the momentum of atypical energy floods his mind in a powerful surge. This novel magic radiates an essence that is not recognizable as his own. As though possessed, Callum helplessly recites the enchantment for several minutes until the words cease and he can open his eyes. The enslaving enchantment finally releases him, leaving Callum dripping with sweat and mentally drained.

The warlock transferred a sizable portion of his own physical and supernatural energy to save Liam and is now sorely depleted.

"Wow," Callum whispers to himself. He cannot help but marvel at the impressive new skill he discovered.

Liam looks at Callum's face with bewilderment. The young hunter's color returned to normal, and his eyes again reflect the spark of life. Callum is relieved to see that the incantation worked. Exhausted, he painfully crawls back to his side of the boxcar without a word. He sinks back against the wall and heaves a weary sigh, suddenly desperate for sleep.

Liam pushes himself off the floor and sits up, gingerly touching his fingertips to his head. He prods the site of a once-mortal wound that is now merely a jagged, pink scar. The thickly crusted blood is the only visible sign of his grievous injury.

As pleased as Callum is that he saved Liam from an agonizing death, he hopes it was not a grave mistake. The hunter is still his enemy and restoring him left the warlock vulnerable. It is now Liam's turn to decide the fate of his companion.

"How's your head now?" Callum asks frailly, letting his hands fall to his sides while stretching his legs. He feels like a run-down battery.

He needs to rest and recover his strength, but Callum is afraid to close his eyes on his revived foe. If Callum knew how tired he would become after casting the healing spell, he might have thought twice.

"It feels much better. But I don't understand...why did you help me?" Liam asks, confused.

"You were dying. It felt like the right thing to do," Callum shrugs weakly. "You can repay the favor by helping me find a way out of here."

"Why would you need my help?" Liam asks. "Your magic can do far more than I can." The hunter seems genuinely worried about Callum's physical state. "You knew that I was tracking you, and you had the upper hand. Why would you sacrifice that advantage to save me? It would have been smarter to let me die."

Surprised by the hunter's inability to understand such an act of compassion, Callum wonders whether Liam has ever been on the receiving end of it before. Has he been so brainwashed by years of service to Quinn that he cannot comprehend this basic element of human nature? Callum's anger toward Liam fades in favor of growing sympathy.

"You've committed some awful crimes in your service to the Order, but I don't think you deserve to die for following commands. I can't explain it, but I sometimes get insights about people. I can sense that you have a desire to do good things. That gave me enough hope for you that I couldn't just sit here and watch you die. I had to help. It's not in my nature to allow someone to suffer."

"You can sense the presence of magic too, can't you?" Liam asks fixedly. It is more of a statement than a question.

Callum frowns, tightening his lips into a rigid line of protest. Mental alarm bells clang, warning him against exposing his closely guarded secrets. The warlock chooses to ignore them.

"Yes," Callum answers, at last, seeing no point in hiding this obvious fact from the hunter.

"Quinn thought you might possess that ability. I learned from my handler that it is suspected you have the same abilities as Kincaid—that is one of his powers. Are you a necromancer too?" Liam's probing comes close to accusing the warlock of something nefarious.

"I don't even know what a necromancer is," mumbles Callum.

Despite fighting fatigue, Callum is still aware enough to feel insulted by Liam's allegation. If that is something Kincaid strives to embrace, it is not a magical skill that Callum wants to share.

"A necromancer is a conjurer. They use black magic to create life that is born from darkness. Anything created by this power is inherently evil. Kincaid has been tapping into that magic for years. He is trying to populate this world with his magical creations, and it is those life forms that have been lurking in the cities and attacking people," Liam explains. "It was my job to hunt and destroy those creatures before I was assigned to your case. The only reason I'm asking is that you two share the same arcane ability, and I need to know if you also have the same motivations."

"Do you think I'm evil?" Callum asks.

He ponders the same question to himself, knowing he has not always lived an honest life. Nevertheless, Callum made a fateful choice to abandon his thievery and start afresh with a new purpose. If not for that decision, he might very well be following the same twisted path as Kincaid. It seems unlikely, though, since guilt about his past still haunts him. But given the right circumstances, would he be strong enough to resist the allure of such power?

"We all have the potential for good and evil. Quinn convinced us that you were dangerous because you had the same magical potential as our enemy. Your abilities made it risky to assume otherwise. So, Quinn ordered us to use whatever force we needed to capture you." Liam's prominent eyebrows furrow with tension, simultaneously trying to conclude Callum's true character.

"I guess you have a choice to make because I really don't have enough strength to resist if you decide to finish your mission."

He is virtually helpless, struggling to stay awake, let alone defend himself, yet he does not think he was wrong to save Liam's life.

Liam studies the warlock for several seconds, wrestling with conflicting beliefs. His mouth pinches into a strict line as he considers his powerless quarry. Then, finally, he makes a choice.

"Get some rest, Callum. When you wake up, we'll work together to get out of this damn place."

"Thank you," is all Callum can say in reply, relieved by the hunter's promise of trust. The warlock immediately settles onto the plank floor and succumbs to deep, restorative sleep.

CHAPTER EIGHTEEN

Callum sleeps for two hours before waking from troubling dreams. His head is still pounding, and his leg still aches, but he is somewhat more refreshed. While Callum is not fully rested, the nap has returned a portion of his strength. Taking advantage of his semi-restored energy, he helps Liam inspect the boxcar's interior. Callum recalls the strange symbols painted on the outside of the train car and describes them to Liam.

"It sounds like runes," the hunter concludes thoughtfully. "They can create an invisible barrier so magic can't penetrate. I guess those dwarves aren't as dumb as they look."

Under normal conditions, Callum could use his powers to unlock the door or simply blast a new exit through one of the walls. In this situation, however, his options are limited. Even if he could create a path of escape, the train is moving too fast. Without seeing beyond the boxcar's walls, the warlock already knows that a desperate leap has a high likelihood of a gruesome end beneath the wheels.

Instead, warlock and hunter devote their diminishing time to crawling along the length of the car. The roof of the dwarven railway car is, like the endless tunnels, too low for standing without stooping. Hoping to find signs of wood rot or water damage that might offer a weak point to break through, they make careful progress down the twenty-foot length until they reach the opposite end.

"Nothing of note here. Do you see anything useful at your end?" Liam asks, raising his voice over the noise of rumbling wheels.

"There's some mildew in the corner here, but it is not enough to cause damage," Callum calls out as he presses his fingertips against the floor planks to test their integrity. The wood is solid beneath his touch.

Both captives continue their search, checking every corner before heading back to their original places by the sliding door. Unfortunately, their hope of finding even a minor flaw is thwarted by superb dwarven craftsmanship. All sides of the boxcar are well built and free of defects.

Liam is first to return to his seat near the locked door.

Discouraged, Callum tenses his face into a frown as he starts to crawl toward his companion.

They are startled by a muffled noise that booms through the tunnel and vibrates the entire boxcar. Although distant, the deep sound reverberates within their confined space. Still pondering the unexpected noise, the pair are caught off guard when the train's brakes are abruptly applied, screeching and grabbing in a frantic attempt to stop. The train car violently jolts as it collides with the connecting hitch of the railcars in front and rams from behind. The car's forward momentum immediately plummets.

The sudden change in acceleration hurls Callum forward. His face takes the brunt of the hard-hitting fall, momentarily dazing him.

The glowing orb that spent most of the trip floating aimlessly between the roof beams is bumped free and bounces wildly until it strikes an end wall and bursts like a bubble. The boxcar is plunged into darkness while the train lurches onward. The earsplitting scream of wheels against tortured steel rails drowns out every other sound. Callum claps his hands over his ears to dampen the horrible noise.

He and Liam leave their stomachs behind when the pitch-black boxcar leaps off the tracks and vaults a couple of feet into the air. The car slams down again and tips sharply to Callum's left before rolling over. With nothing to grab hold of, the two men tumble blindly and crash into a sidewall that suddenly became the new floor. The toppled car plows along the ground until it lurches to a stop. The chaos finally ends in eerie quiet.

For several moments, Callum lies disoriented amid utter blackness and silence. He can taste blood from a split lip, and warm wetness drips onto his hand from a cut above his right eyebrow. Battered and breathless from his ordeal, Callum is amazed to still be alive. Then, when he hears Liam groaning, he turns his attention to locating the hunter.

The air is filled with a fine haze of dust that causes both men to choke. Callum tries to call out to Liam, but all he can manage is a coughing fit. He struggles to sit up and orient himself. At last, the dust begins to settle, and both men can breathe well enough to speak.

"Are you all right?" Liam asks, gasping. His voice indicates he is several feet away.

"Yeah, I think so," Callum grunts, feeling bashed and bruised but thankful that nothing seems broken. Even so, his wounded and swollen leg is nagging him wrathfully after this new trauma.

"Are you injured?" Callum asks. He shifts to his knees and stretches one arm in front of him, sweeping side to side and trying to find the edges of his lightless world.

"No," Liam replies, "but I'm going to be damn sore tomorrow."

"Stay where you are. I'm going to move over to you." Head is still spinning from the upheaval, and Callum does not immediately consider the benefit of his magic to guide him.

The direction of Liam's voice suggests his proximity remains in the center of their cell and is near their only avenue to freedom. Callum hopes the accident did not damage the door's rollers, allowing them to escape if they can break the lock.

"Marco!" Liam calls out.

"Polo!" Callum smiles at the reference to an outdated yet helpful game of blind hide-n-seek.

He clambers over splintered timber, carefully navigating toward Liam's voice. He barely starts to advance when shouts and hurried movements are heard outside the derailed boxcar.

Muffled cries of panic from survivors begin to fill the tunnel. The commotion rapidly escalates to screams of terror, and Callum detects the sharp ring of metal striking metal. He never witnessed a sword battle, but the clashing and clanging suggest something like one. The metallic singing is answered by the bark of gunfire. Callum scrambles faster, gritting his teeth against the pain. He halts, shaking his head and berating himself for not thinking to summon another sphere of light until now. Callum sits on his knees and raises his palm upward. He stares into the darkness and tries to bring his muddled thoughts into focus. Before Callum can summon any arcane energy, bullets cut through the wooden bulkhead, skimming his short hair and forces him to flatten on the floor.

"Shit!" Callum yells as more bullets tear holes in their prison.

"Are they trying to kill us?" Liam hollers back.

Callum glances in the hunter's direction and sees a handful of small puncture holes along the right wall between them. Faint spears of light penetrate the boxcar's pitchy interior. He can barely make out the shadowy form of Liam lying flat six feet away.

"I think they're being attacked," observes Callum.

They anxiously listen as the rate of gunfire increases, accompanied by explosions that rock the derailed train. Callum covers his head with his arms when a larger blast detonates just beyond their boxcar prison. The battered exterior starts to split and crack as heavy blows thud against the planks.

Callum wriggles backward, fearful that the damaged wall

might collapse upon him. Another volley of bullets rips overhead. One shot grazes the back of Callum's shoulder and forcing both men to hug the floor again.

The warlock cautiously raises his face and smells the acrid aroma of smoke filtering into the car from fires burning outside.

"We need to reach that door before we start to cook!" Liam yells over the commotion.

"Not until they stop shooting!" Callum lays flat with his hands protectively shielding the back of his head and neck. Shreds of wooden splinters and dust continue to shower him.

Both men are pinned while the conflict ensues. When the gunfire eventually subsides, it sounds like the struggling dwarves are being pushed back. Callum takes the risk of heaving up onto his elbows to peer through one of the marble-sized holes.

Some of the surviving dwarves are scrambling toward the rear of the train. Their screams echo down the tunnel as they flee.

Without a wide enough field of vision that is clear of the obscuring smoke, Callum cannot see who the attackers are. As soon as the remaining dwarves are gone, they hear the crunch of hurried steps outside the pierced walls.

Callum moves away when he hears several figures climbing atop the car. It only takes a few seconds before footsteps are thundering above his head, converging on the door above Liam.

"Move back," Callum whispers.

He hears Liam shuffling in retreat from the huge door suspended overhead and toward the distant end of the car, just as a violent crunch of fracturing timber resonates from outside.

Callum guesses the lock is being pried loose by these mysterious assailants, and his panic level rises sharply. Could this be Kincaid's crew? Or Quinn's? There is a metallic rattle and chink of tools before the unlatched door is muscled open and floods the cabin with hazy light.

Both prisoners are shrouded by shadows, dust, and smoke. They tuck themselves as far away from the entrance as they can get to avoid being spotted. Unfortunately, the search party is not satisfied with a quick peek, and a silhouetted figure drops down to explore further.

Callum stands on shaking legs and leans against the wall to ensure he stays upright, freeing his hands for defensive retaliation.

Liam is unwilling to remain hidden. The hunter roars and erupts from the shadows, ramming the unsuspecting intruder with his muscular shoulder. Liam and his adversary both tumble to the floor, but the fight is short-lived when three more figures jump into the fray and quickly tackle the feisty hunter.

Even though no one has noticed Callum, the warlock realizes his time for hiding is over. He must defend himself, or at least try to save his impetuous ally. So, the warlock prepares to launch a spell into the heart of the commotion. Bracing himself against the bullet-pitted wall, he raises his right hand as it radiates blue sparks from his fingertips.

Before he can complete the incantation, the partition beside Callum explodes, hurling the warlock across the car and smashing him against the opposite wall. The blasted panel, already full of cracks and bullet holes, disintegrates on impact, and it rains shards of wood upon the warlock until he collapses.

Callum is dazed by the force of the explosion but remains conscious. Despite ringing ears and reeling thoughts, he strains to see through the jagged rupture. A gaping man-sized hole is now at the precise spot where he had been standing.

Three backlit figures clamber through the opening and rush to surround him. Callum is hauled upright and dragged through the shattered wall. He furiously struggles against the arms that hold him and kicks at the lone figure intent on securing his legs. Callum manages a lucky strike to the assailant's face and watches him fall back into the darkness of the toppled boxcar. His resistance is met with merciless force, and the warlock is brutally spun and thrown face-first onto the ground.

His right cheek is squashed against the sharp gravel while his arms are yanked behind his back. Callum strains to free himself, but these opponents are too strong and agile. Someone dives across the back of his knees to restrain him, and Callum screams as his wounded leg crushes under the stranger's weight.

He writhes, unable to think beyond the agony that burns down the length of his calf. But Callum desperately squirms until his arms are bound behind his back, and the heaviness is removed from his legs. Then, wholly spent by pain, Callum stops fighting. He cannot win this battle.

"Are you Callum Walker?" an authoritative voice demands.

Callum is not the least bit inclined to answer the stranger's questions under these circumstances. He can hear Liam nearby, cursing at his captors and battling with furious rancor.

"Are you Callum Walker?" the voice asks again, impatiently.

He considers responding, but Callum seems unable to formulate any comprehendible words. His mind is addled from the trauma of the crash and subsequent explosion, and he feels mentally detached from this surreal environment.

A painful fog swirls through his mind, and his throbbing skull signals it wants to burst. The bustle of activity around him now appears to be happening in slow motion. All Callum knows for sure is that this group has driven the dwarves away, attacked him, dragged him from the train, and then trussed him like a parcel. It does not matter who they are, their actions reveal them as a new enemy, and he accepts the option of silence.

Someone grabs his shoulder to roll him over, and a light blazes down into his eyes. Callum tries to look away from its glare, but his head is gripped and firmly held in place. Fingertips pry his eyelids open, forcing him to look into the intense gleam.

It is only for a few seconds, but Callum's pupils are fully dilated from hours of darkness. When the searing light is removed, all he can do is blink at the dazzling sparks swamping his vision. He can barely discern the sharp-featured face of a man-like figure crouching beside him, holding a colorless stone that glows as bright as a flashlight.

The intrusive assailant continues to probe Callum's various superficial, bleeding scrapes before turning his attention to the warlock's abused leg. The unwelcome examination allows time for the warlock's sight to recover. The magical stone now, thankfully, has been tucked into a pocket.

"Well, Belenor?" grumbles a ramrod-straight, black-haired figure towering behind the kneeling man. He stands cross-armed and scowls down at Callum, impatiently waiting for Belenor's response, who seems in no hurry to provide one.

Belenor turns Callum's head from side to side to examine his collection of cuts and bruises. After a quick inspection, he finally answers, "He has been stunned by the explosion and likely has a concussion. He should recover, Commander Agis, but it will take a while."

"We do not have time for this," Agis barks, turning abruptly on his heels and marching away. "Get him on his feet or carry him if you have to." The commander barks an order over his shoulder. "We need to leave now before those damnable dwarves return."

Two guards waiting nearby step forward and haul Callum from the ground. With a guard under each arm to keep him upright, Callum is pulled in time with their steps. Dazed, he staggers along and heavily leans on the pair of wardens for stability. His eyesight is nearly fully recovered from the blinding assault of light.

"Who are *you*?" Callum asks of the commander. The question drips with truculence.

When he hears Callum speak, Agis halts and turns to look at this impudent prisoner who has suddenly decided to open his mouth.

"We are the mountain elves of Verdon Peaks," Agis says curtly, approaching his prisoner once more with a domineering deportment. "What is *your* name?"

Mountain elves. It makes sense and explains why the attackers look mostly human, with bright eyes, a bit too large, and ears that rise to an elongated point. They are slightly taller than Callum, but he can see that their sharp features almost appear to be artificial. Many carry swords or daggers—a few bear elegant staves topped with decoratively carved fingers of wood that hold colored stones pulsating with magical energy.

"Why do you want to know?" Callum grunts, fighting a wave of dizziness. He is suddenly grateful for the two guards supporting him. If not for them, he would be flat on the ground.

"I am not playing this game," growls Agis. "If you do not wish to answer here, that is your choice, but I hope for your sake that you come around once we cross through the portal. Belenor, he is in your charge. See to his progress."

"Yes, commander," Belenor replies, bowing as Agis spins and stomps toward the front of the train.

They pass many dead and wounded dwarves littering the devastated railway tunnel. While the fires slowly die, red embers fill the exploded craters dotting the tunnel. Most rail cars are damaged beyond salvage, and the metal rails are twisted into fantastic shapes.

The soldiers now busy themselves with gathering their wounded and marching toward the front of the train. Callum's wardens usher him along with the procession.

Amid the chaos, Callum's attention is drawn to Liam's ongoing struggle against his captors. The hunter thrashes to gain freedom, even though his arms are securely tethered behind his back. Callum can feel the intensity of Liam's fear. Whether delivered to Kincaid or returned to Quinn, the hunter is doomed to death. Yet, it appears Liam is desperate to fight for his freedom, and nothing seems to subdue him.

"Sedate him," Agis orders in frustration as he watches his soldiers continue to grapple with their captive.

In compliance with the commander's orders, a tan-robed elf moves toward Liam, wearing a smirk of pleasure. The gangly elf holds a gem-topped staff that rises to the height of his protracted ear tips. He murmurs an incantation and extends the glowing jewel toward the hunter's flailing head. Instantly, Liam's fighting stops, and he goes limp. The elven guards carry him by his shoulders and legs as dead weight, continuing further up the tunnel.

Callum feels an insistent tug from his own guards, urging him to totter along faster. He tries to quicken his hobbling pace while they act as living crutches to hold him up. Still lightheaded and bleary-eyed, Callum keeps moving past a long succession of battlefield scenes.

Victims from both sides of the conflict lay in bloody heaps with gaping wounds and torn limbs. A strange, flute-barreled rifle lies beside a decapitated dwarf. If he had not already been numbed by shock, Callum might have been more disturbed by the carnage around him.

"You are badly limping. Do you need me to tend to your leg?" Belenor asks as he follows close behind.

"I don't trust your help," grumbles Callum with a scowl. "Especially when you won't even bother telling me what the hell this is all about."

"If you tell us your name, then we will answer your questions and explain our motives," Belenor says, echoing his commander's order.

"And what happens if I don't answer?" Callum fires back defiantly, staring straight ahead, and refuses to meet the militia's only hospitable elf.

"Commander Agis will draw memories from your mind and find the answer for himself. Elves have powerful magic, but we would rather not have to resort to that level of intrusion," Belenor explains. "It could be dangerous for you."

Callum realizes that the elves will get their information one way or another and would rather spare himself further grief if possible.

"Fine," he grudgingly relents. "My name is Callum Walker."

He waits for a response from his captors, but they simply carry on as before. Maybe they do not believe him after his initial refusal to cooperate. Whatever the case may be, they continue to guide him even faster, making him grimace with each lumbering step.

Fortunately, it is a short journey. As the troop rounds the end of the smashed locomotive, Callum gawks in surprise at the disfigured steam engine and the massive crater stamped into the railbed directly in the train's path.

The detonation that dented the earth also shattered the engine's front end and carved considerable gouges in the stone walls of the tunnel. An enormous volume of debris hailed down from the destroyed ceiling, and some small fires are still burning. But Callum's eyes are immediately drawn beyond the mangled metal to a swirling vortex of color.

The squad of mountain elves marches straight into the vertical whirlpool. Then, one by one, each soldier vanishes into the maelstrom as though stepping through a painting.

"You should close your eyes," Belenor advises when they near the prismatic eddy.

Callum is not about to reject practical advice, no matter how much he distrusts its source. He closes his eyes and lurches along, relying on his bracing escorts to guide him safely through...whatever this is.

Callum is stunned to feel a bitter wind sting his face and hands and make him shiver uncontrollably despite his tattered jacket.

Opening his eyes, he finds himself transported almost to the peak of a soaring mountain, where he stands on a well-used, snowy trail. Early dawn dimly reflects off pink clouds, illuminating the mountain's white pinnacles in a blushing glow.

Some mountain elves continue along the path, bordered on each side by waist-high bulwarks of snow. The narrow trail rises at a steep angle, in a series of switchback turns ascending to the summit. Callum observes the endpoint—an alpine village comprised of multiple sturdy log buildings. Plumes of wood smoke billows from the tops of their stone chimneys.

Rather than following the rest of the procession, Callum is led to a wooden bench. Belenor brushes away the snow and steps aside so his prisoner can sit. Liam is lugged past by his own pair of guards. The hunter is an awkward burden to his wardens, even while unconscious.

Callum exhales with relief upon easing down as gently as possible. Despite the bone-chilling wind, he remains on the bench until the whole procession of elves finally passes on their trek up to the village. Callum is now alone with his two wardens and Belenor. Clearly, they are waiting for something. Several minutes later, Agis graces them with his domineering presence.

"Well, I hope you feel more like talking now," the elven commander growls. He looms over Callum and frowns down like an angry father on the verge of scolding a child.

"Commander, he has confirmed to me that his name is Callum Walker. However, I cannot tell you if he is lying," Belenor reports.

"Really?" Agis reacts in surprise. "Did Belenor tell you that we have ways of extracting the truth from you?"

"He was pretty sketchy about the details," Callum replies grimly, nervously glancing between Belenor and Agis.

"The Callum Walker we are seeking is rumored to be a human warlock," Agis says sternly. He narrows his eyes at his captive as though judging him to be unworthy of such a title.

"You've gone through a lot of trouble for a rumor," Callum says. He winces as his bound arms, causing his shoulders to ache.

Agis sighs and rolls his eyes. "I do not have the patience for this. Lives have been lost today, and I need to confirm that our venture was not in vain. My methods are not gentle, but they are quick and reliable."

"You asked for my name, and I gave it to you," says Callum, not sure how else to convince these elves he is telling the truth.

"I appreciate that you offered a name, but I am suspicious of your sudden change of heart." Agis fixes Callum with a harsh stare, pulls off his gloves, and hands them to Belenor.

The commander drops to one knee in front of Callum as though about to propose marriage. Instead, his hands reach out for Callum's head.

Grabbing each side of Callum's skull, Agis presses his fingertips firmly against his scalp. Callum attempts to twist his head and break the elf's grasp, forcing Agis to increase the pressure. However, the flanking guards prevent him from leaning back. The commanding elf closes his eyes and bows his head while reciting an ancient incantation.

"*Responsum revelare*," Agis says softly, and Callum begins to see images of his personal history flash through his mind.

From his earliest memories onward, thoughts and scenes race through his consciousness at dizzying speeds. Callum's eyes are wide open, but he can only see the visions of his past. His recollections are nothing more than a series of antic dramas like a movie running at high speed. His mind burns as though the racing memories are too much for his overtaxed brain to cope with. Callum's life rapidly passes before his eyes until it reached a point five years ago. Then, the pace of flickering memories slows and becomes more detailed. He relives many early battles and sees images of magical creatures he vanquished. Viewing both victories and failures, Callum watches his mundane existence drone on while the searing pain in his head makes him scream.

The visions continue to play on, and Callum witnesses his recent experiences and challenges. He catches glimpses of Frey, remembers his visit to the fairy homeland, and endures the goblin fight once again. Callum tries to pull free from Agis' grasp, desperate to escape the unbearable mental onslaught. His nose begins to bleed, and an intense pressure builds within his head, threatening to rend his skull.

Agis forces more memories to emerge from the depths of Callum's psyche, and they flow through the current incidents involving the dwarves and the train. Callum revisits the horror of the crash and the boxcar explosion, and he sees Liam fighting relentlessly for freedom. The events of his life proceed to the moment the portal and arriving at the mountain peak. Only then, Agis abruptly releases his iron grip.

Callum is barely coherent as the guards prop him up against the back of the bench. His head is a furnace of pain, and he closes his eyes tight to help bear the waves of mental agony.

The warlock is slightly aware of a delicate hand placed on his forehead. He misses Belenor's whispered words, attempting to dispel the effects of the enchantment with his own magic.

Eventually, Callum begins to feel some growing relief from the torment inflicted by Agis. He sighs as his muscles relax, yet the warlock still hovers on the edge of consciousness. Nearly half an hour passes before Callum opens his eyes to see Belenor leaning over him, feeling for a pulse in his neck. Agis stands nearby with an apologetic expression painted across his ever-youthful, sculpted face.

"Are you feeling better?" Belenor asks worriedly.

Callum imperceptibly nods. He clears his throat and raises his abused head.

"What the hell was *that*?" Callum asks, hearing the strain in his own voice.

"I am sorry you had to experience that, but we have sacrificed much to find you. It was the only way to be sure you were telling the truth," Agis replies as he massages his own aching temples.

The elven commander unsteadily leans against the wall of packed snow, his features glistening with a film of sweat. He nods an unspoken command to Callum's flanking guards.

Immediately, one of the guards adroitly slides a battle-scarred dagger from a leather sheath at his hip. Then, without explanation, he leans Callum forward and slices the sinewy lashings that bind his arms.

Inwardly rejoicing in the blessed relief of restored circulation, Callum gingerly stretches his shoulders. He cautiously peers at Agis, feeling naked and exposed now that the elf knows everything about him. Since Agis released him, Callum assumes that the intrusion into his mind convinced the commander he is who he claims to be.

"What is it you want with me?" Callum asks. He glares at Agis and tenderly rubs his sore wrists.

He is even more mistrustful of these mountain elves after suffering Agis's mental torture. The commander fixes penitent, wide-set eyes on Callum. The elf presses his thin lips tightly together before sighing through his nose. It is the regretful look of a man, or elf, considering how best to make amends.

"We have been searching for the warlock promised in the prophecy ever since Kincaid was discovered to be a necromancer. His appearance is the first recognized sign that the time of fulfillment was close at hand. Since then, we have been awaiting the second sign—another human sorcerer."

Agis pauses to reflect before continuing. "The Seelie court alerted our monarch that you were confirmed to be the Prophesied One. With only your name to identify you, our search was hampered. We heard about your capture by the mountain dwarves and planned to free you before they could deliver you to Kincaid. That is how and why you are here." Agis speaks with such simple conviction that it is hard not to believe him. "We do not wish to harm you. We only want to help."

"We will have our shaman tend to you when we reach our village," Belenor says, patting Callum's shoulder and offering a friendly smile before straightening up. "Are you able to walk now?"

"I'm not going to let you carry me," Callum says irritably as he wills himself to rise from the bench on trembling legs.

"At least let me provide you some relief," Belenor says. His face draws into a sullen expression. "I am not a shaman, but I am trained as a medic by our magical healers to mend soldiers' injuries in the event of an emergency. I can reduce your pain and help you to reach Velnor Peaks on foot."

Callum considers this for a moment, scrutinizing the helpful elven medic. Then, peering up the daunting half-mile ascent, the warlock grudgingly accepts.

Fifteen minutes later, Callum is plodding steadily up the rest of the mountain. He is still limping, but his pain is now dampened enough that he confidently makes the last leg of the trail unassisted.

Callum is skeptical of these elves' true motives, but for the time being, he is relieved they do not want to kill him, at least not yet.

Time will tell.

CHAPTER NINETEEN

"What do you mean he's gone?!" Quinn screams into the phone on his ostentatious desk. The spider veins flush bright red across his cheeks, and a vein angrily pulses on one side of his thick neck. He knows it is not Eric's fault the warlock has been abducted, but he is the unfortunate messenger who receives the brunt of Quinn's fiery wrath.

"I am sorry, sir. I lost contact with our hunter ten hours ago. I have every available agent searching Duncaster, trying to locate the target again," Eric reports with trepidation.

"Do you have any leads? Or are you completely in the dark?" Quinn blasts back at Eric. He pinches the bridge of his nose and closes his eyes to control his outrage.

"We found evidence that dwarves were involved, and there are several teams of hunters tracking them as we speak. We *will* find Walker again," Eric says as confidently as he can, hoping to reassure his fuming master.

"What about this hunter of yours that's also vanished?" asks Quinn.

"We believe that Liam was taken captive by the dwarves as well."

"If he returns, I want him punished for this failure."

"Yes, master. Of course. I will make sure of it," Eric says obediently.

Quinn huffs and flares his nostrils, then slams down the phone to end the call. The sorcerer pounds his fists on the desk in boiling frustration. His damnable brother has won the loyalty of the dwarves, and if Eric is correct, they have seized the best chance to win this war.

The sorcerer usually maintains a stoic exterior, but this recent string of disappointments has tried his usual calm demeanor. He wants to punish someone for this distressing turn of events, but it seems the inept hunter responsible for this mess is lost to him. Fury clouds his judgment and rules his behavior in recent days, causing Quinn to be more demanding and reckless in his efforts to achieve victory.

The sorcerer looks over at the pendant necklace hanging from a display hook atop his desk. His precious sight stone rests securely between golden claws in the center of the amulet, and its promising revelations are beckoning.

It has been a full day since he sought the stone's guidance, which has already proven its value by showing him the warlock to be in the company of the fairies. While his feeble-minded followers remain oblivious, the stone gives Quinn invaluable direction. Now, he must turn to the amulet once more, seeking critical answers that his feckless subordinates have yet again failed to provide.

Giving in to his urgent desire for knowledge, Quinn grabs the pendant from its ornate hook and stomps strides to the crackling fireplace. He pulls the golden chain over his bald head and lowers himself onto a crimson cushion. Quinn ignores his protesting arthritic knees and hips and forces his blubbery legs to sit cross-legged. Then, tenting his chubby fingers before his chest, he closes his eyes and begins meditating.

For a long while, nothing happens, but when engaged in this exercise, Quinn is uncharacteristically patient. He confidently waits, staring at the darkness within his mind while the stone searches out the information he desires. A revelation finally comes to him—a snow-covered mountain village and a marching line of figures seen from a distance. In visions, the stone carries his astral body to the location of the person he seeks, floating high above but not actually there in physical form. Quinn looks down at the small convoy and notices one member trudging with a pronounced limp.

Quinn focuses, willing his astral form to float closer to the injured man. Now only a short distance away from his target, Quinn confirms that it is indeed Callum Walker. He observes the warlock's pasty pallor. Weariness and pain are written across Callum's bruised and bloodied face.

Quinn shadows Callum's trek to the edge of the elven village, noting the relief etched on the young man's bristly features when he finally arrives. The warlock looks nearly spent from fatigue but drives himself with stubborn defiance, refusing help from the elves that walk with him. It is the same obstinacy that cost Quinn months of intense investigation, confirming his identity and power.

As Quinn shifts his attention to the people accompanying the warlock, he curses his bad fortune—mountain elves.

This discovery is a mixed blessing. Kincaid is still denied access to Callum, but it also means that there is zero chance for his own hunters to conduct a successful capture.

Mountain Elves are masters of their alpine realm and possess powerful magic. These elves have developed an organized defense of their homeland, so any attempt at invasion is met with quick and deadly resistance. He will have to wait until Callum leaves the elven sanctuary before he can hope to snare the warlock.

As Quinn observes his target with hawk-like intensity, the sight stone begins to shift to another vision. As it has happened many times before, the image slowly coalesces.

The sorcerer finds himself standing in a large cavern. His

overworked heart pounds hard against his ribs in anticipation of the nightmarish scene he often sees play out. Every time he uses the stone, it eventually delivers him to this moment. The stone is believed to have a purpose of its own. As if with conscious intent, it is compelled to show the user the moment of their death.

Quinn has memorized this unwelcome vision. Within a cavern, he stands before a soundless column of fire. He does not know what occurred leading up to this moment, but the sorcerer is not alone here. On the opposite side of the pillar of fire, a young human, clothed in a grimy sweatshirt and jeans, calmly stands facing him. In earlier versions of this vision, Quinn was not permitted to see the face of the man confronting him. This time, however, he can clearly identify the dark figure as the warlock, Callum Walker.

In the vision, Callum speaks as he moves from behind the fiery column, but Quinn cannot make out the muted words, no matter how hard he tries. Yet, there is strength in the young man's troubled face, and Quinn recognizes the same determination he saw in his other visions of Callum.

Even though he already witnessed the encounter's outcome, Quinn always experiences the same feelings of dread washing over him. The warlock steps into full view, away from the silent flames, and seconds tick by as he moves closer. Quinn's future self raises an arm to attack, using a magical aid to defend himself. The warlock stops with an alarmed expression on his face. Quinn sees Callum lifting his hand to point behind the sorcerer, then shouts, but he never sees beyond that moment. The ending is always the same. Quinn turns to follow Callum's outstretched finger, and an explosion of dazzling red light steals his life. All he knows is that whatever the cause, it kills him instantly.

When the horrifying divination ends, the sight stone returns Quinn to his earlier view of the warlock. Still, the heart-pounding distress remains for some time. Pushing past his fear,

Quinn lets the vision advance him into the near future. There he finds some hope.

The vision does not tell him exactly when this event is destined to occur, but Quinn can calculate a reasonable time estimate while using the stone. He can make an educated prediction of the date when each forecasted event will transpire. The sorcerer wickedly smiles when he sees Callum's future departure from the elven village. When he watches his hunter, Liam, leaving with the warlock, Quinn's expression becomes hot rage. Furious, not just at Liam's failure but his betrayal.

Taking a deep breath, he removes the pendant, and the magical vision disappears. The sorcerer holds the stone in his hand, grateful for the truth it reveals to him. He has approximately three days to prepare his revenge against Liam's treachery. After that, suffering and oblivion will be the hunter's final reward.

Yes, Liam will pay, and once he robs the warlock of his power, Quinn will also savor seeing Callum Walker die a slow and excruciating death.

CHAPTER TWENTY

T he simple act of laying on a bed causes Callum to experience sensations of bliss. His entire body aches from one injury or another. The moment he reclines into the soft mattress, Callum relaxes fully in luxurious comfort. Looking around, he notes he is not the only resident of the large, airy room. Twenty beds line the walls of the elves' infirmary, and each is occupied by a victim of the vicious battle in the train tunnel.

The warlock spies Liam in a neighboring bed, peacefully sleeping under the effects of a sedation spell. The shaman responsible for his treatment, Leana, inspects the side of his head for wounds that would account for the crusted blood on the hunter's head and neck. She stands up, tapping a finger on her chin and puzzling at the single vivid scar.

"I had to save his life," Callum says, trying to explain.

Leana turns her penetrating green eyes at Callum. "How did you do this?" she asks with amazement.

"I'm not really sure," he replies. Callum tries to recall the exceptionally intense energy he summoned and utilized—still confident that it was not his own power. "I've heard how shamans use arcane energy to heal, so I thought it was worth a shot. I just concentrated on repairing the injury inside his brain, and my magic reversed the damage."

"Belenor tells us you are a warlock," says Leana. She looks at him as though Callum presents a great unsolved mystery. Tilting her pretty, oval face, the shaman frowns and asks, "How is it that a human has access to such magic?"

"I wish I knew," Callum says truthfully, turning away from Leana to stare at the ceiling.

"How does your magic work?" Leana probes.

"The incantations just sort of come to me when I concentrate on what I need." Callum hopes the shaman understands. It is pointless to hide his secrets from the elves—Agis already knows everything about him.

"I...see." Leana raising one thin eyebrow. "Is this how you cast all of your spells?"

"Yes, for the most part. Once, I was able to cast an enchantment without speaking," Callum tells her. Somehow, it feels like a confession.

"Have you ever heard of blood sorcery?"

"Can't say that I have." Callum flashes her a glance, meeting her inquisitive green eyes again. His interest is piqued despite his extreme fatigue. Thankfully, their conversation is happening with a mattress under his battered body, and that is a welcome change.

"In creatures such as elves, fairies, and other beings of this realm, magic is something intangible. Humans would say it is part of our souls, and it gives us life. They would not be wrong. This ethereal source is what powers our magic. It is the way of all magic," says Leana. She smiles kindly at Callum when he pinches his brows in thought. "*Your* arcane source, on the other hand, is both spiritual and physical. From what you have told me, you are born of blood magic. Which means your heart, mind, and soul are the generators of your power. This combination allows your thoughts to guide your spellcasting, and it will give you the gift of insight."

"Oh," Callum says, blankly staring as he processes this information.

"This type of magical ability usually has a negative association. It has been seen in vampires and ancient followers of the occult, but I do not think it has appeared often in living humans. Until Kincaid was born."

"Do necromancers have this kind of power?" Callum asks, closing in on a terrifying theory.

"Yes, it is something that a necromancer can use," Leana answers. "Blood magic is rare and extremely dynamic. Necromancers use the energy in their ichor to conjure new life. But it is forbidden magic because the summoner is playing with the tools of creation. Only a benevolent, divine author can evoke an untainted lifeform. If the conjurer carries the smallest grain of wickedness in their soul, their creations will magnify evil. The poison of the darkness will consume all good in the necromancer's spirit until they are nothing but an unholy shell."

"So, conjuration magic is bad?"

"Not entirely. Conjuration is a valuable tool for spell casters. While the creation of new life is bad, summoning material objects have no effect."

"Okay..." Callum soberly stares at the kindly shaman. His fingers fidget with the coarse wool blanket beneath him as he contemplates.

Amid all this fresh knowledge, Callum is most dismayed to learn that he has more in common with Kincaid than he initially thought.

Whether or not he wants to hear the truth, he realizes it is finally necessary to ask the question gnawing at him ever since his conversation with Liam in the boxcar. "Am *I* a necromancer?"

"No," Leana assures him. "A necromancer is not something you are. It is something you choose to become. It is a learned evil practice that the darkest hearts are attracted to because it offers immense power. You have a rare ability that is at least equivalent in strength to a necromancer. There must be a reason *why* you have this type of magic."

Leana's presence sets Callum's mind at ease. He easily senses her innate kindness and desire to care for those in need of healing. But most importantly, Leana's explanation that he is *not* evil simply because of his blood magic delivers great relief. Callum could not have received better news.

Leana wants to continue their conversation, but other wounded patients await her attention. Callum and Liam are left to sleep, but the shaman promises to visit him later.

Despite his extreme tiredness, Callum's slumber is anything but restful. His dreams are full of explosions and fire, nightmares recounting the trauma of the past few days. Callum helplessly watches the cycle of pain and stress repeat itself. Finally, he sees himself surrounded by faceless enemies closing in, and his fear spikes. The warlock's heart is beating like a jackhammer when he awakens, startled and disoriented.

Drenched in an icy sweat, Callum springs up from his pillow, gasping for breath and clutching a hand to his chest. His sudden movement alarms a young nurse changing the sheets on Liam's empty bed. She drops the linen and runs from the bedside, screaming in fright. Callum feels terrible for scaring the poor elf, but she fled before he could apologize.

Leana is writing at her desk near the far end of the peaceful infirmary when Callum wakes. She maintains her composure, rising and casually walking down the line of mostly vacant beds.

Callum gazes across the ward, barely noticing Leana's approach. Tall windows cast cheerful streams of sunlight across the neat rows of cots and few remaining patients. Dawn was breaking when he first arrived, and he wonders how long he slept. It feels as though he just closed his eyes. Amid Callum's confusion, Leana reaches his bedside and takes a seat on the empty bed Liam had previously occupied.

"I am glad to see you are finally awake," Leana says in greeting. She looks at her patient thoughtfully.

"What time is it?" Callum asks, rubbing his face to wipe away the last traces of sleep. His stubbled chin rasps against his fingers.

Callum is surprised that he feels so much better, despite his stiff muscles and multiple contusions. Even his abused leg feels better. He pushes the blankets aside and lifts his denim pant leg to see fresh, white bandages expertly wrapped from his ankle to his knee.

"It is mid-afternoon," Leana answers quietly.

"I've only slept for half a day then." Callum sighs.

"No, dear. You have slept for thirty-six hours," Leana responds stoically. Callum flashes her a disbelieving stare. "Your body needed rest, and I used some of my magic to speed your healing. The deeper wounds will mend quickly with my medicine. You should be feeling much better now, but you still need some time to recuperate. In another day or two, you will be fine." Leana gives him a pleasant smile and a reassuring nod.

Callum cannot remember ever sleeping so long, but it makes sense considering that he has been deprived of adequate rest for nearly two days.

"You are welcome to stay here until you are fully recovered, or you can see what our community has to offer—as long as you promise to return before nightfall. I need to change your bandages this evening," Leana explains.

"Thank you, Leana. I promise I'll return," says Callum, sporting a sly grin.

"See to it. I would hate to have to hunt you down and drag you back," Leana says with a telling wink. "It has been a long while since I have tied a patient to their cot, but I will not hesitate if it ensures your recovery."

Callum gazes open-mouthed as the curious elf rise and coolly returns to her paperwork. Yet, despite her demeanor, Callum is both cowed and beguiled by Leana's inauspicious remark.

As Callum swings his legs to the floor, he distracts himself

from Leana's unfavorable promise with another puzzling thought
—where is Liam?

~

Callum shields his eyes when he steps into the bright sunshine,
but it does not take long for his vision to adjust. As he descends
the front porch of the infirmary, he tucks his hands into the
pockets of his raggedy green jacket to keep them warm.

The crisp mountaintop air is refreshing, and his breath
circles in a cloud around his face as he meanders down the
narrow roadway. He tries, unsuccessfully, to avoid the many
curious eyes following him or secretly peering through curtained
windows.

The elven village seems tiny, and Callum is surprised to only
count a dozen log buildings around the infirmary. The icy lane
ends at an overlook with a waist-high railing. From this vantage
point, Callum notes his present location is one of many terraced
communities clinging to the sides and peaks of the neighboring
mountains.

The lower levels extend downward like a giant staircase, and
Callum sees many rustic buildings reaching into the distance. A
network of bridges spans the closer crags, stringing them
together like beads on a necklace.

"It's about time you woke up." Liam approaches so quietly, he
startles Callum, who nearly stumbles off the mountain. "At least
I know that you're still alive." The hunter heartily laughs at the
jolt he gave his cohort.

"I hope you've been staying out of trouble," Callum says,
shooting a look of annoyance back at Liam. However, it evaporates when he notices the delicious dish of food Liam is holding.

"I saw you leave the infirmary, and I thought you might be
hungry," Liam says, offering the meal. "Do you remember the
last time you ate?"

The savory aroma of cooked meat intoxicates the ravenous

warlock. Callum takes the meal, pausing only to mumble thanks in Liam's direction before devouring the plateful.

Callum is pleased to see a familiar face and shocked to discover he is grateful for the hunter's company. Leaning his elbows on the wide, wooden railing, Liam peers at the white peaks in silent introspection. Callum observes him carefully while he eats, sensing a difference in his comrade's attitude.

He sets the empty dish on the cedar handrail and turns to look back at the quiet village. The snowy lanes and pathways are nearly vacant now, occupied only by a handful of well-bundled elves who emerge to rush to their destinations and disappear again. Callum and Liam seem to be the last ones out in this freezing winter world without reason.

"I want to thank you for helping me back there on the train," says Liam with a heavy sigh. "I'm still not sure why you did it, but I realize that my master has deliberately given me the wrong impression about you."

"Is that an apology?" Callum asks. He watches another elf chance an inquisitive glance at him before darting across the slippery street and into another log building.

"I'm not going to say I'm sorry for the things I did under false direction," Liam declares. "But I promise you have nothing to fear from me now."

"Thanks." Callum casts an astounded glance at Liam.

The hunter wears a serious frown, but a willingness to make amends is apparent in the young hunter's behavior. Callum is comforted by a kindled hope that Liam may yet prove to be a new friend. Friends are something Callum now knows he could use more of.

"Come on, let me show you around this place before Miss Leana orders you back to bed," Liam says. His melancholy moment seems to have passed, and Quinn's former hunter is suddenly cheerful.

Callum agrees to the grand tour since Liam promises it will

be short. He has neither the energy nor the desire to venture far in the sub-zero alpine air.

Liam shows him the mess hall where he obtained the tasty meal. It is a large concourse with rows of tables and benches. Clusters of elves eat and converse. Their chatter stops as they watch the Prophesied One carry an empty plate down the length of the room to a tempting buffet full of steaming, aromatic food.

A port, red-faced elf is busy wiping counters but turns to greet the new arrivals with a cheery smile and a glance at Callum. The elf quickly looks away as though uncomfortable about being in the presence of the mysterious warlock. Callum is self-conscious about his unwelcome celebrity status among anyone living in the magical realm—at least from those who are not actively trying to kill him.

Next, they visit a clothing shop that makes and mends warm winter garments for such high elevations. The store is operated by an elderly female elf with graying hair and deep laugh lines etched upon her face. She appears very pleased to have Callum patronize her business and rises from her rocking chair to take his hand and gently kiss it.

She insists on outfitting the warlock with a heavy, brown woolen jacket to protect him against the cold. It promises to be far better than the grimy and bedraggled nylon jacket he wore continuously since stealing it from the dentist's office. Callum tries to refuse the generous gift, but the emphatic proprietress takes his disgusting outerwear between her thumb and forefinger and drops it in the fireplace to prevent him from declining. He thanks her profusely and pulls the new jacket over his shirt. Callum is also gifted a pair of red woolen mittens and a matching cap before he and Liam can finally leave the shop.

The next-largest building on this peak is a library. A single room lined with bookcases, filled to the brim with countless scrolls and leather-bound volumes. Callum recognizes the familiar musty odor of old paper from his own bookshop, prowling in search of research materials. It seems like a lifetime ago now.

As in the cafeteria, elves pause and turn to stare at him. The news of the fabled warlock's arrival must have reached every one of the village's inquisitive inhabitants.

Callum locks his shrugged shoulders to his ears and drops his gaze. He would love to inspect the impressive collection of written works, but not under the watchful eyes of half a dozen elves. So, he departs with Liam as soon as possible to escape the unwelcome attention.

Small private homes cluster on the hilltop. Friendly residents offer a cozy place to visit and enjoy some tea and fresh-baked bread as they pass. Callum politely declines the invitations, even though he would have liked to warm his frozen hands and feet. Liam educates him on the complicated bridges and portals connecting all the peaks into a single community, and he points out larger residential districts beyond this mountaintop. He suggests they make a wider excursion, but Callum refuses, and Liam respectfully accepts.

After a lifetime of introversion and near-solitude, Callum is overwhelmed by the universal attention his presence attracts. Here among the elves, he reaches a saturation point where he battles the urge to run and hide from the over-curious stares. Despite Liam's ambitious plan to show Callum the other interconnected elven communities, the warlock requests to return to the infirmary, where they take a seat on the porch steps.

"One of the elders told me the population here is almost one hundred thousand," says Liam, sounding excited by the information.

He had been so upbeat as he guided Callum around the village for the past couple of hours. It is hard not to feel amiable about the hunter's efforts at reconciliation and hints of friendship. Liam is undoubtedly trying hard to atone for the misery he caused.

"So, how do they all stay hidden from humans?" Callum asks.

Although he is not really interested, he wants to appease Liam's desire for company and conversation.

"Apparently, the veil extends like a bubble over the entire magical realm, higher than the tallest mountains and extending deep underground." Liam's explanation is superficial, but it gives Callum something new to ponder.

Liam rambles on with more details about the lives of the mountain elves. However, as the sun sets, Liam lapses into a long, thoughtful pause.

"You know that I can't return to the Order," Liam finally says with a disappointed sigh. "I've failed in my mission twice now, and I'm pretty sure I've royally pissed off my master. I'll be hunted as a fugitive and severely punished if I'm caught."

"Punished?"

"They may lock me in a cell for a few months, but I'm guessing that my consequences will be much worse than that."

"Oh." Callum considers this information for a moment. "What will they do if they catch *me*?"

Liam looks at him with a frown on his square face and concern glinting in his brown eyes. "They'll put you through a series of brutal experiments to test the source of your power. Then they'll extract that essence until they've taken everything they can. No magical creature has ever survived the process." Liam flinches at his culpable guilt in this atrocity as he relates these general details. He mindlessly picks a scab on his knuckle and averts his eyes to the ground.

"So, when they sent you to capture me, you knew your Order was condemning me to death. Why did you agree to it?"

"I didn't know their intentions at first. I thought you were like us, using imbued artifacts to cast magic. My initial task was to confirm your practice of the arcane. After you disappeared, my handler told me what you really are—a natural warlock—and he told me about their lethal plans for you. After learning the truth, my orders to capture you never sat well with me. But I didn't question it. The Order is all I've ever known," Liam replies sadly. Leans over his knees, his posture sags under the weight of self-condemnation. "I was adopted into the organization when I was three years old. I was taught to obey without question and disciplined if I didn't. I believed them when they told me the sacrifice of one man is worth it to save an entire realm of beings. Besides, we're at war."

"I guess it's a good thing for me that you started to question things," says Callum, feeling sympathy for his new friend's sufferings and misguided past.

"I caught them in a lie." Liam shrugs, and a half-hearted smile twitches the corner of his unshaven mouth. The hunter ruefully shakes his head, cursing himself for his years of blind loyalty to a deceitful master.

Warlock and hunter sit in the cold, quietly conversing until the sun disappears and stars punctuate the moonlit sky. It is necessary to temporarily part ways. Liam will stay with a family of elves, but Callum must remain at the infirmary under Leana's care.

The following two days pass in calm serenity. Liam is a wealth of knowledge that he willingly shares with Callum. He reveals everything he knows about David Kincaid but concedes the information is heavily biased, coming from an aggrieved brother. Liam explains that the rival warlords are fraternal twins. While growing up in the human world, they were equally privileged in every way, but one—Kincaid was gifted with natural magic, and Quinn was not. Kincaid flaunted his extraordinary magical power, and Quinn was left to covet his brother's talents.

Quinn's overwhelming jealousy drove him to seek out a teacher in the mystical arts and learn how to channel magic through infused stones and artifacts. It took him many years to find a trustworthy master rather than just another overzealous pretender. When he finally found his desired mentor—an elven hermit who resides in the human world rather than the magical realm—Quinn obsessively immersed himself in his studies.

He became interested in magical creatures that coexisted

upon this Earth. In studying each species, Quinn was disheartened to learn that humans scarcely ever possess natural magic. He hated his twin for being one of the rare few.

While Quinn was discovering that magic had biological sources, Kincaid was learning about the power of dark magic.

Kincaid enjoyed showing off his abilities and gaining admiration among his small circle of friends but soon found little satisfaction performing simple parlor tricks. He wanted to learn more about his potential, so he found himself compelled to study all forms of magic. Although he started with alchemy and healing spells, he considered those to be weak magic. Kincaid believed that his gifts were wasted if he was not challenged.

By the time he stumbled upon the dark arts, he was deeply depressed, so discovering this evil power gave him a revitalized purpose. Dark magic was far stronger than anything else Kincaid encountered. In striving to master it, he found a renewed excitement and direction in his life. Stepping fully into the world of necromancy on the day he conjured his first creature, Kincaid was immediately addicted. The Order later confirmed Kincaid possesses a rare form of magical power originating from his physical life's ichor. Kincaid is a blood sorcerer—like Callum—proven by his capability to invoke life through the power of his own blood.

The war between the brothers truly started when Kincaid, having conjured a small army to serve his ambitions, decided to challenge his brother to a duel. Quinn also developed his own sphere of arcane knowledge and willingly accepted the trial. But in an act of supreme overconfidence, he invited his mentor to watch the test of skills.

Quinn lost the sorcerers' battle against his brother for one simple reason—Kincaid cheated.

Kincaid used a concealed blade to slice his palm, sprinkling droplets of blood across the fighting arena. Using his blood magic to summon the spirits of the dead, two dozen minions rose that day. They seized and held Quinn, forcing him to watch helplessly as his mentor was tortured and slaughtered. Kincaid found it hilarious, of course. But on that day, Quinn vowed to kill his brother in revenge.

"So, Quinn is in it for revenge, and Kincaid is motivated by an appetite for power," Callum concludes, trying to summarize the perplexing conflict.

"The thing about dark magic is that it corrupts the user. It twists their mind and magnifies their most evil characteristics," Liam explains. "Kincaid wants to be the most powerful being alive, and he's resentful of anyone who challenges that self-image." The hunter kicks at a small stone lying free on the shoveled path. It sinks into the waist-high snowbank along the side of the trail as they meander along.

"Meaning me." Callum's face tenses into a troubling frown as enlightenment dawns.

Finally, he understands why there is such interest in his mere existence and the reason for ominous threats against his life.

"Yeah. Kincaid learned about the prophecy regarding you twenty years ago, and he's been searching for you ever since. I guess you would've been a toddler when this all started. He likely has spies in the Order, but we were never able to discover them." Liam sounds despondent at the mention of the organization that served as his surrogate family.

Youthful innocence guaranteed Liam's acceptance of the Order's lies as truth. Their unyielding demand for obedience and rigid training were proclaimed to be forms of affection. Liam shakes his head in dismay, disappointed at his gullibility.

"What I'm trying to say is that Kincaid is scared of you because the prophecy indicates that you will end the war and his potential reign over the magical realm."

"Oh, no pressure there," Callum scoffs, hiding his mounting tension behind sarcasm. In truth, he wishes he could give up his magical gifts and shed his connection to the prophecy. Right now, Callum would give almost anything to go back to his extremely dull life. Though he lived paycheck-to-paycheck, he did not have to fear imminent death at the hands of people he never heard of. The fact that there are so many innocent lives at stake gives him pause to reconsider. Whether he can end this war is not the question. Callum is morally driven to try to save those hopelessly caught in the middle. "I'm thinking it might be time to stop reacting to my enemies and take some serious action."

"Well, if it helps, I can tell you which city Quinn likes to hide in," Liam says thoughtfully.

"That would definitely be useful to know." Callum accepts Liam's help with a nod and grateful smile.

The warlock can sense the sincerity in the hunter's desire to help, and it is comforting to know he has a skilled ally willing to undertake this trial with him. After all, they are equally wanted men.

CHAPTER TWENTY-ONE

D espite some residual leg pain, Callum feels fully restored by his third morning. During his reprieve, the warlock took the opportunity to practice a few choice spells and improve his magical proficiency under Liam's tutelage. Callum also borrowed several tomes from the library. He smuggled them back to the infirmary to read about the realm's history and familiarize himself with his arcane capabilities.

During his time in Verdon Peaks, Agis kept his distance. However, Leana divulged the commander's secretive follow-up on Callum's recovery. On this morning, Callum decides it is time to leave the community of elves, and he seeks out Commander Agis with both a personal request and a specific destination in mind.

Callum leaves the infirmary before dawn, venturing to a distant summit and waiting in the cold for Agis to emerge from his morning council meetings.

Idleness does not suit Callum. While he dallies outside the council building, the warlock removes his bare hands from his pockets and holds his palms upward. It is a good opportunity to practice his newly discovered ability of conjuration. Callum fixes his concentration on his numb hands and visualizes a pair of wool mittens. Vigorous power flows like warm water from his chest, running through his veins and down his arms. The magic diffuses across the skin of his open hands in a thick silver mist. The hazy energy swirls for a few moments then condenses into a tangible structure from an image he held within his thoughts. He pulls the mittens over his frozen fingers as the outer chamber doors open.

"Good morning, Agis," Callum says, stepping forward once the commander emerges from the two-story log building.

The commander looks both astounded and startled to see Callum waiting for him. The other accompanying elves seem equally surprised and excuse themselves so Agis and Callum can speak privately.

"I am pleased to see that you are recovered," Agis says once they are alone. His tone is much less stern than during their first encounter. The commander's beardless face gives him the appearance of youth rather than adulthood. But the wisdom reflected in his eyes expresses an ageless life of hard-won experience. He stands stiffly and peers at Callum in obvious discomfort. Even so, the elf's sable eyes study the warlock carefully, questioning the purpose of this impromptu meeting. "Leana says that you are well enough to leave her care."

"Yeah, about that," Callum replies soberly, seeing the opening he needs. "I think it's time for Liam and me to leave Verdon Peaks. I want to ask if you can send us across the veil to Harbor City."

"It is within my power, but can I ask why?" Agis probes carefully.

Callum clenches his jaw and shuffles his feet, feeling painfully vulnerable in the commander's presence. While he still fumes at Agis's mental violation, Callum must bury his indignation to focus on more urgent matters.

"Liam told me that Quinn has an estate in Harbor City and spends most of his time there. Rather than waiting for him to find me, I think it's time to confront him on my own terms."

"Why not go after Kincaid first?" Agis asks.

Callum considers the question, but neither he nor Liam knows Kincaid's location. Besides, the thought of seeing Kincaid face-to-face is a terrifying prospect that Callum is not quite ready to entertain. "Kincaid's had years to perfect his skills, and I'm just learning to do things that I thought were impossible a short time ago."

"You could stay here and study with our scholars," Agis suggests, knitting his brow with concern at the prospect of the Prophesized One leaving the safety of his community. "We cannot join you in the human cities. There is no way for us to effectively hide our appearance from so many people."

Callum holds firm. "*Fine.* But the war won't wait for me to master my magic. I'm not completely helpless, and I've survived this long with what I've learned on my own. This is my choice. If you won't join me, then at least provide me with transportation."

Agis and Callum trade stares, and for a moment, the warlock wonders if the commander will refuse this request.

Finally, the elf responds, "Very well. I will make the necessary arrangements and meet you at the main village gates by midday."

As arranged, Callum and Liam arrive at the gates and are equipped with food, supplies, and well-wishes from the elves sending them off. The commander patiently waits with Belenor at his side as well as an unknown mage.

Agis steps forward and addresses the departing warlock. "I am sorry to see you go, Callum Walker. If you ever find yourself in the company of elves, speak the name Joric Agis, and I promise you will be protected," the commander vows.

"Thanks," Callum says warily. Agis has kept his promise and proven his good intentions, so Callum's outrage at the elven leader softens.

Agis turns unexpectedly to Liam. "I have something for you, too."

He offers the hunter a small box, opening the lid to reveal six small stones, each glittering in a different color.

"It is not our custom to give humans magical armaments, but we hope that you will employ these to protect and aid our warlock," says Agis. "I assume you know how to use them."

"Uhm...Yeah...Thanks," stammers Liam as he receives the elaborately carved wooden box. Even the container seems precious.

At first glance, Callum is confused by the gift of gemstones. Once he detects the magic residing within them, he realizes this is a far more valuable token than it first appears to be.

Callum learned one important thing about his new friend in their brief time together—it is difficult for Liam to understand and accept acts of kindness.

"It's called a gift," Callum jokingly whispers when Liam seems at odds about what to do. The befuddled hunter glances between the stones and Agis.

"I know that," Liam mutters before hastily stowing the box in the pack the elves thoughtfully provided for each of them.

"As promised, Callum Walker, you will have your portal to Harbor City. I hope you find what you are looking for there," Agis says in farewell. He nods to the unknown mage, walking a short distance along the lane.

The elf enchanter halts. A frigid wind whips the hem of his robes, rippling the fur trim encircling his oversized hood and around his leather boots. Facing away from Agis and the humans, the mage grips his staff in both hands. Within a braid of vines, a glowing white gemstone rests inset.

The enchanter expertly recites an ancient Elven incantation. After several minutes, a familiar colorful vortex begins to form a sword's length in front of him.

Callum's trepidation soars, yet he exhibits no hesitation as he moves toward the wormhole with Liam close behind. He is apprehensive, not because the portal frightens him, but because the journey ahead will be fraught with unforeseen obstacles. Callum is grateful that, this time, he is not alone.

Nevertheless, Callum remains bitter that the elves and the fairies refuse to join forces and assist him. So far, their promises of help seem empty-handed.

Warlock and Hunter arrive at the swirling magical gateway. More prepared this time, Callum keeps his eyes open when he steps into the iridescent whirlpool. The dazzling visual lasts for a split second before he passes the threshold of the vortex. On one side of the magical portal lies the elven stronghold of Verdon Peaks, and beyond lies a quiet back alleyway in Harbor City. The chromatic gateway connects these two physical points, despite existing on opposite sides of the veil.

Callum's nose immediately informs him they arrived next to a pizzeria. Liam joins him a second later. They are both bombarded by the mingled aromas of baking bread, tomato sauce, and savory herbs. Regrettably, there is no time to stop for lunch.

Behind them, the elven portal winks out of existence.

"I can feel his powerful presence here. Quinn is definitely in this city, somewhere," Callum reports to Liam.

"You know that psychic sense of yours really creeps me out," the hunter says.

Callum gives him a curious glance, unsure if Liam is joking.

The hunter continues, ignoring the warlock's momentary confusion. "Listen, we need to find somewhere to set up a base. I think we should split up. You find us a low-budget motel, and I'll get us some cash."

"How are you going to lay your hands on any money?" Callum asks, then instantly regrets the question.

Liam answers with a smirk, "Do you really want to know?"

"Probably not."

"Just meet me back here in an hour," Liam says bluntly,

heading for the bustling street half a block from their secluded position.

"Wait," Callum says. "I have a better idea."

The warlock spots a high-end hotel beyond the end of the alley and across the busy street.

"I've been practicing something that might help," Callum says.

Liam shrugs his broad shoulders. "Okay, I'm game. Show me what you got."

Callum turns his back to shield the action from any pedestrians that may glance down the shaded passageway. He extends his empty hands, palms to the sky.

"*Pecunia. Fidem card,*" he says in a whisper and eagerly watches his empty hands.

As before, arcane energy surges down Callum's arms, and the vaporous magic suffuses from his skin, swirling and consolidating into a physical form.

Before their eyes, a thick stack of human currency appears in one hand, and a credit card materializes in the other. Witnessing this manifestation, Liam's jaw drops. Even Callum secretly admits that it is rather impressive. If only he learned this skill years ago, life could have been less miserable.

Liam smirks. "That's a pretty useful ability to have."

"Yeah, but it takes an awful lot of energy and concentration. Magic isn't free or cheap. Every spell steals some of my strength, and it takes a while to recover. The stronger the magic, the more draining its effects. As useful as it is, it's not something I want to play around with unless necessary."

"Well, if this works, will you at least let me order room service?" Liam jokingly grins. Callum chuckles.

The warlock's plan works flawlessly, although he is unsure where the credit card bill will be sent or who will be paying it. He notices that the name on the card is unfamiliar, but he has no idea if it is attached to a real person. Ultimately, the warlock decides it does not matter—this is war. He scribbles an unreadable signature for the desk clerk and collects a room key card.

Despite the hotel's outward appearance, with its elaborate reception area and bright, decorative hallways, the accommodations are quite basic.

Two queen-sized beds with gaudy, floral quilts fill most of the room, and a single nightstand rests between them. Beneath the window, a side table is flanked by two armchairs sporting the ugliest upholstery both men ever saw. Mass-produced pieces of abstract art adorn the walls. The room's saving grace is that it is far more impressive than Callum's former grungy apartment, and above all, it is a warm shelter. Callum drops his pack on the foot of one bed and dives onto the mattress, burying his face in the pillows.

Liam's security-conscious skillset is on full display. The veteran hunter examines the cheap door lock. Cautiously placing his rucksack on the remaining bed, he then scrutinizes the windows. Like Callum, he regards the room with mild disgust but admits it is better than spending a cold night on the street. They no longer have the option of a cozy elven cottage to protect them from the winter's wrath. Liam grabs the television's remote control and triggers buttons to find a local news station.

As much as he wants to relax, Callum knows there is too much work to do. He ruefully sighs, rolling to the side of the bed, and sits up. Rummaging in the nightstand drawer, he thumbs through a pile of tourist brochures and takeout food menus but fails to find what he really wants.

"I need a city map," Callum announces, knowing that he is about to test his intuitive powers in a way he never attempted before.

"Here," Liam replies. Then, digging into his pack, he produces a glossy pamphlet containing a map of Harbor City. He tosses it at Callum. "I grabbed it from a display rack in the lobby while you were paying for the room. I also have a list of the most popular restaurants and entertainment venues if you're interested." Liam coolly shrugs, declining to turn his attention from the television screen as he speaks.

"I hope you don't consider this a vacation," Callum says with a cheeky grin. He unfolds the map and spreads it across the hideous bedspread.

Harbor City is a sprawling metropolis with a population of just over two million. It offers more than enough venues to provide for their needs and allows ample opportunities to blend into crowds at will.

Callum lived an invisible life for many years, so it will be easy for him to blend into the urban background. His hair, height, weight, and attire have always been typical for a vast portion of the general public. As a result, the warlock is used to being over-looked by society. That is, of course, before Quinn and Kincaid took a particular interest in him and upended his solitary life.

Liam already divulged his knowledge of the expansive legion of hunters dwelling within all the major cities and bordering the veil that runs in a diagonal northeastern line across this human domain. So, it is safe to assume the hunter's former teammates are searching every city for Callum Walker even though he vanished for a few days.

Callum rests his hands on the edges of the map and leans over it to study the intricate pattern of streets. He registers the television is suddenly silent, and he glances over his shoulder to see Liam watching him with curious fascination. The warlock stiffly rises and huffs, staring down at the paper map.

"You know I've spent my entire life concealing my powers," Callum says. "Right now, I'd feel much better doing this without an audience."

"You're going to have to get over your stage fright. Besides, I've seen your power before, and I've also seen your reluctance to use it. That kind of self-doubt will get you killed," Liam warns.

Callum cannot deny his reservations, and at times, hesitation. He is less willing to use his gifts for offense than he is for defense. If he had been more aggressive, he might have been able to avoid injury and captivity. But Callum doubts his own abilities. It was good fortune that elven spies learned about his capture by the dwarves and sheer luck that the mountain elves rescued him when they did. He grudgingly realizes he must abandon uncertainty if he wants to survive this war.

"You're right," Callum finally says with a nod.

He takes a deep breath to steady his nerves and returns to the map, staring at the network of lines, colors, and shapes before closing his eyes and allowing his mind to clear. He needs to focus on Quinn. After a time, Callum feels drawn to the upper-right quadrant of the map and slowly opens his eyes.

The warlock's metaphysical abilities have always been sensitive to strong forces of both magic and evil energy, each of which lay within Quinn. Callum hopes to direct his thoughts, channeling his magic and sixth sense in unison, to find the sorcerer's location. Now, Callum lifts an arm and holds his palm over the map. Leaning forward, he reaches over the northeast district of the city.

"*Perveniunt*," he says softly.

A powerful unseen force yanks his extended arm to the farthest corner of the map. Not expecting such a jolt, Callum slaps his free hand down on the bed to avoid falling. His palm hovers over a region on the outskirts of Harbor City. Stretching his arm as far as he can reach, the warlock peers at the area below his hand and spots a tiny white wisp of light. The wisp highlights a single point, isolating a suburban neighborhood with precision.

Liam hurries to gather a pen and paper from the nightstand and scribbles down map coordinates before the light blinks out. Callum is released from the enchantment and pushes himself back upright, absorbing the significance of what he was able to do.

"I guess we have some reconnaissance to do tonight," Liam says sedately. He hands the note to Callum and returns to his seat and the television as though nothing happened. "By the way, that was really cool," Liam casually adds over his shoulder.

Callum smiles as he refolds the map, admitting only to himself that it *was* an impressive display. He hopes his next challenge will be as successful. He needs all the advantages he can get to face his mortal enemy.

CHAPTER TWENTY-TWO

Eric is uneasy about this meeting, and the location does nothing to lighten his mood. Hugging his coat tight around his barrel chest, he stands with his back pressed against the cold, damp walls somewhere in the impenetrable shadows beneath Harbor City.

He can hear echoes and scurrying movements, but it is far too dark to see anything. The concrete storm drain reeks of rotten garbage and mildew. The floor acts as a basin, holding two inches of gelid, brackish water, and Eric shudders at the thought of the horrible diseases that likely lurk in this cesspool. Given a choice, he would run from this putrid environment, but circumstances compel him to stay.

He initially expected this meeting last week, but the temporary loss of the warlock changed the plan. When the research team at Quinn's main estate detected the residual magical power of the portal in the heart of Harbor City, Eric immediately advised Quinn. As he expected, the information was greeted with great excitement, but Eric was not quite finished making his reports.

Eric also sent a brief, coded message to a secret email address, then anxiously waited for an hour to receive an answer.

When he deciphered the reply and read the instructions, Eric's heart sank over the location his contact chose for their clandestine meeting, but he knew he had to obey.

"Hello, Selkie," a malign voice announces in greeting.

Eric spins toward the speaker, startled at the sight of the dark figure emerging from the shadows. He is certain this person was not there a moment ago.

"I am glad you got our message. What news do you have for our master?" asks the sinister figure.

Eric knows the conspirator from many secret encounters in shadowed corners of the major cities along the veil. He is stationed now in Harbor City, residing at the highly protected property of the Order's primary hub. Eric's was called back here after Callum's capture by the dwarves, remaining close for Quinn to call upon and manage the many field operatives still searching for the warlock.

Alistair and Eric are hostages in this spiteful conflict, striving to survive the violent brotherly feud, but they are far from friends.

Eric is a member of the mythical seal folk, a Selkie—a race distinguished by its affinity for both water and land. His natural form is a water-dwelling seal, but Eric can shed his skin to walk on land as a human.

The Selkies have no extraordinary power, but they possess simple magic to stay hidden in their watery world. Unlike most magical creatures, they reside on this side of the veil, carefully avoiding humans. They lived in peaceful seclusion before the war, but the constant battles for domination have left no magical race untouched. Eric saw members of his family destroyed by crossfire between warring parties, and he watched them die as innocent bystanders. Eric feared is people's survival. So, to protect the remainder of his family, he presented himself as human and entered one side of the conflict to gain valuable war-related intelligence.

In the beginning, Eric could pass along warnings to his

people of marauding armies. As a result, he prevented hundreds of unnecessary deaths among his Selkie kin. It satisfied him to know his involvement had been worthwhile. However, his role in the war evolved when Kincaid sent Alistair to convince Eric to spy for him. As a reward for his efforts, Eric's kin would be safely left out of the conflict. But if he refused, Kincaid promised to destroy every living Selkie and leave Eric to suffer a final murderous assault. Having no other choice, Eric picked the least undesirable option.

Over the years, he grew accustomed to his role as an unwilling but dependable double agent. But to lessen his guilt, he reminds himself that he is still serving the best interests of his family by keeping them alive.

"We have news that the warlock has come out of hiding. He is somewhere in Harbor City," Eric tells Alistair, hardening his expression and trying to calm his frayed nerves.

"Do you know where he is now?" Alistair presses as he steps closer. Faint rays of stray light from overhead gratings partially illuminate his face.

As a vampire, Alistair cannot tolerate direct sunlight but can temporarily endure reflected or diffuse light. Eric hides his nervousness when he sees Alistair's penetrating eyes and needle-sharp fangs slightly visible beneath his upper lip. The vampire never threatens to bite him, but Eric knows Alistair is the servant of a cruel, sadistic master and would not hesitate to follow such an order. Thus, the relationship between the two is uneasy at best.

Clearing his throat, Eric addresses his shadowy contact. "We do not know where he is right now, but we know where he *will* be. Quinn set a trap to lure him to his estate. His best hunters are already waiting for the warlock. I have the address here." Eric holds out a folded slip of paper.

"We can't move if there are hunters around." Alistair lowers his chin and glares.

"Quinn has a plan that will create a diversion, and I will

distract the hunters. If you keep your people at a distance, you can catch the warlock as he flees."

He extends his arm a bit further to encourage the vampire to take the offered note. Alistair stares at him, then scoffs, snatching the paper and quickly pocketing it.

"For your sake, I hope you are right. My master has grown tired of failure. He wants results, or he wants your head," Alistair hisses as he narrows his eyes at Eric.

"If the warlock slips away again, it will be your fault, not mine," Eric retorts.

Alistair lifts his lip in a snarl but cannot deny the truth of Eric's words. The Selkie is handing this prized prey over to the vampires, but a successful capture will be their responsibility. Alistair knows his own people will suffer the severe penalty if Callum Walker is not apprehended this time.

As quickly as he appeared, Alistair turns and races off. His unnatural speed makes it seem like he disappears in a blink with a light breeze and barely a sound.

Eric exhales a sigh and unclenches his muscles. He longs to shed his human form and return to the open seas but will have to wait until his mission on land is finished. One day, if he survives the war, he will go home to rejoin his grateful people and joyfully swim in the cold ocean depths. But as the fighting endlessly drags on, Eric's odds are shrinking.

CHAPTER TWENTY-THREE

As promised, Liam gets to order room service while Callum summons some necessary supplies and surfs the internet on a newly conjured cellphone.

Warlock and hunter deal with the anticipation of their upcoming challenge in different ways, each keeping with their unique personalities. Liam is content to lounge on the bed and watch an action movie while devouring a roast beef sandwich, fries, and caffeinated soda. On the other hand, Callum throws himself into researching the entire neighborhood and the history of the house they will investigate.

His anxiety is heightened, and his mind is alert to all possible approaches and potential escape routes. Even though their mission is strictly reconnaissance, Callum is concerned that something will go wrong. He is uneasy about the expedition but cannot put his impressions into words or calm his apprehension. Callum tries to shrug it off as nervous energy caused by a plan to engage in an activity entirely outside his range of experience. However, Callum understands that since he cannot hide from his growing list of enemies, he must step outside his comfort zone and be more assertive. Hostility is strange behavior for Callum, and he does not embrace it lightly.

"How do you do it?" Callum finally asks, setting his phone down and rubbing tired eyes with his fingers.

"Do what?" Liam responds before taking another big bite of his sandwich.

"How do you stay so calm?"

"Oh, well, if you must know...I'm actually scared shitless," Liam admits, casting Callum a weary glance. "Quinn will have me killed on the spot when he finds out what I'm doing. Right now, I have more to lose than you do."

"Not the way I see it." Callum sighs. He lets his arms drop heavily to his lap and grimly peers at Liam. "Leana told me that the source of my power is in my blood. If I understand correctly, Quinn will have to bleed me dry to steal my magic. I'm pretty sure I'll be just as dead as you if he succeeds. And my death will be a lot more drawn out and agonizing."

"I find it's best not to think of the worst-case scenarios." Liam cringes at the thought of their terrible fates.

"I envy you."

"Why?" Liam casts Calum a bewildering look. "You have more power than anyone I've ever met. Without my talismans or weapons, I'm nothing but a thug. I wish I could be as fortunate as you. Hell, you're the only one that even has a hope of ending this war and freeing the magical races from their suffering. I wish I could be so useful. I'm the one who envies *you*."

Callum had never thought of his situation as fortunate.

For the past week, he has been beaten, kidnapped, and force-fully restrained—not to mention having his mind violated by an elf. He learned he is the only hope of saving millions of lives, human and magical alike. On top of that, he discovered that he is gifted with magic equivalent to his rival in nature and power. Between fighting for survival and running for his life, Callum must come to terms with the fear of surrendering to the same evil that consumes and drives the necromancer's lust for conquest. Callum is frightened of losing himself to the addictive nature of dark magic, a force he now knows can control and destroy him. It is no wonder that his meal stays untouched on the nightstand because of stress-induced indigestion.

When evening arrives, Callum is quite happy to leave the hotel. The stress of waiting is more difficult to endure than the frightening activity of their plan.

Just before departing, Liam loads his pockets with the magical stones that Agis gave him. The pair take a cab to a spot an hour's walk from Quinn's estate and travel the rest of the way on foot. Shrugging against the winter wind in his down-filled jacket to blend in, Callum feels panic starting to cramp his stomach, and all his senses are shouting for him to turn and run. There is something not right about this situation. Still, he ignores the internal screams of warning, preferring to explain it away as anxiety.

When they near the street a few blocks away from their target, Warlock and Hunter hug the alleyways and back lanes where the snow is deep, and the streetlights cannot reach. It is a more challenging approach but ensures they can easily remain hidden until they reach their designated viewpoints and split up. This part of the plan Callum finds least favorable, but he understands the need to investigate Quinn's estate from more than one angle.

While Callum continues north, he glances over his shoulder. He spots Liam's shadowy figure scaling a lattice frame attached to the side of a house. It creaks and groans under his weight but remains intact, allowing the hunter to reach the safety of the rooftop.

Liam disappears over the eaves' edge, carefully crawling and settling into the gentle slope of soft snow packed atop the roof. From here, the hunter can look down over the peaked ridge while remaining hidden from view.

It takes Callum another forty minutes to navigate the dark lanes, heading steadily uphill. Eventually, he reaches a schoolyard and trudges through the thick snow toward the playground equipment. His legs tingle from the cold, so Callum brushes off the layer of snow piled on the upper platform of a two-story play structure. Then, he settles near the edge of the top deck, sitting cross-legged inside a pint-sized archway above a yellow, plastic slide.

This relatively high vantage point gives Callum a straight line of sight through a set of binoculars he conjured before the journey—along with new cellphones that both he and Liam carry. Peering across the powdery white schoolyard and snow-capped rooflines, he can see the two sides of the estate not visible to Liam. As Callum strains his eyes through the binoculars, his phone vibrates into life.

Are you in place? Liam asks with a text.

Just sat down. Callum answers.

Movement inside building, and hunters patrolling the perimeter. What do you see?

Callum peers through the lenses at the mansion. The place is surrounded by a concrete wall that looks taller than he is. Luckily, he is able to look down on the target, and Callum can see roving pairs of hunters with flashlights. He can also sense their magical defenses, even from this distance.

Not looking good. Hunters around back and very well-armed. Callum texts.

Expected that.

Unlike the warlock, Liam is superbly trained for this and well within his element.

Callum identifies the part of the front driveway that passes through a metal security gate before disappearing around the front of the house. His attention is pulled to the front yard and driveway when it is unexpectedly illuminated by glaring floodlights mounted on the facade of the building.

What's happening at the front? Callum messages.

From the opposite side of the house, Liam types, *They might know we're here. Quinn is walking out the door.*

How can they know that? Callum feels a wave of panic and sweeps his alert gaze across the schoolyard. He returns to his surveillance when he sees no signs of an approaching ambush and only his own footprints in the snow.

Quinn can track any magical essence. Not precise enough for an exact location, but he can narrow it down to a few miles.

Would have been good to know before we entered his range.

Callum is unhappy that Liam failed to reveal this capability, but it explains how the hunters tracked him. Even though he was careful to keep his magic hidden, he would have eventually been discovered because of his inherent arcane energy.

Callum curses himself for ignoring the inner voice that warned him of something threatening. Quinn was waiting for them to show up, but how can he know where they were at this precise moment?

How would he know to be watching for us tonight? Callum texts the hunter in frustration, wondering if there is anything else Liam has failed to divulge.

Quinn used a sight stone to find you months ago. Maybe he used it when the Dwarves and Mountain Elves took you.

Liam mentioned the sight stone before, and Callum considers if there is more to this amulet. *Can he see the future with this stone?*

Don't know. But that would explain a lot.

We need to leave now! Callum hopes Liam will understand the urgency that is not easy to express in a text message.

Wait. He has someone with him.

Quinn has now stepped farther away from the house. He stands in the center of the plowed driveway, halfway between the house and the gate. Callum now has a direct line of sight and is surprised to see a woman standing very close to Quinn. The woman frantically glances around as Quinn holds her by the arm, and Callum inhales in shock when he recognizes the cute, blonde barista from the coffee shop.

"What the hell?" The warlock whispers.

≈

Liam can see the terror in Lucy's face, and his heart sinks. He thought he kept their relationship a secret. But as Quinn stands in the roadway with his pudgy fingers locking around Lucy's upper arm, Liam feels panic rising from deep within his core.

"I know you're out there, Liam. I just want to have a chat, so we can settle this like men," Quinn's shouts echo through the cloudy night.

Liam suspects that Quinn may have detected their arrival in Harbor City. However, he cannot figure out how Quinn knew they would choose this moment to survey his estate.

They only came up with their plan a few hours earlier and neither left their hotel room nor spoke to anyone except the room service waiter. Maybe Callum is on to something about the sight stone predicting the future. There are some secrets of the Order that Liam was never privy to. If the stone does foresee the future, he is confident that Quinn would never share that information.

Respond. Need to leave. Now! Callum messages him again, recognizing the severity of a mounting threat.

Liam keeps looking through his lenses, his heart crushed by the anguish in Lucy's face. Then, taking a deep breath, he prepares for what he must do to protect the woman he loves.

Liam descends the lattice into the private yard. He walks along the side of the house, opening the latched gate, and marches out in front of the home where he trespassed. The house is directly across the street from Quinn's guarded mansion, and before he even walks onto the road, hunters are converging on him from all sides.

He stops in the middle of the slippery pavement, facing the wrought iron gate with arms raised in surrender. Liam stoically waits for the other hunters to reach him. He glares at Quinn through the iron bars, halfway across the spacious driveway. The pompous sorcerer grins with evil satisfaction.

The cellphone vibrates from Liam's pocket one last time, but he is unable to read the message while his hands are being cuffed behind his back. He knows his friend will see his sacrifice and be helpless to prevent it. Liam can only hope that Callum will one day understand why this is happening and why he would not resist the hunters as they shove him at the gate. Liam is frog-marched along the driveway, watching the traumatized face of his beloved Lucy at every step.

"I'm sorry it has to come to this," Quinn unapologetically gloats.

He shakes his head as though more disappointed by Liam's performance tonight than by his betrayal. Lucy sobs under her breath, still held in Quinn's grip. Unchecked tears stream down her face.

"He's not what you said he was. He's not evil like your brother." Liam knows his declaration will do nothing to convince Quinn. He holds onto the barest of hope that his fellow hunters might heed the words.

"He's powerful, and he's uncontrollable. The only thing worse than an enemy with a weapon is an enemy that can't be disarmed," Quinn replies through gritted teeth.

Liam sees rage rapidly contort his former master's face, but he is no longer afraid. "You're right, Quinn. Walker is powerful, but he's also disciplined and motivated to help those you disregard. He'll kill you. It's his destiny, but then you already know that don't you?"

When Liam sees Quinn's wrath momentarily turn to a spark of fear, he knows that he is correct. Quinn has seen the future, and with it, his death. The fleeting moment of disclosure is over, and fury returns, fueled by hatred. Liam is relieved to know that although he will not survive to see it, Callum will eventually succeed. So much death and suffering will be avenged—including his own.

Quinn pulls a gold dagger from his belt, and Liam prepares to accept his fate. His sacrifice to save Lucy is the only thing he has left to give her. He remorsefully gazes at his beloved and mouths *I love you*.

As Quinn raises the blade, Liam turns his eyes to the north. Somewhere over the hilltop, he knows Callum is watching. He smiles and nods to his grieving friend.

"*Ferrum Penetrabilior!*" Quinn screams before swinging his deadly skewer.

When the knife plunges into the middle of his chest, Liam gasps at the surprising intensity of pain that engulfs him. Aided with magic, the blade drives right through his heart.

Liam looks down at the handle of the dagger protruding from his sternum, then up at Quinn. The young hunter mockingly grins at his former master, making Quinn's round face turn purple with fury. The world seems to pause, and Liam loses strength in his legs. He collapses in slow motion like a deflated balloon. Blood floods his lungs, and all breath is lost.

Quinn releases Lucy, who buckles to her knees and buries her face in her hands, hysterically weeping. The sorcerer crouches and whispers so only Liam can hear the words he will take to his grave.

"I was never going to let your little girlfriend live. I will kill everyone you care about, including your altruistic warlock. Your death was for nothing."

Liam tries to scream, but his voice is gone.

A moment later, he closes his eyes, and his life drains away with each fading beat of his shredded heart.

CHAPTER TWENTY-FOUR

Watching his friend die at the hand of his mortal enemy, Callum stifles a howl of anguish. He hurls his binoculars in impotent rage, and they disappear into the thick white powder that covers the schoolyard.

Recoiling into the shadows, Callum draws his knees to his chest and clutches the back of his head. His heart aches at the thought of the sadistic violence Liam suffered. Although they met as opponents, circumstance made them allies and friends. That is something Callum has only experienced once before. Frey is gone, and so is Liam. Now, he feels utterly lost.

Callum knows he should immediately leave, but he cannot bring himself to move. Overcome by grief, he lets his arms fall limp and cranes his neck to stare up at the night sky. Fine flakes of snow land unheeded on his burning cheeks. His mind is racing, reliving all that he had seen and the people he met over the past few days. Fairies saved him, tested him, and then cast him back alone on a new life journey. Dwarves kidnapped and imprisoned him. Mountain elves offered help but then refused to join him in the human world. He was promised relief then denied it. Now, he lost the only person willing to fight at his side.

So many innocent races are caught in the middle of this pointless war, each trying to survive and preserve their culture amid brutality and chaos. Those who cannot hide take sides for protection or self-preservation, but they are not evil, and this is not their battle. They are simply collateral damage, as Liam wisely observed. Helpless to escape the conflict that seeks either their domination or their life sacrifice, these are the people that the Prophesized One needs to fight for, but right now, the warlock feels incapable of fighting anything.

Callum wants to retreat and find a place to disappear, leaving behind the heartache that fills his lonely soul. The thought of walking away from everything, ignoring the prophecy written centuries before he was even born, is suddenly very appealing but also terrifying.

He is torn between the urge to flee and his desire to help. Despite his fears, Callum understands that he can no more run than stop breathing. There are countless people, across two realms, now depending on him to be their champion. Regardless of his own wishes, he cannot abandon so many to suffer because of his apathy. Callum is angry at the prophecy that demands so much of him. He is outraged at the fairies and elves and furious at Liam for surrendering himself and taking the easy way out of this war.

Slowly, Callum realizes that he has lingered in the for schoolyard far too long. He wipes the melting flakes of damp snow off his face and climbs down from the play structure, carefully retracing his steps to cover his escape.

He buries his emotions while making his way toward the street, but rather than heading south along his original route, Callum turns east, away from Quinn's mansion. He does not care where he goes, nor does he concern himself with being watchful for hunters. In his current frame of mind, Callum would not hesitate to strike them down. Thankfully, for their sake, he does not encounter any of Quinn's servants.

Callum trudges for nearly an hour, lost in thought, while the falling snow covers his solitary tracks. The temperature is dropping, and Callum begins to shiver despite the protection of his fleece-lined jacket. His legs are past the point of tingling, and his toes are numb inside his boots. If not for the bitter cold, he might have remained adrift in his mind and missed the uncomfortable stillness that now surrounds him.

By the time Callum becomes aware that he is being watched, he has lost his way in the unfamiliar city. He halts and nervously scans the eerie silent street in both directions but cannot see anything out of place in the frosty world.

The streets are devoid of traffic, and parked cars are covered by a blanket of snow. There are no echoing noises in the muffled night, and Callum sees no lights or movement in the closed shops that stretch along both sides of the road. No corridors or alleyways are visible between the buildings, and lampposts illuminate the pristine sidewalks, so he is confident no one can sneak up on foot. It is nearly three in the morning, and to all appearances, the world is sleeping. Yet, the warlock's instinctive awareness alerts him that all is not well, and this time he does not ignore it.

Callum starts to run. The path before him is downhill, and through the deepening snow does not hinder his steps, hidden patches of ice threaten to send him falling on his backside. He slips and skids a few times, but flailing his arms, he manages to right himself and continue. The warlock's keen senses draw his attention across the street and up toward the pursuing threat.

Well above street level, two figures leap and race along the roofline. Both are dressed in form-fitting jackets and dark pants that blend with the color of the night sky. Upon the first appearance, Callum wonders if they are Quinn's hunters. But there is something unusual in how these dark figures move with effortless agility and speed that causes him to abandon his initial theory.

Panic rises in Callum's mind as he psychically perceives the overpowering evil aura of his pursuers—they are not human. The warlock is being stalked by vampires.

Callum's experience with nightwalkers is minimal. He hunted one several years ago after learning of a series of attacks that left victims dead from blood loss. New to his self-appointed calling as a vigilante, the accursed creature nearly killed him during their battle. Callum bears a livid scar on the back of his neck as a reminder of how close he came to death on that occasion. His takeaway from that incident—nightwalkers should never be underestimated.

Far stronger and faster than any human, their cunning and relentless determination when stalking prey is unmatched by any predator. Nothing short of their prey's death will satisfy their bloodlust. Unfortunately, it seems that tonight he is their target. Callum knows he stands a chance in combat against a solo vampire, but two will present a challenge beyond his abilities.

Preoccupied with watching the two nightwalkers skimming the roofline, Callum nearly misses a gentle whump several feet ahead of him. The soft sound draws his attention, and he spots another vampire dropping to the sidewalk from the rooftop directly above.

The warlock skids to a halt, breathless from the pursuit and the sight of an ambushing vampire blocking his path. The obstructing nightwalker smiles with cruel enjoyment at the fear he instills in the warlock. The vicious face and sickening grin send a shiver up Callum's spine. But before Callum can submit to emotion, he raises his right arm to fire a defensive spell. The incantation is interrupted when another figure jumps from the roofline behind him. A powerful arm snakes around Callum's neck to lock him in a chokehold. The warlock's magical words are stolen.

Callum desperately scrambles to claw himself loose from the restraining forearm, lifting him by the throat. He manages to inhale tiny gasps of air. Still, it is not enough to sustain his pounding heart or any intense effort to escape. Panic begins to creep into his mind.

The vampire facing Callum smirks in delight at the unequal physical struggle. As if intent on joining the action, the nightwalker begins to charge toward him. It is a chilling sight to behold something so evil moving toward him while he helplessly battles to break free. Callum pushes past the fear and forces his mind to focus. He thrusts his hand at the approaching enemy, gleaming with white magic, and visualizes what he needs.

No words enter Callum's awareness. Instead, his conceived desire manifests as the nightwalker closes in. Without uttering a sound, Callum experiences a surge of power flowing through his outstretched arm. The luminous energy erupts from his fingers in a vibrant stream, arcing from his body into the attacking vampire. Wild-eyed surprise stuns the undead aggressor when the warlock's attack flings him fifteen feet away. The vampire's flight is violently halted by the clubbed top of a steel parking meter. Cracking bones precede the creature crumpling to the ground in an unmoving heap.

The two vampires barreling along the opposite roofline now descend gracefully to the sidewalk as if floating. They freeze mid-step, gawking at their crumpled comrade.

Even Callum pauses to look, first at his empty hand and then at the foe he conquered with surprising magical might. Inwardly, he is just as confused by what has transpired as the vampires.

The deadly spell was cast without words—verbal or mental. Even though the warlock silently directed his magic before, he always held an incantation in his mind. However, this time, his imagination was the architect of the enchantment, and the arcane energy spawned from pure thought and intent. Callum's fear must have added intensity to his spell, but this increased output has a cost. Fatigue washes over Callum, dulling his sense. The draining effects of his magic leave his body and limbs feel heavy and weak.

The bewildered vampire thug lessens his stranglehold, not because Callum's captor is letting him go, but because of the shocked state of his attacker. Finally, the slackening vice relaxes enough for the warlock to wrench free from the vampire's grasp and wheel around to finish what he started.

The second nightwalker looms two heads taller than Callum and stares slack-jawed at his slain brother without noticing his prey has escaped.

Callum marshals his silent power once again. Without hesitation, he blasts the hulking vampire with dazzling arcane strength. The stunned brute is hurled up and away from Callum. Cartwheeling through the air, the brute smashes against a brick storefront, collapsing into the snow and moaning in agony.

Callum is once again surprised by the unbridled might of this newfound ability. However, he has no time to consider this advantage or the draining toll it levies on his vital life force.

Howls of wrathful indignation catch his attention. The two vampires across the street are now charging in to avenge their undead comrades. There is no point in running, so Callum fights his enervation and braces to continue what had begun as a battle against superior numbers.

Facing his enemy, the warlock drives both fists out before him—his arms still ablaze. He flings his fingers open and fires an explosion of ivory light. A translucent wall fans out as it advances.

For the first time, Callum feels a wave of heat rush through his body like the opening of an oven door. A brief, almost unbearable burning tide flows from the middle of his chest to the tips of his fingers. His flesh stings from the unleashed strength of his firepower, but Callum ignores the pain.

The warlock's third magical attack propels everything in its path into a whirlwind of tumbling hazards. A pair of minivans parked between Callum and the nightwalkers are uprooted and flip, rolling like logs until coming to rest on their roofs. The vampires, a male and female pair, are driven back. They seem undeterred and recover swiftly as the wave of repelling energy dissipates. Then, angered by the warlock's onslaught, the male rushes ahead to resume the assault.

Moving with unnatural swiftness, the vampires' approach is a blur of orchestrated movements that Callum has no real hope of stopping. Before the warlock can strike again, he is bowled over as the leading vampire leaps clear of the wrecked vans and slams Callum to the ground. The snow barely cushions his back as it strikes the hard concrete, followed by his head. White stars erupt across vision, but Callum remains conscious.

The brutal fall is immediately followed by a crushing weight that forces the breath from his lungs and causes his diaphragm to ache. Callum struggles for air as he wrestles with this new foe, but the vampire has a serious strength advantage. Callum's wrists are seized and pinned into the layer of dissolving snow.

"You have to stop him before he can use magic again!" the second vampire bellows, panic straining her voice.

In answer to this command, the nightwalker does the only thing that vampires know how to do. He opens his mouth, baring a set of daggered teeth. Callum wildly thrashes against the strike he knows is coming. The vampire finally releases Callum's left wrist and transfers his firm grasp to the warlock's shoulder. Holding him securely, he buries his fangs into the base of his victim's neck. The action is over before Callum realizes what is happening.

Callum screams as piercing fangs stab his flesh, radiating ragged pain into his skull and toward his chest. The warlock's heart races as the blood drains from his body and is consumed by a voracious vampire.

"That is enough. He is weakened, and that is all we need to control him," the second vampire says, pulling her night brother off his prey.

Callum gasps as dizziness and nausea beset him. The caustic, burning wound throbs, screaming evidence that he is still very much alive.

Fueled by adrenaline, he scurries backward in a crab walk until he reaches a storefront. Cupping an ice-cold hand over his wound, Callum then leans against the grimy bricks for support and rises on wobbly legs.

The vampires glare with dark, eager eyes but do not approach. Callum catches a glimpse of movement to his left. Two more nightwalkers appear at a deserted intersection and run with inhuman haste toward the conflict. Three more shadowy forms appear on rooftops across the street, then drop lightly to the sidewalk. Another pair races toward him from the right. The growing vampire swarm clusters around him but hesitates to edge nearer.

Callum can only prop himself against the brick wall, helplessly watching the pale forms surround him. Anxiety saps more of his physical strength and robs him of his ability to defend himself. Blood trickles down his mangled neck, soaking his shirt and coat. Despite this, the warlock closes his eyes and tries to calm his panicky thoughts. But the burning rawness of his injury steals his ability to concentrate.

"So, this is the famed warlock we have heard so much about," growls one of the newly arrived vampires.

A shell of a man boldly approaches, and Callum's half-closed eyes flicker toward the speaker. The vampire glares with coal-black eyes as he advances, halting only when face-to-face. His lip curls to show his needle-sharp fangs.

"Who are you?" Callum asks weakly, hearing a tremble in his voice and feeling ashamed of his obvious distress.

"You may call me Alistair," the vampire says with distaste. He looks the warlock over as though taking stock of his trophy. "My master has ordered us to collect you for his lord Kincaid, but he wants you alive."

Alistair glances at Callum's hand covering the seeping gash and licks his lips.

"If that's the case, then why did your man try to kill me?"

Callum flashes a glare of false bravado at the vampire who had bitten him.

"Maurice did what he had to do to control you. I assure you that he was not trying to end your life. If he had wanted to kill you, you would already be dead." Alistair regards the warlock with narrowed eyes, then pulls his captive's hand away from the gruesome bite. He visually inspects the wound and frowns at its sight.

Alistair turns to his underling, Maurice, and scowls. "You have damaged him more than necessary. If this human dies because of your failings, I will see to it that you are punished with chains and fire in the pits."

Maurice recoils and stoops, whispering abject apologies as he hangs his head.

Alistair pivots back to Callum, releasing the warlock's wrist. "We must get you back to our lair and tend to your injury. You are useless to us if you die."

"I'd hate to devalue myself," Callum retorts with what little sarcasm he can muster.

He restores his bloody hand to his throbbing neck. Callum is relieved that he is not destined for immediate death. However, the realization triggers fresh worry about their ultimate intentions.

"It is no concern to me. It is our father who requests your live capture. You will eventually die, Warlock. But not this night," Alistair says offhandedly.

Callum understands his enemy's tactical advantage. Dangerously outnumbered and incapacitated, Callum lacks the vigor to fuel his magic to resist them. He might manage to strike down one or two of the nightwalkers, but his feeble revolt would only provoke the others into violence. The vampire's first strike angrily smarts. Any further attack *will* be fatal.

A black SUV rounds a corner, wildly skidding. Alistair moves away from his prey and purposefully strides onto the road to await the careening vehicle's arrival. The driver over-revs the engine, swerving around the pair of mangled minivans and fishtailing before stopping directly in front of Alistair.

Alistair's peers over his shoulder at Callum. "Your ride has arrived, young warlock."

CHAPTER TWENTY-FIVE

Callum slumps in the back seat of the glossy black SUV with Alistair seated beside him. The maniacal driver remains at his post behind the wheel, and a vampire named Silas claims the front passenger seat. When Alistair ordered Callum into the car, there was no point in resisting. He grudgingly complied and is now compressing his blood-soaked jacket against the oozing punctures on his shoulder.

"I have to admit that the prospect of a human with magic is intriguing," Alistair says. "Humans are so frail and hardly worthy of such a powerful gift as yours."

Callum sourly frowns at the comment and slouches further into his seat. He shifts his body in search of any comfortable position. He tries to lean back without putting pressure on his head, where a tender contusion reminds him of his violent fall against the sidewalk.

"Everyone has their weaknesses, even your kind," Callum says bitterly, just as the vehicle skids into a left turn and slides through an empty intersection. The shifting momentum pitches Callum against the passenger door, and he grimaces in pain, clenching his muscles. He grumbles under his breath at the driver's constant disregard for safety.

Alistair shows no compassion for his prisoner's suffering. "You may be right, but we are stronger and faster than feeble men. Despite your valiant efforts tonight, and even with your warlock powers, you are still at our mercy."

"So, I'm guessing this is the first time you've actually had to help anyone bitten by one of your own?" Callum asks. His grumbling voice is heavy with sarcasm.

When the SUV roars around the turn and starts to follow a comparatively straight path along a lonely street, he pushes himself away from the door. Callum settles once more against the back of the back with a weary groan.

"Yes, but this is an unusual situation," Alistair says, distastefully frowning at Callum.

"Not wanting to sound completely ignorant, but am I going to turn into...Uhm...You know?" Callum asks as he casts sidelong glances between Alistair and the other vampires.

The question haunts his thoughts, and he decides to settle the matter as bluntly as possible. Callum registers snickers from the two vampires in the front seat while Alistair rolls his eyes.

"It does not work that way, human. It is *our* blood *you* need to drink, not the other way around," Alistair says. He scowls at this supposedly great warlock's lack of basic knowledge.

"Good." Callum sighs, sinking against his backrest with exaggerated relief. "You bloodsuckers have a bad reputation."

The driver and front passenger shoot furious glares over their shoulders, proof that his deliberate insult hit its mark.

"We are approaching the garage, brother Alistair," Silas announces.

"Good." Alistair skewers Callum with a venomous sneer. "For your safety, warlock, I would keep your slanderous remarks to yourself. There are many ways to suffer that do not end in death."

～

The SUV zooms into an underground parking area beneath a multi-story office building and past a handful of luxury vehicles on the first couple of levels, but the driver continues without stopping. They finally lurch to a halt at the deepest underground level, pulling up next to an olive-green metal door.

Alistair and Silas step out first, and the latter yanks Callum from his seat. The musclebound bodyguard digs his fingers into muscle above the warlock's right elbow, forcing his hostage along. Callum grunts painfully under his breath.

Escort and prisoner wait while Alistair unlocks the mysterious, unmarked door and ushers them into a featureless, concrete anteroom. Granted privileged access, Alistair summons the elevator via a coded access panel. Stepping inside, the vampire commander selects an unmarked button that transports the trio even deeper underground.

The instant the doors close, Alistair turns on Callum. He shoves him against the wall and presses his bony knuckles into the warlock's sternum. Silas releases his grip and apathetically steps aside.

"The only reason you are alive is that my father commands it," Alistair snarls, revealing pent-up rage. "You will do well to remember his mercy when he speaks to you. Any hint of disrespect will cost you dearly."

"I guess I'll only forget once," an uncowed Callum retorts, matching the vampire's indignation with his own fury.

There is no denying Alistair's fiery wrath, but Callum reasons that he is alive because the vampire must be forbidden to act on his own accord. This fact changes the dynamic in his favor, giving the warlock far more power than the nightwalker trying so hard to intimidate him.

Alistair growls and pulls his fist back. Then, skimming Callum's ear, he slams his clenched hand against the stainless-steel wall.

"Remove your jacket. It reeks of your blood," Alistair hisses.

His eyes shoot daggers at Callum as he takes a step back. "You will not need it down here."

Callum wants to refuse out of spite, but Silas steps in and forcibly strips the jacket off to avoid an erupting battle of wills. Alistair turns from them to face the polished elevator door. His slender shoulders are furiously rigid. Silas holds Callum's bloody coat draped over a forearm and resumes his excruciating grip of the warlock's elbow.

Alistair angrily stalks out into what looks like a cavern when the doors open, thundering with the pulsations of heavy bass music. The pounding beat reverberates within Callum's chest and reawakens the ache in his skull. Silas applies finger pressure that propels the warlock through the doors and into the hellish chaos of noise and flashing strobe lights.

The size of a high school gymnasium, this bizarre grotto vibrates with booming rock guitar and screaming lyrics. Dozens of projectors shoot slices of multicolored light over a densely packed mass of writhing bodies. A shrieking chorus keeps time with the music, and the crowd gyrates and bounces in macabre celebration.

Callum and his captors skirt the edge of the mob, hugging the curving perimeter wall. He crunches over fractured ceramic tiles and notices the cracked and pitted concrete walls. Only when he sees fragments of outdated advertising posters, he recognizes the subterranean chamber as a derelict subway station.

A few nearby revelers sniff the air, suddenly alert to the smell of Callum's blood. They pause to hungrily leer at the captive but wisely do nothing as he prodded past them.

Alistair meets any interested nightwalker with a scathing glare that quashes their active curiosity in the warlock. Silas smirks at Callum's uneasiness and tosses the blood-soaked jacket far into the depths of the throng. It vanishes amid an uproar of gnarling shrieks that ignite a bloodlust frenzy.

"We are not all so civilized here," Silas leans closer and shouts over the music.

Callum shudders at the thought of his own body, dead or alive, being ripped to shreds instead of his coat.

Alistair leads them down the length of the forsaken subway terminal, proceeding through a pair of swinging metal doors and into a long, straight corridor. The well-lit hallway, clad in glossy cream tiles, sharply contrasts with the barbaric rave still drumming hypnotically in their wake.

Callum nominally relaxes now that he is beyond the rabble of savage vampires. His right arm still throbs from Silas's constant iron grip, and his shirt is saturated with sticky blood.

Even though Callum thinks the bleeding is slowing, it is already causing him to feel woozy. However, he refuses to reveal any physical disadvantage that these villains could use against him. Callum suspects he will soon have more to worry about than his current state of misery. Without a chance to rest, his physical and magical strength continues to languish.

The journey concludes at an unremarkable steel door, no different than any of the half-dozen in the tiled passageway behind them. Alistair knocks and waits for someone within to allow access.

A husky, young vampire with copper-colored hair cracks open the door to peer out at Alistair and then at Callum. Satisfied, the youth swings the door wide and steps aside, extending his arm toward the inner sanctum and respectfully bowing.

The private gothic suite bears traces of what was once a subway station office. Now cloaked in shadow, the room is dramatically decorated with accents of rich, ruby red. It serves a stately, middle-aged vampire ensconced in a high-backed leather armchair. The pallid figure wears a crimson blazer that matches the color of the blood-red decor. A second chair nearby is occupied by a slightly younger vampire. This handsome, svelte nightwalker sports a dark pinstripe suit and idly sips from a teacup while ogling the human visitor.

Callum is compelled to sit on a jet-black sofa facing the duo of aristocratic hosts. Silas releases his grip when the warlock is seated and takes up station behind the couch next to Alistair. Both watch their superior while they guard Callum carefully.

"Master Vrykalos, father of our western flock, we bring you the warlock, Callum Walker. As I have relayed enroute, he has been injured but remains alive," Alistair respectfully addresses the senior nightwalker who looks at Callum with morbid fascination.

Vrykalos analyzes him with deeply set eyes, arching his manicured eyebrows in keen interest. The master's face is closely shaven, accentuating his hollow cheeks and giving him an anorexic appearance.

"He has been more than just injured, Alistair," Vrykalos observes with dismay. Resting his elbows on the arms of the chair, he rhythmically drums his fingertips together.

"The warlock slayed Lucas and mortally injured Duke," Alistair says cautiously. "Maurice was compelled to bite him in order to subdue him, but I am afraid he did not use enough restraint. The warlock has lost a lot of blood."

"I can see that," Vrykalos says with indifference. "It seems that Kincaid is correct in his assumptions. His ability to overpower your brethren proves this young man's possession of an exceedingly rare power for a human. He appears to have some measure of mastery over his magic. It also appears that either the battle or the bite has robbed much of the warlock's vitality. He looks less than awe-inspiring at this moment."

"I will need to examine his wounds," the second armchair occupant announces, lowering his teacup and eagerly staring at Callum. The younger nightwalker tilts his head as though studying a museum artifact.

"Patience, Isaac. Let us talk first," Vrykalos says without turning his head.

"I don't have anything to say to you." Callum glowers at Vrykalos with pure hostility.

"Why not?" asks Vrykalos, slyly grinning. "I am, after all, a wealth of knowledge regarding your adversary. Would you not like to know how to defeat him?"

"Yeah...like I would believe anything you tell me."

"Not even if I tell you that you and Kincaid have the same gifts? You are both carriers of blood magic." Vrykalos leans forward slightly and suggestively winks.

"I already know that," Callum says. Vrykalos' attempt to gain the conversational upper hand is unimpressive.

Alistair slaps the warlock across the side of his head, not appreciating this blatant lack of respect.

"It is all right, Alistair. Our guest is entitled to his anger," Vrykalos says. He sits back and sighs. "Perhaps the warlock will be interested to know that in all history, blood sorcery has always been associated with evil. There has never been an account of one with such power being able to resist the allure of dark magic."

Callum scoffs at Vrykalos declaration. But the vampire's confirmation mirrors Leana's explanation, making him take notice.

"Ah, it seems you might be curious about this after all?" Vrykalos adds with a trace of amusement.

"No," Callum snaps. "I don't want to have anything to do with necromancy or dark magic."

"Whether you have such a desire or not, dark magic runs through your veins. Blood sorcery and black magic have the same source. It is why your gifts are so powerful without the need for intensive training." Vrykalos pauses, awaiting Callum's reaction.

"What are you talking about?" Callum asks, hating that he appears so captivated by what this damned vampire might know.

"The magic within you draws its force from the same powerful origins. You cannot cast a single spell without tapping into that malevolent essence, which is what it means to be a blood sorcerer. You are, therefore, evil by nature."

Callum says nothing. Staring at the garish wallpaper, he ponders Vrykalos' words and wonders if anything he says is accurate or whether he is feeding him lies to confuse and disarm. It unnerves Callum to think that he could lose himself and be consumed by a malicious power.

"This frightens you?" Vrykalos tilts his head and lifts one corner of his mouth in a half-smirk. The vampire master is apparently intrigued by the depth of concern Callum displays. "Why should it disturb you?"

"I don't...I mean...I just want this war to end," Callum says, stumbling over his words. His mind feels fuzzy under the burden of unspeakable possibilities.

"It will never end," Vrykalos observes bluntly, dropping his hands to his lap and subtly nodding to Alistair.

Alistair swiftly leans over the back of the couch. He grabs a handful of the warlock's unruly brown hair and yanks his head back without warning. Callum fights against the firm grasp.

Preoccupied with Alistair's sudden aggression, the warlock barely registers the tiny pinch of a needle to the side of his neck. Alistair seizes the moment he needs to inject the mystery drug. When the vampire releases his hold, Callum bolts from the couch and spins to face his assailants. Spotting the empty syringe in Alistair's hand, a cold tingle crawls across his skin.

"What the hell?" Callum demands, but he can already feel the drug taking effect.

"You understand that we cannot have you dying while under our guard," Vrykalos says calmly from his posh seat. "Kincaid wants you alive, and he is even less forgiving than I am when it comes to failure. Since it is unlikely you will consent to our remedial aid or accept your imprisonment, we must sedate you. It is for our protection as well as yours. The effects will wear off in a couple of hours."

Callum clumsily turns to see the pompous vampire leaning back as though waiting for their visit to end so he can return to his leisure.

The warlock's legs buckle. He grabs for the sofa as they fail entirely, and he collapses on the wine-hued carpet. Alistair and Silas impassively approach from opposite sides of the ebony couch as a heavy lethargy washed over him. The best Callum can do is helplessly gaze at Isaac as he approaches. Squatting next to him, Isaac pulls the bloody collar of Callum's sweatshirt aside to inspect the painful laceration.

Isaac frowns. "Your man should be punished for his lack of control." He flashes a harsh glower up at Alistair, then tempers his expression and looks to Vrykalos to give his verdict. "These cuts will need suturing. I will do my best, master, but I am not a doctor."

"No matter," Vrykalos dismissively scoffs. "We only need him to live long enough for delivery to Kincaid."

Kincaid is the last thing Callum remembers as the sedative fog takes over. Once his eyes close, he descends into a drug-induced sleep and plunges into a fearful, dreamless state.

CHAPTER TWENTY-SIX

The warlock awakens in near darkness. The only light that appears in the featureless cell penetrates through a small, barred window set in the wooden door. With no idea how long he was unconscious, Callum is still groggy from the vampire's drug when he wakes. His hip and shoulder ache from hours spent curled on one side, lying on the cold stone floor without moving.

Callum carefully rolls onto his back and stretches, wincing as a sharp pain reminds him of the exchange with Maurice. He gingerly touches the site of his ghastly wound and is surprised to find it covered by thick gauze pads.

His filthy, torn shirt is stiff with crusted blood, and he is disgusted to feel the remnants of his collar sticking to his skin when he peels the fabric off his shoulder and chest. Callum gently removes the tape around the bandage and tosses it across the gloomy cell. It hits the floor with a saturated splat. He tenderly palpates a line of crude stitches. Two opposing, crescent-shaped sets of teeth marks cut into his flesh.

These are not mere puncture wounds—that vampire was out for meat. Callum is shocked at how close Maurice came to biting away a large, circular chunk. No wonder he bled so much.

Callum gradually sits up and tests the damage by circling his left arm. He finds that his range of motion is moderately impacted but is more severe when raising his arm higher than his shoulder. Anything beyond causes his muscles to painfully spasm.

A chilling thought occurs to him. Perhaps Kincaid ordered him kept alive because the necromancer wants the pleasure of killing Callum himself.

"Hey, you are not supposed to be here!" someone utters outside the cell. The voice carries as though shouted from the end of a hall.

Callum decides the voice is most likely a vampire stationed to safeguard Vrykalos' valuable prisoner. Still, he wonders who the guard is challenging. The objection is followed by sounds of conflict, and he is both intrigued and alarmed by the erupting activity.

The warlock scrambles to his tiny window. He presses the side of his face against the iron bars but cannot see much more than the concrete wall across the corridor. Curses and painful grunts indicate an escalating commotion, and dancing shadows filter down the dark passage, proving a battle is in progress.

Unexpectedly, the voice of a woman reciting an ancient incantation rises above the fray. A wave of pressurized air flows past his doorway, and the warlock recognizes the familiar signs of arcane energy.

Someone used magic, and it is not a vampire. Callum prudently steps back from his cage door.

The face of a young woman appears in the cell window. Her expression changes from determination to surprise at the sight of him staring back. Although he senses a vampiric aura, Callum appreciates that she is very much alive and human, unlike the rest of the vile creatures in this subterranean stronghold. The amulet on her necklace radiates the deceptive essence, creating the illusion of a nightwalker. It is a perfect disguise against Vrykalos' undead horde. However, Callum's magical perception allows him to see through the arcane camouflage. It also confirms his suspicions about who the woman really is, and he retreats deeper into his gloomy prison.

Having nowhere else to go, Callum prepares to defend himself against Quinn's infiltrating hunters.

"Cain, he's awake!" the woman yells to an unseen accomplice. There is a wary note in her voice as if she is unnerved by her discovery.

Heavy footsteps pound toward the cell. A broad-shouldered man, who easily outmatches the warlock in both height and weight, glares at him through the window.

"We don't have time for this, Jess," Cain barks. He opens the bolted door with a stolen key and fills the entrance with his silhouetted bulk. "Are you Walker, the warlock?"

"You guys need to hand out pictures so you can all stop asking me that question," Callum says sharply. He is annoyed that most of his introductions have begun with a demand to identify himself.

"They'll be here soon. We have to go *now!*" Jess announces. She anxiously glances down the hall toward the guard room from which they entered.

Callum can already hear distant voices approaching, but they are muffled.

"Get over there and block that door," Cain orders gruffly. Jess obeys and disappears. Cain's bulk moves into the cell, his beady eyes ferociously staring. "I'll take care of *you*."

Callum anxiously swallows as the brute clumps toward him. He has faced monsters bigger and far more vicious than this hunter. But after being injured, drugged, and now cornered, the sight of Cain's looming, aggressive form is demoralizing.

"*Pulsus,*" Cain mutters, jabbing his palm toward Callum.

Nothing happens.

Cain looks at his hand, confused by the lack of effect. "*Pulsus,*" he says again, scowling and aiming once more at the warlock.

But there is still nothing.

"Guess you've never encountered a magical ward before." Callum smirks at his attacker's befuddlement.

The warlock recognizes the dampening energy suffusing the chamber. The same suppressive force that radiated from the runes painted on the dwarven train car. Smartly applied by his captors, this unseen power effectively arrests the hunter's magic —as well as his own.

"I can still beat you into submission," Cain growls. Callum's smirk instantly fades.

The musclebound hunter charges across the cramped cell, leading with his shoulder. Callum sidesteps, avoiding the impact by inches. Cain's momentum continues, and his huge body slams into the concrete wall where Callum had stood. Not stopping to see how Cain fares after his collision, the warlock makes a mad dash for the wide open and unguarded prison door.

The warlock acts on this chance for freedom, knowing that if he can escape the warding, he can even the odds against his opponents—or at least try to.

He hears Cain wildly roaring, rebounding from his assault on the wall and plowing after him. But Callum is completely unprepared for what happens next.

As he crosses the threshold, he nearly collides with Jess. Returning to aid her fellow hunter, she almost careens headlong into the fleeing warlock. A trained fighter, Jess reacts immediately and catches Callum with a snapping, roundhouse kick to his upper back as he passes. Although lacking serious force, the strike is enough to send him staggering into the corridor wall.

A furious Cain joins the struggle a moment later.

"Get that portal ready," Cain says with a snarl. He hammers his crushing weight into Callum's back and drives a merciless fist against the warlock's ribs.

Callum cries out as Cain punches his tender flank a second time. The hunter sadistically targets the same area, attempting to break bones.

The warlock spots Jess backpedaling. Callum reaches his hand out and seizes her by the arm to prevent her from leaving. Jess twists free of the warlock's desperate grip, and Cain grabs a handful of Callum's hair, pulling the warlock's head back and smacking the side of his face against the wall. Callum is dazed by the blow and feels warm blood running down his forehead and cheek.

Abruptly turning away, Jess faces the guard room down the hall and the sturdy door beyond. She retrieves an opalescent stone from a pocket, holds it in her outstretched right hand, and frantically recites an elaborate enchantment.

The distant door begins to rattle as vampires arrive, only to find themselves blocked from entering. The nightwalkers shout and crash their bodies against the barrier, distorting the heavy steel beneath the force of their supernatural strength.

Cain jerks the stunned warlock around and shoves his back against the wall. Callum is no longer resisting, but the hunter still relishes launching a resounding uppercut to the warlock's abdomen. Coughing and gasping from aching pain exploding through his stomach, Callum doubles over.

When Jess speaks her final words, the stone ignites with glowing, golden magic, and a portal opens. A familiar vortex of spiraling colors rotates before them just as the door to the guard room, indented and curved, topples from its frame. Cain drags Callum away from the wall and bulldozes forward to follow Jess through the portal. Stepping into the center of the swirling wormhole, they vanish.

The vortex closes like a drawstring, leaving the vampires to scream in impotent rage.

CHAPTER TWENTY-SEVEN

C allum is not surprised to find himself inside the walls of Quinn's mansion. Memories of Liam's gruesome death flood back with agonizing clarity, but he has no time to mourn his friend.

As Cain prods him along, Callum is led, stumbling, to the middle of a two-story foyer. Many hunters hover at its edges, sneering at the hated warlock while they stand guard. Most hold enchanted swords and crossbows, and waves of magical energy radiate from the dozens of artifacts each possesses.

The second tier of hunters is positioned on a balcony encircling the atrium, each ready to defend their master and his lair. A wide staircase provides access to the left and right promenades. Desmond Quinn is slowly descending, obviously delighted to greet this long-sought quarry at last.

Callum's heart pounds as he faces his nemesis. His emotion is fed by the knowledge of what this evil sorcerer is capable of rather than by the man himself.

Quinn is a squat, corpulent man with mottled rosy cheeks and a gleaming bald head. He appears superficially cordial, but Callum has seen this man's depravity first-hand. He is all too aware of Quinn's sadistically cruel soul. Approaching his target, panting, and limping, the sorcerer wildly grins—a true predator toying with its prey. Nonetheless, Callum is determined to face his archenemy with defiant courage.

"I've been looking forward to this moment for months," Quinn cackles, beaming with glee as he nears his prisoner. But prudently, he stops just beyond Callum's reach.

"Your people are pretty persistent," Callum says, willing every atom of contempt he can muster in his unsteady voice. "You never considered just asking me over for coffee and a chat?"

"You confound me, Mr. Walker, by cracking jokes at a time like this," Quinn replies. "You can try to mask your fear with humor, but I've been watching you long enough to know that you're far too serious to play the part of a comedian."

"Go ahead, Quinn. Educate me on what I'm thinking." Callum stands up a little taller, trying hard to maintain his veneer of confidence.

Quinn tweaks one side of his mouth in a lopsided grin. "Why, you're scared. I can see it in your eyes. I possess a sight stone that allows me to see anyone I choose. You, however, remain ignorant of my observations. I've been watching your movements from a distance, Walker. I know you're not nearly as strong as you could be—or as strong as *I* can be."

"And this sight stone can show you the future too, right? Is that how you knew that Liam and I would be watching *you*?" Callum digs, anger rising like a lump in his throat.

Whatever fears Callum felt are now displaced by hatred, and adrenaline gives him the strength to overcome his physical injuries. He glares at Quinn while quieting his thoughts. But before he can launch an enchantment, his efforts are shattered. Cain swiftly grasps the side of Callum's neck and presses his vice-like fingers against the sensitive bite wound.

Callum howls and falls to his knees, grabbing for Cain's wrist to make the agony stop. When the hunter eases his touch, Callum sinks to the polished wood floor on his hands and knees, shaking and pale. His head droops in humiliating defeat. The searing pain Cain created still burns across his neck and shoulder, and fresh blood drips from broken stitches.

Cain crouches beside the warlock and scolds. "The next time you try to attack my master, I'll do something truly unpleasant. Is that understood?"

Callum nods his compliance to avoid further torture. He is unsure how Cain knew of his silent offensive attempt, but it does not matter now.

"Thank you, Cain. I think he gets the point," Quinn says flatly, savoring this moment. "That will be enough for tonight. I want you to take him to the dungeon and let him rest. We'll begin test runs tomorrow morning. I suggest you get some sleep, Walker. You're going to need it."

Quinn sounds ecstatic as he shuffles back to the mammoth staircase. Callum, however, is not done. He rises to his knees and fires a bitter parting shot at Quinn, raising his voice so he can be heard by all.

"Does that stone of yours tell you how you're going to die?"

He knows his question strikes a nerve when the sorcerer freezes in mid-stride. Turning abruptly, he meets Callum's glare with a brief flicker of horror on his ruddy face. In an instant, it is replaced by blazing outrage, but the warlock has his answer. Quinn has seen his death, and the memory of that vision clearly causes him immeasurable dread. Callum smiles at Quinn's hidden terror, knowing that his enemy will meet a deadly fate.

"I'm going to kill you long before that destiny comes to pass, Walker. I have the means to change my future, but can you say the same for yourself?" Quinn shakes with fury as he spits his threatening promise. Both know that every one of his hunters are observing this revealing scene. "Cain, please see to it that our warlock gets some rest."

"Yessir," Cain replies with enthusiasm.

As Quinn stomps back to the staircase, Callum is hauled to his feet and hurried across the foyer to a back passageway. The musclebound hunter takes pleasure in driving the warlock onward, and Callum does his best to comply. His body protests the movement, and his head is aflame. Still, the warlock refuses to let the hunters see his suffering.

Captive and captors walk the gauntlet of hallways, passing through a contemporary kitchen equipped with expensive appliances and rows of stainless-steel workspaces.

Callum thinks about grabbing a carving knife from a nearby utensil rack, but he decides against it. Cain is not alone, and three other hunters accompany him with physical and magical weapons. Death may not be their intention, but accidents happen.

They exit the kitchen and descend a narrow stairway and enter a basement occupied by rows of windowless steel cells. They stretch along the entire length of the mansion, and Callum can hear piteous sobbing and unanswered pleas from several of the cages.

Cain and his acolytes shove Callum along the aisles until they reach a distant wall. At that point, Cain jostles Callum into an open metal box—barely seven feet square—and follows him into the gloomy, magically-warded chamber. He shunts Callum back against the wall and leans forward to wrap his hand around the warlock's throat, fixing his prisoner with an acidic glare.

Choking under the sadist's steel grip, Callum lashes out in panic. He jams a punch into Cain's Adam's apple, and the stranglehold releases. Cain staggers, coughing and holding his throat.

"I warned you," Cain snarls, his speech strains from the abuse to his larynx.

Callum clenches his fists and raises his arms in defense against the lunging hunter. Just as the warlock cocks his arm to punch, another hunter blinds him with the beam of a flashlight. The warlock reflexively shuts his eyes and is unprepared when Cain plows a knee into his groin.

Callum keels over, writhing and moaning.

The hunter stoops and spits before turning and stocking out

of the cell. The heavy door slams, plunging the battered warlock into darkness.

Consumed by excruciating ache and cramps spreading from his hips to his diaphragm, Callum fights to suppress the urge to vomit. The shattering agony in his pelvis lingers for what feels like an eternity. All Callum can do is huddle in silence, waiting for the wretched pain to mercifully subside.

Finally, after a long time, the warlock inhales a trembling breath and gingerly rolls onto his back, cursing every misfortune of his miserable life.

CHAPTER TWENTY-EIGHT

A blanket of darkness surrounds Callum, and the pungent smell of decay poisons the air. Callum shivers as a damp chill fills his metal prison.

He can feel the icy fingers of warding magic dampening his power—not that he has the energy to cast a spell. So, with nothing else to do, Callum lies still for many hours. Yet, the haven of sleep evades him.

His mind churns through gruesome images of what awaits him in the morning. There are no clocks to tally the passage of time, only each breath in and out. Listening to the muffled cries from other captives and encased in his own despair, Callum closes his eyes and turns his thoughts to the last time he felt at peace.

Callum recalls Frey's kind face. The way her cheeks dimple and the genuine affection in her gentle eyes gives Callum some minutes of tranquility. Memories of her compassion and inquisitive spirit remind him of the first moment he ever felt a sense of belonging.

Thinking of her curiously fluttering around his apartment as she studied his world makes him smile. Callum remembers the moment Frey shrank him to the size of a fairy and returned them both to her homeland. He is exceedingly thankful, realizing how much she was willing to sacrifice to save his life. Callum then relives the moment of Frey's tender kiss. He badly wants to linger in this recollection. Not for the intimate appeal, but because Callum found kinship in this turbulent world, even if it was fleeting. His heart longs for the friendship Frey offered, and he clings to the sentiment.

Callum is so absorbed in thought that he scarcely realizes the floor beneath him has morphed into a soft bed of snow-covered moss. He can no longer hear the pitiful cries of other prisoners in Quinn's dungeon, and the awareness makes his eyes fly open. Callum is amazed to discover a nighttime canopy of trees swaying gently overhead instead of rigid steel.

He carefully sits up, testing joints and muscles for fresh spasms and nagging aches. Then, strangely, the fading blackness of his cell is replaced by a muted, moonlit forest. Trees materialize in every direction while the walls of Callum's cell fade and finally vanish. The too-familiar biting chill of winter freezes his breath.

The warlock slowly climbs to his feet, grunting and wincing at the soreness that pervades every part of his body. He uses a tree to steady himself against the jagged migraine that burns inside his skull. Holding his head and moaning in pain and confusion, Callum has no idea what is happening around him.

How can he suddenly find himself in a primeval forest, surrounded by giant oaks, elms, and maples, with a carpet of snow beneath his boots? He is sure that his cage was warded against magic, intuitively detecting the power-draining energy that assailed him for hours.

Callum whips around when he hears quiet movement in the deepest shadows. His eyes probe into the night but can only see tree trunks and overhanging branches. A snap makes him jump and swivel his eyes in the direction of the sound. He grips the rough bark as the single crack of noise is accompanied by the shuffling of undergrowth. Something large is drawing near.

His knuckles turn white as he watches the movement of looming shadow over sable woodland.

Callum wishes he had the strength to run. The warlock cannot identify the advancing creature with only slivers of moonlight piercing the night. Finally, a creature emerges from the darkness, less than eight feet away. At last, Callum clearly sees the form of a noble stallion on stilted powerful legs, plodding and peering down at him with impassioned eyes.

This is a horse like no other Callum has ever seen. With a ghostly coat of brilliant white and a flowing silver mane. A formidable, pointed horn protrudes from the steed's forehead. He had read about unicorns as part of his research but never imagined he would see one.

The magnificent horse attentively watches and radiates a dynamic feeling of peace. Callum senses both concern and compassion. His fear drains away as he looks into the unicorn's empathetic eyes.

I have been waiting for you to arrive. Words speak within Callum's mind, but he knows they belong to the mystical beast. After all the wondrous things Callum has witnessed in this realm, he does not question this strange knowledge.

"You've been waiting for *me?*" Callum whispers in disbelief.

You have suffered greatly and learned much, but your journey is not over.

"This looks a lot like the end to me. I'm injured and lost in a forest in the middle of winter. I'm not sure things can get much worse." The warlock can feel hopelessness wrapping its claws around his soul.

If you fail, worlds will die. This one, and your own.

"I never wanted to be responsible for so many lives. I'm not strong enough to win this fight or protect everyone. Why was I chosen?" Callum asks desperately.

He allows himself to slump to the snowy ground, hugging his knees to his chest and lowering his battered face upon them.

It was not I who decided your fate. Someone else knows you have power more potent than you yet realize. You must have faith to accept your purpose. The unicorn lifts its regal head, gracefully moving nearer and softly snorting.

"I'm useless," says the dejected warlock. "I've been attacked and passed around from one enemy to another, never able to defend myself with this...supposed gift. How can I possibly stop a war?" He grumbles into his knees.

Reflecting on the past, Callum realizes his youth did nothing to prepare him for the prophecy's challenges, nor for the abuse, he suffered as a result. Together, the physical pain and emotional misery are beyond his ability to cope.

From the minute he learned about the prophecy, Callum Walker fought to survive and find the path to his so-called destiny. Now, he is just a failed hero, lacking the will to carry on one day longer. Beyond this encumbering gloom lies an overpowering feeling of isolation. As far as Callum's concerned, he is not the person for this fateful mission.

"I just can't do this anymore." He mournfully shakes his head.

Callum is not sure why this empty feeling of solitude suddenly plagues him after so many years of living alone. Perhaps because of the traumas he suffered in rapid succession or the result of witnessing his new friend's murder such a short time ago. His weary mind wanders through recollections, starting from the earliest awareness of his birth parents' abandonment. He drifts through memories of foster care before embarking on his own path. Experiencing so much hurt, Callum has remained emotionally guarded, steadfastly maintaining introversion.

Yet, he has also found friendship in recent days, first with Frey and then with Liam. This brief bonding was enough to pull Callum out of his dismal shell. That experience of acceptance opened a window on his dark existence, making its loss even more soul-crushing. It is why in his bleakest moments, Callum sought comfort in the one thing that embodied the sentiment of friendship—his memories of Frey.

Everything you have been through has led you to this point. You are here when you are most in need of support. The unicorn lowers its thick neck and nuzzles the warlock's wounded forehead with a velvety nose. *Your adversaries are searching for you at this very moment. They will track you, even here in the magical realm. But help is also on its way. You must keep moving until the sun sets tomorrow. Head north, toward the tallest mountain. It is there that you will discover your true calling, and you will see how you have inspired so many others within this kingdom.*

The stallion raises its pale head when Callum looks up, urgently directing his muzzle over the warlock's left shoulder. *That is the way you must go. But I cannot follow you. I am only your guide.*

Callum feels a soothing calmness enfold him like a quilt, and he marvels at the rare creature. He knows the unicorn must be the one exuding these comforting emotions.

With goodness and faith in your heart, you will be more powerful than your enemies. You have many things still to learn, Callum Walker. I hope the days ahead will prove a rewarding lesson.

Callum's eyes glisten with tears as he watches the steed quietly walk away and fade into the night again.

As cold and sore as he is, Callum forces himself to stand and use some of his meager energy to conjure a warm coat, mittens, and a knitted cap to keep winter at bay. With a full day of cold slogging ahead, it will be scant help at best.

Finally, facing in the direction the unicorn indicated, the warlock sighs and staggers north.

CHAPTER TWENTY-NINE

"How the hell did he escape?" Quinn screams in incoherent rage. The sorcerer repeatedly pounds his fists on the desktop, rattling the many trinkets and ornaments that decorate his innermost sanctum. "I thought you warded every cell so none of our prisoners could use their magic! Especially *him*!"

Eric sits across the desk and responds with extreme caution. "His cell was warded. There is no way Walker should have been able to leave. It had to have been something else. Something more powerful." After making this inconclusive report, Eric can only shrink into his armchair, cowering under Quinn's storm of outrage.

"Something else? Something more powerful? *That's* your answer? Why didn't *I* think of that? You're all *idiots*!" Quinn's face is livid crimson, and the veins on his head and neck protrude.

"Cain assures me that Walker was securely locked in his cell," Eric says, trying to appease Quinn and deflect blame. "Three other hunters, all with years of experience in your service, were with Cain to ensure this was so."

"If that's the case, how do you explain his disappearance?"

Quinn heavily drops into his chair and digs his fat fingers in the leather armrests. He shoots a look of pure hatred at Eric. "I've tolerated these failures long enough! *You* will send a message for me. Cain must be punished. Do it in front of everyone, in the most unpleasant way possible. Make him suffer. Now, get out of my sight! And the next time I see you, it had better be with positive news. Otherwise, I'll be ordering *your* punishment."

"Yes, sir. Thank you, sir," mumbles Eric, fleeing the lavish office before Quinn can change his mind.

The moment he is alone, Quinn sighs and ponders the top drawer of his desk.

He moved the sight stone from its display when he learned that Callum knew of its existence. He assumes that Liam's betrayal provided this knowledge to the warlock, but how did Callum learn that the stone revealed the details of Quinn's final moments? Even Liam did not know about that—although his last remark indicated he may have suspected it.

Quinn hates that he let his composure slip in front of a large portion of the Order. He is certain Callum noted the regrettable split-second display of terror.

The warlock infuriated him for months, but the arcane power he wields is no longer the sorcerer's primary interest. Making sure Callum suffers a prolonged and excruciating death by torture is now at the top of Quinn's demented agenda.

Quinn reaches into a coat pocket and removes an ornate key. Opening the desk drawer, he then withdraws the sight stone.

"This had better be the last time," he murmurs to himself, slipping the chain over his head.

Quinn crosses the room and assumes his customary painful position on the silk cushions in front of the fireplace. His immediate surroundings slip away as the stone takes control. It carries his consciousness throughout the vast human realm and then across the veil until he reaches the lone man, he badly wants to find.

"Got you now," Quinn whispers.

Beaming with spiteful amusement, he begins imagining the list of agonies he will bestow on the troublesome young man.

~

Standing inside the guard room, Vrykalos peers down the short hallway at the open cell door. He takes no notice of the dead vampire guards—his eyes are locked on the empty cage. The smeared blood on the corridor's concrete wall is evidence of the struggle that left Callum beaten before he was whisked away.

Vrykalos is seething with suppressed anger. He is uncertain how Quinn's soldiers could infiltrate his secure domain, but he regards the sorcerer's action as an insult.

"They escaped through a portal cast by an amulet," Alistair reports, guardedly watching as Vrykalos studies the scene.

"Yes. And who do we know that uses amulets?" Vrykalos asks, knowing it is a rhetorical question.

"The hunters who serve Quinn," Alistair answers promptly. "But how did they manage to get in here?"

"That is a good question," says Vrykalos, feeling both violated and enraged that his lair has been penetrated. "The fact that he found our warlock so easily suggests a rare asset. It seems that Quinn may be in possession of a sight stone."

"I thought such artifacts were a myth."

"Sight stones are very real," Vrykalos says, snarling. "Kincaid told me that using a sight stone allows the user to see the target of their desires as though they are walking beside them. We were probably being spied on from the moment we brought the warlock into our midst."

"Could the sorcerer use this power to eavesdrop on vital conversations?" asks Alistair. He looks alarmed by the prospect of their enemy having such a strong advantage.

"The stone can only show you visions of your target and those in the immediate vicinity. It does not allow the user to hear conversations. I thought Quinn was smarter than that."

"Smarter than...what?" a puzzled Alistair asks.

"A sight stone uses dark magic, which makes it extremely irresistible. Over time, it will consume the user's sanity," Vrykalos explains. "This can be a distinct advantage for Kincaid. I will relay this information to the necromancer immediately. In the meantime, you will spy on Quinn. He may lead us to the warlock without even realizing it."

"Very clever, master. I will make it so." Alistair nods and hurries from the guard room, leaving Vrykalos alone.

"Mr. Walker, enjoy your last days. You will be dead within the week," the old vampire hisses. He departs, smiling at the glorious news he will now relate to his dark master.

CHAPTER THIRTY

The sun climbs higher in the early morning sky, and parcels of daylight cut through the canopy of scrawny trees. Callum is approximately a third of the way up the mountain, having just crested the lower ridge of the foothill. Since he began trekking well before dawn, persistent fevers keep him alternately sweating and shivering despite his new attire. As the forest becomes more sparse the higher he ascends, Callum is vulnerable to the bracing wind. But time and Callum trudge on together.

The first leg of his present journey was laborious. The second one is insufferable. Callum struggles with the steepening ascent, slipping on icy patches and occasional slick mud where a film of snow melted.

His throbbing bite wound has become infected, oozing blood and traces of pus. Stubbornly, through his fading strength, Callum muscles his way over rugged terrain until he discovers a well-worn switchback trail offering an easier route to the summit. But he hesitates, realizing that a beaten track means a high-traffic route. The idea of meeting unwelcome company worries Callum.

In his situation, it is wiser and safer to assume any encounter will be negative. In the end, the exhausted warlock relents and takes the trail, lacking the energy and stamina to do otherwise. It is at least a better prospect than succumbing to hypothermia.

As morning advances, unresolved hunger and fatigue wear on Callum and weaken his resolve. Mercifully, he does manage to satisfy his raging thirst at a mountain stream. The glacial water restores him after profusely sweating and risking dehydration. With luck, the path will intersect the tumbling waterway several more times as he climbs.

Nearly two hours later, the stream disappears, and Callum fails to find another source of water. Despite his general high state of fitness, days of constant exertion and heavy battering have exacted a toll. Every time he stops for a brief rest—or falls flat on his face—it is harder to get back up again. By afternoon, the warlock reaches a rocky clearing beyond the thinning tree line.

It is a sun-warmed oasis of slate rock across an open plateau, overlooking a panorama of jagged ice-capped peaks, rolling hills, and winter woodland. At the promise of warmth and reprieve, Callum deviates off the trail. But despite the unicorn's instructions to continue until sunset, Callum is spent. He decides to pause his journey in favor of urgently needed rest.

Callum walks near the sheer cliff edge of the slate plateau. He gingerly lowers himself to the ground in front of a slanting block, dropping the last few inches as his abused legs finally give out.

Looking over an endless expanse, his hope that he might be approaching some type of civilization is dashed. The warlock fears he is lost beyond the reach of any salvation and feels his fever rising again.

The path he was told to follow offers no clue about where it leads. Callum remembers that a person can survive three weeks without food. However, his complete lack of shelter—or energy enough to summon or create such a refuge—means his greatest danger is probably freezing to death.

Callum is not ignorant of his enemies' pursuit either. Quinn is likely watching this very moment with his prophecy stone. His hunters could be guided through the thick forest to return him to the miserable metal prison under his mansion. But after so many hours of strenuous hiking, exhaustion outweighs anxiety, and Callum leans back against his boulder. He stretches out his legs and soaks up as much of the cherished sunshine as he can.

"I just need an hour," he mumbles and surrenders to sleep within seconds.

~

Callum slept soundly but awakens with a start when a shadow blocks the early evening light and prompts him to open his eyelids. Crouching next to him is a young, bronze-skinned elf wearing a heavy wool coat that smells strongly of cedar. The elf gently touched the deep cut above Callum's eye—a souvenir from Cain's gleeful smashing of his face. Dried blood remains glued to his face, and the elf's touch ended the warlock's slumber.

"What the hell!" Callum exclaims. He lashes out in panic and grabs the intruder by one wrist.

The elf's blue eyes grow wide with fear. He wrenches free of the warlock's instinctive but feeble grasp and jumps to his feet, drawing a short sword and leveling its point toward Callum.

The warlock's movements are stiff and sluggish, robbing him of speed and strength. His less-than-agile attempt to sit up also leaves Callum vulnerable to an unseen opponent lurking behind him.

The warlock catches a brief glimpse of a crosswise staff arcing over his head and down past his face. His fixation on the flustered young elf in front of him had distracted his attention. Callum realizes the added danger a moment too late when this second assailant drives the edge of his staff up under the warlock's chin. The sneaky attacker yanks Callum down flat and pins him against the boulder.

Fighting the constricting pressure of the staff on his throat, Callum begins to panic. He grabs the pole weapon with both hands, tugging on it to free himself. The restraint is not quite tight enough to obstruct his breathing, but the ambush makes him gasp during his struggle. Unfortunately, this frightening scenario happened too many times before, always with a bad outcome.

Recovering from his initial fright, the first elf ventures forward again, holding his cutlass ready. The young elf's arm trembles as he glances back and forth between the warlock and his strategically positioned companion.

Shuffling footsteps along the plateau and voices further announce the presence of more attackers. Unable to turn his head, Callum must rely on his hearing to determine the location of the mounting threat.

The blade-wielding elf is the only one in his line of sight. He is either very brave or following orders to investigate the sleeping human. Judging by the elf's cagey demeanor, the warlock assumes it is the latter. But the sharp sword raises the level of danger.

Callum identifies the intruders are elves, not Quinn's hunters. However, they are not outwardly compassionate or friendly. Therefore, he must consider them enemies as well until proven otherwise.

The warlock concentrates his remaining mental energy into a focused, magical fire that causes his arms and hands to radiate a crimson luminance. Flames streak from Callum's fingers, igniting the hardwood staff jammed under his chin.

A scream erupts from his staff-wielding assailant and resonates across the plateau. The blazing staff is instantly dropped and clatters onto the rocks.

Unharmed by his own spell, Callum gathers all his strength and clambers to his feet. He faces the sword-wielding elf, who wisely abandons any notion of defense and darts for safety. The warlock steadies himself against a boulder to compensate for a sudden surge of dizziness. Still, he turns to face whatever new threat is organizing.

A contingent of twenty elven soldiers, some holding swords and staves and others armed with crossbows pointed at his chest, assemble, and are clearly prepared for battle. He hears more movement and hushed voices coming up the trail beyond the tree line. Crunching snow reveals elven reinforcements yet unseen. It appears a small army has converged while Callum dozed.

Although he knows that elves are generally peaceful unless provoked, his experience with Agis and his troops says otherwise. Considering his recent assault, Callum has zero expectations of noble intentions from this group.

A pathway opens as soldiers' part to allow a lone elf, one with graying hair neatly braided down his back, to step from behind the well-armed frontline. This elf appears much older than the rest, and while the warriors wear leather pants and moss-green wool coats, this aged elf is dressed in a woven robe that skirts the ground. His staff is topped with a white gemstone and secured by a web of delicate vines. This staff identifies him as a mage. He sizes up Callum with scrutiny, signifying a position of authority.

"Are you Callum Walker?" the mage demands.

"Tell me who you are first," Callum argues, utterly fed up with repeating this scene yet again.

There is no denying his alarm at seeing this tough elven squad poised to attack. But the warlock is tired, sick, hungry, and completely done with being subjugated. Thus far, his prophetic journey makes him feel like nothing more than human currency, sought after by all and passed between enemies and allies.

Time after time, Callum found momentary respite from physical pain and wrenching loneliness, only to be thrown back to suffer through another desperate battle for his life. He has been beaten, bitten, and thrown into prisons. As far as he is concerned, this is just another enemy looking to exchange him for something else of value. Nothing more.

As Callum glares at the mage, he takes in the nervous faces of the soldiers staring back at him. Every one of them is holding their ground, not advancing but unwilling to retreat. Even the elder mage seems hesitant to step any closer. It is as if the warlock is the one to be truly feared, despite his visible fatigue.

"I need you to answer the question, human. Are you the one called Callum Walker?" the mage asks again, more insistently this time.

"Or what?" Callum fires back. "Are you going to rip into my mind to find the answer? Sorry, but Agis already beat you to it. Go ask him because I'm not telling *you* anything."

The mage recoils and blinks at the mention of the name. His deportment suddenly shifts from one of commanding authority to curiosity.

"You know of the mountain elves of Verdon Peaks?" the mage asks, his tone ebbing to something less severe.

"That is because this man is the warlock we have been seeking. Did you not see him ignite that staff with his power?" a mighty voice booms from behind the vanguard.

Callum spies a towering, athletic form. A man with striking neanderthal features, wiry, black hair, and a full beard to match comes into view. Donning a sheepskin shawl over a shirt of leather and chainmail, this fearsome man and a flanking pair of bodyguards stand a full two heads above the rest of the crowd.

The frontline divides again, allowing the impressive trio to push forward. As their full forms are shown, Callum understands the height discrepancy. These burly men are centaurs. They have a human head, arms, and torso, but their lower half merges into a horse's body. Appearing keenly interested in him, they draw near, and Callum tenses, wary of their intent. Finally, the centaurs halt. The central figure tilts his head as though confused by Callum's confrontational attitude.

"We are not here to hurt you," says the towering centaur. His expression is a mixture of uneasiness and apology. "I am the Chieftain Prince of my clan, my name is Damostom, guardian of the Northern Centaurs. It is a pleasure to finally meet you, young warlock."

Damostom bows his head slightly as he speaks, and his flanking comrades follow his lead.

"And I am Thalan, of the Forest Elves of Caster, and servant of the Northern Kingdom," the mage proudly adds. "We have awaited the Prophesied One's emergence for years. It will be our great pleasure to escort you to the safety of Havishire. Our queen has been eagerly awaiting your arrival and will be delighted to know that you are well."

Callum remembers the unicorn's promise of support. He wants to believe that this is it, but his many tribulations have left him skeptical and on guard. In the shrouding dusk of evening, Callum looks across the line of elven soldiers lowering their weapons and relaxing their hostile stance. A discernable expression of relief flows through the company of elves. Thalan smiles and moves closer but halts as Damostom raises a hand.

"Are you injured?" Damostom asks Callum, pinching his bushy eyebrows together. His gaze assesses the warlock's ashen and haggard appearance.

Callum considers this question for a long, tense moment before crediting the unicorn's claim and trusting these elves and centaurs. After all, the stallion's promise that Callum would meet help seems to be valid.

"I'm not doing so well, but I think I'll live," Callum responds with a weary sigh. He pulls down the neckline of his coat and sweatshirt to reveal the infected vampire bite. It seeps and burns constantly.

Callum knows he suffers the effects of his wounds and is now in dire need of medical help. Keeping the secret of his infirmity would risk his life, and these elves may have access to healing that would alleviate his pain and fevers.

"We have a medic in our midst, but he is only equipped with

bandages and braces to treat injuries, not ointments and elixirs to manage this type of ailment," Thalan explains. The mage hastily relays orders to the nearest soldiers who depart down the trail at a steady run. Callum pulls his bloody collar back up and slumps his shoulders.

The warlock casts a weary look at Thalan and Damostom. Though still fighting his ingrained reservations, Callum is thankful he had found some measure of relief among his new allies. Knowing that he still has some distance to travel, he addresses one of his other urgent needs.

"I could really use some food and water," Callum says through chattering teeth. Now that the sun has set, he feels winter's icy chill despite his winter gear. His shivering is more pronounced than ever, and it is not all due to the sub-zero temperature.

Thalan orders a hearty dinner of bread, nuts, dried meat, and steaming herbal tea to be prepared and brought forth. Damostom continues to observe the warlock with mute concern.

Within minutes, Callum receives a wool blanket to wrap over his coat. It smells like moss and pine and adds another layer against the elements. He welcomes the thick covering and tucks his gloved hands into the folds of fabric. Soon, his fingers tingle with unaccustomed warmth.

The elves and centaurs indulge in an evening repast on the plateau, and Thalan orders the entire squad to set camp so the ailing warlock can benefit from a proper night's rest.

The soldiers light a handful of cozy fires to hold the cold at bay as the moon rises, and the troops happily feast and drink until their bellies are full. Callum quietly eats every morsel offered, relieved to have a meal even if he must endure Damostom's persistent gaze and Thalan's incessant chatter.

"You are lucky we found you when we did," the mage rambles excitedly. "I am leading my troops up to the Slumbering Valley at the summit of this mountain. It is a prominent waypoint for soldiers and travelers. The storehouse supplies are replenished regularly by the queen's order. This final junction is the safest route over the mountain. The northern face directly descends into the woodland plains that surround the city of Havishire. We meant to camp in the upper valley. From there, it's another half-day walk to the elven capital."

Callum partly listens as he stuffs his face. He had not realized how hungry he was until his stomach was finally full. The calories will provide energy for the next stage of his journey.

Thalan stops speaking when one of his soldiers arrives, announcing himself as the medic. He brings Callum a rolled sleeping mat stuffed with sheep's wool and feathers, as well as a steaming cup of steeped tea. Having personally gathered the ingredients, the medic pledges the pungent brew will ease his pain and help him sleep. The medic inspects and bandages Callum's festering bite, frowning, and proclaiming the wound to be septic.

"I guess there's not much we can do about it here," Callum observes.

The kindly elf healer agrees. He respectfully bows and leaves with a promise that he is available to return.

As the warlock gulps down the bitter drink, coughing and shuddering at its disagreeable flavor, his misgivings about these new companions begin to fade.

"Agis had his mage cast a portal, transporting his elves and me over several miles. Why can't you do that now?" Callum asks Thalan, setting down his empty cup. He spreads out his thin woolen mat and reclines, attempting to make himself marginally more comfortable. Whatever medicine was in the tea is fast-acting and potent. Callum can already feel its sedating effects, soothing his aching body and relaxing his mind.

"Only a senior mage has the training or skill to cast such a gateway. It is a delicate art that can be fatal if done incorrectly. I have not attained that level of achievement yet," Thalan explains, disappointment showing on his angular face. "Elves are accustomed to long expeditions. But there are few senior mages in the elven kingdom, and they are reserved for the most important of missions. With Damostom and his warriors guiding us safely through the wilderness, my superiors felt we were blessed with more resources than most regiments."

"You're a guide?" Callum asks Damostom, trying to determine the centaur's position in this company.

"Among other things," Damostom says with a gentle bow and fleeting smile. "My people have a history of allegiances with elves that spans millennia. We also hold the prophecy in high regard. My brothers and I volunteered to aid in the search for you since learning your identity from the elves of Verdon Peaks. Several search parties are scouring the Northern Kingdom as we speak. Some are guided by my brethren. We knew only that the prophecy suggested you would return to the magical realm."

"Oh," Callum says. The combination of medicine and fatigue dull his thoughts and make it hard to stay awake.

Thankfully, Damostom notices the warlock's losing battle with unconsciousness.

"Thalan, do you think it would be prudent to allow our guest to enjoy some needed rest? After all, he is unwell, and we have a difficult trek tomorrow."

"Yes, of course," Thalan stammers, curtly nodding in agreement. "Sleep in peace, Warlock. Take comfort in the fact that my soldiers are here to protect you."

Although grateful for the food and bedding, Callum is not entirely put at ease by his brigade's promise of defense. Quinn and Kincaid have proven their cunning and far-reaching influence over other magical creatures. Knowing this triggers concern about the elves and Centaurs succumbing to his enemy's manipulation. Despite his lack of confidence, Callum takes solace in the relative safety of numbers.

Damostom and Thalan settle down for the night, refusing to leave his side, and a contingent of nearly three dozen elves stand watch. The dangers mounting against him feel lessened, but Callum is wary nonetheless. He cannot count on fate or luck to guard him, nor can these unsuspecting allies. Thalan and Damostom have no idea what the diabolical brothers are capable of.

Only Callum's own prudence will see him succeed against foes threatening every living soul across two worlds. He closes his feverish eyes and surrenders to fitful sleep, accepting his instinct to protect these hapless beings. Now, he just needs to make it to Havishire alive.

CHAPTER THIRTY-ONE

C allum is roused by the noises of soldiers breaking camp
while the sunrise paints the sky in brilliant streaks of
pink and orange. Stiffly, he rises and stretches. It will
take more than a single night's sleep to restore his depleted
energy and heal his injuries. Callum tidies away his sleeping gear
and hands it over to a waiting soldier. Then, he devours another
meal of bread and smoked salmon before the militia commences
its arduous journey.

His fever still raging, Callum struggles to keep pace with the
refreshed soldiers. The warlock distracts himself by watching
the cheerful interactions among the elven troops. They seem
wholly content, bantering in their unique language while casting
many furtive glances at him. The entire group is in high spirits,
and Callum wonders whether this band of elves is always so
annoying upbeat.

He recalls the gruff, serious demeanor of the mountain elves
and their highly conservative culture. They are uncomfortable
with breaking out of their stoic molds unless safely within their
alpine villages. The curious attention from his present companions makes the introverted Callum uneasy, so he turns his attention to the trail and focuses on each grueling step upward.

Hours pass, and Callum pushes on with the rest of the company. Inevitably, the ailing warlock starts falling to the rear of the line.

He fights to summon the strength and keep going, and the constant effort makes him break into cold sweats. Since the thinning forest has vanished at this elevation, there are few handholds to grab, and the snow deepens underfoot. The unfettered wind takes its own toll. Callum's neck wound throbs relentlessly, but he does not complain. It would do him little good.

Despite his quiet suffering, Callum does appreciate being in the company of others again. He listens to their voices, and even though he does not understand the words, their camaraderie improves his surly disposition.

Absorbed by their own conversations, no one notices when Callum drifts back beyond the tail end of the group.

He pauses, doubling over and panting for oxygen to feed his racing heart. His tight chest feels as though it is being squeezed in a vice. He guesses it has been approximately three days since Maurice bit him. Callum sags onto a small boulder to rest, lowering his blanket and opening his coat to prod the swollen injury.

Callum hisses at the lancing pain. Fresh blood and pus soak into his collar, and heat radiating from the infected tissue can be felt over an ever-increasing radius. There is no doubt that his health is failing, and he now admits that his rampant infection has become more severe than he suspected.

The warlock sets his elbows on his knees and buries his ashen face in his hands.

"Callum Walker, why have you stopped?" Damostom asks.

The centaur backtracks from the elven convoy after noticing Callum's absence. His two warriors follow behind as always.

Callum realizes Damostom has been purposely watching him from a distance. He peers up at the looming centaur, intimidated by his impressive stature.

"I didn't want to say anything because it would just cause useless worry. I thought...if I could just make it to Havishire, then I'd be fine. Now, I'm not so sure," Callum says with a sigh, his weary shoulders slumping.

"There is something you must learn about centaurs," Damostom replies, staring at the injured warlock. "We have the gift of discernment, and it allows me to perceive your intense emotions, and thus, your distress. It is why I have been observing you so closely since we first met. I can sense your stubborn determination as well as your anguish and fading strength."

"Is it like an awareness of a person's energetic feelings?" Callum asks, recognizing something in the centaur's explanation.

"Yes," Damostom replies with surprise.

"Can you sense whether someone or something is powerfully evil?"

"Why do you ask this?" Damostom probes, cocking his head.

"Maybe it's intuition, but it feels like more than that. I've had this ability to sense evil and magic, and, if it's strong enough sentiment, emotions as well. It's not something that easy to explain."

Damostom considers this information, then finally responds. "I have not known any other humans before you. Do many of your kind possess this same gift?"

"Some people claim to, but it's difficult to prove, so no one really believes it exists. I imagine if there are people with this ability, they're keeping it a secret like I did."

Callum questioned this strange talent even more than the power of his magic—the two seemed unrelated. Now, he wonders how it is connected to the magical realm.

"How long has it been since receiving your injury?" asks Damostom, frowning with concern.

"It's three days old," Callum admits. He squints up at Damostom through his pounding headache and pulls the wool blanket tighter around his body to stave off the constant cold. "I'm already lightheaded and short of breath, and I can tell you right now I'm not going to make it to Havishire."

Damostom calmly scolds, "I wish you had told us this sooner, rather than trying to shield us from worry."

"I know. I'm sorry." Callum lowers his gaze to the ground, trembling from his fever.

"We are another two hours from the summit. Thalan plans to stop there and allow his soldiers to prepare a meal. Are you able to continue that far?" Damostom glances up, pursing his lips and contemplating the ascending switchback trail.

After resting for a short time, Callum feels marginally better but realizes that the moment he starts climbing again, his struggles will continue. The alternative is riding on the back of a centaur, and the thought of that is unsettling. Callum does not want to have his first riding lesson on the back of a Chieftain royal.

"I'll crawl if I have to," Callum groans and pushes himself upright. He wipes the sweat from his face with the blanket and begins the agonizing upward trudge yet again.

Damostom turns to his warriors and gives an urgent order. His guards nod, launching into a quick gallop. Both warriors race away and disappear up the craggy trail leading to the mountain's peak.

"They're in a big hurry," Callum grunts as he heaves himself up another step.

"I sent them ahead to Havishire Castle. Centaurs travel fast, so they should reach their destination in the next few hours. They will inform the queen of the dire state of your health, and help will be sent to meet us."

"I hope you're right about that."

Callum does not want to die, but the thought enters his mind several times while making the punishing climb. With his body failing, he is anxious about short-term survival.

Damostom stays alongside Callum through his painfully slow progress. They frequently stop to allow Callum to catch his breath and recover whatever strength he can.

It takes nearly twice as long as anticipated before they reach the top. Finally, they are greeted by friendly voices and inviting campfires spreading across a massive clearing. Luckily, the determined warlock defied the odds and reached the mountaintop.

At the summit, the trail ends at the mouth of a U-shaped valley formed in the crater of a dormant volcano. The southern and northern walls of the caldera have been blown away in an ancient eruption, and in its place is a gently sloping vale, framed on two sides by steep, jagged spires of rock.

A carpet of ankle-deep snow covers the dell, punctuated by crisscrossing footpaths and melting circular patches around several campfires. Three simple, log buildings sit in a neat row in the center of the valley. Soldiers file in and out, retrieving armloads of chopped firewood from the supply maintained within.

Clusters of elves rest near crackling fires, soaking up the heat and eating their fill of savory parsnip and potato soup. Patches of scruffy wild grass poke through the defrosted rings surrounding each bonfire.

"We will rest over there," Damostom says, pointing to the right of the main camp.

A lone figure squats before a small firepit, separated from the soldiers for ease of private conversation. Callum agrees and lets Damostom lead him along the snaking paths between camps. They ignore the disquiet gazes from several soldiers, suddenly aware of the warlock's haggard state.

When they reach the embracing warmth of the campfire, Callum meets Thalan once again. The mage is peacefully sipping a bowl of soup, but his expression fades to dismay the second he sets eyes on the warlock.

Callum is as pale as a corpse, and his hair and face are soaked with sweat. Staggering toward the fire for relief, Callum tries to sit but instead falls onto the soggy border of partly melted snow.

Thalan, forgetting his earlier charitability, looks to Damostom for an explanation. The warlock seemed to be in relatively fair condition only hours before, but now he appears ready to curl up and die.

"Callum revealed to me that his illness has become drastically worse since the morning," Damostom explains. "His wound is badly infected."

The centaur drops down on his front legs, tucking them under his body along with his back legs, and sits atop the edge of clean snow.

"I saw your warriors racing past. I assume you sent them ahead to seek aid?" Thalan asks as he observes Callum sitting near the fire and hugging the musty wool blanket around his shivering body.

Meanwhile, Callum blankly stares into the flames, only vaguely aware of the discussion and able to process an occasional word.

"It would take your men half a day to cross the same ground that my warriors can cover in little more than an hour. They should have arrived at the Havishire Castle by now. Hopefully, help is on its way as we speak," Damostom says.

"It's not polite to talk about someone when they're sitting next to you," Callum murmurs.

"Very well, then tell me, why did you minimize your illness?" Thalan asks, clearly irritated.

Callum briefly meets the mage's glare before turning his bloodshot eyes back to the dancing flames.

"I guess it's become a habit. I've been injured and sick before but just learned to deal with it quietly." Callum pauses for a moment to catch his breath. The simple effort required for speech is strenuous. "When you live alone, there's no one around to complain to, much less nurse you back to health."

Thalan and Damostom patiently listen as Callum pauses again, gasping and holding a hand to his aching chest.

"I wasn't being intentionally deceptive," Callum grunts.

As the centaur and mage appear increasingly doubtful of the warlock's survival, a distant shriek erupts from the cloudless sky.

"Well, it seems that fortune is smiling on you, Callum Walker," Damostom says with noticeable relief. "Help is arriving even sooner than expected."

The centaur nimbly unfolds his long, equine legs and rises to a standing position. Damostom's keen eyes track a pair of fast-flying forms against the backdrop of snowy peaks. Thalan rises to join the centaur in welcoming the aid.

Two mighty griffins soar over the flanking mountain ridges, their screeches resonating across the valley. Their eagle-like wings spread ten feet wide, countless feathers rippling as they descend in a racing dive into the crater valley. Then, pulling up effortlessly, they swoop over the campfires and touch down a short distance away.

Thalan remains with the warlock while Damostom breaks into a gallop. The centaur charges along the web of stamped trails toward the graceful and mythical beasts.

Having been told that speed was of the essence, the first rider hurriedly slides from her mount as Damostom approaches. She appreciatively touches the creature's head. Running her fingers over the silky feathers adorning its neck, she stops where the plumage changes to short tan fur across its rump and hind legs. The second rider dismounts and holds her griffin's harness, stroking the animal's plumed neck and wings.

"Are you Damostom?" the lead rider asks, urgently unstrapping medical supplies from behind her griffin's neck and stepping gracefully through the snow. Both aiding elves are strikingly beautiful. They look young, but the wisdom in their eyes contradicts this youthful appearance.

"Yes, I am Damostom. I trust that you are here in response to my request?" the centaur responds and politely bows.

"We are druids from Havishire Castle. We serve Queen Esme. Your centaurs reached our walls and relayed the news that one of your companions is near the threshold of death, and we are here to bring healing. I am Jobella, and this is my assistant Aralynn." Her companion dips her head, saying nothing.

"I am pleased that you have arrived with such haste. Come, I will lead you to your ward."

Callum sits hunching over a steaming meal of warm soup held in his lap. The tin bowl shakes in his trembling hands and, lacking any desire to eat, the warlock sniffs the appealing stew.

"He is human!" Jobella exclaims when she draws close enough to Callum's huddled form.

Callum shoots Jobella a look of irritation. "Sorry to disappoint you," he growls despite a dry, cracking voice.

"I apologize for my rudeness," Jobella says. Her pale cheeks blush with embarrassment, and she ruefully frowns. "I was not told that I was coming to help a human, and I apologize if you thought my words were insulting."

"If you save my life, we'll call it even," Callum fraily mutters and gives her a weak half-hearted grin.

Jobella kneels beside Callum, takes his bowl and sets it aside, then leans in to inspect the scabbed lacerations on his forehead. Her honey hair cascades in a wavy curtain over the thick furs covering her slim shoulders. Riding a griffin in winter must be an exhilarating but frigid exercise.

"What is your name?" Jobella quietly asks.

"You first," Callum croaks weakly.

The druid meets the warlock's glazed eyes. "My name is

Jobella Fairweather, and this is my compeer Aralynn." Jobella smiles pleasantly at him, dimpling both corners of her cherry-red lips. "We are druids trained in the healing arts."

"My name is Callum Walker," he finally offers. He is grateful that she was willing to introduce herself first without hesitation, and the chance of pace puts him at ease.

"Well, Callum, I need you to rest, so that I may restore your health."

He has no strength to protest when Jobella places her palm against his forehead and whispers an incantation. A warm sensation of peace envelops him, his pain is muted, and his eyelids grow too heavy to stay open. The last thing he sees is the lovely face of the druid elf and the concern in her glacial blue eyes. He falls into a dreamless sleep without realizing the healer is worried that her patient might not survive.

Jobella looks back over her shoulder and addresses the anxious mage. "Commander Thalan, I will need two of your soldiers to help with this man," Jobella bluntly demands.

"Whatever you need," Thalan agrees, turning away to wave a summon for his nearest troops.

The druid leaves the commander to relay her needs while gently lowering the unconscious warlock onto his back. She retrieves her satchel, and Aralynn spreads several blankets as near to the fire as possible.

"Aralynn, help me remove his coverings," urgency laces Jobella's words.

The two druids push the warlock's garment from his shoulders, open the blanket, and slide his arms free of his coat. Then, they place them under him as a barrier against the frozen ground. Jobella nervously glances at her druid sister when she catches sight of Callum's bloodstained shirt. Aralynn grimaces and nods in answer to their silent alarm.

"Is it treatable?" Damostom asks as Jobella lifts away the warlock's shirt to see the wound making Callum so desperately ill.

Jobella exhales a long, fretful sigh at the realization of Callum's grim condition. She pulls his shirt back down and answers the centaur with a somber gaze. Jobella slowly shakes her head, then wordlessly returns her attention to her ward.

"This injury is poisoning his body," Jobella observes while assisting Aralynn in cutting away the warlock's stained shirt with a dagger.

Once uncovered, Jobella leans over her unconscious patient's exposed shoulder to see the gruesome damage clearly. "It appears that someone tried to stitch it closed but did not disinfect the gash, so this treatment merely sealed the infection inside. He has shed a great deal of blood from this laceration, which may have worsened his condition. Now, the infection has spread into his blood."

"What does that mean?" Damostom presses, wholly unfamiliar with human physiology. His anxious frown suggests the centaur understands that her findings are not optimistic.

"It means he will die before morning unless I can immediately return him to Havishire. There is not much I can do here at the top of a mountain."

Jobella hates to deliver such a bleak forecast, but to say otherwise would be lying. She knew the extent of the danger as soon as she saw Callum's anemic pallor and inflamed wound.

"Do what you must, but this human is vital to the future of our entire realm," says Thalan, shifting his weight from side to side.

"I am aware of his importance, commander Thalan. My comrade and I will do everything within our abilities," Jobella acknowledges curtly, ignoring an uneasy pair of arriving soldiers gawking at her patient.

With the help of the two eleven troopers, Callum is moved close to the fire to maintain his body heat. Jobella deftly cuts out the remaining stitches and scrapes away the putrid flesh. Aralynn mixes and passes ointments, herbs, and dressings to her druid sister until the warlock's wound is cleaned, coated, and covered. He is swaddled in layers of blankets to prepare him for flight, then wrapped tightly with sturdy cords.

Jobella climbs aboard her mount and clicks her tongue as a signal for the creature to take flight. As they lift off into the night sky, the griffin carefully snatches the bound warlock. Thus, the hope of the magical realm is securely carried in the talons of her mighty griffin.

CHAPTER THIRTY-TWO

Callum slowly awakens to the weight of heavy blankets across his body. Only his head is uncovered, and for the first time in days, he is warm and comfortable. The last thing Callum recalls is sitting up near the heat of a bonfire in the mountain valley. He revels in this blessed relief, wanting to stay in the moment forever—until he realizes he is no longer lying on the ground.

His eyes spring open in alarm. Expecting to see the open sky above, Callum instead looks up at a canopy of delicate fabric supported an enormous four-poster bed frame. He attempts to sit up but recoils from the dull ache in his neck and shoulder that reminds him of his grievous injury.

"Son of a...," Callum starts to say, falling back on the bed. Then, after a few tense moments, he tentatively explores his wound. His fingertips discover soft fabric covering his neck. Although tender, Callum is relieved that his injury feels much less debilitating.

"How are you feeling?" a gentle voice inquires. Callum looks toward Jobella's voice. The druid walks across the unfamiliar room, carrying a wicker basket on her hip. "You had us all quite worried."

"Where am I?" Callum asks as he scans the spacious suite.

Jobella explains as she casually approaches his bedside, "You are at Havishire Castle. My fellow druid and I came to your aid and brought you back here to treat your infection."

"Havishire?" Callum murmurs, distracted by his remarkable bedchamber.

The four-poster bed sits against a stone wall and is decorated with elegant tapestries that mask its rough texture. A high ceiling caps the room, and opposite the bed, an elegant stone fireplace is framed by stained-glass windows that let in cascading sunlight. This room is twice as large as his entire apartment and is lavishly decorated.

"The queen has given you this guest room indefinitely," Jobella says, expansively gesturing with a telling nod.

Callum starts to push a load of blankets away but hastily yanks them back when he discovers that he is naked.

"Where are all my clothes?" he asks Jobella with a mortified expression.

Jobella smiles. She sets the wicker basket on top of his blankets. Investigating, Callum finds his cleaned and folded garments within.

"Your items desperately needed laundering and the castle tailor was able to mend them with some magic. Do you need help dressing?" Jobella asks with professional concern. "I can assist if you are still too sore to—."

"No!" Callum yelps, instantly regretting the sharpness of his tone.

Jobella straightens up, taken aback.

"Wh...what I mean is...I can dress myself, thank you," Callum stammers, offering an inadequate apology.

Callum averts his eyes and droops his head, trying but failing to hide his brightly blushing face. It finally dawns on him that this elven beauty has likely already seen him undressed.

The warlock is a fit and healthy young man with little reason to be embarrassed, but Callum is not a boaster or an exhibitionist. He lives a conservative lifestyle, private and introverted. His naked body is not something he willingly wants to share with strangers.

Jobella slyly smirks at his visible discomfort. "I will take that as a sign you are feeling better. Once you are dressed, the queen wishes to see you." Jobella offers this information with a polite curtsey, then promptly leaves.

Callum sits for a few minutes, rubbing his unexpectantly shaven face. Eventually, he rises and dresses, feeling far more comfortable once back in his hooded sweatshirt and jeans. Even his boots, socks, and underwear have been expertly cleaned. He leaves his jacket, cap, and gloves in the basket, making an educated guess that he will not be leaving the castle's protective walls. After he is clothed, Callum moves to one of the windows. Loosening the hook latch, he allows the pane to swing open. He is astonished to behold a medieval fortress city.

A large courtyard surrounds an enormous castle built with high, stone walls. Elven soldiers pace the wide walkways atop a protective barricade, encircling the keep and its sizable court-yard and connecting with a series of tower battlements. Armed with longbows, each elf carries a full quiver across their back. Barrels of arrows are strategically positioned along the causeway of this inner wall, filled to the brim with arrows to resupply during battle.

From his window, Callum overlooks the front of Havishire Castle. He feasts his eyes upon the low-lying town beyond the imposing castle barricade. The keep's inner sanctum is heavily guarded by armored elves. A gravel roadway passes through an iron and timber gateway, linking the settlement with the inner courtyard.

The sprawling lower town spans Callum's entire field of view, revealing densely packed buildings and houses. The distant edge of the township hugs an outer boundary wall that forms a ring to enclose the entire stronghold. Havishire's many turrets and battlements look down on an expansive, powdered white field, extending beyond the city boundaries and all the way to the edge of dense woodland.

Safely inside the city's sheltering ramparts, snow-covered furrows of dormant gardens await the arrival of spring. Everywhere Callum looks, people are moving around the lower town like roving ants. A well-guarded gatehouse, built into the exterior wall, controls the flow of people, animals, and carts entering and exiting Havishire. The soldiers not on guard practice their fighting skills and marksmanship on dummies in the castle's upper courtyard.

Callum closes the window and backs away. He sweeps his sights once more around the sumptuous room, stricken by how radically distorted and out of control his life has become. Callum feels like a stranger in this magical realm, but everyone here seems to know and revere him. This both perplexes and concerns him.

Jobella told him the queen wants to see him, and Callum waits for an escort to arrive. However, after nearly an hour, he grows tired of being at the mercy of someone else's schedule. The warlock decides to explore the castle on his own rather than restlessly bide his time.

Stepping outside his room, Callum is greeted by a stone-walled corridor lined with wooden benches. Small tables hold candle lanterns, and flags adorn the walls between recessed door-ways. Any elves who happen upon him in the hall regard him with curiosity before hurrying past. Callum ignores the overcautious inhabitants and randomly picks a direction to begin his exploration.

The warlock heads toward an open door at the end of his straight passageway and a narrow stairway beyond. Distant voices rise from below, so he ascends the gloomy stairwell instead, hoping to avoid other castle residents and intrigued leers.

His path is illuminated only by daylight filtering through slit windows as the steps wind upward in a tight spiral and end at a closed door. Having ventured this far, Callum tries the door expecting it to be locked. Surprisingly, it opens.

He steps onto a balcony overlooking a grand sitting room below. A massive fireplace and crackling hearth invite his presence, and a cluster of chairs are arranged around a low, circular table beside it. Callum wanders along the mezzanine, glancing over his shoulders at the door as though afraid it might disappear and leave him trapped. He eventually finds a staircase at the far end that leads down to the main floor.

Descending, Callum marvels at the sitting room's prominent feature—a wall of bookcases beneath the overhanging balcony laden with hundreds of volumes. He eagerly scans some of the titles and discovers that the collection represents a priceless trove of knowledge related to this realm and the magic contained within it. Callum is so absorbed with inspecting the repository of precious information that he does not hear the light footsteps approaching from behind.

"I am happy to see you are on the mend," a quiet voice says.

Callum spins and stumbles back against the shelves, knocking several ancient archives and scrolls to the floor. "You scared the shit out of me," Callum blurts before remembering to place a filter on his human words.

The female elf before him is clothed in elegant, draping fabrics of royal purple with intricate gold embroidery. The elf's fine-boned cheeks flush, and her hands reach automatically to fiddle with a dazzling, jeweled tiara adorning braids of flaxen hair. Though appearing flustered, she maintains an impassive yet regal demeanor.

Callum cringes at his use of profanity in such company. "I'm so sorry," Callum says, turning from the elf's expressionless scrutiny to retrieve the books he tumbled to the floor.

"No, forgive me," she replies. "You were seen heading to this library, and I hurried to meet you here. It was not my intention to frighten you. You may call me Esme. I am queen of the Northern Kingdom." She bends down to help him gather up the books. "I have anxiously followed your progress, and I was very pleased to hear that you were finally awake."

"Finally awake? How long have I been asleep?" Callum asks as he takes the precious volumes Esme passes to him and tucks them back onto the shelf.

"It has been three days since you were brought here." Esme stands and gestures with her hand toward the armchairs, then gracefully strolls toward the hearth and selects a seat close to the fire.

Callum pauses, trying to absorb the fact that he was unconscious for so long. Then, shaking his head in disbelief, he follows her and settles onto a comfortable arm seat facing the queen. He absentmindedly scratches at the bandages that cover his healing wound.

"We have waited many years for your arrival," Queen Esme says, observing the warlock as he intently stares at the fire. Esme hardens her gaze when she realizes he is barely listening to her words. "Your journey here has been burdensome."

"That's putting it mildly," Callum huffs sarcastically.

Despite his royal hostess, the warlock finds himself glancing around at the massive oak trusses and other architectural features. The castle's ancient stones and timbers carry the aura of centuries witnessed within these walls. The result is a strong impression of both history and permanence.

"Though this is not our usual custom, I needed to know that you were indeed the one foretold to us," Queen Esme adds, clearing her throat and lowering her eyes to her lap. "I must admit that I have seen some of your memories, and I am convinced that you are the beacon of hope we have all been waiting for."

"You read my mind while I was sleeping?" Callum asks, flashing her an angry glare and raising his voice. The familiar discomfort of being exposed invades his thoughts—like when Agis had done the same. "I'm just an open book to you then."

He wonders if anyone in elven society has ever heard of

human rights. Instead, everyone sees him as their salvation from this war rather than a man entitled to his own privacy.

"I should never have invaded your mind in that way," Esme apologizes. She inhales deeply to settle her nerves and continues, "But I believed it was necessary under the circumstances."

Callum sharply exhales and slouches in his chair. He hates what Esme did, but what is done is done, and he knows he must find a way to live with it.

"So, if you know everything about me, then you know I'm not a fan of this damn prophecy. But I'm done running from it. I just want this to be over so I can move on. Maybe get rid of the enemies I seem to be collecting unintentionally," he says, scowling at Esme and trying to control his outrage. He needs to bury his anger. There is work to be done.

"I am not as skilled as Commander Agis, so I did not get a complete picture. But I did experience your frustration at the vagueness of the prophecy and your perceived lack of control. It was also apparent how much you despise public adulation."

"And how do you expect me to feel?"

"I would feel honored to have such a powerful gift, knowing that the high gods chose me to liberate the entire world. You should feel privileged that your presence inspires hope. I do not understand your discomfort at receiving such worthy attention. Our world has been suffering for years, victims systematically killed or tortured by both sides of the quarrel. We are outnumbered and scattered across the Earth, alone and afraid just like you." Esme focuses her gaze on her tightly interlaced fingers as though struggling with these difficult facts.

"When the fairies announced that the warlock had been discovered, everyone took heart and began to follow your trail. You think they abandoned you, but they tried to protect you. An hour after you were returned to your own city, Kincaid attacked the fairy village. He followed your unique energy signature and crossed the veil searching for you, but Consul Daphne knew he was coming. She sent you away to protect your life and used her remaining minutes to send a message to the other races, including the mountain elves."

"Frey...," Callum gasps, sitting bolt upright. He instantly feels surging panic and prays that she was safely away from the fairy community before the attack.

"I know some of the survivors made it to our doors—along with others from Ursona who were willing to assist us in our war efforts. I do not know all their names, only that there were many casualties, and several inhabitants of the hamlet are still missing."

Callum leans forward and hides his face in his hands. "I had no idea."

He chokes back his terror at the possibility of having lost his first and dearest friend. Guilt sears him like a flame, and he regrets blaming the fairies who tried to save his life.

"There is something I need to show you, Callum Walker," Esme says, abruptly changing the subject. Rising from her chair, the queen moves toward a door beyond the staircase. She stops halfway across the room and turns, waiting for Callum to follow.

CHAPTER THIRTY-THREE

The extent of Castle Havishire's labyrinth of corridors and passageways is staggering. Callum is soon lost, so he trails close behind the Elven Queen. Some of the hallways are lined with tall, rectangular windows, letting in curtains of light that reflect off polished stone floors. Other passages are windowless and dark, surrounded by ancient black granite burnished smooth by skilled craftsmen. The variety of materials used in construction show that the castle is a continuously expanding domain, and Callum speculates that new sections were added by successive generations of monarchs.

Callum sees others roaming the castle, always stopping to bow or curtsy in tribute to their queen. Most of the courtiers and servants are elves, but he begins to spot other races as they continue.

When the pair finally cease their course, both are standing at a marble railing, looking down at a large, open hall. There are nearly fifty mythical humanoids and various other beings milling in the space. The volume of their voices is magnified by the rafters.

Callum had no idea there were so many different societies in the magical realm, all hidden from human detection by the invisible veil between worlds. Thanks to his research, he recognizes fairies—both human-sized and tiny sprites like Frey—centaurs, elves, dwarves, nymphs, gnomes, and many more. Recognizing the pretentious expressions, extravagant clothing, and inflexible, uptight postures, Callum realizes this is a room of courtiers. Several elven servants weave through the crowd, carrying trays of fluted glasses and elaborate morsels of food.

The collection of so many fantastic, sentient creatures is mind-boggling to Callum, and he stares down at them all in awe.

"These are the leaders of the various dynasties spread across the magical realm. They are here because of *you*," Queen Esme says, studying the warlock's reaction to the stunning assembly.

"They're here to fight along with me?"

"You are their universal symbol of hope. All of them have suffered from this war, in one way or another, and so many more have died. Your existence creates renewed faith, and your presence in Havishire allows me to draw them here from their various domains. This has not happened for nearly two hundred years. Not since the last great war, when my own father rallied the realm and defeated the armies of the south."

"But I don't have the power to stop this war," Callum sighs. Then, turning away from the crowd, he leans against the railing and crosses his arms over his chest.

"Why do you think you were born with your gifts?" Esme probes. "Why did you decide to start hunting monsters in the night?"

"Because no one else could," Callum says, shrugging at her questions.

"It is because your nature is to fight for those who cannot protect themselves."

"I haven't been very successful in that department," Callum says with more than a hint of cynicism.

"You forget that I have seen a portion of your life through your own eyes. I saw someone who has been beaten but comes away stronger and wiser. We cannot learn if we do not fail at first, and we cannot progress if we are not challenged," Esme explains, raising her energetic voice as she speaks. "I have seen you do extraordinary things that even our most accomplished mages cannot."

"I've never trained like your mages. I don't have the same level of mastery." Callum casts her a dubious look.

"From what I have seen, I suspect you are far stronger than you realize. When you are not restricted by your own fears, you can unleash that power at unimaginable levels. Now is not the time for uncertainty," Esme lectures, her uplifted tone drawing the attention of the throng below.

Callum fails to notice the chatter in the great hall slowly diminishing and the eyes peering upward to the balcony.

Some of what she says mirrors Liam's comments about Callum's reservations, making it harder for him to deny Esme's observations.

"Every leader here brings a contingent of military forces to add to my own, ensuring an end to this conflict. You are much more than words etched on a scroll. You are a human gifted with immeasurable arcane energies. You only have to believe in yourself the way others do to see your full potential."

Applause resonates from the crowd below, and it jolts Callum from the railing. Hesitantly, he turns and looks down at the assembly of well-dressed dignitaries and military officials whose attentions are focused on them.

"It is fitting that the human race, which the deities have ordered to be left in peace, will now aid in our protection," Esme addresses the crowd, smiling regally in response to the cheers. She places a firm hand on Callum's right shoulder to encourage him while also preventing him from retreating. She pauses until the chorus of praise ebbs. "This human warlock was born with the power of magic, and he has survived difficult trials, injury, and near-death. He has grown stronger in his wisdom. Although he is not of this realm, Callum Walker has proven himself virtuous by serving and protecting the innocent. Fate led him to us in this time of urgent need as our enemies march toward our doorstep. But now, with his support and the assurance of the prophecy, we can trust in our preordained victory."

"What!" Callum exclaims, gawping at Esme and shouting to be heard over the renewed wave of cheering rising from the lower level.

The decorated officials, many holding ornate chalices of wine and other multi-hued beverages, are entertained and enthralled by the queen's address. A mere wave of her hand is adequate to return the celebrants to their private gala. The rising hum of energized voices and clinking goblets rises above the hall below.

"I wanted you to see this, Callum. I was hoping to inspire your confidence by showing you this coalition of support." Esme turns to Callum with concern on her delicate face. "I brought you to Havishire because this fortification was built to withstand many battles. I believe Havishire is predestined to be the place where this war will be fought and won, and I will lead the final charge. As we speak, Kincaid's forces are reported to be moving in from the south while his brother approaches from the north. With the addition of reinforcements from across the realm, Havishire will withstand the advance of our dual enemies."

"They're coming because *I'm* here," mutters Callum. He retreats just beyond her reach, pacing several steps and shaking his head.

After a few moments, Callum stops. He looks down at the sea of hopeful faces inspired by Queen Esme's words. Callum recalls the thousands of innocent elves sheltering in Havishire's lower levels. What can he possibly do to help all of them?

"We know the brothers are hunting you, and that is precisely why you were guided here. All the events of the past weeks have combined to bring you to this location. This is where you can refine the required skills to fulfill your destiny," Esme says, trying to reassure Callum.

Callum understands the logic in Queen Esme's words. A chain of tragic events that, at face value, appear to be completely random have, in fact, led him to this location at this time. He was spared from death on multiple occasions, and he doubts that anyone can really be that lucky. Or maybe he is just a pawn to be manipulated in an almighty game of life and death.

"How long do I have to prepare?" Callum asks with a scowl, clenching his fists and tensing his body. It is hard to accept the reality that he must sacrifice himself to save the worlds on both sides of the veil. But he must try, even if he fails because doing nothing would be so much worse.

"They will be here in two days."

"Can you allow me some time alone?" Callum asks, resolute in his course of action, whether it is preordained by ancient prophecy or not.

"Of course," Esme replies.

She watches apprehensively as Callum stomps away and disappears around a corner.

Callum understands that Esme is hopeful he will find his conviction. All their lives depend on him and his gifts, and he must be ready to step up. Otherwise, all will be lost.

CHAPTER THIRTY-FOUR

A s expected, Callum loses his way while wandering the gray, stone hallways. However, he is rarely alone, passing castle residents and occasional pampered visitors. Most of them stare in surprise or quickly skitter away as the warlock marches past. When he steps through the same bright lounging room for a second time, Callum realizes that he is moving in a circle.

Exasperated, he drops onto a simple padded bench built into the sill of a recessed window. Sitting sideways, he leans against the wall, pulls one leg up, and drapes his forearm over his bent knee. The spot affords him a perfect view of the castle's courtyard, and he is finally alone.

The yard is covered with snow, packed flat by hours of foot traffic. From his vantage point, Callum can see a row of straw-filled sacks hung as targets and a handful of elven archers and dwarven ax throwers diligently practicing their aim. There is competition between the two races, visible in the stiff postures of the nimble elves and the stern faces of the port dwarves. The elves are professional and deliberate, striking their targets with calm poise, while the dwarves are loud and boisterous, cheering enthusiastically whenever they hit their mark. Both races appear irritated by the behavior of the other. This alliance he is said to have inspired between magical creatures may be an uneasy alliance.

Callum looks to the door at the sound of clomping footsteps. He hopes it is just another wandering castle visitor. Then, when the door swings open, he is dismayed at being denied the solitude he craves.

Damostom ducks his head beneath the top of the door frame as he enters. Upon discovering Callum, he ambles across the room to share the view from the window.

"When you are the only human in Havishire, you cannot go very far without being noticed," Damostom correctly observes. A reassuring smiling stretches across his face. "Although I am pleased you are recovering your health, I can sense you are deeply troubled."

Callum scoffs and resumes staring out the window for several moments before speaking.

"I always thought I had choices in my life. I thought I made the decision to use my powers to fight monsters before I even knew this realm existed or chose to take a stand against Quinn and Kincaid." He feels the heaviness of his obligation like a crushing weight. "Now, I realize that everything I've ever done has been planned without my knowledge."

"Centaurs believe we are all given a unique purpose in life, but it is still our decision to follow that path," Damostom replies. He pauses near the window and peers down at the burdened young man.

"You don't need to worry." Callum casts the centaur a telling sideways glance. "I'll do whatever I can to help protect these people if I can ever find my way around this damn castle."

Damostom laughs heartily at the unexpected joke.

Callum smiles for the first time in a long while and is relieved to share a cheerful moment.

"You look much better with a smile on your face."

Callum grins. "Yeah, it feels better. Now, if I could just get people to stop staring at me."

"Most of the people of this realm have only ever heard stories about humans. You may have to get used to their curiosity and attention," Damostom replies wisely.

The centaur helps Callum navigate the castle, pointing out hidden markers and tapestries that can be used as signposts. Particular wings of the castle display gleaming coats of armor along their walls, while others use red or blue in their tapestries. Using this method, Callum develops a mental map of the castle complex. He even finds his way back to his bedchamber, where he collects his coat.

Damostom directs Callum to the courtyard, showing him the entire grounds and its different training rings and weapon racks. Soldiers of many races are fine-tuning their distinctive fighting techniques. Archers and crossbowmen focus on target practice, and small groups are working on close-combat battle skills. Callum is invited to train in the arenas, but physical combat is not his strong point, so he declines.

Instead, Damostom leads him across the yard to a row of straw dummies where the Elves and Dwarves are still hotly competing.

They abandon their raucous rivalry when Callum approaches. Stepping back to make room, both groups watch Callum, wondering if the unremarkable human before them is actually the mighty warlock.

As he contemplates the line of straw targets impaled on the posts, Callum pauses to appreciate, for the first time, that he can now openly use his gifts rather than secretly wielding magic.

He grins at this new freedom and plants his feet, shifting his weight into a strong stance. His arm extends toward the canvas dummies, palms outward. Then, without uttering a word, an intense white light erupts from his fingertips and expands as it dances across the practice field. The magical energy destroys all the targets simultaneously, delivering such force that dummies and poles explode into a shower of smoldering debris.

No longer skeptical, the Elves and Dwarves are dumbstruck by what they see.

Damostom is also amazed to witness the unfettered power of Callum's arcane energies. Having only ever seen the warlock as frail and sick, the centaur gawks in surprise at the devastating ability the warlock possesses. Damostom motions to the audience of warriors to replace the targets with fresh ones.

Callum watches the pieces of charred hay drift down to Earth, marveling at the destruction he is capable of when he removes his inhibitions.

It is a novel moment, allowing him time to wonder at the magical strength within himself. Just like the ashes drifting in the frosty air, Callum's self-doubt fades. For the first time in his life, he comprehends this gift of power and feels confident in his ability to survive this war.

CHAPTER THIRTY-FIVE

C allum diligently trains over the next few hours, attracting an enthralled audience eager to watch him dispatch each target with unique and devastating spells. He quickly runs out of straw dummies, so he conjures various objects and blasts each one to oblivion. Repetition increases proficiency, and Callum discovers no need to raise an arm to direct his arcane energy. Instead, he directs pulses of power from his chest as though the magic originates from his beating heart, only controlling the force with concentrated thoughts. He ignores the draining effects of his extended magical practice session, and even Callum's rumbling stomach and pounding head are paid scant notice. Headaches, hunger pains, and fatigue can be managed. However, an untimely death cannot be conquered, so it is far more critical to expend energy improving his efficiency and skill.

The warlock practices into the evening hours, freely employing more strength than he ever used before. Dusk crackles with sparks of blue lightning, streams of exploding coral fire, and soaring orbs of vivid violet light.

As darkness settles, each spell causes a hot aching sensation in his chest, as though the energy burns from within. Callum experienced this once before when he attacked the vampires. On that occasion, he ignored the sensation, and it quickly faded. This experience is different, expending magical energy over a long period and with increasing intensity. Callum's heart hammers so forcefully that, on occasion, he needs to pause to recover, holding his chest and gulping the winter air. Thankfully, the moderate distress soon passes.

The thought of stopping his training session occurs, but this is war, and his enemy will not wait for him to recover. Callum pushes himself past the burning pain, bouncing back as fast as possible and then launching another volley of attacks. He becomes quicker and more accurate with every spell, so the warlock is pleased to have achieved major progress when he finally ends his practice.

Callum's talents and power solidify his standing as the human warlock destined to save the realm. The dispersing crowd spreads tales throughout Havishire, planting the seeds of a new legend and affirming the warlock's status as their divinely appointed savior. Callum still has reservations about ending the conflict, but he no longer doubts his power.

"How did you learn to engage your target without speaking?" Damostom quietly asks while following Callum's weary trudge back to the castle.

"It was the vampires who helped me uncover that skill. I needed to defend myself, but I couldn't speak. So, I just visualized what I needed, and it happened." Callum shrugs his shoulders as though it is not extraordinary.

"What you have mastered usually takes centuries to learn, if ever," Damostom tells him. "You seem to have greatly enhanced your skills over the past few hours."

"I've always suppressed my power, but today, I didn't hold back at all."

"You appeared to be struggling at times, having to rest after each attack," says Damostom, thoughtfully eyeing him.

Callum recognizes the centaur's concern, but it is futile to deny the discomfort he felt during his training.

"You're right. The strong magic is tiring. It makes my chest burn, and I have to recover for a few minutes until the pain fades," Callum admits, automatically downplaying its severity. His chest still stings where his shirt brushes the skin, but he ignores the irritation. To lessen the friction caused by contact, he slouches his shoulders. "Might be due to my recent infection. I'm still recuperating."

"You should let Jobella know of your distress. She may be able to help," Damostom suggests.

"I might just do that." Callum nods in agreement.

Damostom escorts Callum through more of the castle, ensuring that he makes it safely to his chamber. The room had been tidied. The bed is now made, a welcoming fire glows in the hearth, and an assortment of food platters wait on a small side table near a comfortable couch.

Sunset is long past, leaving firelight as the room's sole source of illumination. Famished from the day of training, Callum sinks onto the cushions and devours a simple repast of bread, cheese, roast venison, and fruit. Gazing into the flickering embers, the warlock experiences a sense of calm. By choosing to engage himself in this imminent battle, he finally balances his life's purpose with his actions.

Despite the warmth from the fireplace, the chamber is uncomfortably chilly, so Callum climbs into bed fully dressed and wraps the blankets and quilts around himself. It takes more than an hour to calm his busy thoughts and drift into unsettling dreams.

Even from the depths of sleep, Callum senses the profound presence of someone in his room. No sounds reveal an intrusion, only the rising awareness of his sixth sense alerting him to the aura of strong magic.

Jolted awake, he throws off the blankets and springs from his bed. Cursing the near darkness, Callum rapidly blinks, willing his eyes to adjust to the dim moonlight and dying firelight. He hears nothing but his own startled breathing yet instinctively knows he is not alone.

Callum retreats from his bedside. Drawing on his memory of the room, he backs away until he feels a cold, stone wall behind him. The intruder can now only be somewhere in front of him.

"I know you're here," Callum says, squinting into the murk.

Callum raises his right hand from his side, readying his magic to cast an illuminating orb.

Before he can summon his own beacon, a surge of yellow fire suddenly flashes in the hearth and paints the walls in dancing patterns of light.

Callum instinctively shields his eyes against the instant brightness but quickly lowers his hand to reduce his vulnerability. Scanning the room, he spots the figure of a man sitting in a fireside armchair. A heavy black cloak with a hood ensures the man's face remains hidden in shadow.

"Would you please have a seat?" the intruder asks with unexpected politeness. He motions with his arm to the empty chair across the hearth.

"Who are you?" Callum refuses to move.

He swallows hard, fighting a feeling of deep foreboding from the undeniable evil energy that radiates from the intruder.

"You offend me," says the stranger. His voice carries mock disappointment. The figure casually crosses his legs and brushes the creases from his cloak. "You live a dangerous life, Callum Walker, if you don't even recognize your own enemies."

The man waits for Callum to interpret the meaning of his derision.

Panic surges at realizing that this formidable nemesis penetrated Havishire's defenses unopposed and entered Callum's sanctum undetected.

"David Kincaid," Callum utters.

"Very good, Walker," Kincaid answers in a condescending tone. He lowers his hood, exposing a face appearing much older than Callum expected. The necromancer's cropped, gray beard and buzz cut mask his partial baldness. Dark circles around Kincaid's sunken eyes melt into the creases of his withered face. His piercing black gaze is the only thing that betrays his hateful soul. Kincaid looks like a man suffering the draining effects of dark magic, wielding it too often over too many years. His gaunt, bony body shows the physical outcome of such abuse.

"What are you doing here?" Callum furiously glares at the trespasser.

"Relax, Walker. I'm not here to hurt you," Kincaid says indifferently. "I merely came to meet the warlock that has given my brother and me so much grief."

Kincaid again waves his hand at the unoccupied chair. Callum takes a deep, wavering breath and crosses the room to take a seat. The necromancer smirks at the warlock's reluctant cooperation.

"Now, let's talk about this prophecy," Kincaid begins, interlacing his fingers and resting his hands in his lap. "It says that you will end this war, and that is an outcome I can fully support. When Desmond is dead, this war will indeed come to an end."

"What about you?" Callum asks with caution. "What will you do if Quinn is no longer opposing you?"

"Not that it should matter to you, but I intend to rid this realm of all the weak and useless beings that currently reign over it. Once they're gone, I can repopulate this side of the veil with my own creations," Kincaid says nonchalantly. He smiles as though thrilled to play his godlike role.

"No offense, but the people residing here are entitled to keep their homes and lives," says Callum, skewering Kincaid with his eyes.

"You *would* say that. I've heard that you're a man of high morals, fighting for the safety and freedom of the helpless. But my plans shouldn't concern you. Your crusade is focused solely on ending the conflict, and the prophecy does not extend beyond its conclusion."

Callum is dumbstruck by Kincaid's audacity. "I don't care what's written in the prophecy or what it alleges. I won't let you destroy this world so you can rebuild it in your own distorted image."

"Just how do you plan on stopping me?" Kincaid narrows his eyes, mocking Callum's admirable challenge. "I've had years to refine my arcane skills, and I've had great sages to educate me. What can you do that I can't?"

Nothing Kincaid said is a lie, so Callum is left feeling disadvantaged and clueless about how to stop him.

When Callum has nothing to offer in the way of a retort, Kincaid continues to speak, "It seems to me that you are just a terrified young man who's in way over his head."

Callum suspects Kincaid is hiding something, sensing emotional turmoil concealed beneath his facade. "Then why go to all this trouble to visit me?" he asks.

"I came to offer you another option," Kincaid says smoothly as he studies the young warlock's face. "Surrender yourself to me now, and I'll turn my creations on Desmond's army that advances from the north. I give you my word that I'll leave Havishire untouched."

"What do you want with me?" asks Callum, feeling fear boiling within to rival his already potent anger.

"Well, I want to kill you, of course. It's foretold that I will be defeated by you, but if I destroy you first, that destiny will never come to pass. If you submit freely, I'll make it quick and painless. But if my brother seizes you, I promise that your death will be a long and agonizing process."

For the briefest moment, Callum senses the necromancer's emotional mask lowering, and his disguised fear is finally revealed. It is only a glimpse, hardly more than a facial twitch, but just enough that the warlock understands what Kincaid keeps hidden.

"You're afraid of my potential power. You've heard about my growing capabilities, so you've come to entice me into giving myself up," says Callum as he connects the pieces of the puzzle.

Kincaid's instantly tenses and glares at Callum. "How dare you suggest that I possess such weakness. I am the one to be feared!" Kincaid pompously proclaims. Savage outrage stretches the creases of his face and causes his eyes to glow unnaturally red.

"I won't abandon these people. I'll do everything in my power to see you and your brother defeated," Callum says firmly.

He stands and faces his adversary with wrath equal to Kincaid's. Callum blasts a wave of white magic forward from his chest. The necromancer tries to defend himself but is not quick enough to avoid being thrown backward out of his chair.

"You'll pay for this mistake with your life and all of those lives that you've sworn to protect," Kincaid hisses and slowly regains his feet. "*Reditus!*"

Callum shields his eyes against a brilliant flash of purple light that envelopes the necromancer. Kincaid vanishes without a trace when it fades, and Callum's awareness of the intruding presence is also gone.

The warlock collapses back into his chair, dead tired and hurting from his attack on Kincaid. Renewed pain burns within his chest and the area over his heart feels raw to the touch. Callum lifts the front of his shirt and sees a blistering second-degree burn, the size of a quarter. The price his body must pay to use his magical weapons.

The crimson patch covers the spot on his chest directly over his heart. Angry red lines streak outward from the central site of where his power exits his upper body. Callum's pounding heart slowly returns to a normal rhythm, but the exertion leaves him lightheaded. The warlock lowers his shirt and tries to ease his frayed nerves.

Slumping back in his seat, Callum dazedly stares at the overturned chair and wonders what he should do about this new hindrance. He has not seen Jobella since the previous morning, and he has no idea where she resides within the castle.

Callum eventually buries his concerns. After all, there is little he can do at this moment. He will have to wait and seek out Jobella first thing in the morning.

Carefully stoking the fireplace, the warlock returns to bed. Yet, he is not able to turn off the racing thoughts that plague his mind. He is confident Kincaid will not return after experiencing the brunt of Callum's attack. Alone in his chamber, the warlock stares at the flickering firelight dancing across the ceiling until he finally feels his eyelids grow heavy. Soon after, he succumbs to a fitful sleep.

The warlock's rest and recovery are short-lived. Minutes after Callum's eyes close, the castle is rocked by an explosion. A large mirror falls and shatters into hundreds of sparkling shards, and a shower of grit and dust cascades from the ceiling.

For the second time that night, Callum bolts out of bed, knowing the castle must be under attack, and he has a good idea about who is behind it.

CHAPTER THIRTY-SIX

A s Callum hurries through the main corridors of the castle, a buzz of frenzied activity surrounds him. Continuing volleys of explosive strikes rattle the castle walls, panicking hundreds of frantic servants and guests. Everywhere he goes, clouds of dust rain down from shaken ceilings. He must be vigilant to avoid falling paintings, tapestries, and displays of shining armor that crash violently to the floor with every fresh impact. After some time, the initial chaos among castle residents subsides as trained muscle memory restores order.

While Callum rushes through the network of passages, the scramble to reach assigned stations continues until the halls start to empty. The warlock has no clear idea of where he wants to go, so he stops. Leaning over to catch his breath, Callum listens to hostile sounds outside the castle.

Peering through a tall window, he sees smoke rising and the ominous glow of fire ravaging throughout the lower town. Callum knows people are dying and buildings are being destroyed, but he is helpless to assist anyone without information or direction.

Suddenly, a dark form enters his field of view. The obsidian creature soars above Havishire with massive bat-like wings and prepares to deliver another onslaught.

"You've got to be kidding me," Callum says, unable to believe his eyes. Recognizing the monster as a flesh-and-blood dragon, spouting fire and destruction on the helpless inhabitant, he now knows exactly where he needs to be.

Callum is thankful for Damostom's tour and tips on navigating the maze of hallways, but plotting a course is much more challenging while debris continues to fall. Racing down a long hallway, Callum finally sees what he needs—a stairwell leading up to high ground. He maneuvers through heaps of wreckage in his path, clambering over crumbled stonework and broken beams. The warlock is halfway to his goal when a tremendous rumbling resonates throughout the castle.

Significant cracks begin to form in the stonework above his head, and Callum quickens his pace. The ceiling starts to collapse with a deafening roar, and he dives the last few steps to reach the stairwell. A choking dust cloud fills the air. Callum coughs violently but is alive. He scrambles to his feet and scales the spiral staircase two steps at a time, confident he located the correct route.

His choice is confirmed when he reaches the top of a castle tower and enters the center of a circular room. Slits in the perimeter walls are occupied by archers launching a haze of arrows whenever the dragon flies within range. Elven shouts bounce between the soldiers spotting for the archers.

No one seems to notice Callum's arrival amid the commotion, allowing him time for a hasty look around. He sees an open archway that exits onto a gangway extending along the length of a peaked roof. The open pathway connects with an identical turret tower one hundred feet away. No one is fighting on the exposed causeway, so Callum decides it will offer a clear view of his reptilian target.

He darts, unnoticed, across the turret room and through the

archway. From this elevated platform near the very top of the castle, Callum assesses the battle zone around him.

The blaze consuming the lower town still spreads uncontrollably, and the offensive against the castle has demolished much of the spired towers and uppermost floors of the eastern wings of the keep. Gaping holes in the ancient stone walls reveal fires burning within. Perched above the southern border of the keep, Callum looks north to see another turret tower, this one decimated, leaving only rubble and crushed bodies in the smoldering wreckage.

An earsplitting shriek cuts through a smoke-choked sky, and Callum spins to see the dragon circling over the lower town. The mighty winged serpent spits a gout of fire from its yawning mouth at tinder-dry rooftops as it dives, engulfing dozens of hysterical residents fleeing the inferno. Havishire's citizens are being indiscriminately slaughtered by the merciless monster.

Callum is both sickened and enraged by the carnage. He leans over the waist-high wall of the rampart, locking his knees against the coarse sandstone to keep from falling. Watching the sky, he tracks the creature's upward swoop after unleashing its lethal barrage. Callum's thoughts churn with violence before he suddenly chooses a spell and jabs both open hands toward the swarthy beast.

A sphere of silvery light leaps from Callum's hands, tearing through the air and exploding against the dragon's scaly shoulder and powerful wings. A raw, bleeding ulcer shows the magical strike's damage, and the serpent screams in agony. It loses altitude as it writhes and shrieks, yet it does not fall to its doom from the grimy sky. Managing to recover, the dragon beats its great wings and rises into the air once more, madly searching for the source of this unexpected attack.

"Oh, shit," Callum whispers in alarm when the airborne monster inevitably locks eyes on him.

It screeches in fury, slobbering flames like huge drops of acid, and it surges toward the rampart where the exposed warlock stands.

Callum pushes off the wall and runs for the nearest tower but abruptly stops when he realizes the turret will offer no real sanctuary from the angry dragon. His attempt to hide would condemn the elven soldiers within to a fiery death. Callum's only option is to face the demon reptile and defeat it.

The soaring lizard folds its wings back and dives at its prey, taking a deep breath and spewing fire. Then, planting his feet in a wide stance, Callum raises both arms and conjures an arcane, dome-shaped shield.

An invisible wall now protects the exposed pathway and extends beyond the towers. The energy shields those around him from the deadly flames.

Callum feels the intense heat radiating from the liquid fire. It flows over his protective magic, and he instinctively closes his eyes and turns his face away from the scorching temperature.

The aerial assault lasts until the dragon sweeps over the rampart, but its belly connects with the unseen magical barrier. The beast screams in rage and pain as the energy field rips a swath of flesh from its exposed underbelly. The dragon's guts spill across Callum's invisible shield and slide down its curved surface in a gory cascade. Dazed by the impact, Callum is knocked back into the bulwark and doubles over the railing. He looks down upon the dragon's fall and destruction.

The ravaged beast's torn and bleeding corpse plummets, its massive form smashing the smoldering crowns of the rooftops. Already aglow with radiant consuming light, the body of the conjured beast crashes down in a deafening thunder of splintering timber and crumbling stonework. Before it comes to a halt, its mutilated body evaporates into ashes and floats away.

Callum slips to the stone floor, clutching his chest against the burning agony. The warlock's heart beats so fast that it takes his breath away, and he is barely aware of the rejoicing elves rushing toward him. He loses consciousness before they arrive.

"Callum, you *must* wake up," one of the elves says, gently shaking him by the shoulder.

Realizing that someone is calling his name, Callum flutters his eyes open and looks up at a circle of worried elves returning his bewildered gaze. Suddenly overcome by nausea, Callum then rolls to one side and vomits the remnants of his dinner, much to the disgusted shock of a dozen soldiers.

Hauled from the floor, the warlock is helped over to the rampart's wall, where he can sit against the stonework to recover his wits and his dignity.

"What happened?" he asks weakly, resting his head against the wall while draping his leaden arms across his lap.

Although Callum's pulse returned to normal, he feels a deep aching in his heart and lungs, plus a caustic stinging over his sternum. His head spins with persistent dizziness.

"You defeated the dragon!" yells an immensely relieved, gray-haired elf. He appreciatively smiles as others nod their thanks for Callum's selfless victory. "You fell into darkness after that monster struck your magic wall. But not before you tore his belly wide open."

"Did it work? Was I able to protect the towers from the fire?" Callum asks, grimacing as he coughs. He clearly recalls his magical tactic but is still hazy about the result.

"Yes. Your shield kept the flames away from the entire southern roofline. You saved us all," another joyful elf responds.

A great pall of iron-gray smoke hangs over Havishire. Cheers ring out among the elves as they dance in celebration, silhouetted by distant red flames marking the dragon's murderous rampage. Callum does not see this as a great victory. Too many innocent people have lost their lives and homes. He does, however, hope the experience will be a vital learning opportunity. Next time, Queen Esme's forces will be better prepared for a surprise attack, and the outcome will be less catastrophic.

CHAPTER THIRTY-SEVEN

Descending the stairs from the archers' tower, the elves and Callum enter the castle and encounter jubilant rejoicing from survivors inside the keep. Roars of praise and cheers rebound through the halls. Nearly thirty elves, dwarves, and fairies clog the passageway to congratulate the rooftop heroes who killed the dragon and saved the castle.

"The warlock is the true victor this night. His power saved us and defeated the firebird," an elven captain shouts above the adulation.

The gathering revelers swamp Callum as he emerges from the stairwell, and he is alarmed to be raised up and borne above the crowd. His first thought is fear of being dropped, but he realizes that elves, dwarves, and fairies are far stronger than they appear.

Everyone is thrilled by the triumph, and they pitch in to clear the wreckage, singing joyful songs and chattering about the warlock's great valor.

In all the celebration, no one senses that Callum is quietly grief-stricken over the helpless victims of this attack. He does not share their delight, recognizing the dragon for what it is—an ambush set up by Kincaid to test the capability of his loathed warlock opponent. It is no coincidence that the necromancer appeared in his bedchamber only hours before Havishire was attacked.

The impromptu victory procession winds through the beleaguered castle. It culminates into a giant banquet hall already occupied by dozens of noble guests.

Thankfully, the cheering from Callum's entourage fades when they enter the crowded room. An atmosphere of tension fills the hall, created by the troubled occupants who mutter their concerns. Callum is safely lowered to his feet, uncomfortable amid the judgmental stares from nervous officials and irritated commanders. All walks of magical races are assembled here to demand answers from Havishire's queen.

Callum backs away, melting into the throng and retreating to a side wall. He fervently wishes he could disappear.

"Attention, everyone!" Queen Esme bellows from across the great hall as she steps onto a trestle table at the head of the room.

Esme holds her head high as she speaks. Clad in chain mail, she looks like the formidable warrior and leader her people need. The queen's traditional tiara is replaced by a crown of braids that keep her long hair pulled back from her lovely face, now streaked with grime and blood. The restive crowd becomes quiet at the queen's command, and all eyes turn toward her.

"Tonight, we were caught unaware by this cowardly and heinous attack," Esme begins. "But we succeeded despite our enemy's treachery. We held steadfast, and although there were casualties, many lives were saved. I am proud of the swift actions of everyone, and particularly of our warlock. Without his masterful vanquishing of the dragon, Havishire would have suffered even greater death and destruction. This serves to confirm my claim that his presence here will bring us salvation and victory over our adversaries."

"While I fully agree that we should consider this a success, do not celebrate yet. I will direct my servants and soldiers to clear the debris from the castle. And troops have already begun to extinguish the flames within the lower town. Nevertheless, we will not rest while Havishire still burns. There are three hours until sunrise, and I suggest those of you not cleaning rubble or battling fires should take up a vigil to watch the skies. Tomorrow we will mourn our dead, but tonight we must focus on the living."

The queen portrays herself as a pillar of strength and authority, but Callum recognizes her facade. To him, her arrogance is unmistakable.

Queen Esme's orders are immediately obeyed, and the crowd streams out of the banquet hall. Callum hangs back against the wall, trying to stay unnoticed. Even so, many people see him and deliver a grateful pat on the shoulder as they pass. His reputation is bolstered by the queen's continued recognition of his importance.

Esme steps down from her makeshift stage and is surrounded by royal guards while she listens intently to a report from a soldier. Callum recognizes him as the same gray-haired archer who shook him awake when he lost consciousness on the rampart. There is no doubt in his mind that the soldier is telling Esme about his incapacitating agony following the spell that produced victory. As the queen turns to look across the room, she meets Callum's eyes, and he can see disappointment etched across her stern face.

Heaving a sigh of frustration, Callum hunches his shoulders and takes his leave. There is no doubt that Esme is now aware he suffers from the concentrated intensity of his magic. And he is sure that he will hear of her displeasure about his failure to disclose it.

That conversation will have to wait until morning. Right now, the victorious warlock needs time and solitude to ponder everything that happened.

CHAPTER THIRTY-EIGHT

Callum does not immediately return to his bedchamber. After a broken night's sleep and an intense battle, he needs rest, but his thoughts are racing, and adrenaline is still pumping. So, with hands buried in his pockets and his head hanging low, Callum wanders the castle for the next hour.

He hears the quiet mumblings from many dedicated servants and catches bits of scattered English, informing him about the extent of the destruction. While the uppermost levels are almost entirely decimated, he learns that much of Havishire's keep remains intact. Beyond a huge, disordered mess, the southern guest wing survived damage-free, including his own room.

The warlock is convinced Esme will send someone to find him—if only to demand answers for his undisclosed affliction. With a certain degree of confidence, he surmises that the Elven Queen has more pressing matters to coordinate right now. This leaves Callum in no danger of being summoned to a private audience for the next few hours at least. But rather than retire to his room to sleep, Callum hunts for a secluded space to ruminate on his growing suspicions about the outwardly gallant queen.

Retracing his steps, he navigates the hallways back to the archer's tower. He slips past the preoccupied servants, castle guards, and soldiers from the allied armies. A well-organized squad of infantry drags away the largest chunks of rubble. Castle staff sweep and mop floors and return fallen tapestries, paintings, and suits of armor to their rightful places.

There is a uniformly somber countenance worn by the grimy, unsmiling faces hard at work. Callum feels a pang of guilt for failing to offer help, but he would just be an awkward cog in this efficient machine without direction.

The warlock finally reaches the base of a spiral staircase, ascends to the top of the familiar turret tower, and passes through the archway leading to the open rampart.

Callum's remorseful eyes survey the smashed rooftops from the high vantage point, marking the dragon's death throes. The warlock is very aware that the monster's demise was lucky. It was good fortune that the creature gutted itself on Callum's invisible shield. His mind is still assessing the battle's unlikely outcome, wondering how and why it happened. Callum concludes that the dragon's assault was a test of his strength rather than an outright attack on Havishire.

"You have come a long way from the last time we were together," a quiet voice calls out from the shadows of the tower. Someone has followed him.

Whipping around, Callum sharply inhales in shock when a mouse-sized sprite emerges from the gloom. There is no mistaking the pastel-blue fairy that zooms toward him, stopping to hover just in front of his nose. Her oversized eyes express pure joy, and her unbound navy hair kisses the top of her scrawny shoulders.

Frey Pearvale is a wondrous sight after all the carnage Callum witnessed. She looks every bit as charming as he recalls from their last meeting, clad in a short woolen dress cinched around her slim waist by an embossed leather belt and knee-length tan leggings. Her bare arms and shoulders are discreetly covered by a white woven shawl. Frey does not stay still for long, zipping in several excited circles around his head before coming to rest on the top of the stone bulwark beside him.

"What are *you* doing here?" Callum murmurs, his voice cracking slightly. The warlock's mind is a muddle of questions as he squats to her level, next to the short wall.

"My master is offering his services to the Queen of Havishire. Sage Axel Turtlebee has devoted centuries to the study of necromancers. His knowledge is invaluable to the Elven Queen and her allies," Frey responds, biting her lip in an unsuccessful attempt to restrain a beaming smile.

The fairy's expressive eyes reveal her delight at this moment of happenstance, while Callum is stunned by Frey's appearance. Her crystalline wings are like veined glass, drawing together at her back and reflecting the orange glow of Havishire's distant fires. She fixes her teary gaze on Callum's and rapidly blinks up at him, nervously creasing her pretty face.

"Since it is my duty to follow Sage Turtlebee as his servant, this is why I am here."

"I...I had no idea we were this close to each other," Callum says. He chokes back a joyful cry and swipes away a stray tear.

"I have been stationed beside my master, joining him at diplomatic meetings for the last couple of weeks. I slipped away during the confusion of the cleanup, hoping to find you somehow. I followed you up here in secret, but I will have to return soon. This reunion will be short-lived."

"You look...Uhm...Are you being treated well?" Callum asks. He feels his face flushes as he fumbles for words.

Frey giggles, lifting her willowy hand to her mouth to conceal a coy grin. "I am fine, Callum. My master is very kind."

"Oh...well, that's good," Callum says with a sigh, relieved that her punishment is not as cruel as he imagined.

"As happy as I am to see you again, Callum, I also have something important to tell you." Frey lowers her hand from her face and casts a glance toward the barren archway. Then, sensing no one there to threaten them, Frey returns her attention to

Callum. Worry twists her cherub face, and her wings twitch. "You cannot trust the queen. She is blinded by self-interest."

"Yeah, I kind of figured that," Callum says. Relaxing slightly, he settles onto his knees to bring feeling back into his sharply bent legs.

"So, you know Esme deliberately left the lower town undefended?" Frey asks, taken aback that Callum's speculation matches her information.

"What?!" Callum blurts out.

"It is true. The queen commanded that all the allied troops, and Havishire's own soldiers, pull back and protect the castle if an attack occurred. The inner gate was locked to all refugees for fear of citizens storming the keep for protection. I heard this directly from Esme during one of the many strategy meetings my sage and I were part of."

"She sacrificed her own citizens," Callum exclaims, dumfounded. Unfortunately, his misgivings are now fully justified.

"But you also have doubts about her."

Each possessing different pieces of the same puzzle, together they complete a horrifying picture.

"I suspected something wasn't quite right." Callum turns from Frey, sinking down to sit against the rampart's stone wall, drawing his legs to his chest and rubbing his face with both hands. Frey gracefully floats down and settles onto his bent knees.

"What is it you noticed?" Frey asks softly, her face drawn rigid.

He furrows his brows and meets her insistent gaze, frowning at his disturbing insights about the Elven Queen. "When I first met Esme, she led me to a balcony overlooking a crowd of royal guests and commanding officers. She gave a very inspiring speech, but it wasn't for my benefit. When I heard her latest sermon tonight, I realized how egocentric and manipulative she really is." Frey reassuringly pats his knee and listens as Callum continues. "Esme is playing the part of a queen. She is acting out a script that makes her look like a caring leader. But she brushes over the traumatic deaths of her people and lifts herself up at their expense. What you've just told me makes sense. Esme is after one thing—self-glorification."

"I did not hear her speak tonight, but Axel told me the queen has talked at length about earning the same acclaim as her dead father's once she is victorious."

Frey purses her lips and peers over her shoulder at the billowing columns of smoke and flickering fires far below their place of solitude. Callum clears his throat, and Frey ends her moment of introspection.

"Esme had me brought here, knowing full well the enemy would come looking for me." Callum clenches his jaw at this realization. "She uses empty words to rally support for Havishire and her secret agenda. This has all been a clever ploy to build herself up, and Esme is risking the lives of everyone Havishire, and potentially the realm, to feed this insane desire."

"When the armies arrive tomorrow, she will lock the gates again," Frey observes. Her owlish eyes fill with tears as she gazes at Callum. "What can be done to stop this?"

"Where are you staying, Frey?" Callum asks. Slowly inhaling, he tries to steady his outrage at Esme's atrocities. Sharp lines of vexation etch themselves across his forehead.

"I am staying in the servant quarters near my master's suite. It is on the third level of the west wing. Please do not worry about me. Axel is a kind fairy. He treats me like a daughter. I trust him to protect me." Frey's eyes twinkle at the mention of her revered sage's name.

Callum tilts his head, surprised by Frey's admiring reference to her master. All this time, he envisioned Frey to be in miserable subjugation to a tyrant and is pleased to hear this is not the case. Still, the warlock remains uneasy about her arrangement, not to mention Frey's presence at the center of this converging conflict.

Burying these concerns, Callum implores her, "Frey, I need you to promise that you'll find somewhere safe to hide when the battle breaks out. Forget about your punishment and your master. I need to know that you'll be out of harm's way. I lo—." Callum catches himself on the last words, refusing to allow himself to divulge his affection for her. He is afraid to voice his endearment, knowing they can never be together in that way. "I have to go now, Frey," Callum spouts, avoiding her overwrought gaze.

Frey nimbly zips off his knee, allowing him to stand. She flits above the warlock's shoulder as he marches toward the archer's tower.

"Where are you going?" Frey asks as her wings buzz beside his ear.

"I want to see the damage in the lower town for myself," Callum says firmly, pausing at the archway. His shoulder dispiritedly slump. "Maybe I can help or something. I feel like I owe it to these people. I was too slow to defend them."

"Callum, many witnessed you kill the dragon. How much more could you have done?" Faithful Frey curves around to hover directly in front of his face. Her face twists into a grimace of worry, sensing Callum's guilt.

Callum meets her round eyes and shakes his head. "I could have been better prepared. Kincaid came to me only hours before the attack. He wanted me to surrender. If I did, he promised to leave Havishire alone and turn his monsters on Quinn." Callum peers past Frey and stares into the murky shadows of the empty tower. Knowing so many lives were taken because of his oversight, he is plagued with guilt, shame, and remorse.

The warlock returns his weary gaze to Frey, his eyes watering slightly. "I should have known, Frey. I should have done something about it. But instead, I went back to bed."

"You could not have predicted this," Frey insists.

"You're wrong, Frey," Callum says. He balls his hands into

fists and glares into the shadows again. Red-hot flickers of flames flash across his knuckles as he thinks of his failure and Esme's corruption. "The timing of the attack was no accident. Kincaid sent his dragon to test my skill in battle. The monster basically threw itself at my magic."

"Go back to your master, Frey. Don't tell him that we talked. We can't let Esme know that we suspect her. She's already allowed helpless people to die for her vanity, and there is no telling what else she might do."

With a heavy heart, Callum leaves his beloved friend. He hurries down the winding staircase and into the heart of the castle. His thoughts are swimming, but his resolve is absolute. With Frey stranded at Havishire Castle, Callum must succeed in ending this war—one way or another.

CHAPTER THIRTY-NINE

As the sun rises, Callum is well beyond the point of exhaustion. He managed to catch an hour of sleep, hiding in a lonely stairwell. However, the warlock is still painfully groggy. The corridors are relatively clear of debris, and the bustling labor force from the previous night has retired to rest. Since it is now easier to sneak away without being seen, Callum navigates a path through the quiet castle, avoiding guards and sentries until he reaches a busy kitchen and adjoining scullery.

In white aprons, powdered with flour and stained with brown grease, elves toil over their duties and pay no attention to the passing warlock.

Delicious smells permeate the sweltering room and make Callum's mouth water. But he dares not loiter. Instead, he heads through the gallery to a gaping doorway and beyond into a welcoming winter breeze.

He enters a small yard where a trampled dirt path leads to the castle's food storehouses. Callum skirts the edge of the keep until he reaches the front courtyard.

The gloomy morning is quiet, aside from a few diligent soldiers patrolling the castle's inner wall. While he hides behind a dense leafless hedge, Callum gulps several huge breaths, then exhales a magical fog that rises from the frozen ground like a thick, cloudy soup. While the guards can only gawk and stumble around in the grips of this sudden weather phenomenon, Callum uses the haze to scurry across the yard and slip through the open castle gate.

As the warlock makes his way into the lower town, he notices an eerie silence. Everywhere he looks, citizens painstakingly search through the charred remains of their devastated homes. Grief seems permanently carved into their ash-streaked faces.

A few elven soldiers bark orders, their voices blending with those of dwarves, fairies, and centaurs, all trying to help and comfort the survivors.

Although reassuring in terms of compassion and maintaining security, the military presence forces Callum to travel sideroads and devise an intricate route through the stricken town. As a result, the warlock is compelled to see the trauma Havishire's most vulnerable citizens suffered.

He travels unimpeded for over an hour before reaching one of the public gardens, where huddled families curl up near small fires for warmth. Most of the citizens he encountered are in shock. But still, a few recognize him as the human warlock and flash angry stares in his direction. Callum averts his eyes and hurries on, taking stock of the homes and buildings destroyed by the dragon's fire.

Hundreds of structures have been burned to unrecognizable piles of ash and blackened timbers. Many inhabitants are already working to salvage anything of value. Callum cringes at the thought of surviving this initial skirmish, only to suffer a more lingering hardship.

As he passes a stable, Callum catches a pungent whiff of charred horses. Two mares, the barn fire's only survivors, aimlessly wander in a trampled yard nearby, using their hooves to expose the tasteless brown blades of grass beneath the snow.

Callum reaches the main roadway and heads toward the giant

stone gatehouse, now tightly closed to the outside world. However, his progress is arrested by the heart-wrenching sight of long lines of bodies laid out in even rows.

Adults and children lie alongside fallen soldiers of the allied races. All count equally among the dead until their final rites can be coordinated.

The victims rest peacefully on their backs, with hands folded upon their chests and small squares of cloth covering their faces. Many are badly burned, some beyond recognition. A steady procession of somber elves and soldiers from various backgrounds carry more bodies to add to the gruesome yet dignified collection. Each new arrival is placed on the frozen ground, and their limbs gently arranged. Not a word is spoken.

Weeping parents and orphaned children mourn over the bodies of their loved ones. Callum feels a deep sense of guilt tearing at his soul. While the queen brushed over Havishire's innocent dead, much preferring to talk of victory, one inescapable fact remains—these victims were left to fend for themselves. Despite Callum's best efforts, he could not spare them from violent death or heartache.

As Callum stands motionless in the presence of so much anguish, his head explodes in a jarring sharp pain by an unexpected blunt impact of a hurled block. Caught off guard by an unseen citizen elf, Callum grips his battered head and twists toward the source of the assault.

A handful of desperate residents emerge from among the wrecked buildings. They sneer at his unwelcome attendance amid their grief. These elves, who had endured the worst of the dragon's lethal attack, are blaming him for their suffering.

"Cursed warlock! You brought this upon us!" one shouts as he chucks another chunk of broken brick.

Callum dodges the dangerous projectile.

"Begone, human!" another elf yells. His remark repeats among the other enraged voices of the rapidly growing mob.

Soldiers rush to Callum's aid, stepping in front of him to

block the cluster of affronted elves. Unfortunately, the number of grieving victims is too many to hold back. Unwilling to become the prime target of a hostile stoning, Callum retreats toward the castle and runs for his life.

Debris and hateful curses follow Callum's exodus. He runs at full tilt. Taking a direct course along the main road, he barrels through the inner gate and returns to the deceptive safety of the castle courtyard.

A dozen royal guards arrange themselves across the threshold, closing the portcullis and blocking the angry throng. Panting for breath, Callum pauses. He turns to face the utter loathing of a community that blames him for their suffering. Demoralized, Callum is barely aware of his footsteps as he returns to the castle.

Consumed by his weighty thoughts, Callum forgot about his own ailments. When he lifts his hand to his chest, the rough fabric of his shirt stings his blistered flesh, and his breath catches at the sharp pain. He bows his head in misery, wanting to return to his quarters to pass the day in rest and contemplation. The enemy armies are not expected to arrive until later today. Callum has a lot to think about before then.

The warlock does not make it far before his luck takes an even worse turn.

In a castle full of magical creatures abuzz with activity, the warlock's rattled mind is not alert to a trailing menace. Consequently, the two soldiers stalking him remain overlooked until it is too late. When he turns down the familiar hallway leading toward his room, Callum encounters three elven guards waiting for his return.

"Good morning, Callum," Commander Agis says quietly, standing with his troops.

Callum halts and is stunned to see the mountain elves obstructing his path.

"What are *you* doing here?" Callum asks, finding his voice despite a foreboding sense of alarm.

"We are here by order of our queen. My army arrived a few days before you did, but this is a large castle. I am not surprised that we did not encounter one another before now. I only wish we were meeting under better circumstances," Agis says, grimly smiling.

"So you've said before," Callum says, narrowing his eyes at the dubious commander. "What's really going on here?"

Hearing footsteps approaching behind him, Callum peers over his shoulder in time to see the two stalkers appear around the corner and draw to a stop, cutting off any possibility of escape.

"Do not make me do this, Callum," Agis says with a sigh of resignation. "Queen Esme ordered us to escort you to a secure room. She has urgent questions about last night's attack. The queen is also concerned about your state of health. I suggest you come along quietly, for your own sake."

Callum glimpses a twitch of regret in the commander's right eye.

"Why didn't she send Jobella to talk to me instead of you?" Callum asks, stalling for time. He shifts his feet, backing against the corridor wall so he can see both opposing fronts.

"I am here because I told her you would resist her order. It was my archers in the towers who you saved. They told me how you were overcome with agony and how it nearly killed you." Agis takes a hesitant step forward while raising his hand to order his elves to maintain positions. "Your breathing ceased, and your heart stopped. To all appearances, you were dead, and they could do nothing to help. You are only alive now because your body started breathing again."

"I blacked out. That's all," Callum says, pausing to consider Agis' information.

He recalls the terrified faces of the elves on the promenade and how they all looked immensely relieved when he awakened.

"You forget that I have been inside your head, and I know when you are lying, Callum. Please come with us." Agis lifts both arms in a peaceful gesture of surrender. "I promise that we will not harm you. We only wish to see that you receive the healing you need."

Callum absently lifts a hand to his chest, remembering how exhausted and weak he had been on the castle rooftop. What Agis says seems to make sense, but there is something else troubling him.

"What aren't you telling me?" Callum asks, distrustfully glaring.

Agis frowns. His arms fall heavily to his sides before he answers. "Queen Esme wishes to read all of your memories as I did. I informed her that you would not submit to it willingly, so again, here we are."

"Whatever happened to my own personal rights and privacy?" Callum says, sourly outraged. "Or is that only a human concept?"

"Callum, please do not do this," Agis begs. But it is too late for appeals.

Closing his eyes and focusing his frazzled thoughts, Callum channel his magic, feeling its warmth flowing through him. Aware of his coming attack, the elven soldiers rushing footsteps betray their frantic attempts to disarm him before he can unleash his building power. But they are too late.

A burst of dazzling argent energy erupts from Callum's body in all directions, pitching Agis and his soldiers several feet through the air. They land hard on the stone-tiled floor, groaning from the concussive jolt. Callum pushes away from the wall and sprints for freedom.

He moves as quickly as he can while the familiar stabbing pain scalds his chest like acid. Callum was careful not to use a strong spell, but the affliction still strikes like a piercing bullet, stealing his breath away and slowing him down. Still, the warlock manages to stagger past the first dazed elf recovering from his unceremonious landing.

Callum is not moving nearly fast enough to escape the next

soldier, nor does he have any clear destination in mind. A hand grabs his ankle, causing him to lose balance and plummet to the floor.

Nosediving, Callum strikes his face against the stone tiles. A second later, the weight of two elves pins him to the floor. The warlock struggles against this confinement, but when one of Agis' soldiers braces a knee in the center of Callum's back, he screams as his blistering wound is crushed against the tile. The remaining pair of soldiers rush to aid their comrades. Callum's arms are roughly pulled behind his back and his wrists secured with a leather cord.

The elves finally relax their holds once their quarry is firmly restrained. Callum breathes heavily and rolls onto his side.

"I asked you not to fight us," Agis reminds Callum, assisting the warlock to his feet.

Furious, sore, and dejected, Callum has no choice but to compliantly follow along to wherever the Elven Queen awaits.

CHAPTER FORTY

"Callum Walker," Esme says coldly when Callum is led into a windowless room somewhere in the dungeons of Havishire Castle. His uneasiness escalates when he notices the only piece of furniture is a central wooden table. Callum strains against the hands gripping his arms, but they hold steadfast. The druid, Jobella, stands beside her queen and steps forward to meet him.

"Why are you doing this?" Callum demands of Esme.

Still wearing her battle armor, the queen is the same imposing figure she had been the night before. "We are at war. I cannot have secrets if they threaten your life. You are our unifying symbol of our hope," Esme says. She hardens her face at Callum for concealing his injuries. "You are more than a man to these people. Your life far too precious to risk endangerment."

"So that justifies this treatment? Agis has already read my mind once. Just ask him what you need to know," Callum snarls, gritting his teeth and flaring his nostrils.

Jobella moves between Esme and Callum, standing close enough that he sees the bloodshot veins in her weary eyes. She firmly grabs him by the jaw and turns his head to inspect the bleeding gash on his scalp. "What happened here?" she asks with concern.

"One of the angry townsfolk threw something at my head," Callum says, pulling his face free of Jobella's hand and spearing Esme with a fiery glower. "Apparently, they're feeling a bit betrayed by their monarch. They noticed their queen's lack of military support and her orders to lock them out of the castle. I really can't blame them for being pissed off."

He refuses to hide his anger and continues to hatefully glare across the room at the indifferent queen. Esme flinches at the warlock's harsh judgment but quickly recovers her poise.

"The lower town is not essential," Esme says, spitting her words and snarling. "This castle is the only legacy that matters, and it must be defended at all costs."

Callum and Frey both correctly assessed the conceited monarch's priorities. While she is outwardly respectful to her subjects, it is all a performance. Esme is only concerned with her personal conquest, regardless of the expense to innocent lives. Callum's civil liberties are insignificant if they interfere with her lust for triumph.

"Put him on the table," Esme barks her command, maintaining a fierce stare.

Callum puts up a valiant resistance, but in the end, is lifted off his feet and manhandled onto the table as he thrashes. He tries to roll away but is quickly pulled back and held down. Three elves restrain him with hidden leather straps beneath the table. A fourth cinch them tight across his shoulders, belly, knees, and ankles. Flattened on the table, Callum's bound hands dig painfully into his back.

Esme moves to the head of the table and peers down into Callum's face.

"You brought this trouble on yourself," she whispers spitefully.

"Why do you need to read all of my memories?" Callum asks, barely able to breathe beneath the tight tethers. "Jobella can probably tell you what's happening to me. And Agis has all the information you need."

Esme leans forward and speaks softly in his ear, "I need to be stronger to enforce incontestable obedience from my people. I must know the source of your power so that I can have it for my own."

Callum has heard this desire for power spoken to him before. Now, this selfish yearning is coming from someone who he assumed to be an ally. Gaping in silence at the ceiling, he feels a deep loathing for the narcissistic queen.

Esme lifts her head from his ear and smirks at the captive warlock. She places her palms against his head, closes her eyes, and begins to recite an ancient incantation.

"Okay, *your majesty*. You want to find out what's in my head? Let me show you," Callum mutters his vindictive words through grinding teeth.

Before the queen can finish her chant, Callum performs divination of his own. He squeezes his eyes shut and, without resisting her spell, the warlock lets his most painful thoughts surge into the queen's unprepared mind. His torment, sadness, and rage invade her brain like an emotional maelstrom, depicting the worst experiences of his life.

Esme screams in agony and releases Callum's head as if it were red-hot. She staggers backward, seizing her skull in a futile effort to ease the hellish mental backlash of the warlock's self-defense. As she stumbles and falls, the soldiers and Jobella rush to her aid.

Callum uses the diversion to summon his magic and melt the heavy straps holding him down. The tight leather bindings snap like rubber bands, and he rolls off the table and onto his feet. The elves are so distracted by their suffering queen that they do not heed their prisoner escaping his restraints. Only Agis notices that Callum has freed himself.

"What are you doing, Callum?" Agis asks. Stepping back

from his ailing queen, he hastily draws his sword and stands his ground against the warlock.

Suffering the searing ache that slices through his heart, Callum groans and stoops as he staggers back to a cold stone wall. Grimacing, the warlock readies himself for further misery as he employs more magic to break the bindings on his wrists.

The soldiers around the stricken queen are drawn to attention by their commander's voice. They prepared to advance on the liberated warlock, but Agis gruffly orders them to halt. Callum clasps both hands to his chest and slides down the wall to the floor. Jobella rushes to his side. Intense pain steals his voice, exploding from his chest into his head, shoulders, and abdomen. Wavering on the edge of consciousness, Callum is gingerly lowered onto his back.

"Callum, stay with us," Jobella says and patting his reddened cheeks.

Someone grabs the warlock's arms and pulls his hands away from his chest. An instant later, Jobella lifts his shirt and gasps in alarm. But try as she might, there is little she can do to alleviate his suffering.

Callum's pain mercifully subsides after a few minutes, as it is done in the past, and leaves him temporarily weak and sluggish.

"Help me get him back up on the table," Jobella orders once Callum starts to relax.

The soldiers follow Agis's lead, hurrying to lift the human and plant him back on the table he worked so hard to escape.

"I am not finished with him yet," Esme utters—still irate at being denied her direct access into the warlock's mind. She clutches a hand to her head and winces through her ebbing migraine.

"If you want me to save his life, I need everyone to leave. Now!" Jobella barks and fixedly stares at Esme. Clearly, this druid is not intimidated by the scheming monarch.

"Come, your majesty, I will place a guard in the hall to prevent him from escaping," Agis says to the queen. "He is incapable of surviving your interrogation in this state. Let Jobella heal him so you may try again when he is recovered."

Esme petulantly complains yet sees the wisdom of his advice. Agis escorts the queen from the room, and his elven soldiers file out behind them. The heavy door is closed behind them.

"They are gone now," Jobella says in a low voice, ensuring the sentries outside the room cannot hear.

"I'm not dying," Callum says with a grunt. He tries to sit up but fails and elects to remain on the table until his strength returns.

"No, you are not. I exaggerated the truth. How else was I going to get her to leave?"

"I don't understand. Why did you lie?"

"I am trying to help you," Jobella says with a nervous smile. "I do not approve of my queen's methods, but I could not interfere with her commands."

"Esme is trying to steal my magic for herself."

"I know. Before she ordered me down here, Esme asked me if it was possible to draw your magic from you and make it her own. I must admit it was my suggestion that led her to scour your thoughts for an understanding of your abilities," Jobella confesses, lowering her gaze. "I thought it would stall her, but I was wrong. Please forgive me."

Jobella appears genuinely ashamed of her actions, but Callum cannot hold this against her. Instead, he blames Esme for her appalling lack of judgment and egotistical attitude.

Stubborn as ever, Callum struggles and finally manages to sit upright. Jobella anxiously watches but knows he will not easily accept assistance.

"How are you feeling?" she asks, scanning him carefully.

"Like hell, but I'll recover. Just give me a few more minutes," Callum says unconvincingly and braces himself with his hands on the table's rough-hewn edge.

"This is happening because of the strength of your magic," Jobella tells him. "Here, let me help you." She opens a satchel that hangs from a leather shoulder strap and rests upon her narrow hips. Removing a small jar containing a thick, olive-green paste, Jobella scoops out a dollop with her fingers and looks up at him. "Lift your shirt."

Callum hesitates, then does as she asks, trusting that she is not there to hurt him. The druid smears the foul-smelling goo over his marred and blistered skin. He hisses under his breath at the sting of her touch. Thankfully, the malodourous concoction soon begins to provide cooling relief.

"I did not tell the queen, but I recognize that the source of your power is in your blood. Like it is with elves, your heart is the core of your circulatory system, so that is why your affliction is centered within your chest," Jobella explains while returning the cork stopper to her jar of ointment. "Humans are normally incapable of withstanding such powerful energy. That is why your kind are rarely gifted with magic."

"What can I do about it?" Callum asks, gingerly sliding off the table and onto his feet. He is relieved to be free of the pain from his raw flesh, although his heart and lungs ache with each breath. Pushing himself for as long and hard as he felt necessary is finally catching up with him.

"There are others who share this affliction." A sober frown paints Jobella's soft features. "The vampires suffer the same pain when they are transformed—they call it the agony of death. Werewolves are also cursed with a similar torment whenever they shift forms." The druid digs into her shoulder bag again and removes a simple pendant. She raises it before Callum's curious eyes. "The vampires do not care to treat this pain, but were-wolves have found relief by using a common charm such as this one."

A small, clouded gemstone, wrapped in a thin wire, hangs from a gold chain. Callum can discern magical energy emanating from the stone, and its aura is comforting to him. Jobella rises onto her toes to drape the chain over his head. Callum lifts the jeweled charm, and his fingers inspect the cold stone.

"While you wear this amulet, your body will be protected from the overwhelming energy of your magic," Jobella says.

"Thank you." Callum offers her a grateful nod. But as usual, he does not quite know what else to say.

Observing her anxiousness, Callum realizes Jobella must be risking a great deal to aid him.

The druid's smile reveals her understanding. "You can thank me by ending this conflict, Callum Walker."

CHAPTER FORTY-ONE

The elves guarding the passageway are shocked to see Callum emerge from the subterranean chamber. Before the sentry has any chance to react, the warlock dispatches them with a blinding arcane burst, flinging them against the wall. The soldiers crumple to the floor in blissful unconsciousness.

Callum is relieved that Jobella's amulet protects him from the disabling pain of his blood magic. Still, there is no time to linger and celebrate this blessed asset.

"You will not be able to enter the main halls of the keep from the dungeons, nor should you want to. Esme decreed that you must be apprehended on sight," Jobella shares while joining Callum in the long passage.

"How do I get out of the castle then?" Callum asks, glancing down both ends of the lengthy corridor, desperate for direction.

The warlock is not surprised to hear that he can no longer trust any of Havishire's assembled military forces, even those who saved him on the mountain. At least Jobella seems to be working for his benefit. The personal risk the druid is taking gives him plenty of reason to trust her, and his intuition senses her virtuous motivations.

"If you continue this way, it will take you to the barracks." Jobella points to the right. "There will be a sentry stationed there with additional guards, but it is a confined room. If you can constrain them quickly and quietly, there should be no alarm raised. The barracks have their own exit into the courtyard at ground level."

"I guess I'm going to get the practice I need," Callum says sarcastically, feeling uneasy about attacking those who previously assisted him. Loyalty is supposed to be a quality to be prized and honored.

As the warlock starts to trudge to the far end of the hall, he hears Jobella trailing after him. He turns to face her, surprised that she is keen to accompany him.

"It might be safer for you to stay here," Callum suggests.

Jobella delivers a withering look as though she is preparing to counter. "I am perfectly capable of defending myself. In case you have forgotten, I have saved your life twice now, so I am coming to help you. I will not be dissuaded."

"All right then, let's go." Callum has zero appetite for challenging the druid. He also knows he could use the expertise of someone familiar with the castle's complex layout. Jobella seems taken aback by Callum's immediate acceptance of her statement.

"You are not going to argue with me?" she asks as they continue to move steadily down the corridor.

"Why would I? You know this castle better than I do. And I don't have a map, so I could use your guidance."

"Oh. Perhaps I am just used to having to over-assert myself," Jobella says as she advances through the hallway with Callum. "Unless you are the queen, female elves are rarely afforded the same respect or authority as males. I assumed humans are the same."

She sounds both disappointed by and highly critical of the patriarchal society that prevails within Elven culture. Callum belatedly recalls that he is only ever seen male soldiers and male commanders, while most of the castle's servants are female. He also remembers that Jobella can be a rather assertive and intimidating elf when the need is required.

"If that's the case, then why is there an Elven Queen instead of a king?"

"The former king passed from this life without leaving a male heir. Esme was an only child, so the Oracle appointed her queen after her father died. The Oracle's decisions are never challenged."

"What's an oracle?" Callum asks, now breathing heavily from the strenuous events of the past few hours and lack of recuperative rest.

"Your people would call them prophets," Jobella explains. "From birth, Oracles are linked to the dynamic force from which magic is created. They can see and feel the source of power that imbues all of us. They commune with the immortal creators for guidance, which they then pass on to the royal rulers."

"I might pay a visit to this Oracle when this war is over."

"That is impossible, Callum. You must be of royal blood or given express permission from the current monarch. Besides, only a select few know where the Oracle can be found."

"I can always try," Callum says mulishly. Filing this new mission deep among his thoughts, he intends to address it—if he survives the war.

Situated below ground, at the very bottom of the castle tower, lies a circular room nearly sixty feet across. Jobella informs him that this is just one of many barracks throughout Havishire Castle and its adjacent ramparts. Two dozen soldiers sit at a round table, absorbed in a dice game. Behind them, a curved staircase climbs the wall to the ground level.

Callum feels guilty about what he plans on doing but knows he cannot allow any regrets to inhibit him. Far too much is at stake.

Standing outside the wooden door, the warlock peeks through a barred window and listens to the friendly voices within the barrack. He then motions for Jobella to wait behind him in the hallway. She gives him a frosty look, and Callum sighs, realizing that the druid has no intention of doing so.

"Fine. Then at least stay close," Callum says in a frustrated whisper.

Gathering his courage, the warlock shoves the door open and rushes inside the room.

The elves at the table are caught entirely off guard. They bolt from their seats, and all eyes look toward the sudden intrusion. Callum takes full advantage of their hesitation. He raises his right forearm, already alight with a radiant ivory shine, and releases a wave of energy that throws the elves, their chairs, and the table across the room. The jumble of soldiers and furniture collides with a weapons rack and several hay-filled targets, creating a chaotic noise.

"So much for trying to be quiet," Jobella retorts.

"Shit." Callum cringes as the tumultuous racket finally settles. "I didn't mean to use that much force."

The noise alerts the sentry on the floor above. A clamor of rushing footsteps pounds the floorboards and sprinkles a thin layer of dust over the disrupted lower barracks. The fallen guards slowly regroup from Callum's arcane attack.

Sleep, Callum thinks. The command sweeps his right hand in an arc toward the scattered, groaning garrison. One by one, the dice players sag to the floor in gentle slumber.

An arrow whizzes past the warlock's cheek, and Callum instinctively recoils. He spins toward the stairs to see three elves with leveled crossbows, all aimed squarely at his chest.

"Stop right there, Warlock," one of the trio orders. "The next shot will not be a warning!"

"Wait! Do *not* hurt him!" Jobella shouts, stepping between the soldiers and Callum. She raises her arms like wings to obstruct the archers' view of their target.

"What are you doing?" Callum mutters, irritated that Jobella moved into his own line of sight as well.

She ignores his question and stands her ground.

"He is the one foretold to bring an end to this war. Have you been so blind to your orders that you have forgotten this?" asks Jobella, chastising the bemused soldiers.

They look hesitantly at one another, then return their doubtful gaze to the druid.

"The queen has given us orders to arrest this human. We do not intend to kill him, only to lame him and prevent him from leaving," the soldier explains, resolutely maintaining his aim in Callum's direction.

"Has the queen told you *why* she wants to imprison our only weapon against the enemy?" Jobella retorts, lowering her arms and bravely persevering before the guards.

"We do not question our orders. We follow them."

"Then tell me how our queen plans on defending us against an adversary that outnumbers us a hundred to one, without the warlock's protection?" asks Jobella.

"I...do not know," admits the rueful sentry.

All three guards exchange confused glances, appearing equally puzzled by the druid's words. By degrees, the guards begin to lower their weapons and look to Jobella for an explanation. The druid's logic has scored a valid point—the queen's orders seem to severely contradict their own instincts for self-preservation. Jobella peers over her shoulder at Callum with a telling nod. The druid knows that even among the elven kingdom's most loyal subjects, mistrust of the royal leader has taken root and is spreading. Callum is impressed by how masterfully Jobella turns such keen insight to her advantage.

"I am leading the warlock out of Havishire because Queen Esme will see him dead if he stays here," Jobella calmly announces to the irresolute soldiers. "He has a plan to fight the enemy and protect our city from beyond the walls."

She lies so convincingly that even Callum is interested to

know about this great plan he is supposed to execute. The druid is a skillful orator, and Callum feels increasing respect for Jobella. She is knowledgeable and charismatic enough to overcome the old-fashioned limits of Elvish gender inequality.

As the castle's healer, Jobella is a senior and revered member of Esme's staff. Her words carry authority and speak to the sensibilities of these soldiers questioning their own sworn loyalty to the queen. Yet, their primal fear of death is obvious to Callum. Even without his empathic perceptions, he can easily see their turmoil.

Jobella allows the elves time to ponder her words. "Will you please help us?" she finally asks.

"We will let you pass, but that is all we can offer," the sentry says.

The guard then motions for his two comrades to stand down. Druid and Warlock are led up to the second level and provided safe passage past other off-duty elves on the main floor.

Outside the barracks, the afternoon light is brilliant in comparison, and Callum squints as they emerge from the gloom. They arrive in a modest yard, flanked by a stable and a shed. With luck, no one is in the vicinity to witness the pair's exit.

"We need to head to the northern courtyard," Jobella says with urgency. She leads the way along a narrow path separating the castle and stable.

Callum spares a precious few seconds to fix the layout of the stronghold in his mind. Havishire's Castle occupies the northern half of the fortified townsite. Although encircling the entire community, the keep is protected by its own perimeter wall. However, the northernmost courtyard has only a single barricade separating the castle from the open wilderness beyond.

"Over here." Jobella beckons Callum toward a weed-choked drainage hole cut into the wall and covered with a rusted iron grate.

A padlock secures a heavy chain, wrapped several times around the grate and curved anchors built into the stonework.

"It is a tight fit, but this will take you outside the walls," she says. "I cannot follow you any further, but I wish you luck, Warlock."

"Thank you." Callum pauses and looks directly into Jobella's weary blue eyes. "I owe you my life, three times over."

Callum reaches out a hand toward the drain, concentrating his magic on the heavy metal hasp. Then, at the warlock's command, the rust-encased lock unlatches with a quick clunk and drops into the mud. The attached chain begins to uncoil like a snake.

Jobella grabs Callum's arm when he crouches down to inspect the three-foot-wide drain. "Where are you planning to go?"

"I don't know. Maybe I can lead the armies away from Havishire." Callum realizes this tactic will probably bring his young life to a grisly end, but it is the only thing he can think of.

"I have an idea," Jobella suggests. "There is a cave one day's walk west of Havishire. The entrance is hidden behind a waterfall. Only druids know of its existence as it was once a sacred sacrificial temple. Our people have kept it secret and protected. It is believed to hold ancient magical energy."

"Great. A hidden temple that very few people know about. No thanks." Callum feels uneasy about her suggestion, yet some instinct compels him to listen.

"Esme does not know of its existence," Jobella says insistently. "If you travel there and wait, I will have my druid sisters carry a message to Quinn and Kincaid. I will inform the warlords that you are offering yourself as ransom. It is the only way to isolate the sorcerer and necromancer from their forces, and it will help to even the odds for you."

"Are you expecting me to talk to them or kill them?"

"The choice is yours to make. The prophecy only declares that your actions bring an end to the war. It does not foretell how." Jobella's face is a mask of concern, recognizing her plan is fraught with sacrifice and danger.

"You'll only be condemning your messengers to death.

Kincaid and Quinn will be happy to torture them." Callum is reluctant to accept her plan and is uneasy about her eagerness to help if it means asking her comrades to offer up their lives.

"You may feel that you are alone in this journey and have been left without support. I assure you there are those of us willing to die for you. If you survive this war, seek out the druids in High Garth. They are among the few ready to protect you with their lives." Jobella smiles sweetly and loosens her grip on his arm.

For a moment, the warlock wavers, uncomfortable about leaving Jobella without knowing how the furious queen will deal with her.

"Come with me," he says.

"I cannot leave. I must send my messengers. But when this war is over, I will make for High Garth. You can find me there. Now, you must leave before it is too late," Jobella pleads. Blinking back tears, she pushes Callum toward the drainage grate.

Reluctantly, Callum kneels and crawls into the stinking confines of the stone-lined tunnel. A rim of ice grows at the edge of a shallow stream, cracking beneath his weight.

Behind him, he hears the grate screeching shut and the heavy chain and lock being replaced. And then, Jobella's soft voice whispering *goodbye*.

CHAPTER FORTY-TWO

The drainage tunnel is cramped, rank, and slimy. Left with little choice, Callum crawls toward the patch of dim light that represents his exit point. By the time he reaches the grating at the opposite end, his pant legs and sleeves are soaked, and he is nauseated by the stench of rotten scum coating the walls.

Callum's magic again disposes of the lock, and he emerges from the base of the castle wall. Looking back at the breeched tunnel, he decides against leaving it open and exposed—that would risk the safety of Havishire's citizens. Callum focuses his energy on the accumulated turf around the tunnel's mouth, levitating it several feet before dropping it carefully to seal the entrance.

He hurries along the town's outer perimeter. Hugging the wall, Callum moves past the guards patrolling a bulwark high above. He banks on the fact that the archers are fully occupied with scanning the distant tree line across the open fields. This tactic serves Callum well until he reaches the northwest corner of the stronghold.

A belt of wide, open field encircles Havishire like a dry moat, deterring enemies from advancing over the barren ground while

Boyers rain arrows down from above. Callum pauses to catch his breath as he considers the half-mile of snow-covered flatland that lies between him and the shelter of the trees.

An instant before he is ready to dart out in a desperate dash, a horn blares from within the castle walls. The warlock instantly drops to the ground, certain he has been spotted. But the alarm is raised for a far more deadly reason.

Callum hears a chorus of shouting drift across the pristine white field, and from the north, he can make out a battle line of hunters emerging from the forest.

Quinn's army has arrived.

Callum weighs the odds and gambles on the new distraction. He jumps to his feet and sprints for the western woodland. The rutted terrain presents many tripping hazards, but he manages to recover his balance each time and keeps moving, driven by expedience and fear.

No one calls out or tries to skewer him with a well-aimed arrow. His lungs and legs burn from the punishing race. Callum pushes on without stopping until he vanishes into the cover of dormant winter trees. Sagging to rest against the trunk of a giant oak, he heaves to catch his breath in the frosty air.

As the warlock puffs and pants, trumpets sound out a second distress call from somewhere within Havishire. Callum moves far enough from his hiding place to peer at Quinn's brigade of hunters. They stopped advancing, preferring to consolidate their strong position while just beyond the range of the castle's archers.

The warlock scans farther afield, looking past the town walls and toward the south. Now Callum understands the second cause for alarm—a massive army of monstrous beasts charge toward the city walls.

Kincaid's army arrives to join the fight.

Converging in unison, Kincaid's and Quinn's forces are oblivious to the other's presence. Yet, both are poised outside the formidable Elven fortress. Callum's soul is heavy with worry, but he resists the instinct to return to his friend and the city's aid.

Esme made it quite clear she does not need the warlock's visible presence for Havishire's defense. Nonetheless, he is racked with guilt. Above all, he knows that Frey is somewhere in harm's way.

Jobella's plan, however dangerous, is already set in motion. He must stay the course. Escaping the two advancing fronts, Callum turns westward.

As he weaves through the forest, he senses someone is in pursuit. Callum cannot see any hunters chasing him through the winter woods, but he can hear movement and perceives the magical energies of their weapons. Quinn likely sent his arcane warriors to catch or destroy the lone figure fleeing Havishire ahead of the battle. On top of finding a hidden druid temple in the hope of saving millions of lives, the warlock must flee from the sorcerer who vowed to kill him.

Callum still has a good lead on any pursuers, but he knows he is drastically outnumbered.

He scales a small hill, using branches to aid his ascent. But other than trying to shake off the hunters, he lacks any concrete path or direction. There is no way of knowing whether he is even on the right course. Callum halts his climb to gain his bearings. Standing on the top of the rise, an arrow slices through the air over his shoulder.

Shit, that was close.

Not even stopping to think, Callum hurls himself down the icy slope, slipping and sliding in a clumsy, barely controlled descent. Inevitably, one foot catches an exposed rock, and he tumbles. Downward momentum rolls the warlock head over heels through the snow, bouncing off trees and before landing in a groaning heap on the bank of a shallow creek.

The warlock checks for broken bones, but the soft snow has

left him needing only to catch his second wind. Hearing voices approaching the hill's summit, Callum pulls himself up and huddles behind the widest tree available.

"He fell in this direction," someone shouts, reaching the top of the ridge and scanning the bank of the creek below. "I don't see him. Maybe he is still running."

"Let's split up," growls another man. This voice sounds familiar—Cain.

Callum flinches at the memory of his encounters with Cain. Hearing the man's voice again brings back memories of misery and pain.

"Great," Callum mutters to himself, resting his head against the rough tree bark. "Just what I need."

He can hear hurrying movements as the search party separates to continue their hunt. Finally, only a massive, solitary figure remains, carefully navigating the slope down to the creek.

"I know you're here, Walker," Cain taunts him. "It's just you and me. Why don't you stop hiding and face me like a man?"

Callum knows it is futile to remain hidden. Stepping out from behind the tree, he faces his hated foe.

Halfway down the hill, Cain grins with sadistic cruelty and holds a glinting sword. "There you are," the hunter sneers, barely suppressing the rage in his dark eyes.

"Don't do this," Callum warns, slowly shaking his head. He is sure that he cannot escape without killing the powerful man. "I really don't want to fight you."

Cain laughs at Callum's request and continues to scuffle through the snow, finally reaching the bank of the partially frozen creek.

"You have no idea how much trouble you've caused me, Warlock," Cain spits, narrowing his eyes and raising his heavy sword with both hands wrapped around the hilt. "I don't know how you escaped that cell, but you'll pay for the punishment I suffered because of it."

"You're angry because I refused to let myself be tortured to death by your lunatic boss? Do you know how depraved that sounds?" Callum lashes. The warlock steps back until his foot reaches the icebound edge of the stream. "You're angry at me because I didn't want to die?"

"You're a freak," Cain says, snarling. "Humans aren't meant to be born with magic. You're just like Kincaid—inhuman and evil. You don't deserve to live." Cain cruelly smirks, savoring Callum's look of accumulating dread.

Callum cannot believe what he hears. Quinn brainwashed this killing machine so completely that Cain cannot even recognize the basic right to life.

The hunter suddenly lumbers forward, swinging his sword from his shoulder to cleave the warlock in half. Despite this looming threat, Callum is remorseful for what he must do. Without uttering a word, the warlock focuses on Cain's furious attack and thrusts his lambent palm forward. In a split-second, Cain is halted in mid-step, fully conscious but unable to move or speak. The hunter's sword blade is caught in a frozen arc aimed directly at his intended victim's skull.

"I'm sorry you've been so consumed by Quinn's greed that you've lost the ability to think for yourself," Callum says. A rueful frown twists his face as he stretches to reach Cain's magical sword.

Callum pries the weapon from the helpless hunter's grip, causing it to revert to its original form. The warlock curiously inspects the tiny yellow stone resting in his palm. He recognizes the magical gem and feels the energy stored within it.

"If humans were never meant to possess this power, then how do you explain *me*?" Callum asks, looking into the enraged eyes of the corrupted man.

But there can be no reasoning with someone who lost every vestige of humanity.

Callum tosses the arcane artifact into the icy heart of the burbling water, letting nature wash it away. He moves forward to face the immobile Cain.

The warlock prepares himself for what must come next, letting out a long steady breath to build his resolve. He places his hand against Cain's chest and stares with pity into the man's eyes.

"I hope you find peace," Callum whispers.

The hunter's body begins to brighten, and his flesh glows as Callum's magic consumes him. Yet, the killer's rage continues to burn in his eyes. Callum squints as the piercing flare's intensity increases. Then, it abruptly fades, and Cain's body is reduced to dust and ashes, blowing freely in the winter wind.

The warlock's arm falls to his side, and his posture sags. Despite his contrition at taking Cain's life, Callum finds his bearings and turns west. Before taking a step, a solemn, white unicorn appears, standing amid the trees across the creek. He recognizes the stallion regarding him with somber eyes. Callum's tears overflow his eyes, and he quietly sniffles, guilt-ridden over taking a life—even one as violent and unredeemable as Cain's.

"I couldn't save him," Callum says in a murmur, wiping his damp cheeks on the back of his hand.

Part of him is pleased the evil man is dead. The world is now free from his wickedness.

Not everyone can be saved. The unicorn's thoughts resound within his mind.

"I had to kill him," the warlock says dolefully.

I do not hold that against you. It is you that must forgive yourself. There is still work to be done, and I have been waiting here to carry you to your destination. Time is waning, young paladin.

Callum nods his head, ruminating even as he commits himself to this next trial.

Not wanting to waste another minute, Callum leaps over the shallow creek. The unicorn bows to allow the warlock to clamber onto its back. Without delay, they race through the forest, rider tightly clinging to the beast's coarse silvery mane.

Time is not his friend.

CHAPTER FORTY-THREE

Callum is grateful for his swift journey through the forest as the daylight ebbs. Between Jobella's vague directions and the sheer distance involved, it could have taken him days on foot. Instead, Callum leans over the unicorn's mane and hugs its neck to avoid the many overhanging branches that threaten to swat him to the ground.

I have been watching you since last we met. You have become much more powerful. The unicorn's thoughts fill Callum's mind.

"I have no choice now. There are too many people counting on my success," Callum says, feeling uplifted by his determination to save as many innocent lives as he can.

Though here are secrets you have yet to understand, my kin are pleased that you have finally found your purpose.

"You were wrong about one thing. Queen Esme and her elves were not a source of support like you promised."

Was there no one in Havishire who helped you?

"Well, not exactly," Callum considers, recalling the great risks Jobella took to ensure his escape.

Elves and Humans may be of different races, but both are subject to the same faults of character. You must learn to trust your intuition to determine who is working for your benefit rather than close yourself off to the entire world. Friends come in many forms and are often misguided until someone inspires them or shows them the error of their ways.

"Wise advice. I'll keep that in mind," Callum says, vowing to consider trusting his perceptive psychic gift.

Callum relies considerably more on his magical powers than his empathic abilities, but he now wonders if they are equally valuable.

"Is my psychic intuition an accident, or is it related to magic?"

There are no such coincidences. Humans may not be routinely gifted with magic, but it does not mean they are powerless. Many in the magical realm forget that humans are the high gods' chosen protégés. They may not be the firstborn upon this Earth. Still, they are intentionally sheltered from the magical realm by the protective veil. The ancestral deities saw a potential in your race that has yet to be harnessed. When your people are ready, their unique power will be given to them. The question you should be asking is whether your gift of mental perception compliments your magic.

The warlock has never considered this possibility before. He remains silent to ponder its implications for the remainder of his ride to the temple.

After more than an hour hunched over the unicorn's neck, the tireless stallion and warlock rider come to a stop beside a crystal-blue pond fed by a roaring cascade of water. Callum stiffly slides off the unicorn and stretches his aching back and legs.

"How is it that you know about this cavern? Jobella told me the druids are the only ones who do," Callum asks and pauses to look out over the rippling water.

My kin know far more than even the Druids. This is why I was chosen to help you on your journey.

Callum looks into the wise, gentle eyes of the unicorn.

I see, within you, the salvation of all life on this planet. The unicorn lets out a great snort and shakes its powerful head. It winks at Callum and turns to walk away.

"Wait! I need to know what will happen inside this cave," Callum says, pleading for guidance. "What will I find? Will I succeed in ending this war?"

He has the distinct impression that the unicorn knows much more about his immediate future than it lets on.

The stallion pauses and swings its head back toward the warlock. *I will not unveil your destiny, but I promise you will find valuable answers within the temple. Look for the entrance behind the waterfall.*

The unicorn departs, vanishing into the forest in a vigorous trot that barely makes a sound.

Callum peers across the pond at the waterfall, raining down in a glistening curtain. Here the canopy of trees is open, and the rising moon bathes the clearing in its lunar light, reflecting off the undulating water. He clenches his fists and firmly nods, steadying his frayed nerves. Callum cautiously walks around the reservoir in search of the hidden passageway.

The waterfall spills over a high rock wall that hides a narrow, slate ledge. Callum slips behind the cascading spray of water, entering a murky tunnel that plunges into coal-black darkness.

The tunnel appears to be carved by natural forces rather than tools. The glassy floor and walls are polished by years of erosion, and a fine layer of sediment coats the bottom in a film of slick mud. Callum feels his way along the subterranean burrow, dragging his fingers along the damp walls of rock. The blackness almost suffocates him as he gradually descends.

Callum considers using an incantation to light his way but has no idea whether his enemies are watching from somewhere inside the cavern. He can barely make out a glimmering yellow light at the end of the tunnel, twenty feet away. Its glow reflects off the glazed walls. As he inches nearer, Callum becomes aware that his eyes now detect the faintest distinctions between the intensity of shadows. The firelight continues to beckon him onward like a moth drawn to a flame.

Oddly, Callum regrets losing the concealing effects of darkness as he steps to the open archway and beholds the blazing fire beyond. The shaft terminates in a wide, empty cavern. The commanding central feature is an intense pillar of fire rising from a pit.

Callum stands outside the archway and gawks at the perfectly domed chamber of rock, curving two stories high over the vast space, equally as wide as it is high. The smooth floor, an edge-to-edge surface of stone tiles, is a testament to ancient stonemasons' years of intricate, painstaking labor.

There are no structures to interrupt the enormous cavity. Except for the six-foot-wide circular fire pit, the space is empty.

As thick as an oak tree, a twisting column of orange flame spirals upward and disappears into a shaft in the middle of the dome. Although its radiance warms and illuminates the immense cavern, the supernatural fire burns without fuel, sound, or smoke.

Scanning the space carefully, Callum is relieved to see that he is the first to arrive. He still feels uneasy about the plan, but he came too far to turn back now. The warlock musters his courage and steps past the threshold. Under his feet, a border of the inlaid stone tiles is decorated with carved symbols. As soon as Callum crosses this intricate boundary, a feeling of unsteadiness washes over him.

The sensation lasts only a second and causes him to stumble a step, but Callum does not fall. He spins around to look back at the tunnel's mouth, wondering if he triggered a hidden enchantment. The archway looks no different, and he cannot detect any magic.

Callum moves back toward the passage, but as he regains the threshold, he connects with a solid, unseen force blocking his path—an invisible barrier now encompasses the temple.

The warlock reaches out to follow the hidden barrier with his fingers, discovering that it originates from the ring of etched tiles and extends beyond his height. Although he cannot interpret the floor symbols, he strongly suspects this spell is meant to confine unwelcome visitors, but its power is indiscernible. Lucky for Callum, his empathic perception allows him to detect the barricade trapping him inside the druid temple.

Backing several paces away from the wall, Callum focuses on the invisible shield. He tries to strike it with a blast of concentrated magic, hoping to disrupt it, but he cannot summon his power. He repeats the incantation, this time also raising his hand and voicing the innate words that push to the forefront of his thoughts. Once again, nothing happens.

Callum screams, outraged he fell into an ancient snare.

He suddenly wonders if he will be entombed in this cavern for the rest of his life. Only Jobella and the unicorn know of his location. The unicorn already refused any help beyond a swift ride and wishing him good luck. That leaves Jobella as his only hope for getting out of this cavern if she manages to survive. He briefly considers whether she knew about this trap but dismisses the thought. Why would she help him escape only to have him confined in this chamber?

Regardless, Callum is guaranteed to have either a short, painful life or a lingering death without food or water.

He slams his fists against the invisible enclosure, feeling a preternatural structure as unyielding as concrete. Becoming emotionally overwrought, Callum knows he is stranded in this cave while the innocent people of Havishire and the rest of the realm desperately fight for their lives. And all he can do is wait and hope that his two mortal enemies arrive and fall into the same trap.

Sitting on the hard floor, Callum recalls Daphne's mention of a judgment at the end of the prophecy. Could this be his punishment for committing the unforgivable sin of murdering another human?

It takes the warlock a long while to emerge from this replay of guilty thoughts before he raises his eyes from the stone floor. Only then, he notices the domed ceiling has been painted with detailed pictures to frame the space.

Initially, Callum thinks they are creative hieroglyphics, but on closer examination, he realizes it is a story in picture form. This tale is played out in segmented scenes like a comic strip, each panel interspaced with ancient writing. He scans the line of images, astonished to see that someone has portrayed the events of his own life.

Every adventure he endured since meeting Frey is represented in a clockwise pattern around the dome. The visuals capture his major trials: the battle with the shapeshifter, the visit to the fairy village of Whitshell, encounters with the dwarves and vampires, and even his near-fatal illness—all are depicted above his head.

Callum rises to his feet and follows the storyline around the temple.

He studies the images of Havishire and his defeat of the dragon. Callum sees the searing pain of his blood magic represented as a red flame within his chest. The next scene depicts him lying on a table while Esme holds her head following his psychic barrage. After that, the illustrations show his flight from the castle, the killing of Cain, and even his current predicament within this temple. Callum's trepidation increases, but he takes a deep breath and tenses his body before continuing.

The last visuals are rendered in exquisite detail, allowing him to recognize the painted faces. Callum sees Quinn and himself standing on opposite sides of the fire. But in the following image, the sorcerer lies bleeding, and Kincaid enters the cavern. Afraid of seeing how the future ends, Callum turns his back to avoid the final pictures. Inevitably, his need for answers overcomes his sense of dread.

Trembling, Callum peers up to see himself lying on the tiles with Kincaid standing over him. He sighs in despair at the sight of his own violent death.

As he looks closer at the artwork, he makes out what appears to be an outline of a figure standing inside the column of fire.

Though it is shaped like a person, it is impossible to identify the dark form through distortions from the flame.

Callum pivots and intently stares into the twisting cyclone of fire, but he does not see anyone standing inside the rising flames. Yet, his instincts scream that there is something powerful about the unnaturally silent blaze. It is as though it possesses an arcane life of its own, keeping it burning over hundreds of years.

Without knowing it, Callum is caught in an enchantment and is frozen, staring into the column of fire.

CHAPTER FORTY-FOUR

Incarcerated deep beneath Earth's surface, held prisoner by the warded barrier, and robbed of his magical abilities, Callum is oblivious to the passage of time.

He stares at the cycling tower of fire, not realizing he has been ensnared in a trance that keeps him immobilized. The ageless energy within the flame protects him from the agony of waiting. Many hours pass in what feels like a few minutes to Callum.

He emerges from his hypnotic state when the magical barrier is breached by the arrival of his expected enemy.

Callum blinks, returning to awareness. He wonders why he is so tired and feels like he has been on his feet for too long. Then, arching and stretching his aching back, he quickly becomes conscious of another presence entering the massive cave.

Callum cannot see any sign of disturbance in the invisible barrier. However, his empathic sensitivity can detect the disruption that undulates through it and over his head. Standing at the distant end of the cavern but opposite the tunnel entrance, Callum peers through the flame to see Quinn hesitantly walking into the open center space. It is impossible for either man to hide, not that Callum intends to run any longer. But having accepted his fate, he refuses to delay the inevitable confrontation. He gathers his courage, then steps out from behind the burning pedestal.

"Hello Quinn," says Callum, announcing his presence as he moves into sight of his malevolent foe.

Quinn freezes mid-step, alarmed to see the warlock appear. His surprise is fleeting, shifting almost instantly to a look of loathing.

"Callum Walker." Quinn scowls.

Quinn's weight shifts as he swings his thick legs in a falsely confident swagger, his right hand tucked inside the pocket of his overcoat. His corduroy pants swish with each step, and his leather boots thump across the burnished floor.

The sorcerer carefully withdraws his hand, revealing his tight grip wrapping around the butt of a jet-black, semi-automatic pistol. Quinn raises the weapon with slow deliberation until the eye of its lethal barrel is centered on the warlock's chest.

Callum feels a wave of adrenaline rush through his body. His heart lurches into his throat, and his wide eyes lock on the weapon. With infinite care, he then raises his hands in surrender, simultaneously frightened and frustrated by a mortal threat he cannot defend against.

Why would the sorcerer bring a gun to confront a warlock? Quinn has a plethora of magical armaments at his disposal, so using a human-world firearm is unexpected.

Whatever the reason, Quinn seems overjoyed to have caught his victim off guard. Approaching Callum at his leisure, the leader of the Order grins with undisguised delight. Callum has no doubt that the sorcerer could easily hit his target across the short distance separating them.

"I've seen this temple hundreds of times in my visions." Quinn stalks closer to his victim, taking his time to savor the moment. "It took me years to learn its secrets, but it was definitely worth the effort. The only thing I didn't know was its location. Thanks to your druid's hapless messenger, I had the final piece of my puzzle. It seems your little ploy has backfired, young warlock."

Callum's unblinking eyes never leave Quinn's gun.

"You said *visions?* Is this the place you've seen yourself die?" Callum asks, realizing this meeting was predicted by both the sight stone and the cavern's adorning paintings.

Their meeting is not a fanciful coincidence. On the contrary, the degree of dual prediction suggests that a higher power is at work, toying with people in a deadly game and drawing the unwitting pawns toward this moment.

"Not that it will matter much longer, but yes. The sight stone has shown me my death in this place so that I could keep it from happening." Quinn chuckles as though amused by a cruel joke only he can appreciate.

"Is there more than one of those stones in existence?" Callum asks. He struggles to resist the urge to turn and run, but there is nowhere to escape.

"No. I have the only one, and I have no intention of sharing it," Quinn says, halving the distance between them before stopping. He is now easily within reach of his victim.

Swallowing an anxious lump, Callum continues to speak, even as he faces the gun barrel at near point-blank range. "I only ask because it seems that someone else saw your future hundreds of years ago. Look."

Callum points to the painted illustrations overhead.

Forgetting the need to keep his pistol trained on the warlock, Quinn gazes up at the mural portraying his foreseen death in gory detail. The skilled artist captured ample description of the sorcerer's pudgy face, ensuring the dying fool is recognizable as Desmond Quinn. The sorcerer's face goes white, and his previously steady hand begins to tremble. Droplets of cold sweat pepper his cheeks.

"What the hell is that?" Quinn demands. His strained shout rebounds around the domed cavern.

The sorcerer frantically looks around the cave, reading the

familiar story of Callum's journey. Studying the picture of his death for a few tense moments, Quinn then turns his fierce glare back to the warlock.

"That's what your visions showed you, isn't it?" Callum taunts the fretful man.

The warlock is keenly aware of Quinn's horrified expression and wavering pistol. He considers pouncing for the weapon, but he will be riddled with holes if he is too slow. However, Callum also saw his own suffering in the portrait overhead, not caused by Quinn's hand.

Trusting the previous validity of the ancient images, Callum lowers his surrendering hands. He tenses his body in preparation for the right moment to fight.

"You drew that? How did you do that?" Quinn screams in panic, desperately pressing for an answer for the aberration.

"How could I have painted that?" asks Callum. "I have no way of reaching the ceiling, and I don't have anything here to paint pictures with."

"Then how did you know about this place?" Quinn hisses, and flecks of spittle fly from his mouth.

Callum boldly shrugs.

The hefty sorcerer suddenly barrels forward, his wild eyes full of terror. He is quicker than Callum expects from a man of Quinn's considerable girth, but the warlock is prepared.

As an enraged Quinn charges like a riled bull, Callum adroitly sidesteps the lumbering man as an earsplitting boom thunders through the enclosed cavern. A screaming bullet zips over the warlock's right shoulder, missing him by a hair's breadth. But Callum does not stop to ponder how close the lethal projectile came.

He twists and snaps his right boot into Quinn's belly. The sorcerer doubles over with a guttural grunt. The large man lurches for a half step, then stumbles and falls flat with a heavy thump. Quinn sprawls, facedown and unmoving.

For a moment, Callum wonders if he won. Tentatively, the

warlock creeps toward the wretch's prone form. He taps Quinn's boot with the toe of his foot, thinking the sorcerer is incapacitated. Callum is mistaken.

Quinn jerks himself onto his side, swinging both his chunky legs. Both of Callum's feet are swept out from beneath him, and he lands painfully on his back.

The warlock's head strikes the stone tiles, and flashing light invades his vision. Fingers of shooting pain cause him to clutch his skull and writhe long enough to allow Quinn the time he needs to regain the upper hand.

The sorcerer awkwardly scrambles to his hands and knees, crawling toward his stunned quarry in a frenzy. Callum is still reeling when Quinn clambers onto him, straddling his torso and squashing him against the floor. The sorcerer grabs a handful of Callum's hair with his free hand while he drives the cold gun barrel against the warlock's throat.

"You set up this trap in a place where magic is forbidden," Quinn says, snarling. "It took me years to learn about this ancient druid temple. I want to know how you knew about this place and its barrier spell."

"One of the druids in Havishire," Callum breathlessly replies, his voice barely audible as his lungs compress beneath Quinn's bulk. The warlock lowers his arms to the floor and squints up into the flushed, sweat-drenched face. Holding out against the urge to swallow as the steel cylinder grinds against his larynx, Callum manages to draw several short breaths. "I didn't know about the warding until I entered the temple. If I had, I would never have chosen to meet you here."

"Well, well, well. I'm surprised to see you here, brother." a third voice chides from the tunnel archway.

Kincaid.

Preoccupied with almost certain death, Callum fails to notice the necromancer's arrival until too late. Kincaid acts unfazed by the scene before him and strides with authority into the temple and unknowingly through the warding barrier.

Quinn releases his original prey and gracelessly stands to face this new danger, pointing the gun at his brother with both hands.

However, Kincaid is much quicker than his ungainly sibling. The necromancer draws a silver stiletto from a concealed scabbard and flings the knife with expert precision. The deadly dagger whips end over end through the air until it connects with its target. Callum cringes as Quinn's head snaps back and his arms abruptly relax. His gun clatters as it drops to the stone floor, and the sorcerer's body remains upright for an instant longer before collapsing.

Quinn, master of the Order, falls and pins Callum beneath his corpse. The warlock struggles against Quinn's dead weight. Finally managing to shove the lifeless body off him, it flops onto the stone tiles with a soft thud.

Callum spots the dagger as Quinn's body comes to rest on its back. Thrown by the sorcerer's own monstrous brother, its jeweled hilt protrudes deep into Quinn's right eye socket.

Quinn's demise has, inevitably, come to pass.

CHAPTER FORTY-FIVE

Callum swiftly grabs Quinn's gun and scrambles to his knees, leveling the weapon in Kincaid's general direction. The warlock's mind nauseatingly whirls, a side effect of his concussive fall. He blindly squeezes the trigger, firing a deafening shot that completely misses its mark.

Kincaid lurches to his right as the bullet sails by him. The projectile passes unrestricted through the runic barrier and embeds itself in the cavern's stone wall. Without missing a beat, the necromancer draws another blade from beneath his cloak. He pitches the glinting dagger with the speed of a cobra's strike. Callum sharply leans to his left, but the blade manages to graze its razored edge across the warlock's upper arm. Luckily, the cut is merely a shallow slash over his deltoid. Even so, it stings like hell.

Hastily recovering, Callum straightens up again, holding the borrowed gun in his shaky right hand. Kincaid stands motionless near the edge of the temple, widening his stance and fingering another dagger at the ready.

Both men know full well that neither one has a clear advantage. Silence reigns for several tense moments as the two opponents lock eyes in an unrelenting standoff. Callum maintains his trembling aim while Kincaid confidently clutches his knife and smirks at the warlock's unsteady poise.

The murderous necromancer gradually creeps closer. His malicious eyes lack any measure of remorse over Quinn's fate and expose the soulless heart of a monster. In contrast to the false diplomacy at their first meeting, Kincaid finally reveals his truest nature and scowls with vile contempt.

There is not one iota of humanity left in the man, which is more frightening to Callum than Quinn and his gun.

"I was surprised to hear that you've decided to surrender yourself after your adamant refusal," Kincaid says, diverting his path to gradually circle around the armed warlock. "Your little trap made perfect sense once I saw my fathead brother."

"I was half-hoping to figure out a truce," says Callum, hearing the tension in his dry voice. He is on edge. Every muscle is taut, and his jaw anxiously twitches.

"Yes, of course. More talking," Kincaid huffs. The nostrils of his pencil-thin nose flare below his glowering eyes. "Your naivety continues to blind you, even when the time for words is long past. Then again, that's all you're good at, isn't it, Walker?"

The necromancer continues to pace in a slow spiral, trying to conceal his gradual advance toward Callum.

"If that's all I could do, then how did I survive this long?" Callum retorts as he tracks the necromancer's movement.

Callum's thoughts remain fixed on the pistol in his grasp, but he has already missed once. The warlock does not want to give away his complete lack of marksmanship by fumbling a second shot—it is wiser to keep Kincaid guessing. The necromancer's effortless kill shot from fifteen paces out proves a proficiency that Callum would be wise to respect.

"Sheer luck, I'm afraid, nothing more," Kincaid says with a derisive laugh. "I find it hilarious that you really thought your little scheme would be enough to outwit both my brother and me."

"I had to try something you wouldn't expect. Besides, it got you both here. So, yeah. I'd say it worked," Callum says with a wry face.

"So, if your little chat didn't work, what then? Were you going to kill us both?" Kincaid jeers at the prospect of any feeble attack by the warlock.

"If it came to that," Callum's voice is bold and as cold as ice, while inside, he is a nervous wreck. "But I realized I didn't have to kill you the moment I walked through that archway and discovered this temple is actually a prison for people like us, people with magic."

Kincaid recoils and halts his pacing as the impact of Callum's statement strikes home. Risking a glance back at the entrance, the necromancer returns his fierce gaze to Callum. Then, dramatically raising his free arm toward his intended victim, one palm open to aim his power, Kincaid speaks a string of incomprehensible words.

Nothing happens.

He tries the same incantation again with the same results, then drops his arm and glares at the warlock.

"What is this, Walker?" Kincaid is livid. "I can't detect any shield spell."

"I guess you and I aren't quite as similar as others believe," Callum observes. "The warding isn't a traditional spell. It's something...supernatural. I sensed it because I can perceive the extrasensory energy of magic and life, and others don't. Including *you*."

"What?" spits Kincaid, trying unsuccessfully to appear amused.

"It's metaphysical, not magical."

"That's impossible." Kincaid sneers, swatting the air dismissively with his free hand. "I've studied the existence of psychic phenomena extensively and found it inconclusive at best."

Callum can see Kincaid's anger over challenging his vast knowledge and understanding of magic. The necromancer seems to struggle with some internal presumption, and he looks around the cavern mystified. Once he notices the murals on the curved ceiling, he pauses and gawks.

With Kincaid's attention momentarily drawn to the painted panels, Callum considers his own options.

Given a reverse of their situations, Kincaid would not hesitate to take the deadly shot. Callum, however, has reservations about cold-blooded murder, even in this desperate hour. On the other hand, he has received enough hostility for one lifetime and refuses to go down without a fight. Callum understands he will never leave this cave alive, but neither will Kincaid. Whatever happens here, the warlock knows he played an essential part in ending the brothers' reign of chaos and death.

With that in mind, the warlock steadies his wavering hand and squeezes the trigger.

The bullet grazes the necromancer, piercing folds of clothing and skimming Kincaid's upper thigh, clearly spared by Callum's lack of skill. Howling in both pain and rage, the necromancer claps his left hand to the flesh wound and swings his ready dagger with deadly intent.

The stiletto flashes with lightning speed. Callum tries to duck the whizzing blade, but the percussive pistol fire leaves him disoriented. The sharp knife flies past his face, slicing a gash across an earlobe. Reflexively, the warlock reaches for his damaged ear with his gun hand, wincing and cursing in anger. Callum's painful distraction leaves him blind to Kincaid's determined hobble toward him.

As the necromancer hastens closer, he draws another knife from beneath his cloak. Kincaid promptly launches this third skewer with maximum force, and it strikes with devastating effect.

Callum screams as the third dagger—thrown from only a few feet away—sinks its point into the muscles of his right shoulder. The expertly aimed blade disables the warlock's right arm, and it falls to his side. The gun, again, clatters to the floor.

Callum scrambles to removes the knife, barely succeeding in

yanking it free when Kincaid makes physical contact. Although partially lame, Kincaid lashes out a vicious kick that connects savagely with Callum's face.

The warlock crumples into a moaning heap, and the deadly dagger falls from his hand. But Kincaid is not nearly finished with him.

The necromancer kneels beside Callum, grumbling under his breath at the biting sting of his bullet wound, and clutches the front of the warlock's shirt. Reeling from the brutal kick, Callum's injured nose gushes blood. He lost much of his fighting spirit, but he is still conscious.

Callum weakly grabs at the deceptively strong arm raising his upper body from the floor. Blinking through watery eyes, the warlock defiantly looks into the necromancer's maniacal gaze, burning with fury.

"Do you know why I use a knife to kill?" Kincaid snarls.

"Because you're a coward," Callum says, spitting his words through bloodied lips and grit teeth.

"No. It's because no one expects it of me," Kincaid says nonchalantly.

His hostility turns to self-assurance as he picks up the blade Callum dropped. The necromancer lifts the delicate dagger to admire the stain of crimson blood on its razor-sharp tip. Then, he shifts his sights back to his pierced and battered victim.

"I can savor the moment and kill you quickly like I did with my brother, or I can make you suffer. I'm the one controlling your fate, and you have no choice in the matter."

"Go to hell," Callum utters at his enemy.

Kincaid lowers the stiletto to Callum's unprotected stomach. The warlock reaches for the necromancer's wrist but has little strength to resist. High on power, Kincaid laughs as he deliberately takes his time spearing the dagger into Callum's gut, sinking it all the way to its hilt. The impalement delivers a merciless, sharp-edged agony and steals the warlock's breath.

Callum instinctively gasps for air despite the excruciating

pain, and Kincaid roars in delight. Releasing the warlock's shirt, the necromancer lets his dying subject fall limp on the cavern floor. Kincaid sadistically twists the blade, further torturing his helpless prey before ripping the silver dagger out. Callum's blood wells and pools, reflecting the light of the silent, blazing pillar.

Callum moans and squeezes a feeble hand over the mortal gash. Shrinking into a huddling mass, he tries to roll away, but Kincaid pulls him face up again. The necromancer holds the dripping crimson blade above Callum's face, waiting for him to fully realize these are his final minutes of life.

"You surprise me," Kincaid proclaims, almost conversationally. "You *had* a powerful potential and a great destiny, but you squander it. You had to know that you were no match for me, with or without magic."

The necromancer's cruel temper gives way to clinical fascination as he stares at the nemesis who once posed such a dire threat.

"I'm willing to die protecting everyone you promised to kill," Callum grunts.

"What a waste," says Kincaid, shaking his head mockingly and clicking his tongue. "Tell me this...how does it feel to be completely at my mercy, Walker? You've tried so hard to resist death, only to face it now, knowing you can't avoid this moment."

"I feel sorry for you." Callum's voice is barely even a whisper. "You're already dead...you just don't know it yet."

"Typical martyr."

Kincaid straightens and raises the dagger with both hands high over his head, ready to drive it deep into the center of Callum's chest.

Accepting his fate, Callum finds deep solace in knowing that his sacrifice and entrapment of his enemies, however unintentional, will bring the brother's war to an end. Yet, even though he will die, Callum has ensured the continuing survival of human and magical life on his planet.

The prophecy will be fulfilled.

Callum closes his eyes and waits for the fatal blow, welcoming the end of his pain.

His thoughts serenely turn to Frey.

The final, piercing attack never comes. Instead, Callum hears the dagger rattle harmlessly to the stone floor beside his head.

Gradually, Callum raises his eyelids just enough to see a bizarre spectacle. Kincaid is dangling in the air with his flailing arms and legs enmeshed in the folds of his cloak. His plight is caused by the mighty arm of a male figure standing close by Callum. One sinewy hand grips the wriggling necromancer by the throat and effortlessly lifts him into the air.

This herculean newcomer towers over Kincaid with a discernable torso, head, and limbs but lacks identifying features. From the waist down, the being resembles a churning formation of smoke in the process of coalescing into two brawny legs. Within seconds, the terrifying man-like creature completes its physical form. Before them, stands a figure dressed only in leather leggings, with bare, bronze skin rippling over a chiseled torso and arms.

Holding Kincaid in a commanding yet non-fatal grasp, the figure begins to alter its distorted exterior.

The necromancer's desperation escalates to panic. While the terrifying humanoid holds Kincaid in its grasp, its near feature-less expressions transfigure.

Kincaid's eyes bulge while details of the giant's stoic body and face emerge. The mesomorphic man stares at the pathetic necromancer with pure animosity.

"Wh...Who are you?" Kincaid asks, straining to speak.

"I am Anulap, the deity of magic and master of knowledge," the man's baritone voice echoes with unnatural volume and causes the cavern to shake. "I am here to pass judgment upon you, David Kincaid."

"Judgment?" Kincaid squeaks.

"I have seen what you have done with the gifts naturally bestowed upon you, and I know the intentions of your cold and treacherous heart. I bear witness to your efforts to rid the world of beings you deem inferior and unworthy. You have caused much death and suffering. For this, I judge you on behalf of my divine authority."

"David Kincaid, I hereby I condemn you to the void, where you will eternally suffer the same fate as your victims, both living and dead."

"Wai—" Kincaid shrieks, but his final word is lost.

Anulap, without hesitation, flings the wretched, pleading human into the ethereal flame.

Kincaid's tortured screams reverberate throughout the temple as his body is consumed by the eternal fire. Callum clenches his eyes shut, unwilling to witness the necromancer's torment. He feels no relief at Kincaid's richly deserved death. In its place, the dying warlock has only immense pity for the anguish of this person who made so many wrong choices throughout their warped life. The howls of excruciation linger until finally vanquished by the unnatural fire.

Only when the cavern becomes silent again does Callum feel at peace—the magical realm and his own human world are safe. And Frey along with them.

The warlock gradually peers up at the white-haired divinity now kneeling beside him. The seething yellow column backlights the deity like a glowing corona. Callum never saw Anulap emerge from the flame, yet he knows it to be true. This arrival was depicted on the temple dome, along with all the other predicted events. He beholds the sky-blue eyes and rugged smiling face looking down at him, and Callum feels no fear.

Kincaid's unnaturally conjured horde will already be

dissolving in the consuming light, and Quinn's hunter army is left leaderless on the battlefield.

Callum knows that he is about to die. As blood spills from his wounds and adds to the spreading puddle beneath him, Callum can feel his life draining along with it.

"Do not be so willing to give in to death," Anulap speaks softly now, and his scarred and bearded face expresses a tenderness he denied to Kincaid. "You have been courageous throughout your many trials, and though they have pushed you beyond what you could bear, you have prevailed. Despite fear and hostility, you aspire to protect the innocent, embracing your fate and the mortal sacrifice you knew you must make. I am very pleased with your choices, Callum Walker, and I have deemed you worthy of your inherent gifts."

His speech comes slowly now. "Did you give me magic?" Callum whispers.

"No, Callum. Your magic is accessed through your ancestry."

"Then who are you?"

"I am older than time," Anulap tells him. "I am what you humans would call a celestial god, and I have awaited your birth for centuries. Your heart is unequaled among men, and you have demonstrated your inherent purity and goodness through your actions. I knew only that a man would eventually be born beyond the veil, but I could not identify who it was. When your birth came to light, I knew that *my prophecy* would come to pass. From a distance, I have proudly watched you throughout your life."

While he speaks, Anulap gently moves Callum's bloodied hands away from his stomach, and places own his giant palm over the fatal wound. A warm, cerulean light radiates down the deity's thick arm as his preeminent magic diffuses into Callum's perishing body. It spreads through him like a comforting blanket and envelopes him in calming energy. The warlock's miserable afflictions steadily fade as his deadly wound is mended— although his incredible fatigue does not abate.

"It is time to rest now, Callum Walker. You have done *well*."

Callum is unable to resist his overwhelming exhaustion, so his eyes droop and close. He vaguely wonders if he will ever wake up again.

With that last thought, the warlock shrugs off his fears and allows himself to be swallowed by darkness.

CHAPTER FORTY-SIX

"Do you recognize this place?"

Anulap's voice wakes Callum from sweet slumber. He flutters his eyes against the morning light filtering through the canopy of trees.

"I'm in the forest," Callum says as he slowly regaining his senses.

He is surprised to be free of the confines of the druid temple and astonished to realize all his pain is gone. Anulap sits cross-legged, leaning back on his hands and peering with serene pleasure at the sun-dappled wilderness all around him.

"Did you bring me here?" Callum asks.

Callum gingerly rises and looks down at his bloodstained clothes, expecting the bodily soreness he has grown so accustomed to. Instead, Callum lifts his shirt and sees the laceration that had so nearly claimed his life is mended, and only a thumblength scar remains. His other injuries are also healed, a testament to the deity's incredible restorative power.

"This is where your heart wants to be. The first place that you felt at peace. It is where you were drawn to when you were in your darkest moment when Quinn had you trapped in his prison. This is where you felt most comforted," Anulap calmly explains.

"Why this place? I remember this forest, but I don't know why it's important."

Callum looks around, recalling the familiarity of the trees from his first unexpected visit.

"I am not surprised that you do not recall the significance of this place. You were only two years old when you were brought here. Your parents feared the potential of your gifts, and so they sadly left you to your fate in this forest," Anulap says. "It was the first time you met Estar."

"Estar?" Callum asks. The name is distantly memorable.

"Look, here he comes," Anulap announces, pointing to a gap between trees.

The familiar white unicorn emerges from the thick woods. His majestic head is held high, and his gentle eyes look upon Callum with deep affection.

"Estar is your first and oldest friend. He was with you in those early days, protecting you from the dangers of the forest. He kept you safe and was the first soul in this harsh and dangerous world to show you kindness. He comforted you when you were most vulnerable and guided you back to your civilization. It was there that your human kin fostered your young life."

"I was thinking about Frey when I came here last time. I thought it was my memory of her that rescued me from Quinn's cell," says Callum, looking to Anulap for answers.

"You were not drawn to her specifically. Instead, it was the desire to free yourself from the loneliness that saved you. In your darkest moments, you sought the first friendship and belonging you experienced from this precise location. This was where Estar was waiting for your return."

Callum watches the unicorn step into the forest glade, sensing the stallion's adoration and pride directed at him.

"Estar has watched you from afar since you were abandoned

by your parents, as have I. We were waiting for you to accept your great destiny and power."

"What about my parents?"

Anulap sighs and casts Callum a solemn look. "Your parents were not inherently bad, but they were frightened of what your powers represented. Your abilities, although immature, were terrifying. So, they left you here in a moment of weakness and panic, and that decision haunted them until the day they died."

Callum turns and meets Anulap's sorrowful expression. The deity nods slowly, confirming that his parents have perished.

"It is because of this early alienation that you struggle with loneliness and mistrust," Anulap continues gently. "I need you to understand that although there are those who will forsake you, there are also those who need your support and many more who will endeavor to assist you. Trust your instincts, for they will guide you with wisdom."

"Did you grant me the ability of discernment?" Callum asks. His head is swimming with newfound knowledge, and he longs for more answers.

"It is beyond my power to bestow gifts such as yours. I know you have many questions, Callum, but some things will remain unknown for now. Even I do not know everything. But I will tell you that your journey is not over should you choose to continue."

"Choose?"

"Yes. You have a decision to make." Anulap guardedly smiles as though unsure of what Callum will decide. "Beyond this meeting, I cannot see the future, so I offer you the choice. You can return with me to the great beyond, never again to suffer grief or pain. Or you can continue to protect all those who have been left broken and vulnerable by this senseless conflict."

Estar quietly snorts, and Callum watches the massive creature bow its head, blinking in respectful patience and awaiting his decision.

"So, my options are passing on or living," Callum clarifies, turning from Estar to Anulap.

The possibility of finding tranquility and belonging is a tempting proposition. However, Callum cannot set aside the knowledge of many people who are still subjugated by evil powers, seeking control and domination. Although fierce enemies, Kincaid and Quinn were not the only ones threatening the innocent. Callum expels a heavy breath, understanding that his work is far from finished.

"I can't leave while there are people out there in need of protection. As much as I would love to find eternal comfort, I could never enjoy it with the guilt of knowing I would condemn others to suffer. Now that I know they exist, I have to help them." Callum slowly shakes his head. For better or worse, his choice is made.

"Very well. But know that whenever you are ready, you have only to call upon my name," Anulap says, rising to his feet.

Reaching out his hand, Anulap offers to help Callum stand. The moment their fingers touch, Callum feels a spark of energy surge up his arm, traveling across his entire network of nerves like static electricity.

"What was that?" Callum asks, stunned by the fading surge.

"Consider it a gift. When I saw that you were born with the ability to tap into magical energy, I could not allow your strength to go unchecked. I used my own magic to limit your tolerance of powerful spells. Because of your inherited ability, you could have accessed vast magical potential if not for this physical restriction. I have now withdrawn my limiting curse and returned your fortitude to wield the most powerful of spells. You are worthy of your legacy. There is no longer a need to wear that amulet around your neck."

Anulap concludes this lengthy explanation, placing his free hand upon Callum's shoulder like a parent offering comfort. "You must use your gifts to protect. Do not fall victim to the darkness. Estar will be your guide for a short time. Listen to his lessons and heed his instructions. Unfortunately, I must leave you now but seek me out if you are ever in need."

"Wait! I need to know..." Callum starts, furrowing his brow with worry. His heart is aching for some good news. "Is Frey safe?"

"Yes, your fairy friend is alive and well, as is the druid, Jobella," Anulap replies, grinning warmly.

Anulap takes a step back, and his form begins to glow. Shimmering light increases in intensity, making Callum shield his eyes until the brightness fades. When he looks again, the deity is gone.

Callum removes the now redundant pendant Jobella gave him. Holding it in his open hand, he contemplates the gem before letting it slide from his fingers into the forest's natural litter. Estar lifts his head expectantly at the warlock.

"I need to ask a favor of you," says Callum, and Estar nods. "Can you take me to a place called High Garth?"

I am here to serve you, Callum, the warlock.

Within minutes, he is astride the galloping unicorn, approaching a different future and another chance at life. This time, he is without a prophetic guide, but Callum is consoled by the fact that he found a place to belong, a world that will accept him, and very soon, people who will welcome him.

Whatever fate holds in store for him, the warlock is ready to face it.

END

ABOUT THE AUTHOR

J. M. Shaw lives in Airdrie, Alberta, with her husband and two young children. She and her sons learned they are on the autism spectrum and together are sharing a journey of understanding, acceptance, and life-long learning. She pours her experience in medical technology, personal training, martial arts, airsoft, and running into her creative fiction. *The Ascension* is her debut novel in the Callum Walker series.

CPSIA information can be obtained
at www.ICGtesting.com
Printed in the USA
LVHW071057090623
749201LV00004B/7